Works by Michael J. Sullivan

THE LEGENDS OF THE FIRST EMPIRE
Age of Myth • *Age of Swords* • *Age of War*
Age of Legend • *Age of Death*
Forthcoming: *Age of Empyre* (May 2020)

THE RISE AND THE FALL
Nolyn (Summer 2020) • *Farilane* (Summer 2021)
Esrahaddon (Summer 2022)

THE RIYRIA REVELATIONS
Theft of Swords (contains *The Crown Conspiracy* & *Avempartha*)
Rise of Empire (contains *Nyphron Rising* & *The Emerald Storm*)
Heir of Novron (contains *Wintertide* & *Percepliquis*)

THE RIYRIA CHRONICLES
The Crown Tower • *The Rose and the Thorn*
The Death of Dulgath • *The Disappearance of Winter's Daughter*
Forthcoming: *Drumindor*

STANDALONE NOVELS
Hollow World (Sci-fi Thriller)

SHORT STORY ANTHOLOGIES
Heroes Wanted: "The Ashmoore Affair" (Fantasy: Riyria Chronicles)
Unfettered: "The Jester" (Fantasy: Riyria Chronicles)
Unbound: "The Game" (Fantasy: Contemporary)
Unfettered II: "Little Wren and the Big Forest" (Fantasy: Legends)
Blackguards: "Professional Integrity" (Fantasy: Riyria Chronicles)
The End: Visions of the Apocalypse: "Burning Alexandria" (Dystopian Sci-fi)
Triumph Over Tragedy: "Traditions" (Fantasy: Tales from Elan)
The Fantasy Faction Anthology: "Autumn Mist" (Fantasy: Contemporary)

Age of Death © 2020 by Michael J. Sullivan
Cover illustration © 2019 by Marc Simonetti
Cover design © 2020 Michael J. Sullivan
Map © 2016 by David Lindroth
Interior design © 2020 by Robin Sullivan
978-1944145392
All rights reserved.

Published in the United States by Riyria Enterprises, LLC and distributed through Grim Oak Press.

Learn more about Michael's writings at www.riyria.com
To contact Michael, email him at michael@michaelsullivan-author.com

MICHAEL'S NOVELS INCLUDE:
The First Empire Series: Age of Myth • Age of Swords • Age of War • Age of Legend • Age of Death • Age of Empyre
The Riyria Revelations: Theft of Swords • Rise of Empire • Heir of Novron
The Riyria Chronicles: The Crown Tower • The Rose and the Thorn • The Death of Dulgath • The Disappearance of Winter's Daughter
Standalone Titles: Hollow World

First Edition
Printed in the United States of America

2 4 6 8 9 7 5 3 1

Published by
RIYRIA
ENTERPRISES

Distributed by:

GRIM
OAK

Age OF Death

Age OF Death

BOOK FIVE OF

The Legends of the First Empire

MICHAEL J. SULLIVAN

This book is dedicated to John Patrick Sullivan, my brother, who introduced me to fantasy when I was just a boy.

Contents

Contents

Author's Note

Well, we are getting down to the wire—just two books left! Let me start by mentioning a few things from my last author's note. First, if you have read the prior books but need a refresher on what has happened so far, you can find recaps for each at www.firstempireseries.com/book-recaps. And second, you can also take a gander at the "Glossary of Terms and Names," which can also be found online at www.firstempireseries.com/age-of-death-glossary. It's written to be spoiler-free, and it's updated for each book to provide additional details as more secrets are revealed. Why has it been moved online? There are several reasons, and they all revolve around how large and complex the glossary has become. For people on ereaders, its inclusion gives an inaccurate indication regarding how much story is left, and some people have complained about that. For those who read physical books, waiting until it was fully compiled would have delayed the printing and would have pushed back not only this book but the next as well. Given that, it seemed like moving the glossary was worth doing.

With that addressed, I want to take just a moment to talk about the writing of this book because it has a lot to do with how the second part of the Legends series was structured. As I mentioned in my last book, this series was supposed to end with *Age of War*, and that book does indeed tie up a great many loose threads, but not all of them. When I started what I thought would be the last book, an idea had popped up that would give me the possibility to dig into the bedrock of Elan and delve into the origin story of my world. I knew it wouldn't be a short tale, and I wasn't even sure if I would be able to reveal the whole yarn (because there was so much to tell), but I thought I needed to try.

With this new direction, the fourth book grew, and grew, and then grew even more. Also, my wife (whom I'm sure you know by now is a genius and my most trusted critic) indicated that the writing was "too close to the bone" and "much too rushed."

The "too close" statement might need some clarification. What Robin pointed out is that while I had the plot points well-established, there wasn't enough flesh on the skeleton. In my desire to fit everything in, I had been sacrificing the narrative and missing excellent opportunities for emotional impact. On reflection, I saw (as so often is the case) that she was absolutely right. So, guess what, the book started to grow once more.

Eventually, the story became too large to fit into a single book. Yes, we could have played around with font size, the spacing between lines, or used thin paper. But even with such concessions, we would be right up against the two-and-a-half-inch spine width that limits most printers. We would also have to leave out some desired front and back matter like my author's note and Robin's afterword. We didn't want to make those changes because I still read printed books, and I think the look and feel of them matter. If the font is too small and the line spacing too tight, I don't enjoy reading the physical copy. And I wanted to love all versions of my book.

So, after much deliberation, we decided to break the fourth book into two parts. The only problem was that there wasn't an appropriate stopping place around the half-way mark. You see, when I wrote the story, I wasn't concerned with page count, or word count, or book count. I was telling the tale in the best way I could to make a good story. My job was to write a compelling tale, and *how* that saga would eventually be published wasn't foremost in my mind.

Eventually, I had to turn my attention to the more practical side of getting the books into people's hands. When looking objectively at the entire story, it became evident that we had a three-act play, and two breaking points stood out. But the balance was a problem. I could have made one regular-sized book and one double-dipper volume, but that didn't feel right to me. Plus, I liked the idea of two trilogies under the umbrella of a single epic tale. Also, as a storyteller I liked where the two climaxes occurred, and I thought they had great drama.

Besides the story aspects, making the last part of the series three books instead of two would split the first half and second half of the story evenly. From a balance and symmetry perspective, I liked that. Having one book that was essentially twice as long as the other stories just felt lopsided in a way that I can't fully explain. So, since we were in a position to control such things, we did exactly that. We followed the convention of *The Lord of the Rings* and made one long story that was split between three volumes.

So, problem solved. But there was another issue. Unlike my previous books (each of which was a self-contained episode), the second half of my Legends series would end with cliffhangers. I expected bad reviews (and I did receive a few), but I had a much larger number of positive reviews praising the book. Also, I knew that once all the books were released, the cliffhanger aspect wouldn't be nearly as big a deal. The trick, then, was to get the books out as quickly as possible.

Now, as many already know, Del Rey signed the first half of the Legends series and published them one book a year (June 2016, July 2017, July 2018). That's the schedule most traditional publishers standardize on, but I wasn't going the traditional route so I wanted to accelerate the release dates. My thought was to put out a book every six months (a rate I had previously used when self-published), but Robin wanted to be even more aggressive. She wanted the full second half to come out in a year or less. As is often the case, Robin won, and we'll have all three books published within ten months. Here are the dates:

- *Age of Legend* – July 2019
- *Age of Death* – February 2020
- *Age of Empyre* – May 2020

But even that accelerated schedule wasn't quick enough for Robin, so we'll continue our tradition of giving Kickstarter backers the books several months before the retail release. Those who preordered during the *Age of Death* Kickstarter received the story in October 2019. We don't yet have a date for the *Age of Empyre* project, but backers of it will get the last book in February instead of May.

That's really all you need to know when starting this book, but I will repeat something I've said in other author's notes: I have greatly appreciated receiving all the amazing emails, so please keep them coming to michael@michaelsullivan-author.com. It's never a bother hearing from readers—it's an honor and a privilege.

Now that this preamble is over, let's all gather in a circle around the lodge's cozy eternal flame as I invite you back to an age of myths and legends, to a time when humans were known as Rhunes and elves were once believed to be gods. In this particular case, allow me to take you to the *Age of Death*.

Michael J. Sullivan
October 2019

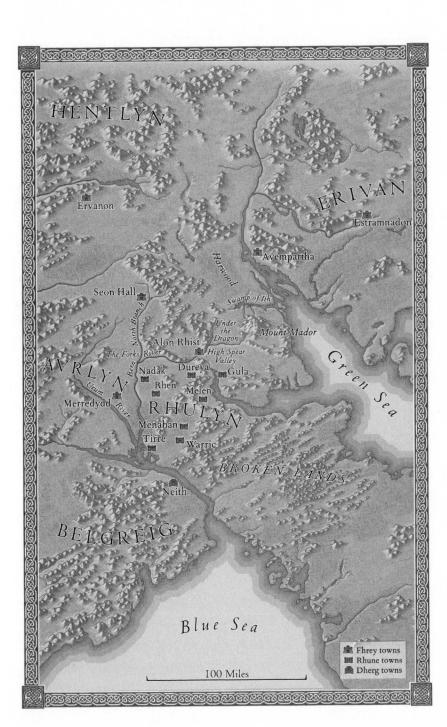

HENTLYN

ERIVAN

Ervanon

Estramnadon

Harwood

Avempartha

Seon Hall

Swamp of Ith

North Branch

Under the Dragon

Mount Mador

Green Sea

Alon Rhist

The Forks River

High Spear Valley

AVRLYN

Bern

Nadak

Dureya

Gula

Utum River

Rhen

Melen

Merredydd

RHULYN

Menahan

Tirre

Warric

BROKEN LANDS

Neith

BELGREIG

Blue Sea

Fhrey towns
Rhune towns
Dherg towns

100 Miles

Age OF Death

CHAPTER ONE

The Great Gate

The good news is that death is not the end, but that is also the bad news.

— THE BOOK OF BRIN

Oh dear Mari, what have I done? Brin's thought came too late. The pool had her. There was a distinct sucking sound as she was drawn into its center. She could feel the muck around her feet, a sensation like entering the throat of a toothless serpent, pulling her down. The icy chill, colder than anything she'd ever felt, inched up her legs and continued past her waist. What trapped her wasn't liquid nor mud, but rather a thick freezing tar that seemed alive. She shook with terror as, inch by inch, the goo crept up her chest, making it difficult to breathe.

Tesh cried out as if he, too, were dying—the loss of Brin's life ending his own.

How can I do this? He really loves me, and I—

Like the hand of a corpse from a nightmare, the muck slid around her neck. Sinking farther, Brin tilted her head back in a last desperate attempt to keep her face above the murky pool. When the slime covered her mouth and eyes, she could no longer suppress the scream.

With her mouth filled with muck, the shriek was silent. Tesh would never know that her last word had been his name. After the shout, Brin refused to inhale. The instinct not to draw in a breath while underwater proved stronger than her desire for air.

Heroic thoughts, which had given her the courage to enter the pool, vanished from her mind; reason, reflection, and contemplation soon followed. What remained was a staccato rhythm of imagery: sunshine on leaves, rain in a bucket, chopped carrots, her mother's laughter, an icy pond. As her mind froze in terror, her body lashed out, kicking and thrashing in a hopeless struggle to survive. Reaching up, her hand briefly broke the surface. She felt air—air!

So close.

And so short-lived, as her fingers were consumed once more.

Her arms slowed, growing weak. Her legs refused to listen to her mind and stopped moving.

Additional images emerged: fire in the lodge, sheep in a windstorm, Tesh's hand in hers, words on a page.

While trying to breathe *might* kill her, her body determined that *not* breathing certainly would, so she inhaled. Sludge entered through her nose and mouth. Further attempts to bring in more air stopped with all the suddenness of a bird hitting a window. An involuntary cough sought to clear her airways, but it was as futile as a frightened child shouting at a tempest.

The panic dissipated. A calm enveloped her as she hung motionless in a cold, timeless expanse.

Slowly, her mind returned. Thoughts coalesced into ideas once more, and the first was the most obvious.

I made a mistake—my last mistake.

Brin waited patiently, knowing death was overdue.

More time passed. Nothing happened.

Is it over? Am I . . . ?

The darkness was so absolute that Brin wasn't sure if her eyes were open or closed—a ridiculous thought because she couldn't tell if she had eyes anymore.

Am I dead? I must be.

The thought surfaced with a peculiar calm acceptance, an oddly reasoned conclusion to a most unusual situation. The deduction wasn't obvious, as she still had no clear indication of death. The panic had departed, as had the discomfort of choking, and she no longer felt cold. But by themselves these things didn't definitively signify death. She briefly considered that she might still be alive and had merely passed out.

She tried moving her arms and legs, and they resumed obeying her commands. These limbs reported that she was in a liquid, but it wasn't the thick slime of the pool.

Water. I'm in water.

A moment later, her head breached the surface. Brin took an involuntary breath and began to bob and splash.

Have I somehow survived? Did I . . . ?

Everything was still black, but some things were self-evident. She wasn't in the pool, nor anywhere on the island, and no longer with the witch. Tesh was gone, forever beyond her reach.

The River of Death.

Brin knew the stories. Those who had almost died told of a powerful, dark waterway that carried them toward a bright light. Brin didn't see any glow, and she didn't feel dead. She had her arms and legs, and she was just as bad at swimming as always. Relaxing her efforts, she stopped kicking and let her arms fall limp. Rather than sinking, she floated and bobbed. In that stillness, she couldn't perceive anything: no light, no sound, no smell, no taste or feeling. Brin found herself drowning in nothingness, and in that void, she had to wonder, *Am I only imagining the existence of arms and legs?* With nothing to interact with, she had no means to confirm anything, no ability to refute a growing fear.

Do I still exist? With that came a second, even more horrifying thought. *Was there* ever *someone named Brin? Did any of what I remember of my life actually happen?*

She had no clear answers. Thoughts needed frameworks, references, and foundations. She had none. Along with her senses, she felt herself slipping away.

Am I . . . ?

The sensation of the water vanished. The feeling of bobbing disappeared.

Do I exist?

Without connection, Brin couldn't maintain any sense of herself.

I'm not drowning. I'm dissolving.

What little had been left of her dispersed, broke up, and melted. She faded, nearly vanished, and then—

A light appeared.

Brin saw it. A mere pinprick, like a far-distant star.

Something else exists—so I can, too. I'm not completely gone.

The glint grew. Its radiance revealed the river, a dark, inky snake that wound through a massive rock canyon. Seeing the walls, watching them slide past, Brin knew she was moving, going somewhere. In the reassurance that swelled within her, Brin had a moment to think, to remember. Instantly, she was stabbed by the memory of Tesh, of the cry he'd let out. The sound had stayed with her. That horrible scream had followed her all the way down.

I'm sorry, Brin thought, as the light grew bigger and brighter.

Neither yellow nor orange, the glow possessed a lackluster, pale quality, like a late afternoon in deep winter when the sun was lost behind a blanket of clouds. As she drew closer, the illumination made it possible to see farther, and she discerned the impossibly high walls of jagged stone that rose to either side. Where the river ended was a pool and a beach bathed in light. The movement of silhouetted figures caught her attention.

People! Yes, there are most definitely others.

The light was behind them, so all she saw were silhouettes, hundreds standing together in a crowd. Beyond them, Brin spotted the source of the glow emanating from behind a great gate and a pair of towering doors. They were closed, but the brilliance was so powerful that it bled through the gaps between the door and the frame.

Unexpectedly, Brin's feet touched a sandy bottom. She was dragged along for a bit, then she caught her footing and stood.

"Brin!" Roan shouted while coming toward her. Her friend didn't look dead. Roan appeared just as she had before entering the pool, not a bit of muck visible as she pulled Brin from the water.

"Stupid girl." Moya came over and hugged Brin tightly. Breaking the embrace, Moya reached up and brushed away one of Brin's stray hairs. "I told you not to come. Ordered you. Why? Why didn't you listen?"

"I realized something that I hadn't before but should have. Muriel's name was listed in the Agave tablets along with Ferrol, Drome, and Mari. If she is a god, then her father would be, too. Tressa was right about Malcolm and he wanted me to come."

"So, you're a believer now, too? And that faith was enough to kill yourself over?"

"That's only part of it. Malcolm told me *The Book of Brin* might be the most important thing ever created by mankind. He knew I would write everything down. He wants me to tell the truth, and he thinks I'll find it down here."

"You still shouldn't have done it." Moya's voice was tense. "Persephone will never forgive me."

"She will if we succeed."

"Slim chance of that."

Together, they walked over to join Gifford, Tressa, and Rain, who stood in a tight cluster overlooking the pool and the crowd at the door. They all glanced at her, smiling cheerlessly and nodding as if they shared a solemn secret. Brin knew what it was. They were together, but they were also dead.

Rain still had his pick, Moya her bow, and Tressa wore the same oversized shirt she'd taken from Gelston, a bit of rope binding it around her waist. Brin hadn't finished the garment she'd promised to Tressa for learning to read, and it gave her a stab of regret that the woman would endure all of eternity in such a shabby outfit.

Moya studied Brin, then peered over the Keeper's shoulder at the water. Her eyes darkened. "Tesh?"

Brin shook her head and pretended to smile. "He let me go," she said in a cheery tone that sounded forced, even to herself.

Moya gave her a sad nod.

"He tried to stop me. It took a while to convince him. I was worried you might have left already, and I wouldn't know how to find you."

"Not much chance of that." Gifford gestured at the mob gathered near the great doors. "There appears to be a wait to get in."

Roan spun abruptly. "Gifford?" She stared at him in fascination.

"What?"

"You just—what did you say?"

Gifford shrugged. "I was just thinking that there must have been a big battle to have so many people waiting."

"You did it again!" Roan hopped on her toes in excitement.

"Did what?"

"Gifford, say my name."

His brows furrowed. He glanced at the rest of them, confused. "Roan, what are you—" Then, his eyes went wide, and his mouth hung open.

"You can speak like everyone else." Roan reached up and caressed his lips.

"Roan," he said, louder this time. "Roan, Roan, *Rrr-oan!*"

Gifford threw his arms around his wife, and the two hugged and laughed.

Brin found herself smiling. All of them were grinning except— "Where's Tekchin?"

"He went to the gate——" Something caught Moya's attention from the direction of the crowd, and she waved her bow over her head. "Here he comes."

The Fhrey trotted over, moving with the same ease he had exhibited in life. "It's locked up good and tight. No one can get in, and they don't know why. The consensus is something is wrong."

"I'd say so." Moya frowned. "We go through all the trouble of dying just to get stuck here? Are we even sure where the gate goes?"

"Yep. It's Phyre, all right. That gate is usually open," he explained. "The light from inside attracts the newly dead. When they get close enough, they find family and friends waiting."

"How do you know all that?"

"There's a woman over that way who has been here before——but she was sucked back into her body. At least that's what she told me. And according to some guy who died from a fever in southern Rhulyn, the doors have been closed for a long time."

"Any idea how long?"

Tekchin gestured at the darkness behind them. "How can you tell?"

Moya led the others toward the doors. The crowd was nearly all Rhunes, and she became unsettled by the large number of children. Tekchin was the only Fhrey, but there were a fair number of dwarfs. The common thread was that they all looked frightened, lost, and confused.

Everyone here is dead.

The idea would take some time for Moya to get used to. None of them looked like ghosts. They were just people, although oddly dressed. Few besides those in her group wore traveling clothes. Most of the ladies were draped in gowns, and the men sported what had to have been their best tunics. None of them had cloaks or packs or so much as a bag, but they all had stones. Some hung around their necks, but most were clenched tightly in fists.

"Make way, make way!" Tekchin plowed through the mass of people, who dutifully let them pass. He used an outstretched hand like the prow of a ship to cut through the sea of spirits. No one appeared offended at his forcefulness. On the contrary, the party's determined movement must have provided an air of authority because people approached with pleas.

"There's been a mistake," a man told them as they brushed by. He was dressed in shredded clothes that dangled in tatters. Unlike most of the others, he had no stone. "I shouldn't be here. I wasn't even sick. I was out in the forest . . ."

They walked out of hearing range, and Moya was grateful she didn't find out how that scenario played out.

"My babies, my babies . . ." They came upon a weeping woman, who sat rocking and hugging herself. She looked right at Moya. "How will they live without me?"

A finely dressed woman with her arms folded tightly across her chest glared at them and then at the gate. "Are we expected to just wait here for eternity? If people keep dying, it's going to get mighty crowded on this beach."

Tekchin reached back and took Moya's hand as they pushed into a denser section of the crowd. Drawing near the gate, she realized that the entrance was even bigger than it had appeared at a distance. Above the doors, three figures were carved from stone. The trio stood shoulder to shoulder, looking down on them: one male dwarf and two females, a Rhune and a Fhrey. At their feet, creatures were depicted perched on the lintel, throwing rocks. Below them were the great doors themselves. Far taller than those of Alon Rhist—bigger even than the great entrance to Neith—these were massive and appeared to be cast from gold. Each door was decorated with relief sculptures of people struggling in all manner of misfortune. Some were falling from great heights. Others raised defensive arms while being pelted by the stones thrown from those on the lintel. Still more were stabbed, strangled, or beheaded. Moya couldn't help noticing a panel near the bottom where a woman was being overwhelmed by huge, crushing waves. One arm reached up for help that would never come.

Light seeped out around the edges of the doors and bathed the beach with its only source of illumination.

It's like the moon is trapped back there.

"What's your hurry?" a dwarf asked as Tekchin pushed past. "Got someplace to be, do you?"

The Galantian gave the complainer a nasty look, and nothing else was said. He handed out a few more shoves and glares until they reached the gate. Moya moved right up against the doors, touching the cold stone and feeling the face of the drowning woman. "Such comforting carvings they have. Makes you want to rush right in. Who do you think those three at the top are?"

"No idea," Tekchin replied. "But as for getting in, do you have a plan?" He gave her a questioning look along with a mischievous smile. Most everything Tekchin served up came with some version of an amused grin. For him, life was an unending adventure. Death hadn't tarnished his attitude, and Moya was grateful for that.

He loves me. The great Galantian, the-onetime-god-from-across-the-river, loves me, Moya—the uncontrollable daughter of Audrey the washerwoman.

She still couldn't get over that Tekchin had forfeited more than a thousand years of life for her. In all the time they'd spent together, he'd refused to say, "I love you." But in that one amazing moment of self-sacrifice when he'd scooped her up and carried her to the pool, he'd proven his devotion.

Moya stared up at the towering pair of doors, then shrugged. She looked at those nearby. "Anyone tried knocking?"

"Are you insane?" the impatient woman asked.

Moya nodded. "Probably." Reaching up, she found a smooth area and gave the door three solid slaps with the palm of her hand.

The noise was louder than expected, but nothing happened.

Moya gave the gates a solid shove, which did nothing except push her backward.

The testy woman rolled her eyes.

"Worth a try," Moya concluded. She rose on her toes to see the river that lay beyond those gathered. More were arriving. Heads bobbed along like debris, and the newly arrived climbed out at a sandy bank.

"There must be a few hundred here—maybe more." She looked at a man in a nightshirt. The gown's chest and armpits were stained yellow. His mustache and beard looked hard, coated with dried mucus. "How long do we have to wait?"

"Like I know?" He pulled on his filthy garment with a scowl. "I was in bed, sleeping. Then I wake up to this!"

Moya scowled right back. "Oh, you poor dear. Died in your own bed, did you? How sad. Some of us drowned in a disgusting pool of slime. And that sad bastard back there"—she pointed at the man in the tattered clothes—"looks like he was mauled by a bear. And have you looked at these gates? Seen these images? You should think of all the ways you could have gone." She shook her head. "Died in your sleep. Honestly!"

The man backed up and slipped into the crowd, leaving the base of the doors to them.

With Mucus Beard gone, she looked to Rain. "Okay, so how does it work, exactly? The *you-know-what*, I mean?"

The dwarf straightened up as if guilty of something. "What? Oh, ah—right." Like Moya, he, too, took a second to be certain no one was around. Then lowering his voice, he said, "So, a key goes into a lock."

"What's that?" Moya asked.

"Ah, well, they appear as openings, little holes that the key fits into."

They all scanned the vast and confusing face of the panels. "There are dozens of them," Moya said. She pointed. "There's a cave up there, a doorway over here. Which is the right one?"

"Could try all of them," Gifford said.

Moya shook her head. "Can't really be experimenting in front of an audience. No one is supposed to know, remember?"

"You're right," Tressa said. "So, let's just wait forever, which down here isn't just a figure of speech."

Moya frowned at her. "The idea that death would make you less of a bitch was just too much to hope for, wasn't it?"

"I am what I am," Tressa said while dramatically sweeping her hands down her sides as if showing off a new dress.

"Won't be at the top," Rain said. "Too hard to use. Most locks are within easy reach for convenience. Look there." He pointed partway up near the center of the right-hand-side panel at a scene where a bear mauled three men. Near it, the sun was depicted as a man with wild hair. His mouth was wide open, revealing a hole in the stone. "That's Eton, and she has his key."

He turned to Tressa. "Slide it in teeth first, the part with the jagged edges, then turn it around like this." He rotated his wrist.

"Maybe you should do it," Tressa said as fear crept into her voice. "You know how it works."

"No," Moya interjected. "Malcolm gave it to you, and you're the one who got us into this. So don't try pushing your responsibility onto others."

Tressa looked up at the gaping mouth, then back at the crowd. "If I reach up, people will see."

Tressa looked at Moya as if she held all the answers to life's many riddles. She didn't, and even if she did, being dead meant the rules had changed.

Roan whispered into Gifford's ear. "I'll handle that," he declared. "Just be ready."

"For what?" Moya asked, and before she could say more, Gifford walked down the slope into the crowd.

"What's he doing?" she asked Roan.

Roan smiled. "Just watch."

Gifford tore his leg brace off, threw it aside, and strode out straight and tall down to the bank of the river. Then he shouted, "Hello, everyone!" Reaching into the bag that was still at his side, he pulled out three stones. "I wonder if any of you know me. I'm Gifford of Dahl Rhen. I was once a potter."

"I do!" exclaimed a woman from the crowd, as if she'd won a prize. "Bought a bowl in Vernes by a potter named Gifford of Rhen. Good pot. Real good pot." Confusion dawned, and she added, "But I was told a cripple had made it."

"Indeed!" Gifford shouted. "That would be me. I'm that very same wretch. All my life I could never talk right. I had a terrible speech impediment. Couldn't even say the name of my beautiful wife. It's Roan, by the way—RrrOAN!" he roared. "While alive, I couldn't say *right* or *rain, ridiculous* or *terrible.*" Gifford grinned immeasurably, his smile reflected on the faces of those in the crowd.

Roan stood beside Moya and Brin, watching in rapture, her hands clasped together in front of her mouth. She bounced on her toes and appeared to be on the verge of both laughing and crying.

"Yes, I was an awful mess. My back was as twisted as a carrot grown in a rock-filled garden. I couldn't even walk without help. People in my dahl used to call me The Goblin because of how I shambled around. A terrible, wretched thing I was, but watch this!"

Gifford began juggling the three stones Suri had given him. The crowd paid closer attention now, following the stones as they flew high into the air. Moya guessed that such entertainment was a welcome change for those who had been waiting on the beach for who knew how long. Everyone watched, including Tressa.

"Hey!" Moya called out through clenched teeth, shaking the woman's arm. "Now! Do it! Hurry!"

"Oh, right." Tressa plunged a hand down her shirt and retrieved the twisted bit of metal hanging from a chain.

"And now, watch this!" Gifford shouted.

Moya didn't see what he was doing, but the crowd was impressed enough to let out a combined, "Oohhhh," which was followed by an, "Ahhhh!"

Tressa inserted the key into Eton's mouth and twisted. There was a *clank*—a loud one. When Moya looked around, all eyes were still on Gifford, who was catching the rocks behind his back.

Tressa withdrew the key and shoved it down her shirt.

Moya gave each door a slight push, and they began to swing inward, the light growing. This caught the crowd's attention, and everyone turned to look.

The doors continued to part as if drawn back by giants. As the gap widened, the brilliance blinded everyone.

CHAPTER TWO

Finding Fault

For every mistake, someone must be responsible and punishment exacted. To think otherwise is to believe we are not the center of the universe, and the world does not revolve around us.

— THE BOOK OF BRIN

A cold wind cut through Persephone's breckon mor as she stood beneath the shrouded morning sun. Dust-mote snow floated wistfully in the air, playful and pretty. The not-quite-snow turned the grassy mound a lighter shade of green. Although she was only a couple hundred yards from the camp, Persephone was confident in her privacy. She stood on the lee side of the beast. Nearly everyone was still terrified of the winged serpent that rested, but didn't sleep, on the hill's crest. The great beast's eyes were closed, and while Persephone visited often, the dragon never moved, and it had only spoken that one time. Once had been enough.

Persephone kept her distance from the creature. She was terrified by it, yet she visited nearly every day. In the morning hours or late at night when no one would see, she climbed the hill to stand before the beast and confess her fears and failures as well as confide her hopes and dreams. She knew it could hear and understand—believed that somehow *he* listened, too. Persephone didn't have the slightest clue how the magic worked, but she felt certain that when she spoke to the dragon, Raithe heard.

"They should have returned by now," she told the beast. "I'm worried. They were only supposed to scout out the swamp and then come right back. That should have taken only a day, two or three at the most."

She wrung the fingers of one hand and then the other. "I sent Moya to watch over them and Tekchin went, too. With Tesh along, they should have been fine. So, why aren't they back?" She hadn't expected an answer, and she didn't receive one. The dragon didn't even open its eyes. "Why did I let them go?"

Persephone sighed out a cloud into the frosty air, her eyes focusing on the beast's massive claws. "Because I was terrified the sky would darken with more of your kind; that's why. I'm still afraid." Looking up at the gray sky and feeling the gentle kiss of snow on her cheeks, Persephone pictured vast, black shadows, swarms as numerous as locusts. "We need another miracle, Raithe."

Persephone dropped to her knees, hands clutching her arms, head bowed as if praying. "I've no more faith in Nyphron's plans than my own. We sent Elysan to the north to speak with the giants, and half of the second legion marched south to look for an easier way across the river. I don't have high hopes for either. Lately, it seems like all we do is send people into the wilderness to be swallowed. I'm out of ideas. *We're* out of ideas. While he'll never admit it, not to himself and not to me, I think Nyphron feels the same desperation—a sense that the tide has shifted once more, and we'll be drowned this time. It all feels so hopeless and absurd. When we first heard the Fhrey were coming to destroy the dahls, it was easy to accept our loss. In Tirre, when we had no keenig and no weapons to fight with, it made sense to expect that we would perish. Even in Alon Rhist, success was such a distant dream. Yet somehow, we always survived. There have been so many near misses—so many miracles."

Persephone thought about all the famines, diseases, and skirmishes among the clans that Rhen had endured during her lifetime. None of them compared to the perils they'd faced over the last few years. Humanity seemed like a weak flame that the wind was determined to extinguish, but each time a gust arose, something got in the way—an unexpected stroke of luck that under normal circumstances would have been impossible.

"It's almost as if—"

From behind, Persephone heard a labored breath and the crunch of grass. Turning, she spied the tall, thin figure of a man bundled in a cloak. He used a spear like a walking stick while climbing the hill—a familiar yet unexpected sight.

"Malcolm?"

"Good morning," he said brightly. "I thought I might find you here."

Pushing to her feet, Persephone stared at the man, and she was overcome with a strange mix of happiness and irritation. "I haven't seen you in years. Where have you been?"

"Many places actually: Tirre, Caric, Neith, and a little point of land that juts out into the Green Sea."

"In case you haven't heard, there's a war on. What made you leave? We needed every available man."

Malcolm finished his climb, leaned on the spear, and smiled at her. "I missed you, too."

"I—" She felt embarrassed. "I'm sorry. I didn't mean to scold. I did miss you very much."

This was truer than even Persephone had realized, and she gave him a hug worthy of the old friend he had become. But Malcolm was more than that. Before he had disappeared, Raithe's unassuming tagalong had grown into a valued adviser. After the Battle of Grandford, Roan had mentioned something about him being special, but Roan's observations were often obscure and hard to understand.

Persephone had initially noticed Malcolm's hidden talent firsthand when he'd predicted the birth of Nolyn. And he hadn't merely guessed she might have a child soon. He'd told her she would give birth to Nyphron's son in a tent on the bank of the Bern River in the High Spear Valley during the first battle of the next spring. A bold claim at the time given that she was still in Alon Rhist and unsure if she would ever see Nyphron again, much less marry him. Persephone had known seers in the past, and as such, she was untroubled by his apparent, albeit recently developed, foresight. Suri and Tura used bones and spoke in vague, cryptic terms, admitting they didn't know *exactly* what would happen, but Malcolm's predictions were made as precise statements of fact.

Persephone let go of Malcolm, and she offered a sad smile. "It's just that things aren't going well, and I'm . . ."

He nodded, a knowing smile at the corner of his mouth. "You're terrified. You're worried that the Fhrey will obliterate all of mankind."

Persephone blinked. "Well, yeah."

"But that's not *all* you are thinking. Is it?"

"Isn't that enough?"

"For most, it would be, but the chances of Rhunes prevailing against the Fhrey have always been slim. Your fears are rooted closer to your heart." Malcolm looked at the dragon. "You believe Raithe's blood is on your hands, that sending Suri to Avempartha was pure stupidity, and that letting your closest friends disappear into the Swamp of Ith will result in nothing but their deaths."

His words cut, but she retorted, "Maybe I was premature about saying I missed you." All of what he said was true, but hearing it spoken aloud, and by a friend, was devastating. "Did you come back just to remind me what a failure I am?"

His eyes left the creature and returned to her, his lower lip offering sympathy. "Not at all. I'm here, among other things, to show you just how wrong you are."

"How can you say that? I sent birds, foolishly seeking peace. I should have realized that the fane didn't want Suri to negotiate. I've given up our most valuable weapon, and Lothian will get her to reveal the secret of dragons. I lost this war, Malcolm. I've ruined everything."

He shook his head. "This war won't be won or lost by birds or dragons, nor by greed or hate, but by the courage and virtue of an unlikely few who will forfeit everything to save the future. That's how it works, you know?

The proud, the greedy, the vengeful are never the ones to change the world—not for the better, at least. They can't; they don't have the tools. It's like asking a fish to fly. It's not in their nature to sacrifice for others. But those who went to the swamp understand the importance of doing what's needed when the time comes, and they're not the only ones."

"What do you mean?"

"You, Persephone. Your sacrifices have made a difference, and they will continue to do so."

She let out a sad laugh. "Me? Maybe I did some good in the past. The trip to Neith and moving to Alon Rhist gave us some time, but I've done nothing of value for years."

"Really? Is that what you think?" He glanced at the dragon. "Why did you choose Nyphron over Raithe?"

"I don't see how my choice of husband has a bearing on anything."

"I do, and you do, too. Why are you so reluctant to say it out loud? Tell me."

She didn't want to answer, but with so many gone, she was down to just a few people she could speak freely with, and Malcolm was one of those. She sighed, embarrassed to admit it. "Because he was the best for the job."

"Which one? Lover? Father? Confidant?"

"No." She returned to staring at the grass.

"Well?"

Persephone was a bit surprised by his insistence. Malcolm had never been so confrontational before. "Ruler," she finally said.

"Yes." Malcolm nodded. "Not exactly the trait most women would look for in a man. But why does that matter? The Rhunes have their chieftains."

"The world has changed. We can't go back to the fractured clans that we once were, not now that we've seen the benefit of a single ruler."

"But you are already keenig. You are the leader of all the Rhunes, aren't you?"

"For now, but I'm forty years old. I'll be lucky to see Nolyn grow to be a man. When I thought there was a chance we would win, I saw Nyphron as a steady hand, a fair hand. He isn't much of a husband, not passionate or devoted, but he is strong, rational, and our best chance for a better future. He will likely live for another thousand years. In that time, he will bring stability and do great things for us as a people."

"And that's why you sacrificed your future—the happiness you might have known with Raithe. You did it for the good of the world and for generations yet to come. And you will keep doing so for the rest of your life."

Persephone took a hard breath and shook her head. "If it had only been my burden, that would have been one thing, but it wasn't. It's because of me that Raithe is gone. I took away his life!"

"No, you didn't." Just as Persephone had developed a preoccupation with the grass between her feet, Malcolm looked to the clouds as if bad weather were approaching. "Raithe didn't die because you rejected him. What's more, Suri didn't go to Avempartha because you asked her, and Brin, Moya, Roan, and Gifford didn't leave because you let them. Take a moment to think. Set aside your devotion to regret and guilt and consider that all these things may have come to pass because that's how it had to be. Everyone has their part to play. Their *own* part. It's not because of *you;* it's because of *them.* They are sacrificing for the greater good, just as you have done."

"So, is that your way of saying the whole world doesn't revolve around me?"

He smiled. "More or less. My point is that while much of what has happened is to your credit, the things you see as failures are not your fault. None of it is. Not the war, not Raithe's death, nor Suri's capture."

"Whose fault is it, then?"

Malcolm hesitated, then looked around as if he'd heard something. "Where is Nolyn?" he asked, as if just noticing they were alone.

"What?" Persephone was stunned at the abrupt turn in the conversation.

"I know it's early, but don't little boys rise with the dawn?"

"He's with Justine."

Malcolm nodded. "Of course," he said with a lingering tone that was bloated with insinuation.

"What?"

Malcolm frowned. There was judgment, negative and disapproving. "I was just wondering—does Nyphron spend *any* time with the child?"

"You're avoiding my question."

"Hmm?" he said.

Persephone folded her arms. "Whose fault is it, Malcolm?"

The man with the spear frowned. His shoulders drooped, and he sighed. *"Fault.* It's an interesting word, don't you think? When you became keenig, you didn't ask whose fault *that* was, but I'm quite certain the Gula leaders did. A fault is only leveled when something bad happens. Success is free of such a burden. Perhaps it might be best to await judgment on events before laying blame where there may not be room for it."

Tura would just have said, *I don't know.* No doubt, Suri would have brought up butterflies or clouds or something even more nonsensical. Malcolm knew the answer—of that she was certain—but he was holding back.

Why? she wondered.

Persephone stared at him as a new thought began to form in her mind. Seers were those who could sometimes read mystical signs that gave them an insight into the future. To her knowledge, none of them was ever capable of shaping events to come.

Is that even possible?

When Tressa had mentioned it was Malcolm who told her about a passageway that could be used to rescue Suri, Persephone hadn't thought much about it. But now . . .

Malcolm had been with Raithe when Shegon was killed, the turning point when Rhunes began to question the divinity of the Fhrey. When she first met Raithe, it had been Malcolm who had helped persuade Raithe to return to Dahl Rhen, and just in time to face Nyphron and his Galantians.

Also, when Arion came to take Nyphron into custody, Malcolm hit her with a rock, keeping both the Galantian leader and the Miralyith in Dahl Rhen.

Can these all just be coincidences?

"Malcolm? How did you know Suri would be captured years before it happened?" she asked.

"That's not what you really want to know, is it?"

He was right; it wasn't. "Is there still a chance for the survival of mankind?"

The funny-looking man with the sharp nose and lanky frame nodded. "I'm not saying it's a certainty. And while I was gone, I discovered things that make matters even more precarious. But I'm here to tell you that plans have been set in motion, and I still have faith. I want you to have some, too."

"You're talking about the people who went to the swamp, aren't you? Are they all right? What has happened to them?"

"You may want to sit down."

"Oh dear Mari." Persephone wavered. Returning to her knees, she waited before him like the guilty under an executioner's ax.

Malcolm knelt down as well and took hold of her hands. "Moya, Tekchin, Brin, Roan, Gifford, Tressa, and Rain—they are . . ."

"What?"

He shifted uncomfortably.

"Tell me!" she shouted.

"They're . . . dead."

Persephone felt as if her heart had stopped, as if time did as well.

"That's not possible. Can't be. It can't. They only went to look—just to scout, nothing else. They didn't go to fight."

"You're right. There was no skirmish. They drowned."

Persephone was frantically shaking her head. "All of them? No . . . no . . ."

Oh dear Mari, not them, too. How many more have to die?

"But . . ." Malcolm paused, then added with a measured smile, "it's okay."

She wasn't certain she had heard him correctly, but his face—that weak smile—was backing up his words. No, not words, *word*. "By the will of Elan, how can *that* be okay?"

"Because"—Malcolm straightened up and squared his shoulders—"there's a good chance they'll come back."

She stared at him. This time she had no trouble looking into his eyes. "Are you insane?"

He shook his head and held up his hands to calm her, or at least fend her off. "It, ah . . . won't be easy. In fact, it's going to be a lot harder now than I first expected."

"You *knew* they would go?" The understanding dawned on her hard enough to shorten her breath. *"You* planned it." She began shaking her head. "This isn't my fault—it's yours!"

"Yes." He nodded. "All of it is, but it's not over yet. Allow me to explain where they went. You see, Persephone, I sent them to—"

"Their deaths. You killed them!"

"True." He held up a finger. "But I'm sending help."

CHAPTER THREE

Masters of Secrets

Education is never without cost; all the truly valuable lessons leave a scar.

— THE BOOK OF BRIN

All of the dead fanes had their own crypts, decorated with images illustrating their many achievements. Those hallowed halls were not only eternal resting places but tributes to the leaders' greatness as well. Each one was a marvel of architecture, and members of the Eilywin tribe had spared no expense in their construction. All five burial chambers stood in a place of honor just off Florella Plaza in the center of Estramnadon, so every Fhrey could easily visit and be suitably awed and inspired.

Few ever came.

This lack of devotion saddened Imaly, providing further proof that the Fhrey society was a structure with a crumbling foundation and, as a result, was on the verge of collapse. Yet the seldom-visited crypts also provided a much-needed resource—a convenient, deserted sanctuary.

"Why are we here?" Nanagal asked as Imaly closed the door to the mausoleum that housed Gylindora Fane, sealing them in.

"Nanagal, you're an Eilywin," Imaly said brightly. "Could you please build another fire in that brazier in the corner? It's rather dim in here, wouldn't you agree?"

"One doesn't *build* a fire. It just needs to be lit."

"Oh yes, how clever of you. Well, can you do that then, dear? You're tall enough to reach the brazier." She smiled at him.

"You didn't answer Nanagal's question, Imaly," Hermon stated. Stocky and unusually hairy for a Fhrey, he had failed to shave that day, and his face had a shadow. "Are we going to commune with the dead? Try to speak to your great-grandmother?" He looked at Volhoric. "Is such a thing sanctioned by Ferrol?"

"Absolutely not," the high priest replied with folded arms.

"We aren't here for any such nonsense," Imaly said hotly. "For Ferrol's sake, we're in my ancestor's tomb. Show a little respect, won't you?"

"Then, why?" Hermon asked.

"We are holding a meeting."

The brazier ignited, and the interior of the crypt brightened. A flickering yellow glow played to remarkable effect off the gold and silver gilding. The rear of the vault became visible and with it the sarcophagus of Gylindora. The stone image on the lid looked nothing like her. Too stiff, it lacked any real artistry and failed to capture the true essence of the first fane.

"A meeting?" Nanagal questioned, letting go of the fire starter that swayed from its cord. "You might not be aware of this, but we have a perfectly fine meeting place just down the street. It's called the Airenthenon—nice place, pillars, benches—built for exactly this kind of assembly."

"No, not *this* kind," Imaly assured.

Almost all the other senior tribal leaders were in attendance: Nanagal of the Eilywin, Osla of the Asendwayr, Hermon of the Gwydry, and Volhoric of the Umalyn. Despite the absence of Vidar of the Miralyith, they had enough councilors for a quorum. And even though the members of the Aquila were not meeting in the Airenthenon, their decisions would be binding.

"I've asked you here because this august body may be the only thing that stands between our society and complete annihilation. I need to assess your opinions about Fane Lothian and his ability to rule—your *true* opinions."

"And you found it necessary to seek that out here?" Osla asked. Having only recently joined the Aquila, she rarely spoke, and Imaly found it interesting that she was the first to respond. Those who were more experienced waited.

"Yes," Imaly said. "What we do in the Airenthenon is public knowledge. What we say here *stays here.*" These last two words she said with enough bite to suggest a threat.

"What exactly do you want to know?" Nanagal asked with all the tonality of non-commitment. Nanagal was no fool, but he didn't care for hypotheticals. He preferred everything laid out, clear and irrevocable.

"How many of you approve of the fane's performance since he took the throne?"

No one spoke.

"I agree with you," Imaly declared. "Since his ascension, we have suffered a Miralyith rebellion that nearly destroyed the Airenthenon, an open revolt of the Instarya tribe, and a war that may very well destroy our entire civilization. And he's only been fane for a few years, a mere heartbeat in the full reign of a fane. None of this was necessary or inevitable, and all of it was the direct result of his actions or the lack thereof."

Imaly brushed the front of her asica to smooth out a wrinkle and give them time to savor the aroma of the meal she had set before them. "And why has his reign been such a failure? Because Lothian does not seek our counsel. Since taking the throne, he has rarely graced the Airenthenon with his presence except to deliver edicts, ultimatums, or sweeping declarations. This is not how it is supposed to be. The Aquila was formed to assist our leader, to help guide decisions utilizing our combined wisdom. But Lothian wishes no such assistance, wants no insight. His performance thus far has demonstrated his poor judgment."

"What are you getting at, Imaly?" Again, it was Osla who asked—being the only one who truly didn't understand.

"Why, nothing—yet. I am merely asking a question. But perhaps I should rephrase it, so let me put forth the following: If it were possible to have a different fane, would you want one?"

"Lothian was chosen by Ferrol," Osla said, as if this self-evident proof made Imaly's hypothetical inquiry moot.

Imaly watched for, but didn't see, the same mindless devotion to tradition in the others' eyes. Having hatched the plan together with Imaly, Volhoric was already converted. So it was Nanagal and Hermon she waited on. Neither spoke, each stabbing back at her with suspicious eyes.

"Ferrol didn't act alone in picking Lothian," she continued, "and perhaps we were the ones who failed our lord by not choosing a better challenger than Zephyron. But this isn't about the past. It's about the future. So will no one answer my simple, harmless question?" Imaly folded her arms and leaned back against the ornate tile wall.

"You're speaking of treason," Osla said.

"No, dear. I'm only asking a question. We are merely having a conversation. No one is suggesting we arm ourselves and storm the palace—*that* would be treason. I'm only asking for opinions and soliciting the combined wisdom of the Aquila. That's why it was created, isn't that so?"

"And yet we are meeting here and not in the Airenthenon, so don't try to pretend you are just making harmless inquiries," Osla accused.

Imaly bowed her head, conceding the point. "Be that as it may, I've still not received an answer."

Nanagal stepped forward. "I suppose that would depend on who would replace him." Unlike Imaly's casual posture, which was carefully chosen to suggest confidence, his was stiff and straight.

"A valid point, but then let me ask this: What would Lothian need to do in order for you to prefer *any Fhrey* other than him?"

This prompted a series of smiles and near laughs.

Nanagal shrugged at the absurdity. "I don't know. I suppose if he went insane and became incapable of reasoned thought."

"So, you concede that under certain circumstances removal of the fane may be necessary? What if he threatened the very existence of the Fhrey as a people? Would you be willing to take steps to remove him in such a case?"

The smiles faded.

Nanagal looked to Volhoric. "Would insanity constitute a breaking of the covenant with Ferrol? In such a circumstance, wouldn't our lord demand removal of the fane?"

Volhoric shook his head. "Going strictly by Ferrol's Law, the fane can do whatever he desires, whether sane or not. Tradition alone—not Ferrol's edict—demands that he work for the benefit of the Fhrey. I suppose it is possible he could summarily execute every single Fhrey if he chose to do so." He raised a finger. "Likewise, however, only tradition demands that we obey him. Ferrol's Law doesn't explicitly require our obedience."

Imaly pressed, "Given Lothian's inability to effectively rule, do we let him continue, or is it our responsibility to see that a just and capable leader is in control? If left unchecked, Lothian could, indeed, exterminate our entire race. Do you think Ferrol wants that to happen? Should we not intervene?"

They looked to one another.

For what? Help? Support? Guidance?

In the past, Imaly had always appreciated how pliable the members of the Aquila were, but at that moment, she wished for a bit more backbone.

"I'm not sure," Nanagal said. He looked around at the others. "Ferrol's wishes aren't explicitly clear, are they?"

"So, you'd ignore such behavior? A mad fane slaughtering all of us?" Imaly asked. "And wouldn't that be the same as condoning such behavior? But being members of the Aquila, don't you have a responsibility to the tribes you represent?"

"Well, I don't—"

Volhoric stepped in, "In such a circumstance, I think it would be our duty to our Lord Ferrol to remove him."

"Yes." Nanagal reluctantly nodded. "Yes, I suppose so."

Imaly looked at Hermon.

"I have to agree with Nanagal," he said.

Imaly thought, *Of course you do. You always do.*

Osla appeared deep in thought as she stared at her feet, hands clenched before her. "I agree, but . . . I submit that we are only speaking in hypotheticals. Lothian's threat has not yet risen to the level Imaly has put forth. Incompetent he may be, but that has resulted in a stalemate between ourselves and the Rhune. I see no evidence that we are about to be overwhelmed by them at the present. There is no serious threat to our people as a whole. Besides, I don't understand. How would we even . . ." She paused. "Is there a provision in the law for the Aquila to remove a fane from the throne?"

"No," Volhoric said.

"Then how could we—"

"We would have to kill him," Imaly said without hesitation.

Osla's face dropped, her jaw dangling. "That would require breaking Ferrol's Law."

"Yes, it would," Imaly agreed. "A small price to pay to save all of Erivan, I submit. We are the leaders of our tribes. We are the ones entrusted with the responsibility of protecting our civilization, and sometimes that burden requires more than just sitting in a lavish building and doing only what is safe."

The echo of her words lingered for a moment, and then silence filled the tomb as they stared, horrified, at Imaly.

Gylindora had once told her that one of the secrets of crafting baskets was to know how far a reed would bend before it broke. The trick with a particularly stiff one was to soak it overnight, or even longer if necessary. This made it more flexible.

I've done enough for now, she thought.

"Well, this has been a good discussion, hasn't it? And I concur with Osla. Times are not yet so dire, and as I said, all this has only been speculation. Nothing we need to concern ourselves with at the moment. It's just a thought to ponder for another time that, Ferrol willing, may never come." Imaly opened the door, letting the light of day in. "I want to thank each of you for coming."

∂

With a pair of ropes looped beneath the coffin, Vasek's team lifted the casket and set it to one side of the gaping hole. Volhoric had denied Vasek access to the Estramnadon cemetery, but the forest just outside the city had served him well.

The box Vasek had put the mystic in was an actual coffin, a six-sided crate tapered from shoulders to ankles. While Lothian had ordered Suri to be taken to "The Hole"—a set of small cells under the Lion Corps' barracks—it was the fane's command to *bury her* that had given the Master of Secrets the idea to try something even more drastic. Her reported aversion to small spaces seemed like the best leverage and had the added benefit of avoiding physical damage, which always carried additional risk.

He'd picked a coffin that was a tight fit, leaving her no room to move. Constricting the Rhune in the smallest space possible would yield the greatest results. The sound and smell of dirt dropped on the lid, the loss of light bleeding in through the cracks, and the total silence of a grave was a mixture he felt certain would be perfect to convince her to talk.

Timing was key. Too little and the subject would still resist; too much and the Rhune might no longer possess the ability to communicate. His was a dangerous venture, for both the Rhune and for himself. Should he break or kill the fane's prize, Vasek suspected Lothian might make *him* the next occupant of that crate.

The Master of Secrets took no pleasure in his work. He had no feelings about Rhunes one way or the other. The stories about them being wild animals—vicious, cruel, and mindless—were nothing more than propaganda. He knew this because he'd created most of the tales himself. The purpose was to depict the Rhunes as ferocious but inferior.

This combination would generate fear in the Fhrey population, but not despair. Motivation was the goal, desperation the enemy. Lothian needed his people's support, not their anger. The fane was their absolute ruler, Ferrol's embodiment on Elan, but terror tore down even the most sacred of symbols.

As always, Vasek was merely solving a problem given to him by the fane. His task was to obtain a secret from the Rhune's mind. Had the fane asked him to extract the yolk from an egg, he would have gone about that task with similar logic. And yet in the remote alcoves of his mind, Vasek hoped the Rhune survived being *cracked* for the same reason that people regretted accidentally killing a ladybug after mistaking it for a mosquito.

No sound came from inside the box, and Vasek felt his stomach sink.

It has only been two hours!

Pry bars were applied to the lid, and Vasek prepared himself for the sight of a dead Rhune and possibly his own future. The lid came free, slid aside, and there she was, eyes closed, hands at her sides, her chest rising and falling, slowly, evenly.

She's alive!

This thought was quickly followed by an equally surprising one: *She's sleeping.*

Much of life fell short of expectations. Spring wasn't as wondrous as the one dreamed about during a harsh winter, a broken bone was never as painful as imagined, and Suri strongly suspected that death would be the biggest disappointment of all. Everyone spent a good part of their life thinking about what happened when they died. Stories were told by firelight, and all of the tales were larger than life, which was pretty ironic when she thought about it. Reality couldn't possibly compete with decades of anticipation. These were the thoughts going through Suri's head when they put her into the coffin.

The sealing of the box had been difficult to endure, but matters got worse when they began dropping shovelfuls of soil onto the lid. Some of the dirt slipped through the seams between the wooden boards, including the poorly fitted joint directly over her face. With her hands trapped at her sides, she was forced to turn her head to keep breathing. That's when she knew she would die. This thought didn't come as a surprise, but the fact that she wasn't screaming did.

At first, she'd thought, *This is it. My worst nightmare finally faced.*

For most of her life, Suri had been uncomfortable with walls, caves, and any confined place because of an incident that had happened when she was six years old. She had entered a hole that she couldn't get out of, an opening dug into a sandy bluff near a riverbank. Suri was pretty sure it was a fox's den. Being young and small, she was certain she could fit, and she desperately wanted to see how foxes lived. She'd been told they were clever, so she imagined tiny tables—miniatures of the one she and Tura used—set with minuscule cups and plates.

Do they have little beds? Candles? Formal clothes they hide from everyone else that they only wear on special nights when the forest holds secret celebrations?

Suri had long suspected that the Crescent Forest creatures held private parties they didn't talk about when she was around. That hole had been her chance to expose the truth of it, and afterward, she planned to confront the first animal she came across and ask them why she had never been invited.

The problem, she discovered, was that she wasn't as small as a fox. Partway in, she got stuck. When she tried to push her way out, the sandy dirt broke loose and collapsed around her. The more she tried to get out, the worse her situation became. The opening filled up. Everything became dark, and the air was thick with the smell of soil. She'd screamed until her tortured throat refused to make any more sounds. Tura had saved her. The old mystic had found and dug her out . . . three days later.

Ever since, Suri had been terrified of any small place that she wasn't certain she could get out of. She'd lost part of herself in that fox's hole. Left it behind, perhaps, or maybe it had died—smothered in the dirt. Suri slept outside from then on, and she only went into Tura's house on the coldest of nights.

And so she found it odd that as the sounds of the dropped dirt became more and more muffled—as she was buried deeper and deeper—there was no screaming. The panic had failed to come.

I should be losing my mind. Why isn't that happening? Why am I so calm?

This was, after all, number one on Suri's list of worst possibilities, her greatest nightmare.

Except it's not anymore.

Suri had no problem jumping off waterfalls, facing a pack of wolves, or climbing towering trees in storms, but it hadn't always been that way. In the primordial depths of her memories, she remembered a time when she had been scared of such things. Minna had given her courage. The little wolf pup had been fearless. Suri couldn't allow herself to be outdone by a pup, so pride had pushed her to confront her terrors, and she discovered fear was a cowardly bully—all bluster, no substance. After one successful jump off the waterfall, Suri couldn't understand what she'd been so worried about.

Being in tight places like small rooms or the cage that had transported her to the Fhrey capital had *almost* been like being buried alive, but *similar* wasn't the same. Fear of the real thing had haunted her, and it was the anticipation—that unknown factor—which had always paralyzed her. Suri hadn't been forced to face the greatest fear of her childhood, not head-on, not until Vasek's men actually buried her.

So, what has changed?

It didn't take long to puzzle it out. Suri wasn't six anymore, and the time in the grave taught her to see fear for what it was—a child's terror. Suri had evolved, and in doing so, she'd learned there were far greater horrors.

Compared with making a gilarabrywn, being buried alive is nothing.

With that realization came another: It'd been days since she'd had a good night's sleep, and since she was lying down in the dark, she took a nap.

✑

"How is she?" Imaly asked. The Curator of the Aquila was careful to keep her voice low and her eyes on the Garden Door.

"The same condition I suspect you would be in if imprisoned and denied food and water." Vasek, the Master of Secrets, kept his customary even tone, the one carefully cultivated to offer no glimpse into his true feelings. "She's seen better days, I am certain."

The two sat side by side on one of the dozens of stone benches in the Garden that formed the center of the Fhrey city of Estramnadon. Imaly sat to the left, her arm on the rest, he to the far right—close enough to speak quietly, far enough to suggest they might not be together.

Autumn was giving way to winter. The normally lush arboretum had been stripped of its leaves, reduced to naked branches of drab browns, blacks, and grays. The cultural and religious center of the Fhrey universe had also been stripped of its visitors. This was good because it granted the two privacy, but it was bad since so many empty seats prompted the question: Why are they sharing a bench if they aren't together? Still, that wasn't an issue since only one other person was in sight.

Trilos sat in his usual place. He didn't appear to care about the weather; nor did he seem to take any notice of them as they sat on the bench farthest from him.

"I'm not concerned about her physical condition," Imaly whispered. "What about her attitude?"

"One holds hands with the other, don't you think?"

"I wouldn't be asking if I knew the answer. She's a Rhune. I have no understanding of them."

"I'm no expert, either."

Imaly had been careful in choosing allies. Volhoric was necessary since he controlled access to the horn. Makareta was her secret weapon, but if

Imaly could have picked only one associate, one partner in crime, it would have been Vasek, even though he was the greatest threat. Being intelligent and experienced, he was also the most likely to betray her.

"What are the chances of this Rhune relinquishing the secret of dragons?" Imaly asked.

"Low," he replied confidently. "I seriously doubt she has that knowledge at all. It'd be beyond stupid to send a person who possesses the information we need the most, and my sources report that Nyphron is no idiot. The gift wrapping is a bit too perfect. I suspect a trap. She's probably here on some sort of suicide mission. Her purpose is likely sabotage, information gathering, or maybe even an assassination attempt. Although I can't see how that Rhune could pose a threat to anyone, let alone the fane. Still, it worries me that I haven't been able to determine the nature of her threat."

"But what if she does know?"

"Then she would try her best not to tell us."

"Do you think you can force it out of her?"

Vasek hesitated. "This morning I would have said yes, but now, I'm not so certain."

"Why? What happened?"

"We dug her up, expecting her to do anything to avoid being put in the coffin again, but—"

"You did what?" Imaly forgot about pretending they weren't together and turned to stare directly at him. "You *buried* her? In the ground? Are you insane? She could have died!"

Still looking at the door, Vasek replied in his infuriatingly calm voice, "She was only down there for a few hours. The coffin had enough air for twice that long. I had been led to believe the Rhune was terrified of small places, but apparently not."

"That was an incredibly risky gamble. How do you know how much air is in a coffin?"

"How I came by that knowledge is not something you want to know, trust me."

"Is she all right?"

"She's fine. It would appear the rumor was inaccurate. The Rhune took the opportunity to take a nap."

"Thank Ferrol for that. She could be important after we . . . well, you know." She looked around. They were well out of Trilos's hearing range, but Imaly was uncomfortable speaking plainly in public.

Vasek appeared to agree and quietly replied, "How is the *well-you-know* coming?"

Imaly rubbed her palms together, warming them. "It's a work in progress but showing great promise."

"That means nothing," Vasek said. "Show me results, and I'll consider taking measures to support your success."

"So, you would rather align yourself with Lothian? Do you believe he can win this war? You already admitted your doubts about the Rhune possessing the knowledge he seeks. And even if she has it, your powers of persuasion haven't worked. Lothian is dangling from a thread that is the promise of dragons. Do you believe we can win this war without them?"

"No." His answer was what she expected, but the speed at which he delivered it was not. He hadn't even bothered to think. Vasek had already, perhaps long ago, come to this conclusion.

"No chance at all?" she asked.

"We don't have enough Miralyith to guard all of Erivan. Eventually, Nyphron will realize this—or maybe he already has, but he's just stubborn about crossing the Nidwalden. Eventually, he will send an army around our Miralyith. They might already be on their way. We have only minor defenses to our south, the east, and the far north. Our population shrinks while the Rhune are free to spread into Avrlyn and multiply." He shook his head. "Short of Ferrol personally intervening on our behalf, I don't think we have any chance at all."

"Vasek, when Lothian was off to Alon Rhist, I received an overture from the Rhunes, sent by a bird. It proposed peace between our peoples. If—and granted it's a big assumption—but if we manage to succeed in our plan, we will still have a war to deal with, one you admit we can't win. On the outside chance we impress ourselves and succeed, I'd like to be on better terms with this Rhune. So, might I suggest treating her better?"

"You want me to defy the fane's order?"

She sighed. "No, the fane told you to extract the secret of dragons, but you don't believe she knows it. You can't obtain what doesn't exist. But if we can't win without dragons, wouldn't it make sense to consider a peaceful resolution with the Rhunes? If Lothian questions you, tell him you are trying a new tactic because the last one failed. Explain that sometimes kindness can obtain what cruelty cannot."

"What do you suggest? I have her to tea?"

"It'd be a good start, but why don't you stop treating her as an enemy and welcome her as a guest? You could arrange for food, a bath, better clothes, and a comfortable place to stay."

Vasek frowned. "Like where?"

"I don't know. You're the Master of Secrets."

Vasek leaned back on the bench to ponder this. "I suppose I could arrange for a better room at the palace."

Imaly sat up suddenly, her back coming free of the rear of the bench. She covered the act by pretending to brush something off her lap, as if a late autumn bee had landed on her. "No," she said forcefully. "Not there. Let's keep her away from Lothian, for Ferrol's sake."

"You want to take her in?"

"Absolutely not." Imaly was horrified at the thought of trying to house both the Rhune and Makareta—whom she had yet to tell Vasek about. "Given that she is under your charge, why not give her a guest room at your house?"

"*Mine?*"

"You live alone. It'd be perfect. And what better way to mend a broken fence than to accept her into your own home?"

"I don't—"

"We'll all need to make sacrifices, Vasek."

"And what will you be sacrificing?"

Makareta's trusting face popped into Imaly's head, saddening her. But years in the body politic kept her expression neutral.

"My life, I suspect, which will end in an extremely painful way. If I fail to remove Lothian from office, all fingers will point my way. And we both know how publicly Lothian likes to execute traitors. But that is not my greatest concern."

"No? What is?"

"That you are wrong, and this Rhune really does know how to create dragons. What do you think will happen if that is the case?"

"Well, assuming I can't charm the secret out of her, Lothian will take measures into his own hands. He'll use his own *powers of persuasion,* and she'll tell him what she knows. Then Lothian *will* win this war, become a new hero to his people just as Fenelyus did, and that will eliminate your opportunity to remove the Miralyith from power."

Imaly nodded. "And given that, we should find out for certain what she does or doesn't know."

℘

"Buried in a coffin! Is she dead?" Volhoric asked Imaly. "Did that fool Vasek kill her?"

The high priest had been waiting outside the Garden, pretending to prune the hedges that surrounded it. He had a small pile of twigs at his feet and a tiny saw that he waved and jabbed to articulate his comments.

"No, she's fine," Imaly replied, pulling back. She was concerned Volhoric might accidentally hit her with his pruner.

"Seriously? How could anyone be all right after that! We need her on *our* side—or at least sympathetic to our cause. She's our only path to peace. Did you explain that?"

"I did."

Volhoric lowered the garden tool and sighed. "What's Vasek going to do now, start chopping off fingers?"

"That might have been his next approach, but I persuaded him to try a different course. We can't have her hating us."

He looked at the saw with remorse. "I think that tree has already fallen."

"I'm sure it has, but the good news is that any animosity she possesses is with Lothian, and that *could* work to our favor. But that's not our immediate concern."

"What is?"

Imaly bent down and picked up a handful of little branches that the priest had been cutting. She held them pointedly. "We need to stand that tree up again, which is where you come in."

"Me?" He stared at the twigs. "What do you want me to do?"

"You're the head of the Umalyn tribe. I need the cooperation of one of your disciples—a priestess of Ferrol. I need her to speak to the Rhune and make her feel at ease."

"I take it you have someone in mind?"

"Yes." She clapped the branches against her open palm. "I suspect Nyree is the only one in Estramnadon whom the Rhune might be willing to trust."

Volhoric's eyes widened. "Are you serious?"

"Yes. Why?"

He dragged a hand over his face. "Because I can think of no one more ill-suited to the task."

"What's wrong with her?"

"She's as zealous as they come, utterly unyielding, and as cold as the frozen Shinara River in the depths of winter. Even if I could convince her that making friends with a Rhune would save Erivan, I doubt she could manage it. She's a terrible liar."

"Oh, no! She can't lie." Imaly dropped the twigs and held up both hands. "This Rhune has already suffered from several deceptions. She'll be expecting that. We need Nyree to be authentic, so don't give her any instructions other than that she is to follow Vasek's directions."

Volhoric stared at Imaly, dumbfounded. He shook his head, his saw arm limp at his side. "How is that going to end in anything other than disaster?"

"It's been said that this Rhune had been close friends with Arion—she was there when the Miralyith died. I'm hoping that their shared loss of a loved one will generate a common bond and shared pain."

"Only one problem with that," Volhoric said, as he brushed at the hedge, dusting off the remaining dead leaves. "Nyree hated Arion."

"But Arion was her daughter," Imaly said incredulously.

Volhoric nodded. "As cold as the Shinara, I tell you."

CHAPTER FOUR

Loved Ones Lost and Found

In that world beyond the veil of death, we found that those we had thought to be lost forever had only been misplaced.

— THE BOOK OF BRIN

Moya was thirty-two when she died, and while that certainly wasn't young for an unmarried, childless woman, it wasn't get-your-things-in-order old. As a result, the afterlife wasn't a topic Moya had given much thought to. Still, she'd heard the stories. Great warriors went to Alysin, the afterlife's paradise; everyone else was divided between Rel and Nifrel. The good went to the former, the bad to the latter. Nifrel was rumored to be a place of retribution, endless torture, and anguish. Moya never thought Rel would be much better, especially given it had been described to her as a sunless existence filled with sadness and regret. Moya heard all of this from her mother, and as Audrey had a reputation for poor judgment as well as a negative view of everyone's future, Moya guessed that her mother's descriptions were probably wrong. Death could just as easily be a wondrous place flowing with abundant food and drink. She honestly had no idea what to expect, no preconceived notion of what the afterlife would be like—dark probably, hazy perhaps, cold certainly. Everyone knew Phyre was underground, and Moya's visit to Neith suggested all three.

The light shining through the gate surprised her, but passing through it was like entering an illuminated house on a dark night. From the outside and at a distance, the interior looked as bright as a star. Once inside, it wasn't nearly so brilliant, but the outside changed into a dark opaque of utter black.

Rel, as it happened, was not a dark, cold cavern; nor was it like living in an orchard with apples on every tree and fountains filled with foaming beer. In her youth, Moya had never thought much of their neighbor, the Crescent Forest. But having left Dahl Rhen and seeing a wider world of barren, dusty plains, Moya had discovered a fondness for trees, a nostalgia that had fermented from childhood bitter to adulthood sweet. These trees were different from those in Rhen. Moya found their massive height and aged appearance as comforting as an old cloak rediscovered at the start of a long journey.

Aside from the forests, the land was hilly, but not unbearably so. A pleasant stream meandered through, snaking around the rocks and hills. In the distance, mountains rose and were unlike anything Moya had ever seen. Huge, snow-swept stony teeth made a wall, as if Mount Mador had given birth to a brood of equal-height children. Above it all was a sky of sorts, but Moya saw no sun nor any hint of blue. Diffused white light illuminated everything such that there were no shadows and no warmth. Moya's mother had been right about that much: The afterlife appeared to be sunless.

"Huh," mused Rain as they all took their first look at the eternal world.

Only a single utterance, and perhaps not even a word at all, but Moya felt it summed up what she, too, was feeling.

"I was expecting a bit more," Tekchin said, sounding disappointed, his eyes peering off into the distant heights.

"I was expecting less," Tressa admitted with a tone of relief. "Or perhaps, more of something else."

"I think it's grand," Gifford declared, beaming a perfectly straight smile.

"No sun . . . so what makes the light?" Roan asked softly, presumably to herself.

Brin had nothing to say, but her head shifted, and her eyes darted, struggling to take it all in.

On the far side of the gate began a road, a fine street made of white bricks—chalk or perhaps alabaster. Along its edges waited another crowd. This one was larger than those previously trapped outside. Moya's first thought was that they were trying to get out, but she soon realized that wasn't the case. The moment the gate opened, the newly dead poured in and were swarmed by mothers, fathers, grandparents, and children. Shocked recognition was followed by hugs and tears—a series of grand reunions. Introductions were the next order of business. In the vast crowd of pushing bodies, Moya didn't so much see as hear them.

"This is your great-grandfather, Cobalt Sire! You never met him. He's who you were named after. Died a'fore you were born."

"I'm your mother. I died giving you life. Seems like it was only yesterday, and now look at you!"

Moya's initial fears that someone might have seen Tressa using the key had vanished. In those precious moments of reunion, everything else had been forgotten.

"Brin! Brin!" a familiar voice yelled. "Brin!"

Before Moya knew what was happening, Brin had bolted forward into the arms of a familiar man and woman. Moya had mentally accepted that she was in Rel and that this was the afterlife, but not until that instant did it sink to her gut. Watching Delwin and Sarah hug their daughter, Moya felt punched in the stomach.

This is real. We truly are dead.

Sarah and Delwin weren't alone. A familiar black-and-white dog bounded up, happily barking. Moya remembered a sad old sheepdog who had lived a life of leisure after growing too old to herd. This Darby wasn't that one. This dog was young and spirited, but Sarah and Delwin looked exactly the same as when they had died. Moya knew she was missing something—many somethings, she guessed—and she suspected the dog was a clue. Gifford's ability to speak normally might be one, too.

I'm terrible at riddles.

A handsome Fhrey in white robes approached Tekchin and clapped him warmly on the shoulder. "Tekchinry!" He grinned.

"Prylo?" Shocked, Tekchin stared at the Fhrey. Then he said to Moya, "This is my father. He died in the Dherg War."

"Pleased to meet you, sir."

"Prylo, where's Mother?"

The Fhrey rolled his eyes. "She's still alive, you fool!"

Off to Moya's left, Rain was mobbed by a dozen dwarfs that surrounded him. They hugged, slapped, and generally berated the digger.

"Oh, so have you finally dug deep enough?"

"Look! He's brought his pick, he has! Fool of a boy."

"Those days are over, laddie! You've reached the bottom at last."

The comments sounded hurtful, which concerned Moya, but they came with smiles and hugs.

Something is not quite right about the Dherg.

After Sarah had let go of Brin, Delwin swung his daughter up in his arms the way he had done a thousand times when alive. Watching the familiar scene brought back the old, ugly pang of envy she'd forgotten.

Moya, who had earned her keep with Brin's family by spinning wool, used to watch when Delwin came in after a long day with the sheep. Sarah would welcome her husband with kisses. Then Brin would rush over with something to show. All of it—the smell of the food, the smiles, the happiness and love—had driven Moya to slip outside; she had to, or they might have seen her crying and ask why. Moya hadn't wanted to explain how empty it made her feel knowing she would never experience anything like what they had.

Watching Brin's reunion, Moya felt the same emptiness. She looked for her own mother, but Audrey was nowhere to be seen.

Some things never change.

Sarah spotted Moya. With a sympathetic look, the woman—who had been more of a mother than Audrey—ran over and hugged her tightly. Trapped as she was in Sarah's embrace, Moya couldn't hide her tears.

"It's okay," Sarah said. "Everything is fine now."

Sarah held onto Moya, a moment filled with the nostalgia of a crackling hearth and the comforting smell of wool and baking bread—the shelter Moya had long ago found in a neighbor's home.

"Your mother *will* come. Those who have had strong emotional ties with someone who dies know when it has happened. That's why we are here. There's a ringing, the same sort you hear if you've ever been close to fainting. Audrey was here earlier but she . . . well . . ."

"She hates me," Moya replied. "Never forgave me for being such a terrible daughter."

Sarah looked embarrassed, as if company had dropped by while her home was a mess. "It's nothing like that. I'm sure. It's just that the gate has been closed, and no one knew for how long, so some left. I'm certain Audrey will be back." Sarah wiped Moya's tears away. "Anyway, we're here, and you can stay with us until you and your mother find each other."

"Oh—Mom," Brin said, wiping her cheeks and eyes, "I'm sorry, but we won't be staying. We're only passing through."

This drew surprised looks from both parents.

"Ah, honey . . ." Sarah began.

"You do understand that you're—that *you died?* Right?" Delwin asked.

"Of course I do, and I have to admit that I'm not looking forward to doing that twice."

"Twice?" Sarah said. With a puzzled expression, she glanced at her husband.

Moya laughed awkwardly. "You know Brin, always joking."

Sarah looked at her the same way she used to when Moya and Brin came home covered in mud—her what-have-you-two-been-up-to expression. That look also said, *And this is your fault—I know it.* Then, as if she remembered something had been cooking too long, Sarah clapped hands to her cheeks and looked around at the others. "Why are you all here at once? Have the Fhrey invaded the Dragon Camp?"

"No, it's not that. It's just . . . hey, wait. How do you know about the camp? I lived there after—after . . ." Brin faltered.

"After we died, yes." Sarah nodded.

All around them, people had finished their greetings and were moving off, walking up the brick road toward where Moya noticed clusters of buildings—little roundhouses like the ones in Dahl Rhen. Most of the people she didn't recognize, but some teased her memory, faces vaguely recalled from childhood but now unplaceable.

"Other people die, too, dear," Sarah explained. "They bring news with them." She paused, a pang of sadness filling her eyes. "A lot of people have died recently, what with the war and all. We've heard wonderful stories about you, Persephone, Moya, Roan, and Gifford, and your romance with the Dureyan boy Tesh—who I assume is no longer a boy. We were hoping to hear about becoming grandparents soon. I guess that won't happen now."

"And speaking of no longer a boy . . . neither is this one." Delwin clapped Gifford on the back, staggering the potter. "*You've* straightened out, haven't you?"

"Yes, sir."

"Why don't we all go home?" Sarah said, coaxing them with waves of her arms as if they were sheep. "We can sit by the fire, and you can tell us all that is happening in the world. Our place is just up that way." Sarah pointed up the brick road where Moya saw a well that she could swear was exactly the same as the one that had once stood near the center of Dahl Rhen, the well where the legendary Bucket Raid occurred and where she once coaxed Tekchin to fill waterskins for her.

I'm Tekchin, the handsomest and most skilled of the Galantians.

That scar suggests otherwise on both counts.

"That well looks exactly like the one where we used to live. How is that possible?" Moya asked.

"It's there because we all remember it," Sarah explained. "It's still our common well, but now we draw something other than water from it. Something deeper and more vital. Memories are important here. They help form the world around us."

Turning to Brin, she added, "Your grandmother Brinhilda is waiting with the children. I asked them to stay. Didn't want to overwhelm. Some people bring the whole clan, but I know how confusing coming down here can be. I thought it might be you; a mother's intuition doesn't end with death, and I remember that you were never a diver, always a wader."

Sarah took hold of Brin's hand and started off.

"Wait!" Gifford said.

They all stopped and looked at him. The potter was staring into the depths of the dispersing crowd, where a small woman was slowly revealed. She was young and thin and wore her hair straight and short. As the throng peeled away, the woman stepped slowly forward, approaching hesitantly, her hands shaking, tears welling—her sight locked on—

"Roan?" Reanna said in a soft voice while inching toward her.

Mother and daughter were so alike, though disturbingly, Roan looked a bit older. Moya had to remind herself that Roan's mother had died young.

They didn't embrace, not at first. When they did, their hug lacked the wild abandon that Sarah and Brin had shared. Instead, they crept up, hands out but clenched. Then slowly, haltingly, Roan's mother closed the distance and took Roan in her arms as if her daughter were a fine porcelain figurine. They stayed that way for a time, then slowly Reanna began to stroke her daughter's hair.

As she did, Roan cried. Moya had rarely seen her friend that way. Roan didn't just weep, she sobbed.

The two huddled with shoulders hunched and backs bowed. Lifetimes of cowering had turned these women, who might otherwise have been beautiful and proud, into lesser versions of themselves.

While alive, they hadn't merely cast tiny shadows upon the world; they were shadows.

Moya adjusted her grip on her bow as she scanned the faces around them. She pointed at Roan and Reanna, and said, "Anyone know where Iver the Carver has taken root?" She peered down the brick road, hoping to catch a glimpse of the monster who, for far too long, she had mistaken for a man. "I'd like to put an arrow or maybe six or seven into that worthless excuse of a man."

"What's an arrow?" Delwin asked.

"This." She held one up.

"Is that supposed to cause pain?"

"It's been known to."

"It won't here," Sarah said. "In Rel, pain is muted like the light. And I've never seen Iver—not around here. He might be farther in. Most of us don't travel far. We like our little village. Come, let me show you."

Gifford didn't want to intrude. He left Roan alone with her mother and walked up the brick road with the others, but he stopped at the well so he could keep his wife in sight. Seeing mother and daughter together was both wonderful and devastating—a tragic miracle of sorts. The two were a marvel, like a shattered mountain that left behind the breathtaking beauty of an exposed cliff. He watched them the way he might stare at a rainbow, trying to grasp the whole of it. When he realized he was staring, he turned away to grant them privacy.

He discovered he was standing in what appeared to be a village remarkably like Dahl Rhen. Many of the houses were similar to those he remembered. Where they fell short of identical was in their perfection and lack of wear. They all sported thick, straight timbers and fresh thatch of bright blond. And not a single roofline listed or bowed. The other notable difference was the vast number of buildings—thousands, maybe tens of thousands—that radiated out from the well's central location. All of them were classic Rhulyn-Rhune roundhouses, but then again, not quite. Gifford spotted cook fires outside the homes, just as there should be, but he didn't smell food or even smoke.

A good many people in the crowd waved at Gifford and the others as they walked past, everyone smiling, all friendly. None of them was thin, pale, or sickly. No one limped or coughed. He searched the faces for his father, who was little more than a vague memory, and he hoped to finally meet his mother. All he knew about her came from others. By all accounts, Aria was amazing. She'd died at sixteen but had left a deep and wide mark on everyone who knew her. Brave, kind, and wise were the words most often used to describe her, and over the years, Gifford had come to idolize this woman who knowingly sacrificed herself so he could live. He wanted to meet her, if only to say thank you, but he didn't know what she looked like, and she wouldn't be able to recognize him, either.

Did she come to the gate but hadn't realized who she was there for? Maybe we passed by each other without even knowing.

No, he concluded. Surely, Delwin and Sarah knew Aria, and they would have reunited mother and son. Now that he thought of it, he wondered why Brin's parents had said that Audrey would be back for Moya, but they hadn't said the same about his family.

What does that mean? Has something happened to them?

Maybe his parents were like Meeks, wandering the world of Elan and never finding their way into Phyre. The thought made Gifford feel suddenly alone.

Brin had gone into her parents' home. Moya stood with Tekchin, speaking to a handful of Fhrey, who seemed fascinated and a bit disconcerted by Moya. Rain continued to chat with his fellow dwarfs. Oddly, everyone was speaking in Rhunic.

Maybe they're using their native languages, but because I'm dead, I can understand them. Perhaps when I talk, they are hearing Fhrey or Belgriclungreian.

Smiling at the idea of speaking Fhrey and wondering what that must sound like, Gifford spotted Tressa resting beside the well. He went over and sat on an overturned bucket. "Misfits together again, huh? Just like sitting in front of Hopeless House."

"No," Tressa replied. "You were expelled from there."

"What? Why? Because I can speak better?"

Tressa shook her head. "No. We kicked you out years ago."

"Really? Who's *we?*"

"Me, I guess. I'm the only one left, aren't I? Anyway, you have her." Tressa pointed at Roan. Mother and daughter continued to speak, foreheads touching. "Oh, yeah, and there was that thing about saving all of mankind that you did a few years back. That really ruined your worthless status. People think you're a hero now. Can't have heroes in Hopeless House."

"You're not worthless, Tressa."

"I don't see a line forming to thank me for all the good I did with my life."

"It isn't over."

"Yeah, it is," Tressa said with a terrible certainty. "And what a mess I made of it, huh?"

"What did you do that was so awful? You married badly—must be millions who have done that."

Tressa shook her head. "I can't blame it on Konniger. If I didn't know what he was up to, I should have, isn't that right? I mean, what kind of wife doesn't know when her husband is out killing people? And I've always left a bad taste in everyone's mouth even before I met him. Folks started calling me a bitch when I was eight years old—eight! I don't know why. Didn't even realize what it meant. I tried to be a good person, brought back the Killians' cow when she got lost. I was out all night, tore my dress, and took a beating from my father over it. The stupid animal had gotten caught in thickets, probably would have broken her leg and died. No one saw me, though, so I didn't get any credit. And I was the one who made Heath Coswall return Tope Highland's knife—that nice one he had, remember? I made Heath give it back; said I'd tell if he didn't. He did, and I kept my promise, never said a word. Of course, no one knew it was me. I kinda thought that was a good thing, you know? I guess I was wrong. Been wrong a lot. Funny how you get to see things so clearly right after you can't do anything about them."

Roan was looking their way, waving for Gifford to come over.

He stood up, thrilled at how easy it was to get to his feet. He took a step, then stopped. "Come with me," he said to Tressa.

"You don't have to be nice to me, Gifford. It's okay."

"No, it's not. And yeah, I do."

"Why?"

"Because I like you."

Tressa laughed. "I took the Second Chair from Persephone, remember? And Konniger and I were useless even though we were supposed to be in charge. And I tried to marry Moya to the Stump. You didn't forget that, did you?"

Gifford scowled. "You work at making it hard to like you, Tressa."

"So, don't."

"But I—"

"Don't." Tressa stood up. "I know you think I deserve what I got. You all do. Everyone does. Some folks—like you—are just a little more polite about it, I guess. But I don't want pity. I'd rather be hated." She stormed off.

The interior of Brin's mother's home was eerily similar to the one where Brin had grown up. Her murals—the ones she had painted on the walls—and the handprints of the child she had once been were all there. The details were remarkable, and if they were the result of memory, Brin finally understood where she had gotten her Keeper's talent from.

The moment Brin entered, she was rushed by a small mob. Five children nearly tackled her. They were dressed in wool, woven in the pattern of Dahl Rhen. Each focused on her with excitement.

"Everyone, this is your baby sister, Brin," Sarah said, then she pointed at each of the children in turn as she introduced them. "This is Will, that's

Dell, over there is Wren, Dale, and this little one here is Meadow. They died before you were born. Wren lived the longest."

"I got sick," the little girl said. "You beat my record by fourteen years."

The family features were there; each child looked a little like Brin, same eyes, same mouth, and yet they were unique—original paintings born of a common artist. Brin knew she'd had brothers and sisters, but details had been cast into the gloom of childhood myth. Now, they were talking to her.

"I—" Was all Brin got out before Meadow hugged her. She was the youngest, her face all eyes and cheeks.

"Was it . . . was it awful?" Dell asked. "Your death, I mean. Was it violent?"

"Dell!" Sarah reprimanded. "What kind of question is that?"

Brin recalled stories about Dell, Sarah's firstborn. He was named after their father, and everyone called him Little Dell, a moniker the boy was said to have hated.

"Sorry. I was just curious."

Brin didn't know what to say. She knew she couldn't provide details because eventually the key would be brought up, and she thought it was best to not say anything about that, even to her own family.

Thankfully, she didn't have to explain, because Sarah changed the subject. "This is your grandmother Brinhilda," Sarah said as she introduced a woman who failed to meet any expectations. Brin had always imagined her grandmother as an evil crone, the Tetlin Witch's uglier sister. This woman was pretty and younger than Sarah.

"I would have come to the gate," Brinhilda said, "but you wouldn't have recognized me even though I was the one who provided you with your name. I've been waiting a long time to meet you, dear." Another hug was delivered.

"Your uncles and their families will be stopping by later, I expect," Sarah said. "Everyone will want news about what's happening in the world, so you can expect to be hounded. It'll give you something to do, for a while, at least. Too many days are just like the ones that came before. It's quite boring with so little to do."

"Why is that?" Brin looked around.

"This is a place of waiting." Her father spoke loudly, and as if to prove the point, he sat down in a chair by the well-stocked fire pit. "A place without want."

"But that's good, isn't it? I mean, you don't have to toil, right? There's no need to cut wood or farm. You both worked so hard in life, you deserve some rest. All your problems and fears are gone."

"And we have nothing to do," Sarah said. "I used to look forward to a time when you kids would be grown, and your father and I would finally be able to relax. At some point, I realized it would never happen. There would always be something needing attention. That's what life is, dealing with one problem and then the next. It's striving and suffering to obtain a goal, only to find another one waiting beyond it. I thought life was misery because of the unending succession of trials and tribulations. But now, I see that challenges are what life is all about. Take them away and . . . there's no point. It's like life is a game, but now the competition is over. We're still here, waiting and hearing about others who can still play. It's not terrible, but neither is it enjoyable."

"It's better in some ways," Delwin said. "We've sort of forgotten about it, but you're right. The fear and worry are gone. You have a lot of time to rest, to talk, and to think."

Brin got the impression her father was doing his best to sell a bad idea.

"And maybe that's all Rel is for, a time to pause and reflect, to think about our lives, what we did wrong and what we could have done better."

Sarah wiped clean hands on a spotless towel. "Our existence and the world wasn't supposed to be like this. It's broken, and we'll continue this way until it's fixed. At least that's what people say. Everyone was supposed to live forever—up there." She pointed at the ceiling.

"Brin?" Moya called from outside. "We need to go."

For a moment, Brin almost thought it was years ago, and Moya was coming to invite her on an adventure, a hike down the river or a firefly-illuminated trip along the forest's eaves—neither of which she had written about in her book, but perhaps she should have.

My book! I haven't told them!

"I'm writing down all the events of our world!" she blurted out, then shook her head at her own stupidity. They couldn't possibly understand. "I'm making marks on—"

"Brin!" Moya shouted in a tone that wasn't the orphaned daughter staying with Brin's family; this was the voice of the Shield of the Keenig calling.

"What's wrong?" Brin cleared the doorway, surprised to discover most of the group outside.

"We *need* to get moving." Moya gave a cautious look around before adding in a quieter voice, "We're in trouble." She tilted her head toward Rain. "There's a rumor among the dwarfs that the ruler of this realm is looking for the ones who opened the gate he had ordered sealed."

"Rel has a ruler?"

Moya nodded. "And apparently he's not happy."

"Where's Tressa?" Brin asked.

"I was hoping she was with you."

Brin shook her head. "You don't suppose she was . . . I mean, do you think . . ."

"I don't know, but we have to find her . . . and fast."

Tressa had wandered back toward the gate. She wasn't looking for someone, not really, and she was grateful that Konniger and her parents hadn't shown up. She didn't want to see any of them. Taking a seat in the grass, she pretended to fix a perfectly fine strap of her sandal to appear busy so no one would intrude. But perhaps it just made her look like an idiot who couldn't fix whatever was wrong with such a complicated thing as a strap. Sitting there, she felt remarkably like the only kid at Wintertide who didn't get a present. The embarrassment she felt didn't come from not receiving something; it came from knowing that everyone else did.

Tressa knew what everyone who looked her way was thinking.

How did she *get in here?*

She doesn't belong.

There's another place for the likes of her.

The next place, she thought and puzzled over why she wasn't already in Nifrel.

Tressa had no idea how she knew, maybe the same way she had known that Malcolm was a god, but she was positive that once she entered into the next realm of Phyre she would never leave. That was the place for her, *Nif-Rel*—*below* Rel—the bottom. She'd find plenty of friends there—friends *and* family.

How does it usually work? Do people destined for the other realms magically pop into Nifrel or Alysin when they cross through the Rel Gate? Maybe there is some sort of delay while spirits are sorted. Or perhaps someone will come and escort me to my final resting place.

Tressa didn't think any of those ideas were right, and she considered whether the existence of the key was somehow interfering with the natural order. All she really knew for sure was that she wasn't likely to work out the mystery. Maybe Roan could, but not her.

What happens if I just don't go to Nifrel?

She could give the key to Moya and stay in Rel forever, cheat death—sort of. The problem was, it sounded too much like something Konniger would come up with. His plans never worked. Besides . . .

Malcolm sent me. That has to count for something, doesn't it?

She wore the key. She still didn't know why he had given it to her, or why the others hadn't taken it. She wanted to believe it was her second chance, an opportunity to change things, but she also conceded that was just wishful thinking. Malcolm hadn't said anything, never so much as dropped a hint in that direction. All she had was a feeling that stood back-to-back with the other one, the certainty that everything would end in Nifrel.

Is it either-or?

She sighed and frowned. Probably one, *then* the other. That made more sense. Malcolm needed her, and when she was done, he'd toss her aside like a picked-clean chicken bone.

No one's fault but my own.

She thought of many reasons why that wasn't true, but she was also aware that she was attempting to fool herself. And while Tressa was many things, she wasn't an idiot. People always provided justifications for their actions and found their behavior acceptable, even if they hated others for doing the same things. But that sort of deception had become too hard to maintain. Everything had been so clear when she stepped into the pool in the swamp, but her perception was growing fuzzy again. New thoughts, fresh doubts, had had time to creep in.

If Malcolm is a god and knows everything, why does he let things get so messed up in the first place? Why do good people have to die? Why, for instance, did he kill—

"Tressa?" She heard the voice, stood up, and turned.

Gelston stood a few feet away, staring at her. He looked exactly as he used to whenever she showed up at Hopeless House. She would knock, but he wouldn't answer. Then she'd let herself in. When he saw her, he would stand there, his face blank, no one home. On good days, he'd remember her name, but usually, that was all he recalled. On bad days, he wouldn't know her at all, and he'd yell and scream, telling her to leave his house. That last part had always baffled her since it wasn't.

Tressa braced herself for the worst because Gelston wore his confused face, the one that had always preceded the yelling. But that didn't happen this time. Instead, he did something unexpected and so totally bewildering that it left Tressa at a loss.

He cried.

Tears welled up and spilled down his cheeks. The man didn't try to stop, didn't so much as wipe at them. He just stood there until she, too, started to tear up. Then without warning, Gelston came over and wrapped her in his arms, pulling her tight. He was tall, and her face was pressed into his chest. She felt his big hand on the back of her head, cradling it. His body spasmed with sobs, his arms holding her close, embracing her like he . . .

"Thank you, Tressa," Gelston managed to whisper when he was able to suck in and hold a breath—a breath he clearly didn't need. "I tried . . . I wanted . . . I wanted to tell you that for so very long." He gasped again. "Oh Grand Mother, thank you for letting me catch her. I can never express how—I can't ever thank you enough for what you did. I was so frightened that you might run right through Rel on your way to the Door, and I wouldn't get the chance to tell you."

He let go, and she lifted her head to meet his eyes.

"You know?"

"I was with you when Malcolm explained everything, remember?" Gelston said in a shaking voice. "I was there, but I couldn't say anything. Ever since my accident, I felt so alone. It was beyond frightening. Then you came. And I was so horrible to you. I couldn't control what my body was doing. I yelled, screamed, and threw things. I even hit you, didn't I? No." He shook his head. "It was worse than that. I *beat* you. Oh, I did. I remember a time when you could barely open your eyes. You came back the next day, and you could hardly see." Horror filled his face.

Tressa wiped her eyes, sniffled, and nodded. "It wasn't your fault. You were scared and thought I was an intruder. You—you thought I was a crazy woman breaking into your home. Of course you did; why wouldn't you?"

Gelston shook his head as tears slipped free again, running fast now that the riverbeds were established. "I'm *so* sorry. Oh, Tressa. And you never told anyone."

She shrugged. "No one listens to me, and besides, it was nobody's business but our own. It wasn't really you. I knew that."

"And you came back—day after day. I was so afraid you wouldn't. But you always did, no exceptions. You were my one light in an ocean of darkness. Tressa . . ." He took her face in his hands. "I love you, Tressa."

He hugged her again, and as he did, she realized they weren't alone anymore.

She drew back to see them all. Roan, Gifford, Brin, Tekchin, Rain, and Moya were watching.

"And there it goes," Moya told her. "Years of carefully cultivated bitchiness—gone—wiped out by a simple act of kindness."

"Kiss my ass, Moya!"

It was then that she heard a ringing, a sound in her ears that made it difficult to hear anything else. From the looks on the faces of the others, they heard it, too.

Someone they knew had died and was at the gate.

CHAPTER FIVE

The Swan Priestess

Suri and Arion had complicated relationships with their mothers. Maybe that was part of their bond. The mystic had only spent a few hours with hers, and the Miralyith wished she could have said the same.

— THE BOOK OF BRIN

Suri's new room, where she had been moved to after her brief stint as a seed planted in the forest, was the nicest accommodations she'd been provided so far. She liked that it wasn't as grandiose as her chambers in the tower of Avempartha. This room had a pleasant, lived-in quality. The comfortable bed comprised a mattress, wooden headboard, and a quilt with a diamond pattern in brown and white. The floor was wood, its finish worn, revealing a path that led from the door to the bed. The walls were constructed of beams and plaster, the windows a single thick pane of glass. A table and some shelves completed the furnishings, but they were bare. Suri had noticed areas free of dust that told a story of personal items hastily removed. She would have been happier with a bed of grass and a ceiling of stars, but her days of panic were behind her.

She found some string left on a shelf and made a loop. It had been years since she'd played the game, and it was enjoyable to sit on the bed and create various patterns with her fingers. Her diversion was interrupted when the door opened, and Vasek and a woman entered.

Suri thought the stranger was small, even for a Fhrey. Her long neck, delicate features, and graceful movements were like a swan in the same way Arion's had been. Looking closely, Suri noticed that the similarity didn't stop there. She had the same small nose, thin lips, expressive eyes, and high cheekbones. The only significant departure was the hair. Arion had kept her head bald, but this visitor's hair was long and pure white.

Definitely a swan.

This echo of Arion entered the room carrying a bundle wrapped in twine and accompanied by Vasek, who appeared huge and clumsy when standing beside her. Suri got off the bed and stood. She hoped it would be taken as a sign of respect, the first step in carrying out Arion's plan.

"This is Nyree," Vasek said. As always, his tone was neither friendly nor cold, merely a polite indifference. This was a job to him, a task of many. Perhaps he was the jailer to hundreds. "The leader of our religious tribe thought you might like to meet her. She's Arion's mother."

Nyree looked at Vasek, confused. "It can't understand you. It's a Rhune."

Arion's what?

On a few occasions, Suri and Arion had talked about their mothers, expressing regrets and sharing tales. Arion had said that she and Nyree were . . . *distant.*

Suri was surprised that while Nyree's voice was identical to Arion's, her tone was the exact opposite. Where Arion had been warm and approachable, Nyree laced her words with frosty superiority. The Fhrey was annoyed to be there, and she wanted Vasek to know about her displeasure.

Distant.

"I assure you *she* can speak Fhrey, but find out for yourself." Vasek gestured in Suri's direction.

Nyree looked aghast. "Surely, you don't expect *me* to speak to *it?*"

"I do."

Nyree's brows shot up, and her mouth made a little pretentious O. "Don't be absurd. I'm not going to pretend to hold a conversation with an animal!"

Suri spoke then, "I'm not an animal, although I've had conversations with many of them, and most are quite pleasant. Sure, every now and then you come across a badger that is in a foul mood, or a squirrel who is too busy to chat. But for the most part, I find them to be quite cordial."

Nyree stepped backward.

Seeing the Fhrey's stunned expression, Suri indulged in a rare smile. She realized Vasek was trying to manipulate her. He was trying to coax Suri into talking, and she was willing to oblige. The reason wasn't to shock Nyree, nor because Suri had been alone for so long. She did it because communicating with the Fhrey was what Arion had wanted. Persephone had asked her to act as a vehicle for peace, but Arion had foreseen a greater purpose. She had believed that Suri could change minds; that she could destroy misconceptions that had been born of ignorance. Even if Persephone won the war, or if a grudging peace were reached, the hatred between Rhunes and Fhrey would still exist; it might even intensify. The Fhrey would merely endure the truce. They wouldn't embrace it because they didn't see humans as equals. The first step to real understanding between their two peoples was to show them how wrong they were. Nyree looked to be an ideal opportunity. Arion's *distant* mother was a perfect example of the *real* war, the one that perhaps only Suri and Arion could see.

"I'll leave the two of you to get acquainted." Vasek paused at the threshold and reached out to close the door behind him.

"Don't!" Nyree and Suri said in unison, then they looked at each other in surprise. Nyree stared at Suri, appalled, as if by joining her in that one-word protest, Suri had somehow sullied Nyree's reputation.

Suri hadn't protested because of her fear, but because the room was stiflingly warm and that pleasant breeze that had entered with Nyree would be snuffed out.

Nyree, Suri suspected, had other reasons. The woman inched back toward the exit. "You will not lock me in here alone with this thing! It's disgusting—perverse! A perfect example of what comes from having a godless Miralyith for a fane."

Vasek frowned at her. "Volhoric is the one who ordered you here. Shall I fetch him so he can remind you of the vows you've made?"

Nyree stopped inching. She squeezed the bundle as a deep scowl crossed her lips.

"Stay here. Talk to *her*," Vasek demanded.

"What do you want me to say? And why me? I don't know anything about *their* kind. I'm a priestess, not an interrogator. I don't know what you want from me. This is *insane.*"

"It's very simple, Nyree." Vasek spoke in a patient tone. "I want you to talk to her. Speak words. Converse. You understand the concept, yes? I want you to get to know each other."

"It's a Rhune! A *Rhune!* What could possibly come from talking to it?"

"She was a friend of your daughter's. Volhoric thought you could be a bridge. Why don't you ask her about Arion?"

"You *can't* be serious." Nyree looked at Vasek as if she might be sick. She shook her head.

He offered a sympathetic smile. "It's your duty. Do it for Ferrol."

"Don't presume to know the will of our lord, you ignorant little worm!"

The insult bounced off Vasek's bulwark of a façade. "Volhoric and other senior members of the Aquila feel this is important, so you will do as they ask. Do it for your fane, for your people, for Erivan, for Volhoric. I honestly don't care where you find the strength, but you *will* do it. It's not like we are asking you to get her to divulge secrets. We're only asking for you to become acquainted with each other. Be civil. Consider yourself a representative of our people. Be nice."

"How long must I stay?"

"As long as it takes."

ৎৄ

Nyree stood rigid, still holding the bundle to her chest, staring at Suri with nervous eyes.

Vasek had long since left, but the Fhrey hadn't moved or spoken. Suri didn't press. Nyree reminded her of a cornered rabbit, and it was best to wait for her to get as comfortable as possible.

Suri was impressed that Vasek had heeded their wishes and left the door open. She saw it as a sign of trust. Maybe it wasn't a huge leap of faith, and he might be waiting just out of sight. But she wouldn't step foot near the exit. Trying to escape would be seen as a breach of his goodwill, and she wanted to prove herself worthy of his gesture.

Nyree had looked at the door enough times that Suri thought the Fhrey would be the one to take flight.

Wouldn't that be ironic? Suri smiled.

"What are you grinning at?" Nyree scolded, as if smiling were a crime.

"Just thinking that most people would expect me to be the one wanting to escape."

Nyree's scowl morphed into a suspicious study. "It's some kind of magic, isn't it?" She looked around at the ceiling and the walls. Nyree leaned out, trying to see around Suri without moving her feet from her spot. "It's Miralyith trickery. They're around here somewhere, making it seem like you can speak."

"Miralyith don't use *trickery*. And it isn't magic. It's called the Art, although I don't know of any weave that can make a person talk. Still, Artists *can* do many things: raise mountains, control weather, reroute rivers. Oh, did you know Arion did that once? Yes, she told me that she fell off a horse into a stream, and it made her so angry that she couldn't help herself. I think you are confusing Artists with magicians, who *do* use trickery and call what they do magic."

Nyree's head tilted. Her eyes narrowed. "You sound like—" She stopped herself, uncertainty creeping into her eyes.

"Arion spoke about you. She said you two didn't get along because she left the Umalyn to become a Miralyith. She mentioned you're a leader in your tribe. She said it's your job to talk to Ferrol or something like that."

"Something *like that?*" Nyree said with enough pride to fill an ocean. "I'm a *priestess* of our lord Ferrol."

"Yeah." Suri nodded. "That's what she said. She mentioned you felt betrayed when she didn't follow your lead. She was sorry for that. Said she missed you."

Nyree glared. She looked mad, but Suri couldn't understand why. Maybe she had hit on a nerve, so she tried a different approach. "Arion helped teach me Fhrey. I wasn't good at first, but she was an excellent teacher, even if she could be a real pain. With her, it was always *me* this and *I* that, as if it mattered. After all, she knew what I meant."

"It *does* matter." Nyree straightened her back. "Carelessness is unacceptable in any form." She appraised Suri and added, "As is sloppiness."

Suri looked down at the oversized dress she'd gotten from Treya. The rag had never been nice and was now a disaster of stains and wrinkles. After being exhumed from the grave, Vasek had treated Suri unusually well. She received two meals a day, moved into her new room, and was afforded a good deal of privacy. The one thing she hadn't received was new clothing.

Suri took note of Nyree's perfectly white asica. Not a fold out of place. "You take a bath every day, don't you?"

"Twice a day—as any civilized person does."

Suri nodded and held up her filthy rag. "You assume this is who I am because I'm a Rhune. Perhaps it hasn't occurred to you that I am not allowed to bathe, was stripped of my nicer clothes, locked in a cage, and dragged here against my will. You might look like this if someone did that to you. Arion told me you were judgmental, and I can understand your contempt. But how could you hate your own daughter? Arion was as close to perfection as anyone I ever met, but she still wasn't good enough for you."

Nyree glared.

"She only wanted your approval. Arion told me about the last time the two of you spoke. How she wanted to smooth things over. She feared it would be the last time the two of you would ever see each other, and she was right. Don't you have any regrets? Now that she's gone, do you wish you could tell her you were sorry?"

Nyree remained rigid, lips squeezed tight.

If this is what having a mother is like, I'm glad I never got to know mine.

"She couldn't understand why you refused to accept her."

Nyree pivoted sharply and took one step toward the doorway, then stopped. She stood there with her back to Suri for several heartbeats before whirling around. Her face was red as an apple. "Arion betrayed me! I raised her properly, gave her everything. She was going to be the first female Umalyn High Priestess. I was going to see to that. She was intelligent, beautiful, charming, and capable. Arion could have been the greatest of our order. She could have been fane. The first Umalyn ruler of our people! Instead, she . . ."

Nyree started to cry. She gritted her teeth and jerked away the tears. "Instead, *my daughter,*" she said with disgust, "to whom I devoted a lifetime, became a *Miralyith.*" She shook her head in anger. "I can't do this. I can't stay here." Nyree took another step toward the exit.

"She loved you," Suri said.

"Stop it! Just stop!" Nyree screamed so loudly that Suri jerked back, bumping against the wall.

Tears ran down Nyree's face too quickly to be wiped away.

"All I said was—"

"She didn't love me. Never! It was I who loved her and was willing to devote all that I was, all that I had accomplished for her benefit! But she refused my help, rejected me and our tribe."

"No, that wasn't it. She was just being who she was instead of who *you* wanted her to be."

"You know nothing! Nothing about me or my daughter. You are a heathen and a savage. Don't you dare think you can educate me on Arion and what she was or wasn't."

Nyree threw the bundle at Suri and fled the room.

"Did Arion ever ask *you* to become a Miralyith? Would you have thought she had your best interests in mind if she had?" Suri shouted after her.

She waited, but it was Vasek's face that reemerged in the doorway. "That didn't go so well," he said.

"I won't tell you how to make dragons."

"I wasn't asking you to." He pointed to the bundle. "In her haste, Nyree neglected to properly give you her gift. It's new clothes. Oh, and from now on, a bath will be prepared if you wish. All you have to do is ask."

"That won't do the trick, either. It doesn't matter how well you treat me."

Vasek thought about this for a moment. Then he cast a glance in the direction that Nyree had fled. "I'm not sure how you misconstrued a visit from Nyree as an indication of me being nice. If I were you, I would suspect this had been a well-calculated torture, and although you likely won't believe me, I'll state for the record that wasn't our intention. Perhaps Volhoric was too naïve. He doesn't have my years of experience in studying how people like Nyree react."

He shook his head and offered a sad sigh. "Like most of Nyree's tribe, the Umalyn are rigid in their thinking. Once she believes something, no amount of argument, or even proof, can change her mind. Just as you saw, the more you press the more defensive and deaf she becomes. A closed mind is like a door that can't be opened—it might as well be a wall." He turned to leave, then paused. "You might consider that while walls are made to keep people out and to protect, these barriers also isolate, making them an impediment to a lasting peace."

CHAPTER SIX

The Invitation

It is strange how some things are exactly how you imagined, and others are not. Odder still are those that are both.

— THE BOOK OF BRIN

The crowd gathering at the Great Gate of Rel was massive. At first, Moya feared there had been a huge battle and many were arriving at once. But she hadn't heard a series of rings, and intuition whispered that there had been only a single death, and the throng was an indication that someone important had died.

Having discovered that the ruler of Rel had people looking for Moya's party, she considered using the distraction to slip away. One thing that stopped her was the knowledge she'd gained from the shepherd's community of Dahl Rhen. Everyone knew that when a wolf pack hunted a particular area, it was the foolish, and soon to be dead, sheep that separated itself from the flock.

And then there were her curiosity and trepidation. She wanted to learn who had passed, but she was also terrified to find out. Moya hadn't been the only one who had heard the signal, and that provided a clue. Brin, Gifford, Tressa, and Roan had heard it, too. Rain and Tekchin had not, making the list of possibilities short, and none of them good.

"It's Suri, isn't it? We've failed." Brin's voice was filled with concern as they all huddled together, trying to blend in with the rest of the crowd.

"We don't know that," Moya said while silently thinking, *It could be Persephone, and I don't know which would be worse.*

Moya directed them to wait near the rear to avoid getting penned in. They only needed to know who had arrived. Afterward, they could disperse with the rest of the crowd and just keep going. She wasn't certain exactly where to head but thought following the road would be a good place to start.

"She's told them the secret, and they've killed her."

"Calm down, Brin. We don't—"

Moya spotted Tura waiting in the crowd, and her reserve of hope shrank. Looking over the waves of faces, she recognized Cobb, Bergin, Filson, Tope Highland and his sons, and the whole Killian family—minus the still-living Brigham. The Bakers, the Whipples, Holiman Hunt, and most of the Wedons were there. He was out front with a handsome young man Moya didn't recognize.

Holiman doesn't know Suri. So it has to be Persephone.

With that knowledge, she realized that there had been a *worse* option, and the gods had chosen it.

Just then, several of those who had gathered noticed her. Shock was followed by bewilderment and even a dash of irritation, as if Moya had done something shameful by dying.

"Moya?"

She turned to see Arion. The Fhrey looked exactly as she always had, still wearing the asica she'd been buried in. "Are you here because Suri has—"

"That's them." The mauled-to-death fellow they'd met outside the gate was talking to a small group of people dressed in flowing gray robes. He pointed toward Moya, then added, "The gate opened after they arrived."

The six robed figures headed directly their way. They weren't Fhrey, but they moved with the same elegance and grace. All were clean-shaven and tall, so they weren't Dherg, either, but they bore the same stony stare and granite jawlines. These were something else. Something Moya had never seen before.

The ruler of Rel has people looking for us.

Tekchin moved close as one of the six stepped forward. The man—as that's what Moya decided he most resembled—had the same green eyes as Muriel. His hair was straight, slick, and black, as if he had dipped it in a vat of Brin's ink. The man's skin was alabaster white, and his gray robes billowed despite the lack of a breeze.

"His Most Immaculate, Serene, and Renowned Majesty of Rel has decided to favor you with an audience. You will accompany us to his wondrous presence."

"How nice," Moya said. "But we're busy at the moment. Please tell *His Majesty* that we'll have to meet some other time."

The man's brows rose in surprise, then his eyes narrowed in seriousness. "It's not a request."

"Not overly polite, either," Moya added, and she enjoyed seeing his brows rise once more.

"Watch your words. His Majesty reigns supreme here." The man in gray swept his arm forward, indicating they should walk back up the brick road toward the village.

"Good for him." Moya stayed where she was.

The others did likewise.

Moya felt everyone's eyes on her. She was upstaging the main event with this unexpected warm-up act. A long moment lingered. Maybe it was only the length of a heartbeat, but Moya no longer had that meter to judge by.

"You will obey your lord," the ink-headed, alabaster man declared with insulting certainty.

Moya knew she wasn't smart. Her mother had reminded her of that little fact from the time she was born. She wasn't creative or physically strong, and she couldn't make a dress, shear a sheep, or cook a decent meal.

Until discovering the bow, she hadn't been good, or even adequate, at anything—except causing trouble. She didn't mean to be difficult and most of the time regretted her actions, but something in her refused to bend. No one owned Moya. No man, no woman, no Fhrey or Dherg, and no ruler of the afterlife was going to make her bow.

"Tell *your* lord that if he wishes the privilege of our company, he will ask nicely. I'm accustomed to being courted with a *please* and *thank you.*"

The creepy, pale man—although he might have just looked pale because his face was framed in that intensely black hair—stared in confusion. "You *will* follow me *now,*" Ink-Head demanded and turned his back.

"Kiss my ass," Moya said.

Brin's hand touched Moya's back. The Keeper of Ways was only lightly patting, but in hand-language, her fingers were screaming.

The man whipped back around and glared at Moya with enough intensity that she almost reached for an arrow. Tekchin shifted his stance, hand rising to the pommel of his sword.

"What does your master want with them?" Arion asked.

"None of your business, Fhrey," Ink-Head replied without looking at her.

Moya knew that because they were dead the rules were different, but it was still shocking to see anyone speak to Arion with such disregard. Perhaps in death she was no longer the terrifying Miralyith she'd once been, or maybe they merely didn't know her well enough.

"These are friends of mine, which is why I'm making it my business," Arion explained, using her ridiculously even tone that proclaimed refinement and grace. "And besides, when I first arrived, *I* didn't receive an invitation to bask in the grace of his wondrous presence, so I'm feeling a bit snubbed."

"They *will* obey His Majesty's command," Ink-Head insisted.

"Or what?" Arion asked. She'd spoken the words matter-of-factly, but their meaning was clear. The shocked expression on the gray-clad half dozen revealed that perhaps they did know Arion, at least by reputation.

"His Majesty will not appreciate your interference, *Fhrey.*"

"Ezerton, we've been over this. I prefer to be called Arion, and if Drome has a problem with my actions, he can bring it up with me personally. I don't conduct conversations through intermediaries."

"Did you say *Drome?*" Rain asked. "You don't mean . . ."

Arion nodded. "God of the Belgriclungreians—yes."

Rain, who was usually as steadfast as a hundred-year-old elm, staggered.

Ezerton glared at Arion. "Our ruler will punish you for this interference."

Arion smiled back. Had Moya been too far away to hear their words and forced to interpret their exchange only through body language, she would swear they were holding two different conversations. "Ezerton, you are aware there is nothing remotely true in that statement. He's not *my* ruler, and I honestly don't believe he'll risk losing his best skib partner over something as inconsequential as this."

"This is not trivial, and you will address me as the Word of Drome."

Arion rolled her eyes. "Run along and find someone else to bother. Can't you see we are waiting to greet a loved one?"

With a harrumph, Ezerton, or the Word of Drome, turned and led his retinue up the brick road, moving at a brisk pace.

Arion watched them retreat, then faced Moya with a frown. "That might not have been wise."

Moya huffed. "Don't like people assuming they can tell me what to do."

"You know what bothers me?" Tekchin asked.

Roan, who hadn't said anything since returning from her visit with Reanna, volunteered an answer. "The fact that all of them have an odd number of ties down the front of their left boots but an even number on their right ones?"

Everyone turned so suddenly to look at her that Roan shrank back. "That wasn't it?"

"No—ah—I wasn't thinking that," Tekchin replied. "I was going to say that none of them was carrying any weapons—no weapons, no armor."

"Everyone is already dead, and Sarah said you don't feel pain here," Moya reminded them. "So why bother? It's not like they can harm us."

Tekchin grinned. "Which goes both ways, I suspect. If things turned ugly, I was planning on severing heads. That might not be permanent, but I figure it would slow them down, right?"

"What's wrong with you people?" Arion asked, aghast.

"Raised badly," Moya said. "That's my excuse, at least." She paused to smile at Roan. "You know, I completely missed that about the bootlaces."

"Really?" Roan said in disbelief. "It was all I could think about. It's still driving me crazy. Why would anyone design them that way?"

"Moya, I know I appeared flippant just now with Ezerton, but you really need to be careful," Arion said. "Drome *is* the undisputed ruler here. Usually, he's a good-natured administrator and spends most of his time entertaining himself in his castle, but he is an Aesira, and I don't take it as a good sign that he's interested in you."

Moya wasn't suitably impressed. "Who cares? If he doesn't like my attitude, he can kill me—oh wait—no, he can't. I'm already dead."

"Well, actually . . ." Arion said and hesitated.

Moya didn't like the sound of those two words. "Actually, what?"

"Death in Rel isn't so bad. You are reunited with those you love, there is no fear of pain or growing old, but there *are* dangers in Phyre. Permanent ones."

"Such as?"

"You can stop *being.*"

"How's that?" Gifford asked.

"We exist only as long as we believe we do, but without faith, you can fade."

"How could anyone not believe they exist?" Moya asked.

"It's easier than you might think." Arion's tone dropped, and Moya didn't like the change. The Fhrey had sounded so pleasant up until then. Her new manner felt like an unexpected cold wind. "When living, little annoyances such as hunger or a need for sleep are reminders that you're alive. But Rel doesn't have such irritants, so it's possible to doubt you exist at all. Here, we are reminded of our existence through interaction with others. If you take that away, it's easy to lose your sense of self."

"Tell me about it," Tressa said.

Moya ignored her. "But that's not something Drome can *do* to us, right?"

Arion shrugged. "Not really. Truth is, Drome isn't so terrible. He's not crazy like his sister. He's scared of her, I think. Drome likes his realm quiet and stable, but you're new here and *already* causing trouble. I'm just saying that it's not smart to poke a bear while you're in his cave."

"That's fine. We don't plan on staying." Moya grinned at her. "We are heading on to Nifrel." Arion didn't appear surprised to learn this, and Moya wondered why. "You don't happen to know where the entrance is, do you?"

"Everyone does. Well, anyone who has been here for any period of time." She pointed toward the retreating figures in gray. "That road ends at it. Running from one side of Rel to the other, it links the two. In fact . . . the Nifrel Gate is right next to Drome's castle."

Moya lost her grin.

"There she is!" The shout came from the front of those assembled, and it drew all of their attentions. Kid Gorgeous—the young fellow standing out front next to Holiman Hunt—had made the outburst as he pointed toward the river.

Moya pushed forward until she reached the front and saw the recently deceased come out of the dark water. There was no mistaking who it was, and while she felt saddened, she was also relieved that it wasn't Persephone or Suri.

"Padera, my love. It took you long enough!"

The handsome kid rushed forward and the two embraced, kissing as lovers.

Everyone applauded.

Moya waited, watching the reunion and sighing in relief. Brin came over to join her. The Keeper looked confused. When the lovers broke apart, the old woman noticed the pair. "Moya? Brin? By the Grand Mother, what are you two doing here?"

"I suppose we could say the same about you," Moya said.

"Hardly. I'm long overdue, so that shouldn't be such a surprise." The rest of the party joined them, and the old woman appeared shocked. "I'd heard you were going to a swamp, but honestly, I didn't think it was dangerous. Brin didn't make it sound that way."

"It's a long story," Brin said. "But you . . . you were fine when I left. You had a bit of a cold, but I didn't think it was anything serious, and now you're here and looking so—"

"Brin." Padera waved her hand, interrupting the girl. "You're going to think this is odd, but I have a message for you. I thought it was for when you got back, but finding you here . . . well . . ."

"It's from Malcolm, isn't it?" Tressa said.

Padera looked over, surprised. "It is. How did you know?"

"Oh, bother that! What did he say?"

"Simmer down. You're dead and still just as pushy as ever."

"Get on with it, old woman."

Padera turned away from Tressa and focused on Brin. "I was tired—body and soul—and just getting into bed when he came in. I was surprised because he'd been gone for years, and most men just don't walk into a woman's tent uninvited."

The face of the handsome young man who had kissed Padera hardened.

She patted his hand and gave him a warm smile. "Wasn't anything like that. Not to worry. Oh, everyone, this is my husband. Melvin, this is Brin, Roan, Gifford, Moya, Tressa, and the two foreigners over there are Tekchin and Rain."

The kid looked to be no more than eighteen, but he was built like a Dherg fortress, with long, beautiful hair the color of late-season maple syrup.

"*This* is your husband?" Moya asked.

Padera grinned her toothless smile and nodded. "Ain't he something?"

"He's so . . ." Moya swallowed. "Young. No offense, Padera, but watching your old mushed-up face smooching him is a sight I could have done without."

Melvin looked confused. "She looks exactly the way she did on our wedding day."

Padera laughed, looked down at her hands, and ran one over the back of the other. "Yep, it's smooth as a baby's bottom. I'm glad to be rid of the dark spots and thin skin. I was the Moya of my day, and Melvin was . . ." She looked at her husband and shook her head. "Nope, there never was another Melvin."

"What are you two talking about? Padera hasn't changed at all," Moya said.

"None of us have ever met Melvin, so we're probably seeing him the way *Padera* remembers him," Roan said in her usual muttering voice, the one she reserved for talking to herself. "Or maybe we see Melvin's own impression of how he imagines himself. Could be either, really. But it doesn't explain why Moya still sees Padera as old. To me, she's young and beautiful."

Tressa's annoyance grew once more. "By Mari's fat ass, I don't care who looks like what; you said Malcolm sent a message. What was it, woman!"

"Oh right. Well, as I was saying, the night I died Malcolm came by. I was feeling poorly, so I wasn't in a mood for visitors. I went right on with curling up in my covers, and he just stood there staring at me. Odd became strange, and I saw a look of sadness in his eyes. Then he said, 'The next time you see Brin, tell her, "When trees walk and stones talk."'"

"And?" Brin asked.

"That's all there was. I thought there should be more, too, but he said that was the whole message."

"But that makes no sense. There must be something I need to do when that happens. There has to be more."

"Nope. That's all. At the time, I figured he was drunk. Then he did something really strange." Padera gave a sheepish glance toward Melvin, and Moya saw her blush. "He kissed me."

Melvin opened his mouth to speak.

She stopped him. "Not that sort of kiss. It was . . ." She hesitated, and her eyes watered. "Anyway, after that, he left, and I went to sleep. The next thing I know, I'm in a river with a stone, heading toward a light, and now I'm here."

Moya's mind was pulled back to the swamp and the discussion she'd had with Muriel.

Our little Malcolm, who has trouble putting his own boots on, can arrange help for us in Rel?

If he wants to, yes.

In Rel, goodbyes were as rare as birthday parties, and Sarah and Delwin were mystified by their daughter's departure, asking where she thought they were going. Rather than attempt a lengthy and awkward explanation, Moya asked for Padera's help. The woman, who Moya still saw as an ancient matriarch, assured everyone that those who'd arrived with Moya had some place they needed to be. As hoped, that ended the discussion. While Dahl Rhen's oldest resident had only just arrived in Phyre, everyone still accepted her wisdom. So it was with hugs and lingering waves that Moya managed to get them moving.

In accordance with Arion's directions, they followed the brick road deeper into Rel. Gifford had suggested they ask Arion to join them, but Moya felt the fewer who knew about the key the better. Tressa also pointed out that if Malcolm thought they needed Arion along, he would have said so. The bright-white stones made Moya's boots *clack* in a manner she found pleasing. Having trudged through field and swamp, the idea of a pleasant stroll along a smooth road was inviting. Given that nothing could be worse than drowning in the witch's pool, Moya felt confident in her expectations for a brighter future.

After passing numerous homes and spotting side streets that revealed even more buildings, they moved beyond the Rhen village. More communities appeared, such as the plaster frame homes of Nadak. Then came the Dureyan mud-brick houses, which stood to either side, looking sorely out of place along the pristine brick.

Gifford pointed at a man who was splitting a log as they walked by. "Why do you think they are doing that? Chopping wood, I mean? It's not cold, and I doubt anyone eats, so there is no reason for a cook fire."

"To them, it's a joy," Brin explained. "Tesh always complained that there was so little wood in Dureya that it was considered a luxury."

"Still seems a bit, well, boring," Tekchin said. He frowned at another man who was stacking the pieces. "I like a good wine, but I wouldn't want to drink it constantly."

Brin looked at Tekchin, as if what he'd said was profound. "My mother complained about the monotony as well. Said it wasn't supposed to be this way. Apparently, something broke."

"Broke? Like what?" Gifford asked.

"She didn't say. Maybe she doesn't know."

"Malcolm does," Tressa proudly announced.

"Give it a break, will ya, Tressa," Moya said, her voice weary. "You've told us a hundred times about the marvel that is Malcolm. It's way past old."

"No, she's right," Roan interjected. "He brought it up. In the smithy the night when Suri made the gilarabrywn, Malcolm said the world was broken."

Tekchin snorted. "That'd be quite a feat. In what way is it supposed to be busted? Seemed fine to me."

"I don't think he actually explained that part." Roan looked to the others. "But I remember he said that he was the one who broke it."

Moya laughed. "Malcolm broke the whole world, did he?"

Roan nodded, straight-faced, but she had also once declared that the world had to be round. With Roan, there was no line dividing imagination from fact.

"Did he say how?" Tekchin asked with a bemused interest.

All those with a means of knowing shook their heads.

Moya spoke up, "And you didn't press the issue?"

"There was a lot going on," Tressa said. "The Fhrey were about to attack, Suri was preparing to kill her best friend, and Raithe was about to die, so—"

"Raithe!" Moya said, looking out among the many mud-brick houses.

"You see him?" Brin asked.

"No. But I just realized he wasn't at the gate or your parents' place. Don't you find that strange?"

"Maybe he's not dead, not entirely," Tressa said. "Maybe he's still in the dragon—part of him anyway."

"Or maybe we just missed him," Tekchin countered. "Moya's mother wasn't there, either. To be honest, I can't see how people ever find one another. That ringing lets you know someone has died—but you don't know who, or even what they will look like. Consider how many millions of Rhunes, Fhrey, Dherg, Moklins, Grenmorians, and who knows what else have died over the millennia. Phyre ought to be packed tight. I know I contributed my fair share to the afterlife's population. The Galantians have slaughtered hundreds and we were only eight warriors. Think of the wars! Moving at all should be nearly impossible, and yet—look at this place— it's quite spacious, and all the people we knew were nearby."

"Hair and nails," Roan said.

Everyone looked back to where she and Gifford walked hand in hand, but it was Moya who spoke. "Roan?"

"Huh?" She'd been watching her feet and stepping carefully to avoid gaps between the bricks.

Moya smiled at her. "You said that out loud, hon. The thing about hair and nails. What does it mean?"

"Oh, ah . . . I was just thinking that the reason Rel isn't crowded is because it's always growing, getting bigger. When more is needed, it's created at the source—in the case of Rel, that would be the river."

"And everything just moves down? That doesn't sound right."

"Well, I don't know for sure. Maybe the river pulls back, but it's like Tekchin said, if the size of Phyre was fixed, it would eventually fill up. So it has to expand. That just makes sense, and it would account for a number of things, wouldn't it?"

Years of experience told Moya that Roan always assumed everyone saw what she did, and Moya found it strange that Roan—who usually noticed everything—never picked up on how consistently this assumption was proven wrong. "What kind of *things*, Roan?"

"Well, people keep getting born, and they all die, so that means an ever-growing and infinite number of souls. Having new arrivals walk all the way to the end would be silly. It'd be more efficient to add space where they come in. So, the area closest to the gate is filled with people who died recently, while those farther out would have done so further in the past." She gestured at the mud-brick houses. "Nadak was destroyed after Dureya, and Rhen was attacked after that. As a result, we passed through those areas in reverse order. In a way, we are walking backward through time, at least in regard to the dead."

"But my parents were killed before the war, and a lot of people died in the Battle of Grandford," Brin said. "Why didn't we have to walk through them to get to my parents' house?"

"Maybe you did, at least some of them. But just like in Elan, people move around and settle in communities. If your parents had died a hundred years ago, they might be somewhere in Rel that resembled a forest like the Crescent. They may have gone for a walk, found neighbors there, and moved to be near them. They would be a bit farther away, but not too far when you consider the amount of time that has passed since the world began. They'd still be relatively close to where we came in. Now, if you needed to find Gath of Odeon, I suspect that would have been harder, and you'd be forced to travel farther."

"That's why Brin's parents and Farmer Wedon have homes near one another even though they died a few years apart," Gifford concluded.

"Yes, exactly," Roan said and smiled.

They walked on. More communities came and went. Not all were human. Some were Dherg, others Fhrey. Many paths branched off the brick road as if it were the trunk of a tree, then they grew out to either side, creating their own network of roads and trails. Moya noticed some settlements completely disconnected from the brick road, isolated in far-off pastures, forests, and swamps. Although they were too far to see details, Moya concluded that the architecture was different from any they'd seen so far.

Why live in a swamp? she wondered.

Moya remembered what Tekchin had said about those who died and curiosity took hold. "What's a Moklin?" she asked him.

"Means *Blind Ones.* You know them as goblins."

"You think *goblins* come *here* when they die?" she asked, shocked. "You believe *they* have souls?"

"How should I know?"

Moya looked back at the swamp. *Maybe they do.*

The trip from the river was always uphill, which Moya thought was odd since everyone knew that Nifrel was below Rel. She concluded that while the entrance might be up high, Nifrel itself could extend a long way down.

Unless it has nothing to do with location. Perhaps Nifrel is below Rel *in other ways.*

As they gained height and looked back, they saw how the lowland nearest the Rel Gate was easily the most populated. Densely clustered roundhouses dominated the landscape, spreading out in a haphazard fashion along the meandering brick road. They spilled out like silt after a flood. Amid that human sediment were little stone-wrought communities of dwarfs, and speckled here and there were a smattering of brick-and-timber homes like the Fhrey dwellings of Alon Rhist.

Thinking about Roan's idea that Rel grew over time, she noticed that some sections along the road were more thinly populated, while others were dense.

Am I looking at famines and good years? Times of war and peace?

The farther they went, the higher they climbed, and the sparser the population became. Even the buildings grew cruder, more primitive.

"I don't understand where all this stuff comes from," Brin said, pointing to the multitude of homes stretching as far as they could see. "My parents' home was just like the one I grew up in."

"Not exactly," Gifford said. "It was nicer."

Brin nodded. "Yeah, I suppose. But how do people wish things into existence?"

Roan pulled on her hair and stared at her feet as she walked. "Arion said we exist because we believe we do." She thought a bit more. "When we died, we left our bodies in Elan, and yet . . ." She poked herself. "I have a body." She looked up. "Moya has her bow and Rain his pickax. But they aren't real. They have them because they believe they do—we look the way we do for the same reason—we believe it. Perhaps in a world lacking substance, willpower and faith can shape our surroundings."

"And the reason all the houses are nicer than the real thing?" Gifford asked.

"Pride," Tressa explained. "No one is going to make their home anything other than perfect if given a choice, right?"

"Really?" Moya smirked. "Then how come you're still wearing that miserable shirt? Or am I seeing only what I expect?"

Tressa looked down at herself and shrugged. "You see what I am."

"We see what you believe," Gifford said.

"Maybe," Rain said, "but there are two sides to every wall, aren't there?"

Roan nodded. "Every impression is built from our sense of self, but also from the expectations of others."

"You lost me, Roan," Moya said.

"Oh . . . well, it's like Padera, isn't it?"

"Is it?"

"Yes!" Gifford exclaimed with a big grin. "It is. Roan, you're a genius. That's why Moya saw Padera as old, but you saw her as young."

Moya glared at Tekchin, who looked as confused as she felt. "Don't you dare figure this out before me."

The Fhrey shook his head. "Not a chance of that. I never was known as the smart Galantian—just the best looking." He winked at her.

"It's like this," Gifford explained. "The reason Moya saw Padera as old is because that's how she remembers her. Moya's memory is more powerful than Padera's perception of herself. That makes sense because Moya's opinions—her willpower is . . . well, she's . . ."

"Bullheaded," Tekchin supplied.

Gifford swallowed, looking embarrassed. "I would have said *strong.*"

"How did you see Padera?" Moya glared at Tekchin.

"Oh, we're both pure bull."

Roan nodded in agreement, then her eyes went wide, and she let out a little gasp.

"What?" Moya asked.

"I just thought of something."

"Yes, we know that. The question is, *what* was it?"

"Oh . . . I thought of the well in the middle of the brick road. Did you see it?"

"I think we all did. So?"

Roan looked at Moya, confused. "It's in the middle of the road—right *on* the brick."

Moya frowned and shook her head. "Am I the only stupid one here? Is anyone else following her?"

A series of identical gestures followed, making Moya feel better, and Roan blinked several times, bewildered.

"Why is it significant that the well is on the brick road?"

"Because I don't think this road exists any more than Sarah's home or your bow."

Moya gave a glance around and was happy to see five faces looking back that were still just as muddled as she felt. "Need a bit more, Roan."

"Really?"

"Ah, yeah."

"Oh, okay. The well is *on top* of the brick, it was *made* after the one who created the paving stones. And I'm going to assume that's the ruler of this realm."

Tekchin nodded. "You're saying someone altered Drome's work. So, that someone must have more power than a god. Who in Rhen could do that?"

"Oh, I know!" Brin had the answer. "It's everyone. That's what my mother meant when she said they draw something other than water from the well. She mentioned it was deeper and more vital. It's the community. It's all of them."

Moya was about to ask what exactly Brin's mother drew from this waterless well when she heard the ringing once more.

"Someone has died," Gifford announced. "I hear ringing."

"I think we all do," Moya added.

Even Tekchin and Rain appeared to hear it this time, and Moya felt certain that wasn't a good sign.

"Who do you think it is?" Brin's face displayed a devastated expression.

"It's not Suri," Moya insisted. "It's not. And we aren't going back to look. We have a job to do, and we've wasted too much time already. C'mon."

کو

They walked along the bricks in silence after that, each lost in thought. Moya had a pretty good idea what was on their minds. She didn't want to know who was climbing up the riverbank at Rel's Great Gate. Whoever it was, there was nothing Moya could do for them. Suri, if she was still alive, was another matter. They had died for the mission that Malcolm and Tressa had cooked up, and her only path was forward.

You are brave, Muriel had told her. *I can tell that just from the short time I've known you. Your fortitude is the sort of thing that will be important in Phyre.*

Moya was disturbed by the silence that was more than a lack of noise. It was the absence of life. While alive, even when isolated in a room, she couldn't block out the din of a living world: Wind rustled thatch; voices carried, and birdsongs wafted in through windows. When she had been in Neith—deep underground—there was still her beating heart and the sound of breathing. She'd never noticed them before, but now their absence was maddening. After climbing the last steep hill, Moya should have been panting for air. She wasn't even out of breath.

She broke the stifling silence. "Is anyone else having problems getting used to this whole not-breathing thing?"

"I feel like I am; breathing that is," Tekchin said.

"But you don't have to." Moya turned so that she was walking backward and spread out her arms, inviting them to view how far they had come. "Look at that. See how high we've climbed. Is anyone tired? Anyone sore? It's creepy—creepy, I tell you."

They never once strayed from the white road, and it never faltered. As they rose higher, the brick lane serpentined ever upward. Despite the switchbacks, they covered the distance between the Rel Gate and the mountains in a short time—or so Moya thought. Without a moving sun, a need for sleep or rest—or the beating of a heart—time became impossible to judge. Covering the distance might have taken hours, days, or weeks.

Moya had no way to make a determination except by remembering various milestones they had passed. All she was certain of is they had come far, and they were high above the valley, plains, and hills. Ahead, jagged walls of gray stone were covered in snow.

Villages continued to come and go, but they were tiny things now, and not at all like those back in the valley. In the highlands, humans were shorter and hairier, and their crude huts consisted of stretched animal skins and bent tree branches. The Fhrey's ears were less pointed, and they wore modest cloth wraps and lived in simple mud-brick structures. The Dherg, who were oddly tall, sought shelter in caves. And there was another group, a strange-looking race with large eyes and long arms. They wore robes of red. All of these people glared with angry eyes as they chipped rocks and shaved sticks. Then for a long time there were no more villages, no more people. The higher altitudes brought with them a world of pure, uninhabited wilderness.

As they entered the mountains, the road narrowed. Once wide enough for five to walk abreast, they now had to go single file, making their way through twisted gaps and along cliff ledges that provided fabulous views of the valley.

What happens if I fall? Moya wondered. *Will I plummet thousands of feet, hit the ground, and then what? Bounce and get up? Will I just have to start over?*

As they climbed higher, Moya saw snow on the ground. She looked up at the pale sky.

Did that snow fall? Or has it always been here?

Clearing one more switchback, a great fortress came into sight. Made entirely of stone, the building wasn't cut into the mountain like Neith, nor was it raised up the way Avempartha was said to have been. Castle Rel was the mountain itself. More than twice the size of Mador, the stronghold extended into clouds that, until that moment, Moya hadn't known were there. Made of obsidian and alabaster, the castle was a forest of white and black spires that pierced and defied the gray sky with undeniable insult.

The perfect spear-like towers appeared to be weapons thrusting at the very nature of the underworld. Rage was at the heart of the design, a bristling symbol of defiance. In a place of peaceful surrender, Castle Rel was an expletive in stone. And Moya had to admit it was beautiful. Lines were straighter than any she'd seen before. Curves were exact, and the construction bore a balance so perfect that it made Moya smile against her will. She'd never seen anything so delightful and so disturbing at the same time—a beautiful flower made entirely of thorns.

"Whoa." Tekchin craned his neck, trying to see the top. "Now, *that's* something."

Rain gaped as he moved to the front of their little troop. "It's perfect."

"It's scary," Brin said.

"I'm with you on this one," Gifford added.

"There's the Nifrel Gate." Roan pointed to where the road ended.

Directly across from the castle's entrance, a great arched gateway stood, supporting what looked to be a sheet of black glass. In front of it, a small contingent of gray-clad beings blocked its access.

"Probably wishing you hadn't insulted Ezerton right now, huh?" Tressa asked her.

"Oh, like you would have done any different."

"You're taking pride in being as stupid as me, now?"

Moya opened her mouth, but realized she had nothing to say.

"What do we do?" Brin asked.

"Looks like, what? Twenty? Thirty?" Moya asked.

"How many arrows you got?" Tekchin inquired.

"Eight."

"And they've got weapons now," Gifford said.

The men at the gate formed up in straight lines and began to walk in their direction. No running, no rush; they moved slowly and in perfect formation.

Moya frowned, turned back to Tekchin, and sighed. "Arion said Drome was usually good-natured, right?"

"She did."

"And we don't know why he wanted to see us, so it might not be anything bad."

"That's true."

As the soldiers came closer, Moya saw it was Ezerton approaching. Just as Gifford had said, this time he wore a sword.

"You will follow me, now," he ordered and turned toward the castle.

The group of men split, forming two lines. Ezerton walked between them.

Moya took Tekchin's hand. "Stay close to me."

"Like a tick on a hound's ear."

She looked over.

Tekchin shrugged. "It's what I used to tell Nyphron. Sounded better with him."

As the party approached the castle, the soldiers reformed and followed from behind. Looking at the entrance, seeing the open archway like a wide mouth ready to swallow everyone whole, Moya realized three things. A lot of people had called the Fhrey gods. A few Miralyith thought themselves to be gods. But when a Fhrey Miralyith dwelling in the afterlife said someone was a god, you should listen. Moya squeezed Tekchin's hand as they stepped over the threshold and went in.

CHAPTER SEVEN

End of an Era

If I had been Nyphron, I would have chosen a tree. A tree does not strike fear into the hearts of one's enemies, nor does it inspire anything besides peace and growth, so I am guessing that is why he went with a dragon.

— THE BOOK OF BRIN

A thin veil of snow dusted the ground, except for the mound of freshly turned soil that was a dark scar upon the land. The barrow before Persephone was one of many that had transformed a flat field into a mounded plain, as if it had suffered a terrible pox. She supposed it had. So many years of war had raised an abundant, bitter crop.

"Cold," Nolyn complained. He pulled on her finger.

"Hush, little man," Justine said from behind them.

Little man? Is that new?

Persephone couldn't remember having heard it before. She approved. *It's good he's reminded. Someday he might forget.*

"Shall I take him back, ma'am?" Justine asked.

Persephone looked at her son. His cheeks and ears were red from the wind, a stream glistening under his nose, his mouth pulled down in a miserable frown. Nolyn had suffered through the farewell, and he'd cast his handful of dirt into the hole. His duty was done. Keeping him there was selfish, but holding his hand had helped.

"Yes," she said. "Thank you."

She felt him let go, heard her son trotting away.

"Don't stay too long, ma'am," Justine said. "Getting cold."

"Yes," Persephone replied without turning. "It is."

As Justine led Nolyn away, Persephone was the last one standing in the field. Few had been there at all. Persephone had long believed that when Padera finally died, her funeral would be massive, but she had outlived everyone. With her death went an era. The old woman had been the last true remnant of the past—that time of stone weapons and gods across the river.

Farmer Wedon's two boys, Brent and Oscar, who were now men, and Viv Baker's daughter, Hest, who was betrothed to the last of the Killian boys, had all attended the funeral. And of course, there was Habet, who remained a comforting constant in the universe. All of them had been born in Dahl Rhen, but they were young, too young to remember how it was. They had only one foot in the old world. Most of their weight was on their other leg. The days of gathering in the lodge in winter to listen as Maeve told the stories of Gath of Odeon were over. No longer did anyone sit shoulder to shoulder in the flickering light with friends and neighbors, sharing roast lamb. And the innocence of knowing that tomorrow would be the same as today would never come again.

They are all gone.

Persephone dropped to her knees, clutching the fabric of her breckon mor tightly to her neck.

Padera, Reglan, Mahn, Maeve, Sarah, Delwin, Gelston, Aria, and . . . no, not them!

Persephone shook her head. She still had hope that those who'd gone to the swamp could come back because Malcolm told her they might. This strange proclamation gave her an extremely tenuous thread to hold on to. And as absurd as it sounded, and as impossible as it might seem,

Persephone clutched it as if that hope alone stood between herself and the brink of insanity. But with each passing day, even that hope wavered, the thread frayed.

Persephone looked back at the camp and sighed.

Why—in a camp filled with people—do I feel so alone?

She loved Nolyn, was blessed with Justine, and comforted by Habet. They kept her going, but the people she had loved the most, the ones she'd fought and bled with, were gone. Without them, she felt weak and naked.

Winter had arrived, and even old Padera had abandoned her. That's when Persephone realized the truth of it.

Padera isn't the last of the era—I am. Without Brin and her book, everything I once knew and loved will be forgotten. After I die, the days of Dahl Rhen will be an age of myth.

"How are they doing, Padera?" Persephone asked the dirt. "Tell them to hurry, won't you? Tell them they must come back because I need them. I need them all."

Persephone began to cry, but she wasn't sure who the tears were for.

❧

Nyphron walked the empty, open plain between what had become known as the Dragon Camp and the forest.

A dragon. That should be my symbol, my standard.

He'd had nothing to do with the beast. He hadn't conjured it, nor asked for it to be summoned. If he'd known such things were possible, he would have ordered twenty. They only had the one, but that singular winged beast had saved everyone at Alon Rhist and kept the Dragon Camp safe through many years of war. People saw it as a symbol of strength and protection.

Nyphron frowned. *They're supposed to see* me *that way.*

That had been the plan, but Nyphron's plans hadn't been working out so well.

He paused his meandering stroll through the field when he caught sight of bone. A hand—or what had been one—lay mostly covered in grass and a dusting of snow. Only the fingertips poked up, as if the skeletal owner were trapped and trying to claw his way to the surface. This was the site of the last of the open battles where the fane's forces had foolishly attempted to stop them from entering the trees. As they always had done in the fields, his chariots ruled, and he had won the day.

But not the war.

"Who were you, I wonder?" he asked the hand. "Rhune or Fhrey? Friend or foe?"

Whoever it had been, Nyphron felt a kinship—the buried person's plans hadn't worked out, either.

Returning to his chariot, he leaned against the wheel, looking east at the forest. He had come out there to be alone, to think, not about dragons—not anymore. What had once been his possible salvation would now be his undoing. The fane would have dragons—of that, he had no doubt—but he didn't have them yet. That was also a certainty. Lothian wouldn't waste even a moment sending his new weapon across the river—and he would ask for as many as he wished and get them. As the sky was clear of everything except snow, Nyphron knew there was still time . . . but for what?

What should I do next?

The flurries lent a hazy gray to the world. Not a real snow yet, only a ghostly preview of the season to come. And while he could see the trees, he saw nothing else.

"I've had lousy luck of late," he said. Then speaking to the white bony fingers, he added, "You can understand that, can't you? For you, it was what? A sword? An arrow? For me, it'll likely be the teeth of a dragon."

Yes, he thought again, *my symbol should have been a dragon.*

He should have thought of it years ago. His emblem of leadership needed to proclaim strength and power. Lions and bears were typical, but he was supposed to be the ruler of kings and fanes. His symbol had to be greater, and what was more powerful than a dragon? And if the Rhunes chose to bestow the adoration he deserved on a conjured beast, that was fine. Just as he had acquired power over the Ten Clans by marrying Persephone, so, too, would he have gained the reverence he desired by linking himself to a dragon. In a few centuries, no one would have known the difference. Nyphron the Dragon, the defender of the people: The two titles would be the same. From what he knew of the Rhunes, it might only take a few decades. They were a forgetful lot.

Nyphron caught movement coming from the camp. A figure in a hooded cloak walked toward him. The person was alone—and it was a man. He could tell that much by the awkward gait.

"Sorry to intrude," Malcolm called when closer. Then he paused, threw back his hood, and created a massive cloud of fog as he struggled to catch his breath.

No, not a man after all.

He honestly had no idea what Malcolm was. He looked like a Rhune, moved like one, but he wasn't. What he actually was remained a mystery. The only reason Nyphron hadn't banished the not-a-man was that he had disappeared on his own.

"I thought you'd left."

"Came back for the funeral and . . . other things."

Malcolm took notice of the skeletal hand. "Friend of yours?"

Nyphron wasn't amused. "So, why aren't you at the ceremony?"

"I was. It's over."

"Do you expect me to believe that you left for all those years, and it was the death of an old woman that brought you back?"

"Her name was Padera," Malcolm reminded him. "But as I said, I'm here for other reasons as well." He glanced down at the bony fingers. "You know, lend a hand where I can. Check on things, make any necessary adjustments."

"You're not going to ask me to make another vow, are you? Because I traded that for a promise that's not looking like it'll come to fruition."

Malcolm shook his head and offered a sad smile. "No, it's not that. Would you find it odd if I said I'm concerned about you?"

Despite his depression, that made Nyphron laugh.

"Think what you will," Malcolm said. "But your welfare and success are very important to me."

"Since when?"

"Since your father died." Malcolm stared at the bony hand with an unsettled expression that puzzled Nyphron.

How can he appear so prissy? So human?

"Are you saying I risk suffering his same fate? Because that's not exactly news to me. The war is going badly, and it's only a matter of time before Lothian repeats the denigration of my father on me. Now if you don't mind, I came up here to be away from people. And that includes you, whatever you are."

Malcolm turned his attention to Nyphron. "You came up here to think. I came to help you do that."

"I'm certain I am capable of doing that on my own."

"You're disillusioned, disappointed, and depressed because you suspect everything is lost. But worst of all, you're losing faith in me."

"I never *had* any faith in you."

Malcolm raised his arms and then let them fall with a sigh. "See—this has always been my problem. Why can't the world be filled with Tressas?"

"What?"

"Never mind. The point is, I promised that you would be ruler of Elan, and you will."

"You've been gone, so you might not know this, but Suri is going to give Lothian dragons."

"No, Suri's capture is not news to me. I've known about it for a long time. Before it happened, in fact."

Nyphron was sure Malcolm was just babbling nonsense now. But his implicit agreement about Lothian obtaining dragons was a surprise. He had expected an argument. The lack of debate left him confused, and he lost track of his thoughts for a moment.

He likes to keep me off-balance, but why?

Nyphron had learned from experience never to trust anyone, or more accurately, to trust them only as far as was safe. That distance could only be accomplished by knowing the person. While Malcolm had been around during Nyphron's early years, he knew nothing of his father's servant. He caught the thread of his thoughts again. "We have no defense against dragons, and without Suri, we can't hope to survive."

"Right again. You're pretty good at this."

Nyphron frowned. "Did you come up here to make me feel worse? To revel in my pain?"

Malcolm sighed. "I hate it when people don't hear me. No, I suppose they hear, they just don't listen. Look, I told you I came to help, but lying to you wouldn't accomplish that."

Malcolm looked around for a place to sit, but found nothing and frowned. "So yes, the outcome of this war is teetering, and as hard as it may be for you to do, I think you need to relax and let matters run their course. I don't need any further meddling from you."

"Meddling? What makes you think I'm planning on doing anything?"

"Because you're Nyphron, not Petragar. And because I know that you sent Elysan north on a secret mission."

"Not so secret if *you* know about it."

Malcolm gave him that disturbing stare that wasn't quite human—because humans wouldn't dare look at him so boldly. Doing so required a lack of mortal fear that men didn't possess.

"I tried to build a bridge," Nyphron said. "That didn't work. Persephone suggested a tunnel, but the Dherg nixed that idea. They said they'd prefer to be buried by their own people rather than the Miralyith. Can't say I blame them."

"Yes, and you also sent a contingent south toward the base of the falls, looking for a ford across the river. See? Meddling. As a result, there will be more unnecessary deaths as neither of the parties will survive."

"You can't know that."

"Ghazel to the south and giants to the north. Both have a fondness for human meat, and they've been known to eat a Fhrey or two."

"I sent *a lot* of men—half of the Second Legion, in fact."

"Won't matter."

"Well then, I will place my hope on Elysan. You see, my problem isn't the river, but the water itself. Can't put Dherg runes on water—this has become the mantra of all those I send to the Harwood. But what if I got rid of the water?"

Malcolm shook his head. "He won't be able to recruit giants to dam the river in the north."

"Dam it, divert it, drink it—I don't care what they do just as long as it stops flowing long enough for me to get troops to the Estramnadon side. Furgenrok has some truly huge relatives. Not that he, himself, isn't large, but some of his uncles—the ones who have been asleep for centuries—could cut off the water by cupping it with their hands. If Elysan can convince them, they could shut off the flow, the Nidwalden would run dry, at least for a time, and the Techylors could spearhead the attack by slaughtering the Miralyith in Avempartha. Then the army can pour across the empty riverbed and flood Erivan."

"And you hope to do this before Lothian starts making dragons."

"That's the idea."

"Odds of success?"

"Dismal. The giants of Hentlyn hate us. They have no reason to help. So, I told Elysan to promise them anything."

"Anything?"

Nyphron shrugged. "What do we care? If they stop the water, I'll wipe out the only force on Elan that can threaten me. And after the fane dies, the giants will be yoked into slavery, or if subjugation proves too troublesome, they will be erased."

"And did Persephone agree to this plan?"

Despite aiding Nyphron's cause with the idea of an opportunistic marriage with Persephone, Nyphron knew that Malcolm preferred her to him. He displayed a little smile. "She doesn't need to know."

"You don't think she might want to weigh in on the *erasure* of a race, since that is what the Fhrey are trying to do to her people?"

"I don't think her knowing will be necessary, since the war with the giants won't start until well after she's dead."

Malcolm's eyebrows shot up. "You aren't saying—"

Nyphron laughed, and it felt surprisingly good. Seeing Malcolm knocked off-balance was the most fun he'd had in months. "I'm not planning on killing the woman. She's my wife, you know."

"Men have killed their wives before and over lesser offenses than sending their only hope into the hands of the enemy."

"I'm not a man."

Malcolm said nothing. He continued to stare, unconvinced.

Nyphron rolled his eyes. "Truthfully, I like Persephone. She's been a good wife and mother."

"What about keenig?"

He nodded. "That too."

"Because she leaves the military decisions to you?"

"As is sensible. While I hate to admit it, the pairing has been a good one. She has no ego to butt against, no desire for glory. If I had to ally myself with a man, or even an Instarya like Sikar or Tekchin, we would have come to blows by now. Persephone is wiser than I first imagined. No, what I meant is that the Grenmorian problem will likely not be addressed for another fifty or sixty years, and by then, I doubt Persephone will still be with us."

To this, Malcolm merely nodded.

"But you don't think Elysan will be successful," Nyphron said.

"The Fhrey, and in particular the Instarya, don't have a good reputation in the north."

"And what about the army we sent south?" Nyphron asked. "We merely ordered them to establish a secure route across the lower river, then scout a way to scale the cliff on the far side. What makes you think that won't succeed?"

114 • *Michael J. Sullivan*

Malcolm turned to face east, as if he could see something in the flurries that Nyphron could not. "The world to the southeast—the Broken Lands and isles—are the scarred and flooded remains of the ancient shattered lands. They belong to the Uber-Ran. They always have."

"Uber-Ran?"

"Your people call them Moklins—the Blind Ones; humans named them goblins; the Belgriclungreians dubbed them ghazel. But they call themselves Uber-ran—Ones of Uber, the Faithful Children of Uberlin, the Great Ones. They are the loyal, the devout, the only followers who didn't abandon the first ruler of Elan."

"Who was that?"

"Rex Uberlin."

Nyphron smirked. "Children of an evil god they may be, but they're still just goblins, primitive and unruly."

"Like everyone, they were different once. Loyal to their king, but he didn't return their faith in kind. Abandoned and leaderless, they were twisted by the selfish and cruel example left to them. Given enough time, sediment settles to the bottom of any cup." Malcolm continued to stare east for a moment, then he turned back with an apologetic smile. "Call them what you will, but the party you sent will be eaten. You can count on that."

"We'll see."

The wind picked up and howled across the plain. Snow thickened and danced among the rocks. Nyphron looked once more toward the forest. "I can't see the river. Waiting for a signal from the Techylors is maddening."

"Why not go there yourself?"

Nyphron shook his head and frowned. "I don't dare. Running a war from the rear is"—he sighed—"so very frustrating. Far more so than I ever would have believed. But if I were on the bank and the water did stop . . ." He laid a hand on his sword, and in doing so, he realized he couldn't remember the last time he'd drawn it.

"That Law of Ferrol's is a problem, isn't it?" Malcolm said with a smug smile. "But you shouldn't worry too much. As I promised, you will be the ruler of the world. We have a deal, remember?"

"Are you ever going to tell me what you want?"

"I'll let you know soon. Just remember that I was right then, and nothing has changed with regards to you becoming emperor."

"I'll be what?"

"You aren't familiar with the term *empyre?* Probably not, it comes from the Eilywin tribe and has nothing to do with conquest. It means 'to join together, to build, to unify.' The Eilywin are all about living in balance. It's their word for creating an environment in which people can live together in harmony with nature, the gods, and with one another. That's what I want to create. You will help me build an empyre for everyone."

"*You* want to create?" Nyphron said.

Malcolm ignored him. "Just consider what could be done if wars were a thing of the past and everyone worked together."

"Sounds boring." He stared at Malcolm, sizing him up once more. The tall, lanky not-a-man lacked fear, but displayed no attributes to explain why. Disturbing is what he was, like a fish that talked. Such things weren't supposed to be possible, yet there he stood—the talking fish promising to fulfill Nyphron's greatest dreams . . . for a price. "Why do I get the impression there's something you *aren't* telling me? You're like one of those demons that grant wishes, but not the way one would expect. If you ask to never grow old—they kill you. Is that it?"

Malcolm raised his hood and smiled, not a happy expression but one of endured regret. "Life doesn't always turn out the way we want, but that doesn't mean it isn't for the best. Remember that, too. It might help." He looked up at the sky. "No . . . it probably won't. There's no sense in the demon explaining why death is better than immortality. That's something that has to be experienced to be understood."

CHAPTER EIGHT

Unanswered Questions

I now understand that Aesira is another word for god. There are five, which oddly feels like both too few and too many.

— THE BOOK OF BRIN

Entering the home of Drome, Moya was greeted by two rows of five massive pillars. To either side, broad marble staircases curved like two giants' arms hugging the grand entry hall. From the checkered-tile floor to the soaring walls and arches, everything was either black or white. Even the torches didn't flicker with the familiar yellow of fire. Instead, they radiated an unwavering pale brilliance that reminded Moya of how snow reflected a winter's gray sky. For all her mother's tales of woe about Phyre, Audrey had failed to mention that the underworld was run by a tyrannical black-and-white-loving overlord. Not that it mattered because Moya wouldn't have believed the stories, but in retrospect, she would have appreciated the warning.

They found no one inside. The vast and imposing entrance was empty of anything except stone. The soldiers remained in the vestibule while Ezerton continued to lead the way up the stairs. As it happened, both sets circled to the same balcony and met at a single archway. Before it, the polished floor was made up of geometric patterns of a copper-colored stone, at the center of which lay a design like the sun. Rays sprayed out in a way that was similar to the art Moya had seen in Neith. To either side, statues soared. On the left, a man held a short sword in one hand and a torch in the other. The opposing figure was the same man, but this time he held a triangular tool in one hand and a hammer in the other. A bright light emanated from the chamber within.

While the climb hadn't been far, Moya felt exhausted. "Anyone else winded?"

"I feel . . . heavy," Tekchin said. "Tired, even."

The others nodded.

"We don't have bodies, so how can we be fatigued? Roan? What's going on?"

"Don't know."

"It's like the rules are changing on us," Moya said.

"What's that light, do you suppose?" Gifford asked, squinting at the archway.

"Well, we don't have eyes," Roan said. "So it's something we are interpreting. Power maybe?"

"It's the presence of Drome," Rain concluded.

"Seriously? He gives off his own light?" Moya rolled her eyes.

"Why not? He is a god, after all."

"Malcolm doesn't glow." Moya glanced at Tressa, taunting her, but she didn't bother to reply.

Ezerton stopped at the archway. "Behold, Lord God Drome of Rel." He beckoned them to enter.

Feeling less sure of herself than she ever had, Moya took slow steps forward. The interior brilliance was blinding, and she put up a hand in defense. Peering through spread fingers, she determined they were entering a white-marbled throne room. Instead of pillars, the roof—if there was one—was held up by statues of giants. Their arms strained to keep the sky in place. Rivers of liquid gold and silver spilled from indescribable heights, falling in cascades and splashing their way down sculptured walls. In the center of everything, a grand chair was placed on a dais at the top of yet another set of stairs.

Upon it sat Drome.

Grand, grinning, and terrifying, he looked to be so solid, broad, and heavy that he might have been another statue—if not for the energy he radiated. High cheekbones held up by cheerful anticipation, wide-set eyes, and a flat nose were all wreathed by a bristling mane. His hair was gold with streaks of silver that suggested the graying of age, yet while Moya was certain this being *was* old, the color of his hair and beard had nothing to do with that impression.

"What shades of Elan have entered my home?" the god asked.

That could have been worse, Moya thought. *He hasn't snuffed us out of existence. Maybe I misjudged Ink-Head's intentions. Perhaps I should stop thinking of him as Ink-Head, or possibly stop thinking altogether.*

Nothing else was said for quite some time, and Moya stood there, listening to the splash of the precious-metal falls.

Drome shifted his feet, drawing his heels in toward the base of his throne, and he leaned forward so that the long braids of his beard made a coil on the floor. He pointed at each as he counted them off. "Moya, Tekchin, Brin . . ." He hesitated. "Ah—Roan! Yes, Roan and Gifford." His eyes settled on Tressa, and they narrowed. "Hmm, who are—oh, yes, Konniger's wife." His sight slid off her in an instant as something caught his eye. "And of course, Rain!" His gaze remained on the dwarf for a time, and his smile grew brighter. "Nice to see one of my own."

The god sat back and crossed his legs, revealing a pair of stocky, hairy, muscled calves beneath purple, gold, and silver robes. "Normally, I would welcome you to my realm, but of course you aren't—*welcome,* that is. You are intruders, trespassers, troublemakers—rabble-rousers up to no good and no doubt here for nefarious purposes. Never before have I shut the Rel Gate, but when my sister warned me of your coming, I took her advice. As twins, we have divided all that makes us what we are. She hoarded the shrewdness, and I got everything else." He focused on Rain again. "*You* know what I mean."

Rain showed no indication of anything other than perhaps having voluntarily turned to stone.

"Now, let's get to the point of this visit." Drome leaned forward once more, this time placing both of his large squarish hands on the sturdy throne's arms, pushing himself to a more upright position. "How did you get in?"

Drome waited, but no one said a word.

"Did someone help you? Someone on the inside? Arion perhaps?" As Drome's voice rose, so did Moya's fear.

She recalled Arion's words, *Drome is the undisputed ruler here . . . he is an Aesira, and I don't take it as a good sign that he's interested in you.*

What's an Aesira? Moya wondered, *and why do I feel that it's bad?*

Just looking at Drome, at the light he radiated, which according to Roan might be an expression of his power, made Moya suspect that letting him build up to a frenzy wasn't a good idea.

Her first impulse was to tell him. More than just a thought, it was a compulsion, an almost undeniable desire. Giving him what he asked for would save them—all of them. So strong was the need to grant him his wish that Moya's mouth opened. But her propensity for standing up when she was told to sit down, for saying no when everyone else said yes, stopped her.

Despite her reputation, Moya hadn't slept with all the boys in Dahl Rhen. She'd said yes to Heath Coswall but only that one time. Moya had felt sorry for the boy because he'd cried while begging on his knees. He'd proclaimed his love and said that the pain of not being with her was too great. Being young and stupid, she'd picked poorly, and Heath turned out to be a bastard and then some. He spread rumors of her seducing him because there was no way he was going to tell the truth about that night. Moya was angry, but her mother was furious. Seeing how much it pained Audrey, Moya didn't dispute the rumors, which grew like crabgrass in a garden. It wasn't long before everyone was sure she had said yes to anyone who had asked, but she hadn't. After Heath's lie, she said no hundreds of times. Each one brought stunned looks that she enjoyed seeing. Saying no—refusing to obey, go along, or appease—became ingrained in her and helped to erase in her own mind that one foolish mistake. Over time, it became part of her character. Defiance was one of the pillars of who she was. Being dead hadn't changed that.

For all his power and glory, Drome was one more male asking, *Will you?* No—he was *demanding* that she obey. God or not, Moya's mouth twisted into her usual wry smile. "Rel is where people go when they die. We died. Being a god and all, I assumed you knew how that worked."

Drome narrowed his gaze, but rather than explode, he settled back, and the hint of a smile graced his lips. "Few people are able to stand before my light, much less sass me. You know full well what I'm asking. I locked the gate. How did you open it?"

Moya batted her eyes. "Maybe it didn't latch all that well because it opened when I pushed. But now that you bring it up, why did you seal it? I heard you're the undisputed ruler here. It seems odd that you would take orders from your sister."

"It wasn't an order, just a comment." The god studied her for a long time, and with remarkable calm, he said, "You are an only child, Moya, daughter of Audrey. You can't begin to understand what it's like to have a sister, much less an evil twin. Ferrol is—well, let's put it out there, shall we? She's awful—a hideous, horrible, detestable, vicious, cruel being. But she *is* smart. She was the first one to leave Erebus, and she took all the other brilliant minds with her. But she's not as smart as she thinks she is. Ferrol thought her exodus would mortally wound Uberlin." Drome broke into a smile that burst into a laugh. He slapped a thigh, and the noise shook the room and made Moya stagger. "We almost didn't know she'd left! All those great intellects—we didn't need a one of them." He continued to laugh, rocking in his chair. Then he calmed down, twisted his lips, and looked at them once more. "But she does have her moments, times of wisdom and insight. So no, little Rhune, I didn't *take orders*, but I was intrigued by her request. If she wanted you, there must be a good reason. But I'm the one who has the prize . . . something you should be grateful for. Now I am faced with two curiosities: Why does my sister seek you, and how did you open a sealed gate? Who would like to help me solve these puzzles?" Drome looked at each of them, waiting for a volunteer.

No one spoke or raised a hand.

The god looked genuinely disappointed, even a bit hurt.

"I can understand being frightened. You think I'm some sort of monster, don't you?" Drome sounded unduly persecuted. "I can empathize. Especially after mentioning how terrible my sister is and revealing that we are twins. But I'm not cruel like her. You're all so young. You have no idea what real fear is. You didn't exist when Uberlin ruled the world with razor-sharp fingers and stone boots. His word was law, unbreakable and absolute. And his retribution was swift and brutal."

Drome sat back and chuckled. "The funny thing is, you and I are so much alike. You defy me, just as I once stood against Uberlin. During his reign, *we*—me, my brother, and sisters—were the heroes out to save the world from an evil tyrant. But Trilos was killed and in response Ferrol left. Being the first to break away, she inherited such lovely real estate." He laughed, vibrating the stone.

With great pride, Drome said, *"I* was the second to leave, and I took every artisan in Erebus with me. *That* didn't go unnoticed, let me assure you."

"So, Erebus is a place?" Brin asked. Moya didn't think Brin meant to ask the question. She spoke so softly that it was certain the Keeper of Ways was speaking to herself, but her excitement had gotten the better of her.

Drome heard her and leaned forward again, looking down. He smiled at Brin like a friendly old man who was happy to discover a child had been paying attention. "You're the Keeper, aren't you?"

Brin didn't say anything, but she didn't retreat, didn't take her eyes off him. She would have had tea with a raow if it promised a good story, and this one had to be the best ever.

"Oh, yes! Erebus was a city—no, that's not right—it was *the* city, the birthplace of everyone. Well, okay, not everyone. The Typhons were already locked up by then, and their children were wandering around somewhere eating rocks or whatever. Eton didn't care about them, I guess. But everyone else was in Erebus, such a beautiful place, a perfect place. Then Uberlin's greed and arrogance ruined everything."

"What did he do?" Brin asked.

Drome narrowed his bushy brows at her. "I'd bet you'd like to know, wouldn't you? Not just about the great Rex Uberlin, but all of it—the whole story. Would you like to know how Eton and Elan gave birth to Light, Water, Time, the Four Winds, the three Typhons, and the most beloved of all, Alurya? Or should I tell you why Eton created the underworld and buried Erl, Toth, and Gar?

"No, I think you'd rather I start with why Elan stole five of Eton's teeth and what became of them. That's where the tale really begins. That one explains how a family went to war against one another, leaving a mother bereft, barren, and estranged from her husband. And that, dear girl, is a very sad tale indeed." Drome slapped the arms of his chair. "Uberlin was the first to make a throne. Did you know that? He invented it. Rex Uberlin—King Great One. I fought in the First War.

"Oh, Brin, we can trade. You tell me how you opened my gate, and I'll fill all the shadows with light. You tell me what I want to know, and I'll tell you what you need. How does that sound?"

"Sorry." Moya shook her head. "There's nothing we need to know. We just came to say thank you for the invitation to visit. It was nice meeting you. Please say goodbye to the Word of Drome for us when you see him. Oh, and don't bother getting up. We can find our own way out."

Moya took a step but only one. Her feet stopped, and she nearly fell. Looking down, she saw she was standing ankle-deep in the stone of the floor. Gasps caused her to look back, and she found that all of the others were suffering from the same affliction, as if the marble had melted into a wading pool and then had instantly frozen solid.

"Answer my questions!" Drome shouted this time, causing the room to shake.

Moya could feel an imaginary heart beating in her non-existent ears, and the desire to offer up the key returned once more.

"Does it concern the Golrok?" Drome asked.

Continued silence—and of course, no one moved.

Drome rubbed his beard, considering them. Then he got off his throne, walked down the steps, and stood before Rain. In an inexplicably calm manner, Rain watched the god as if Drome were putting on a not-too-entertaining show—the dwarf's usual, ever-present expression. It took being trapped in the underworld when facing a glowing god of unfathomable power to make Moya realize how consistently out of place that expression had always been. Maybe this stone face was a dwarven virtue that Rain embodied to the fullest. It certainly explained why folks thought Dherg were descended from rocks.

"I am your god, Rain. Tell me how you entered this realm."

Moya cringed. *How can anyone refuse their own god?*

"Through the gate," Rain said without pause. "Was open when I got to it."

Drome narrowed his eyes and studied the dwarf. *"How* was it opened?"

They all watched Rain as the god took an intimidating step toward him. "How?"

Moya couldn't fault him if he broke. She wanted to do the same, and Drome wasn't even her god. In many ways, she hoped Rain would tell, so it would be over. Just being in the god's presence was becoming painful in the same way it would be to watch someone chew on a knife's blade. It wasn't *her* teeth, but she would still pray for it to stop.

Go on, tell him already! Do it so we can—

Wings fluttered overhead, and everyone looked up, including Drome.

Into the room of polished stone and flowing precious-metal waterfalls, a bird flew. A crow. Its wingbeats thumped and echoed as loudly and ominously as drums. It circled the perimeter once, then landed on the throne. It eyed them in the creepy, sidelong manner that birds sometimes use, then it let out a *caw!* The sound was shrill, reflecting off the harsh, unyielding stone.

Drome regarded the bird for a moment, then scowled.

"Fine," he said and looked back at those mired in the black-and-white stone floor. "I'm in no rush, but I think *you* might be." Moya wasn't certain whether he spoke to them or the bird.

Drome smiled. "I have eternity on my side. Stay here for as long as you like. I don't mind the wait. But you won't leave until you tell me what neither you"—he turned and looked at the crow—"nor apparently my sister, wants me to know."

He clapped his hands. Out of the floor, sheets of stone rose, walling them off, closing them in. After reaching a height twice theirs, they came together in a ceiling that formed a dome. A tiny window formed on one side. Too small to put a fist through, it allowed a single shaft of light to shine directly on Moya's face. She didn't think its placement was coincidental.

"When you are ready to answer my questions, just tell Goll, he'll let me know."

Goll? Is that the bird? Ink-Head's first or last name? Someone else?

Moya stood with feet still trapped, forced to face the throne of Drome for what could very well be eternity.

How long has it been since we've died? How much time is left before Suri tells the fane the secret of dragons or is killed? When will our bodies in the muck of the swamp decay? How long before we're really and permanently dead?

From outside the prison, the crow squawked again.

CHAPTER NINE

An Equal Trade

For many, telling the truth is a given; for the rest, conversations are a quest for lies and hidden meanings.

— THE BOOK OF BRIN

The door opened, and Nyree entered for the second time. She was alone and still dressed in that snow-white asica, but she wore a different expression. She kept her head down, casting furtive glances at Suri the way a guilty child might approach an angry parent.

"I, ah . . ." she began, hesitated, then closed the door. Whatever she was going to say this time, she wanted privacy. Then Nyree took three steps inside. "The last time I was here, I ah . . ." Nyree continued to struggle. Her face shifted from one awkward grimace to the next. "You caught me off guard, and I reacted badly." Her tone was one of an apology, and it sounded sincere.

Nyree took three more steps, two more than on her previous visit. "You, ah . . . you look better," Nyree finally said.

Suri glanced down at herself. Vasek had made good on his promise of a bath, which Suri accepted both because she was filthy beyond even her own standards and because she still hoped to make a good impression on the Fhrey. The new clothes—which were supposed to appear as a gift from Nyree but clearly came from Vasek—were simple linen. While they fit poorly, they were clean and comfortable.

"I suppose you are wondering why I am back?" Nyree asked.

Suri wasn't, but she was grateful for another conversation. Despite everything, she still had hope for Arion's plan, and she thought Nyree was her most likely candidate.

The Fhrey weaved her fingers together, holding her hands to her chest. "I came because I want to know why Arion betrayed us. It's a question I've never been able to answer for myself, and perhaps you can. Why did she forsake her heritage and Ferrol? How could she join the Rhunes and become a traitor to her people? You were right about me being upset that she chose to be a Miralyith. That was reprehensible, but I can understand her decision. They are the ruling class now, and Arion always wanted power and prestige."

"I don't think we are talking about the same person," Suri said. "Arion never wanted those things. She liked string games, baths, and a good cup of tea. And she didn't become a Miralyith to side with those in control, she did so because that's who she was. She was the most remarkable person I've ever met. I wish you had known her the way I did."

"But that doesn't explain why she turned against her own people. Why did she do that?"

"She didn't."

Nyree's open, inviting demeanor vanished in a flash of fury. "Of course she did! She killed hundreds of her own people!"

Suri shook her head. "No. That's not so."

Nyree threw out an arm, pointing violently at one of the walls, making her sleeve ride up to the elbow. "She made a dragon that slaughtered our army and nearly killed the fane!"

Again, Suri shook her head. "No. Arion would never do such a thing, even if she could. As it happens, she didn't know how."

Nyree opened her mouth and just left it that way for a moment. Then she folded her arms and stared at Suri for a long while.

Suri hesitated to say anything. She didn't want to risk upsetting Nyree further. Still, she had to take the risk. This silence might be her only chance. "When your daughter came to Rhulyn, she discovered an amazing secret," Suri began gently. "You see, just like you—just like everyone here—she believed Rhunes were like animals or something. She learned she was wrong, that we were people who had thoughts, feelings, hopes, dreams, and fears. That was a surprise to her. But what really shocked Arion was that we, too, could use the Art."

Nyree narrowed her eyes, a little frown forming. "You mean like a Miralyith?"

"Yes, just like that. Arion tutored me, but I already knew some things before she arrived." Suri ran her fingers through her hair and made a lopsided grin. "She wanted me to shave my head, too, but I refused. Bathing was sacrifice enough."

Nyree looked skeptical.

"You don't believe me, do you?"

"No, I do not. If you could use magic, then why would you allow yourself to be held as a prisoner?"

Suri pulled on her collar. "This is marked with symbols called the Orinfar. They create a barrier between me and the Art. As long as this is on, I can't create weaves. I agreed to this collar because it was the only way I could get an audience with your fane. Arion thought if Lothian could see us, see me, that he would realize that Rhunes have just as much right to live as the Fhrey. I came here in good faith to talk about stopping the war. I risked my life to make peace between our peoples because *that* is what your daughter wanted."

Nyree shook her head. "No. No—that can't be. She fought against our people. She broke Ferrol's Law! She killed hundreds of the fane's men at Alon Rhist by creating that dragon."

"She didn't. The thing you call a dragon was made by me. Arion never took a life, Fhrey or otherwise. Yes, she helped defend the Rhunes, but she never attacked. Never. I can't say the same about Lothian and his son. I was there when your daughter died. She pushed me aside and saved my life. Mawyndulë attacked and killed her."

"The prince? *He* was the one—"

Suri nodded. "Killed her as a traitor—but she never was. All Arion ever sought was peace."

Nyree studied Suri for a long moment, then inched closer and peered at the collar.

"So . . . if that thing was taken off?" She pointed at the restraint on Suri's neck. "What would happen?"

Suri smiled. "Things would be much different."

Imaly sat on the stool nearest the hearth, trying to lose the chill that came from walking to Vasek's house in the freezing rain, while she listened to Nyree give her account of her latest meeting with Suri. The Master of Secrets' home—a tiny, humble residence for such an important figure—was located a full half mile from the central square. Imaly imagined the frustration Vasek experienced when forced to hike to the palace to supply the fane with his daily reports.

Most people might have suspected that Vasek's poor opinion of the fane had been the direct result of Lothian burning him, but Imaly guessed it was actually the result of a thousand little cuts delivered over the course of centuries that had severed his leash. Whatever the case, she was glad that Vasek was siding with her, at least for now.

The house was austere, lacking mementos as one would expect from a Master of Secrets, but that didn't explain everything. Not only did it lack knickknacks, paintings, and pillows, but there were also no plants and only a few pieces of furniture. The stool Imaly perched on was the only seat. There was no table and only a tiny shelf upon which rested a single empty cup. Vasek lived like a man prepared to disappear at a moment's notice—a tree with no roots.

By contrast, Nyree was a different species altogether. She was all roots. The priestess continued to live in the same small village where she'd been born, rarely ever leaving it. Imaly hadn't seen Nyree in more than a century, but it didn't matter. The priestess was one of those people who never changed. Fhrey were blessed with lives that lasted thousands of years, yet few did much with all that time. Even Vasek, who seemed untethered from his role, hadn't altered course. People found comfortable corners, and unless something forced them to move, they settled in and stayed put. Nyree was an extreme example. She'd found success early in the Umalyn tribe, and her childhood beliefs merged so neatly into adult life that her career choice could have been—and certainly was, in Nyree's mind—divine destiny. When a glove fit that well, there was no need to look further. Certainty inevitably followed. In Nyree's colorless house of drawn drapes and locked doors, the world remained comfortably black and white.

Once the priestess had finished her report, Vasek said, "Thank you, Nyree. We appreciate your assistance in this matter, and we will tell Volhoric how helpful you have been. I don't think you'll need to come back."

Imaly was surprised by this but wanted to show a united front. She nodded. "Yes. Go on home. We can take matters from here."

They waited for Nyree, who hesitated to leave. The priestess ran her tongue along the edge of her front teeth.

"Something else?" Vasek asked.

"Ah . . . just one thing more. Suri said that Arion . . ." A pause followed in which doubt appeared to replace two thousand years of certainty.

Suri? That's the first time Nyree has used the Rhune's name.

The priestess continued, "Well, she said Arion only defended herself from attacks. According to her, my daughter never broke Ferrol's Law. That means she wasn't a traitor. If that's so, can the fane make a public statement to clear my daughter's name?"

And remove the stain she put on you and your reputation? Imaly thought.

"We'll take it under advisement. Again, thank you for your time. Goodbye, Nyree," Vasek said.

Once she was gone and the door closed, Imaly faced Vasek. "Why did you send her home?"

"Because Lothian's patience wears thin. I've not been able to show him any progress, and he'll soon be taking matters into his own hands."

"That would be most unfortunate, especially since we now know the Rhune came here seeking peace."

"Do we? What makes you think the Rhune is telling the truth? I don't believe a word of it, and I see no reason you should, either."

"But she confirmed what Lothian said. She admitted that she can make dragons."

"Which means absolutely nothing, other than she maintains the lie she came here with. I see no reason to change my opinion on the matter."

"I confess I've never known whom to believe. You've made valid points to the contrary, but Lothian and Mawyndulë have long supported that it was a Rhune, not Arion, who made the dragon. And the Rhune that we have in custody—the very one credited with that feat—has substantiated the claim."

"I think the key word there is *claim*. The existence of a Rhune Miralyith is hard enough to conceive, but how could one of her kind possess more knowledge than the fane—the son of the first Artist? On the other hand, Arion was a master of the Art, a teacher at the academy. She defeated Gryndal, and Fenelyus often referred to her as Cenzlyor. Isn't she the more logical source of the dragon? But beyond the speculation about who *knows* how to make them, there is one indisputable fact."

"Which is what?"

"There is only one. Why? Obviously, Arion's death prevented her from supplying Nyphron with more. If this Rhune can do what she says, we wouldn't be having this discussion. Dragons would have already darkened our skies and obliterated our race. Since we are still alive, how do you explain this?"

Imaly shook her head. "I can't, but that's not the only thing I can't figure out."

"Such as?"

"Nyree mentioned a collar. Is there one?"

"Yes, but that doesn't mean it prevents her from doing magic. I could claim the shoes I wear stop me from being able to fly, but it doesn't make it so."

"Then why does she wear it? I was under the impression she traveled here in a cage. I see no need for a collar. Has it ever been used to restrain her in any way? Was she previously chained, and whoever released her forgot to remove it?"

Vasek considered this for a moment, his eyes shifting side-to-side in thought. "Actually, as I think about it . . . the collar lacks a means of attaching a chain or rope—beyond a simple loop."

"And do you have the key?"

"No, but I have no need for one."

"If there is no need to take it off, then there shouldn't have been any reason to have put it on. Wouldn't you agree?"

Vasek didn't answer.

"Does it have markings?"

"Not that I've noticed."

Again, Imaly heard the disquieting voice of Trilos. *What you're missing is that you don't have enough pieces on the board to achieve your goal. You're going to need a second Miralyith, Imaly, or it isn't going to work. What you are ignorant of, what you're failing to realize, is that the Miralyith doesn't need to be a Fhrey.*

If anyone other than Trilos had said those words, Imaly would have forgotten them. Now, they were all she could think about.

Imaly noticed Vasek pondering. Unlike Nyree, even when he settled on an assumption, he never closed the door completely on any possibility, no matter how absurd. She got up from the stool and went to the window.

The freezing rain continued to fall. Ice had begun to coat branches, and the street glistened.

"What are you thinking?" Vasek asked.

"That it is time I spoke with this Rhune." Imaly nodded, making the decision, confirming it in her own head.

"What are you hoping to discover?"

"The truth."

The Fhrey were a quiet lot. Suri never heard their footsteps, although she knew someone was always standing guard. The door to her room was closed, but as far as she knew, it wasn't bolted. Still, just having it shut was enough to bother her, even if it wasn't in the same way it used to. Suri didn't feel the gut-clenching fear anymore, but the memory lingered like the bad taste of something that had once made her ill. The space was comfortable, and sunlight entered through a window. Even so, there was no ignoring that she was a prisoner, and no one enjoyed being held captive.

That afternoon the sun's light was weak, muted by poor weather. She could hear the faint rattle of hail on the roof and glass panes. On a day such as this, she likely would have stayed inside anyway, but that would have been her choice. Having the option made all the difference.

When the door opened, Suri expected to see Nyree again, or if not her then Vasek. Instead, a tall and stocky stranger with gray hair and a broad face fumbled with the door, her asica catching on the latch.

Not at all swanlike.

"Good afternoon. My name is Imaly," she said in a voice that was loud and deep. "I am the Curator of the Aquila. I would like to speak with you. May I come in?"

May you what? Suri blinked in confusion but nodded just the same.

The Fhrey presented her a pleasant smile, then she did what no other Fhrey had. She walked across the room and extended a hand. "You're called Suri. Is that correct?"

Suri stared at the Curator's open palm, a big meaty thing, wrinkled and discolored.

"I'm told shaking hands is a Rhune custom," Imaly explained. "Something about validating you aren't hiding a weapon—a proof of trust."

Suri had never shaken hands before but gave it a try. Imaly's fingers wrapped around hers, softer and warmer than expected. The woman gave Suri's hand a stout up-and-down motion before letting go. For two people who had never attempted the ritual before, Suri felt they did well.

Imaly motioned to the bed. "May I sit?"

Suri nodded, and the strange—but clearly polite—Fhrey settled herself at the foot of the bed, clasping her hands neatly in her lap. "Please, sit with me. This might take a while."

This? Suri wondered what *this* might be.

"Before we begin, I have something for you." She reached into the folds of her asica and withdrew a small but familiar bag. "Vasek says this was delivered with you. Jerydd must have thought it would be of use. It's yours, yes?"

Suri took it, nodding. Opening the mouth, she reached in and pulled out the small knit hat, which brought a smile to her lips.

"First off, I want to apologize for how you've been mistreated. None of this was my doing, and when I heard, I took measures to correct the situation. I'm assuming this room is comfortable? Have your meals improved?"

"Yes," Suri replied, her fingers exploring the little holes amid the stitches in the yarn of Arion's knit hat.

"Good." Imaly dipped her head and looked at her clasped hands for just a moment. Then, she raised her eyes and once more focused on Suri. "Now, as I understand it, you came to negotiate peace. This was a meeting previously agreed upon between your leader and mine via pigeons, but as it turned out, Lothian lied to you. The whole thing was a trap designed to obtain the secret to making dragons. Is that so?"

A sense of cautious relief rose in Suri. *First she asks permission to enter, and now this?*

"You are correct," Suri said. "And the first one to admit it."

Imaly smiled. "That's because I am in favor of peace between our people, and I'm hoping"—she shook her head and sighed as if disgusted to the core—"to salvage what I can from Lothian's debacle."

Suri had only a vague idea what *salvage* meant and no clue about *debacle*, but she felt it was best not to admit her ignorance since this was the first Fhrey to treat her like a person.

"The impediment to peace is Lothian. He won't heed my advice, and he'll never concede to a peaceful resolution. The fane will not accept anything but the complete annihilation of the Rhunes and the Instarya. As fane and a Miralyith, he sees himself as a god, and deities don't compromise." She lowered her voice. "It is just one of the reasons I, and several others, hope to remove him from power. Replace him. Unfortunately, that is not an easy thing to do."

"If you could remove this, I can help." Suri pulled on the collar that remained snug to her neck—not tight enough to choke, but swallowing wasn't easy.

Imaly's sight shifted to the collar. "What would you do if I did?"

"You mean, would I blow apart these walls and rain fire on this city?"

The friendly smile vanished, and the Curator of the Aquila straightened up, her eyes widening. She nodded very slowly. "Yes, that is exactly what I'm asking."

Suri looked past her at the freezing rain assaulting the window. She had more than thought about it. Suri had fantasized what it would be like to reconnect with the Art. How glorious it would be to pull in the power, let it build, and then release it in a sudden burst.

That would get their attention, demand their respect. They would listen to me just as Gronbach had. Except . . .

"I came here for a reason, and that's not it."

Imaly studied her. "I wish I could believe you."

"I can say the same thing about you, and I have more reason to doubt your sincerity. You admitted that I was lied to and mistreated. I trusted your fane, and he betrayed me. If you truly wish to *salvage* things . . ." She pulled again on the collar. "Taking this off would be a good first step."

Imaly continued to stare at the metal ring and frowned. "That would be more difficult than you'd think."

"A chisel or a saw should do the trick."

Imaly smiled. "That's not what I meant. I wasn't speaking of the physical removal of . . ." She paused, and her brows narrowed as she stared at Suri's neck. Something had caught her eye, something new. Imaly lifted a hand toward the collar, then paused. "May I?"

Again with the polite manners.

Suri responded with a shrug.

Imaly touched the collar. Suri felt it move very slightly and heard metal click. For a moment, Suri wondered if she had unclasped it, but the ring didn't loosen. Nothing changed.

"How strange," Imaly said after drawing her hand back. "The lock holding your collar closed has no keyhole."

"What does that mean?"

"It means it can't be taken off, short of, well . . . as you mentioned, cutting it."

Imaly pressed her lips together, concerned about something.

Suri couldn't guess what it was and figured Imaly wasn't prepared to say, so she waited.

Imaly's face calmed—a decision made or postponed. Then she glanced at the door and asked, "Suri, why did Nyphron send you? He isn't stupid, and letting someone come here who knows how to make dragons is a massive tactical blunder. Why would he risk someone so valuable?"

Suri snorted. "Nyphron didn't send me, and he's never thought of me as valuable. For years, he's called me worthless because I've refused to make any more gilarabrywns. That's what you call dragons. In many ways, he and your fane are alike. Neither one is interested in peace. But Arion was, and Persephone is, and she's the one who sent me. Well, *sent* probably isn't the right word. She asked and I said yes. I agreed because that is what Arion wished."

"Who is Persephone?"

"She is the leader of our people. We call her the keenig, which is similar to your fane. Nyphron is the commander of *her* army."

Imaly struggled to remain indifferent to this, but Suri saw surprise. The elderly Fhrey paused a long time before continuing. "Still, wasn't this Persephone person afraid that you—that we would force you to tell us the secret of dragons?"

"Perhaps. I don't know. She only seemed worried about me being killed, but I had the Art, so neither of us was too afraid. I suppose the hope of saving lives and finally living in peace was too great a prize to pass up out of fear. Of course, neither one of us expected this collar. And the secret to dragons—as you call them—isn't as valuable as you might think. Creating one comes at a terrible price."

"What do you mean?"

"A sacrifice. Not of a lamb or goat, but the life of an innocent person, a good person. Someone you care about."

Imaly's eyes widened. "Are you saying that every time the fane makes a dragon, it would necessitate him sacrificing—a *Fhrey?* An innocent Fhrey?"

"I would think so." Suri nodded. "I doubt Lothian cares about Rhunes or dwarfs."

Imaly looked suddenly winded. She sucked in a breath, then her eyes searched the corners of the room as if seeing things previously hidden. "Suri, when I came in here, I was afraid of two things. The first was that you didn't know how to create dragons and that Lothian would kill you while trying to extract information you didn't possess."

"And the second?"

"That you did know the secret, Lothian would get it out of you, and he would use that knowledge to destroy your people."

"I can see why that would be bad for us, but why is that a problem for you?"

"Because this conflict, this war, provides an excellent opportunity to remove Lothian from the throne. If it ends with him victorious, we will have missed our chance to replace him. He is a curse upon our race because he elevates his tribe over the rest of the Fhrey. This is not Ferrol's will. Since long before you arrived—even before the war—I've searched for a means of deposing him and restoring our civilization, but I had one insurmountable problem, and I think you just solved it. If Lothian kills innocent Fhrey, he will provide me with justification to remove him. Once he is gone, we can have peace. All you need to do is give Lothian the secret he desires, and his own lust for power, his arrogance, will fix everything."

"So you say." Suri frowned. "But I feel like a squirrel who doesn't believe the wolf when he insists his mouth is a nice, safe place to sleep."

"But I'm offering what you came here for. Peace."

Suri smiled, but shook her head. "Me too, but you are getting peace *and* the ability to conquer us. If I'm trading a bowlful of strawberries, I won't accept a few acorns in return."

"So, what would you suggest?"

Suri shrugged. "Dragons would give Lothian the power to rule over the Rhunes. I would need something like that—something that would provide me the same power over the Fhrey."

Imaly thought a moment. "There is something, but . . ." She sighed.

"What's wrong?"

"I can give you what you ask for, but it would still require you giving the fane what he desires first."

Suri frowned.

"I'm sorry, but it must be done in that order," Imaly said. "It's the only way this will work."

"You sound like Jerydd just before he put this collar on me."

Imaly scowled and straightened up. She replied with what appeared to be genuine offense, "I am *not* Jerydd."

"I don't know who you are." Suri once more let her fingers run over the woven yarn of Arion's hat. "We've just met. But what I do know is that you're asking me for power in return for a promise, and your people have already betrayed me twice. Either you see me as an ignorant Rhune who can be easily tricked, or you think I have a terrible memory. How can I possibly believe you?"

Once more, Imaly's eyes returned to the collar. "What if I took that off? What if I removed it *before* you gave up the secret? Doing so would restore your magic, correct? Make you as powerful as a Miralyith? You could strike me dead if you wanted, right? I'd be doing what you did. I'd be putting my life in jeopardy for the hope of peace. Would that provide enough proof for you to trust me?"

Suri hesitated, but just for show. What Imaly didn't know—perhaps couldn't imagine—was that if the collar were removed, Suri could ensure the bargain was honored. The balance of power would shift: *They* would have the promise of dragons to come, but she would *be* the dragon on their doorstep—a doorstep currently bereft of Miralyith. Each would have the ability to destroy the other.

"Yes, that would work. Remove this collar, and we can make a trade. So, what is it that you offer?"

"Did Arion ever mention something called the Horn of Gylindora?"

CHAPTER TEN

Goll

*It had been scary but thrilling, unpleasant but endurable, difficult
but manageable. Then, well . . . then everything changed. Now, all
I remember is the screams and the tears.*

— THE BOOK OF BRIN

In her head, Brin struggled to repeat everything Drome had said. There
had been so much of it that she feared losing something. Repetition was a
technique Maeve had taught her to strengthen memory.

Same as lifting heavy bales of hay: The more you do it, the easier it gets.

She had just witnessed a conversation with Drome, god of the
Belgriclungreians and the ruler of Rel.

A real god! Erebus was a city—a city! The original home of mankind—of
every *kind*.

All of it shocked and overwhelmed her. Initially, she hadn't believed
a word, but that had only been pride, her own stubbornness to let go of
centuries of false tradition. When she finally did, the pieces came together.

Some think the Fhrey, Rhune, and Dherg are all related. Malcolm had
said this years ago in Roan's roundhouse, back when everyone thought he
was nothing but an awkward ex-slave with a big appetite.

The children of Erebus revolted and fought against their own father. That was one of Brin's translations from the Agave tablets. Originally, she had equated *Erebus* and *father* with an actual person rather than the place they had come from, the home where they were born. Brin reeled with the knowledge.

If Erebus is a place, is it possible to find it? It would be in the far east. All legends spoke of people coming from there, fleeing some ancient evil. The first keenig, Gath of Odeon, was said to have led all the human clans across the sea to Rhulyn during a time of great danger.

Brin was terrified of forgetting what she'd learned because she knew Drome's casually spoken words were more than an accounting of the past. She feared they might well be an insight into the present and likely a warning for the future. Without pen and pages, she relied on the old ways.

It's all about organization, Maeve had told her. *The mind of a Keeper is a series of rooms, and the walls in each are lined with little drawers. To remember any single thing, you must put it in a particular place. The trick is to use groups. Individual words can be combined into a sentence; a group of sentences tells a story. Context comes from placement, and where you put something is crucial. Anything can be found if you know where to look.*

"Rain?" Roan asked. "What are you thinking?"

The digger was staring at his feet trapped in the stone. "Ya said it was possible to alter this place if ya believed ya could, right?"

"Rain," Moya said, "I saw you cut through a wall of stone in Neith in less than a few minutes."

"This isn't the same thing," Rain replied. He scratched his beard and ran his tongue along the inside of his lower lip as he continued to evaluate the state of his feet.

"No, it's not," she agreed. "In fact, that's not even stone. Not really. It's just an idea, right?"

"Aye," the dwarf said. "Just an idea."

"Maybe it's like the Art," Gifford said. "Arion taught me about the importance of confidence, that believing you can do something is most of the battle."

"Same applies when fighting, too," Tekchin declared. "It saved my ass many times during centuries campaigning with Nyphron."

Rain nodded. "Well, I dunno about either of those things, but there's nothing I'm more confident about than digging rock." He slipped the pickax off his back and hefted it. "Sure looks like rock to me." With his elegant compact swing, Rain brought the point of the pick down.

Struggling to concentrate, Brin was startled by the loud *crack,* made all the more ear-piercing by the enclosed walls. The sound wasn't metal on stone, but rather the impact of two competing ideas: the will of a god and the desire for freedom from one of his faithful. The result was a chip of stone and a divot in the marble floor.

"That's not much," Moya said.

"Aye, but it's something," Rain assured her and brought the pick around again. The divine marble grudgingly gave way. Flakes shot across their tiny prison and pinged off the walls. Stroke after stroke widened the hole until Rain at last had one foot free and then the other.

He grinned at himself. "Being able to move will make this a lot easier to do the rest of ya."

He approached Moya, who winced as he shattered the floor near her ankles. "Careful," she said. "I might need those toes."

Brin once more struggled to block them out, to focus. She had work to do, important work. If she ever returned to the world of the living, the knowledge she carried would be more valuable than any buried treasure. But there was so much, and so little of it was comprehensible. She sensed an idea trapped in the recesses of her mind—a frightening and elusive thought hovering just beyond consciousness. It wasn't unlike the irritation of knowing she left something undone but having no inkling what that might be.

"Tetlin's ass!" Moya cursed.

Brin thought Rain had nicked Moya, but she was already free of the stone. Moya had crossed to the little window and peered out.

"What?" Tekchin asked while Rain went to work on the stone around the Galantian's feet.

"The wall is about five feet thick."

"Great. And time isn't on our side," Tekchin said.

Moya pressed her face against the little window, blocking the light and leaving the rest of them in darkness.

"What do you see out there?" Tekchin asked.

"Well . . . Drome is gone. Don't see him anywhere, but—oh, hello!" Moya jerked her head back just as something hammered into the wall with a *clang*.

Brin felt a tremor through the stone. Moya fell back, allowing the light to stream in once more, but the opening was quickly blocked as something outside moved closer. There was just enough illumination for Brin to catch sight of a massive eye peering in. It blinked twice and then moved away.

"What in Ferrol's name was that?" Tekchin asked.

"I think it was Goll," Moya replied.

"Cut me loose, Rain," Tekchin said. "I want to see this."

Rain doubled his effort on the Fhrey's feet. The dwarf had a good rhythm going, and he worked with speed and precision.

Ping, Ping, Ping.

The pounding was aggravating as Brin continued to struggle with her Keeper duties.

Erebus was a city, the birthplace of everyone.

But Brin knew that wasn't right, not exactly. There was something that came before, Drome had mentioned . . .

Ping, Ping, Ping.

Brin squeezed her fists in frustration, as she focused on trying to remember Drome's words.

So, who wasn't there?

When Tekchin's second foot finally broke free, he inched forward, tentatively looking out the window from a distance. "So, we have a guard now? Looks big."

"It is," Moya said and made no attempt to return to the window. "Has claws, too, and sharp teeth. No nose, big ears, and only one eye, a very *big* one."

"I don't think I like Goll," Gifford said.

"He certainly doesn't sound"—Tressa winced as Rain went to work on her feet—"like the friendly sort."

"Grenmorian?" Rain asked in between swings.

Tekchin shrugged. "Maybe, but I doubt it. Grenmorians have two eyes, no claws, and a terrible smell. I know; I used to room with one."

"A Typhon?" Rain inquired.

That's it! Brin grinned in relief. *That's who wasn't in Erebus.*

"What are they?" Brin asked.

"Typhons? You don't know?" Tekchin looked at her, surprised. "But you're the . . ."

Brin shook her head, feeling a bit embarrassed. "My mentor died unexpectedly. Either she didn't know, or she hadn't gotten to that part of our lessons."

Tekchin shrugged. "Grygor told me some. He said there are three of them, Erl, Toth, and Gar, and they made the Grenmorians. The Typhons are the giants' gods—older than ours, he said. But I wouldn't count on that being true. With Grygor, all things Grenmorian were bigger and better than anything Fhrey." Tekchin shook his head. "But no, Goll can't be a Typhon. He just looks like an unusually large giant with strange features. The way Grygor described Typhons, they weren't so much giants as forces of nature—and they certainly wouldn't serve the likes of Drome."

"Well, that's good—right?" Moya was nodding.

With that jog of memory, Brin recollected more. *Would you like to know how Eton and Elan gave birth to Light, Water, Time, the Four Winds, the three Typhons, and the most beloved of all, Alurya?* Brin grinned in the dark at her triumph of recall, but the hammering of the pick was echoing in her head, as if something else was struggling to break free.

Or should I tell you why Eton created the underworld and buried Erl, Toth, and Gar? No, I think you'd rather I start with why Elan stole five of Eton's teeth and what became of them. That's where the tale really begins. That one explains how a family went to war against one another, leaving a mother bereft, barren, and estranged from her husband.

Brin didn't know how, but she felt all these things were linked in some way. Drome wasn't randomly teasing her with tidbits of treasure; he had been telling her something—just the sort of *something* that a Keeper of Ways ought to be able to understand. She had no idea why he bothered to hint rather than being direct, unless he thought she wouldn't believe. Few can accept the value of something given, but something earned is cherished.

"Okay, so assuming Rain can cut through this wall," Moya began, "how are we going to get past good old Goll?"

"Only one eye, and big, you could close it easily with an arrow," Tekchin suggested. "Just get him to peek in again. Shoot through the little window, then we can run out and down the stairs."

"What about those soldiers who escorted us in? Won't they be downstairs?" Tressa asked. "How are we going to get past them?"

Moya twisted her mouth into a frown, and in a spiteful tone, she said, "Geez, Tressa, give me a break, will ya. It's my first trip to the afterlife, so excuse me if I don't have all the answers."

"Honestly, I really thought you did."

"Oh," Moya said as if she'd accidentally walked into a wall. "Ah . . . sorry . . . I'm not used to the post-bitch version of you."

Once more, Brin tried to ignore her surroundings—disruptive as it was. That nagging question, that elusive thought refused to be found, and with each passing moment, she felt added urgency to grasp it.

Rain brought his pick down at Gifford's feet, and in that moment, Brin recalled Drome hitting the arm of his—

Uberlin was the first to make a throne. Did you know that? He invented it.

Brin paused, confused. *Why did Drome mention that? Why is it important?*

Rex Uberlin—King Great One. I fought in the First War . . . You tell me what I want to know, and I'll tell you what you need.

What I need? Why would I need to know about thrones, the first city, and an evil god named Uberlin?

Rain had finished freeing Gifford and was working on Roan, which left only Brin. She hoped Rain had been perfecting his technique. Like Moya, she wanted to keep her toes—even if they were only ten little ideas.

Rain set his pick down for a breather, which confused Brin. The heaviness that they had felt in Drome's presence was gone, and Rain shouldn't need a rest. The dwarf stretched his back, then picked up his pick again. "Probably doing this for nothing. Being a god, won't Drome just summon us to his side?"

"It has been my experience that gods—that anyone, for that matter— are never as all-powerful as people think." Then, looking at Tekchin, Moya added, "I once thought he was a god. Talk about disappointment."

Tekchin raised his brows and opened his mouth in mock surprise.

Rain began chipping away near Brin's feet, making her flinch with each impact of the pick. Swing after swing the dwarf created the smallest of chips. He paused, looked at the end of his pick, and huffed. The point was noticeably flattened.

"What's wrong?" Brin asked.

The dwarf sighed and shook his head.

"Can't you free her?" Moya came closer to see.

"I suspect I can get 'er out, but"—he looked at the walls—"did you say these are five feet thick? I'm not sure me pick will last."

Moya frowned and bit her lip. "Keep going. Just do the best you can."

Rain hefted the pickax once more and resumed swinging, pelting Brin's calves with sharp shards.

Brin couldn't watch. The sight of him and that big pick hammering near her ankles—even though they weren't really her feet—was too much to bear. Each impact caused her to jerk uncontrollably. Watching him wasn't something she could bring herself to do. Instead, she focused on the one person she could clearly see—Moya.

Holding tightly to her bow with both hands, Moya stared at the window of their prison, where it seemed they would be trapped forever. The light fell on her face, making it bright and disembodied in the dark.

So brave.

Her jaw was clenched, eyes clear and fixed. Bravery was fortitude and determination in the face of terror. To be unafraid was to be stupid. If they couldn't get free, if they couldn't get to Nifrel, Suri would die, they would lose the war, and humanity would be wiped out. They had each jumped into the pool believing they could do something to change all that and maybe come back out again. Now, not only did that look unlikely, it appeared that they had ruined what meager afterlife they might have enjoyed. Instead of dwelling with their family and friends in an eternal village that mimicked life, they would remain forever sealed in a marble tomb. Moya knew all of this, but none of it was on her face. That was bravery.

Brin wasn't brave, and she was pleased that the light was nowhere near her. She wasn't crying, nothing so childish as that, but she was certain her expression was a miserable one. If Brin had been adrift in an ocean storm, Moya would have been the rock she swam for.

"I wonder how far we've come," Gifford said, and he looked up at the darkness. "Up there, I mean, in Elan. Do you think we've crossed the Nidwalden already? Or maybe it doesn't work that way."

"Gifford!" Moya spun and pointed at the man as if he were guilty of some crime. "Can *you* do anything? Use magic to increase the size of the hole or something?"

Gifford shook his head. "There's no power here, nothing to draw from."

Moya nodded. "It was like that in the Agave, but Arion was able to—"

"She drew power from us," Roan clarified. "From our life force, but none of us are alive anymore."

"So . . . wait." Moya looked down at her hands, her brows furrowing. "How did Drome put up these walls? How did he lock our feet in stone? That seems like magic."

"He's Drome," Rain said, as if that should end the discussion. "He's a god. This is his realm."

Brin looked down and saw that her left foot was close to coming loose.

"Then that's it." Tekchin threw up his hands in defeat. "We either give it up, or we'll stay here forever."

"We can't give *it* up," Tressa said.

"We don't have a choice. It makes no sense to keep it now."

Moya glanced his way. "We can't succeed without it."

"We can't succeed at all."

"We also won't be able to get out of Phyre," Brin reminded them. "Handing it over would mean a death sentence for all of us."

"You're being foolish." Tressa spoke with absolute confidence. "Malcolm wouldn't have sent us unless—"

"Drome is as much a god as Malcolm!" Moya countered, and then shook her head. "I can't believe I just said that."

Malcolm is a god. The words rang in Brin's head as loud as the hammering at her feet, where one foot was coming free.

I'm not familiar with a god named Malcolm. Is he new? Brin recalled Muriel's words.

"What is Malcolm the god of?" Brin asked.

Moya looked at her as if Brin had morphed into Roan.

"It's what Muriel asked us, remember? All the gods rule over something. Ferrol is the god of the Fhrey, Drome the god of the . . . Belgr . . . Belgric . . . ah, Rain's people. Mari is our god. The Typhons are the gods of the giants, Eton is the god of the sky. Elan is the god of the world. So, if Malcolm is a god, what is he the god of? What did he create?"

"Interesting question, Brin, but I don't see how it helps us"—Moya focused a disapproving gaze on Tressa—"although it does suggest that maybe Malcolm isn't a god after all."

"He is," Tressa insisted, "And he would have foreseen our imprisonment."

Moya slapped the wall. "Then he should have told us how to get out of here!"

"He did," Roan said, once more using her private-dialogue voice.

"You're twisting and chewing your hair, Roan," Moya said with a growing smile. "Tell me something is going on in that famous head of yours."

Roan shrugged. "Not much."

"*Not much* from you has been known to turn the tides of war. We're sort of desperate, so forgive me if I seem a little excited."

"It's just that . . ." Roan focused on Tressa, as if speaking to her alone. "Well, didn't you say the key could open any lock in Phyre? Not just doors, right? And we are *locked in.*"

"Only in a manner of speaking," Rain said. "And you can't insert a key into a manner of speaking."

Tressa's hand fluttered to her chest as her eyes widened. "Has to be."

She quickly stepped forward into the light, her hand reaching into her shirt.

Moya stopped her. "Hold on. What are you planning on doing?"

"I don't know," Tressa said. "Just gonna touch the key to the wall and pray, I guess."

Moya licked her lips. "Not yet." She peeked out the little window, then began to string her bow. "In the unlikely event this works, we still have Goll to deal with."

"It *will* work," Tressa said.

Moya frowned. "I'm actually starting to believe you, but it's *so* frustrating. Why didn't Malcolm just come with us?"

"He can't," Tressa said. "He told me so. He's immortal. It's the same with Muriel. Only the dead are allowed."

He cursed me with immortality, Brin remembered Muriel saying. *I hate him.*

That was the final tiny crack that launched the landslide. With it, all the pieces came together in one perfect and terrible pile, each stacking up in proper order.

Muriel had said, *I hate him with every particle of my being.*

Her mother had mentioned, *Our existence and the world wasn't supposed to be like this. It's broken, and we'll continue this way until it's fixed.*

Drome told them, *Then Uberlin's greed and arrogance ruined everything.*

And most damning of all was Malcolm's admission that he was the one who broke the world.

Brin gasped as the thought materialized. *Oh Blessed Mari! Malcolm is Uberlin!*

"I suppose that makes sense," Moya said.

Brin looked up in shock but quickly realized Moya was replying to Tressa. That didn't matter; she finally figured out what Drome felt she needed.

Malcolm is the god of evil.

Rain stopped chiseling and looked up at her. "Yer free."

Moya waited, peering out through the narrow slit until she could see Goll. The mountainous being didn't stand in one place. He wandered around with no perceptible pattern, pausing in places for no reason, then moving on to another spot. The one-eyed creature busied himself by occasionally slapping his own head, coughing, or swiping through the air at nothing. Watching him, Moya estimated his intelligence at just above a particularly dull lump of coal.

Having just one eye didn't help. Truth be told, the eye bothered Moya. Not only did it lack a partner, but it was far too large. The problem wasn't that the eye was bigger than Moya's entire head, but that it was out of proportion for Goll's. It took up too much space, dominating his forehead and extending way past where a nose ought to be. That prominent feature was complemented by a ruthlessly fanged mouth, and both barely fit onto Goll's egg-shaped noggin.

Roan was the one who called what they were about to try a *plan* because that was the way her mind worked. Moya considered it a desperate gamble because that was how she considered things. Most of her life—the best parts—had been one reckless risk after another. Gambling became a compulsive habit for those who had enjoyed even minor success, and Moya's chance-taking had promoted her from village hussy to Keenig's Shield, a position so revered that men often referred to her as *sir*. She had no idea if they forgot themselves or felt a feminine honorific beneath the station, but the sentiment was genuine. They respected her. No one could take that away; not a dead mother, not a chieftain or husband, not even a one-eyed brute. The chance-taking was intensified by the fact that she was involved with another obsessive-compulsive gambler. They fed off each other. Yawns, laughter, tears, jumping off cliffs—all were contagious. Most people wouldn't understand that last one, but Tekchin and Moya did—and they were about to do it again.

She fitted one of her eight remaining arrows to her bow, then her lips found Tekchin's in the dark. His were moist and firm. No hesitation there—never had been. He wasn't a god, but close enough.

"I just want to say it was an honor dying with all of you." Moya stepped away, taking position directly in the light. She took a moment to look at Rain, Roan, Brin, Gifford, and lastly Tressa. "And I do mean *all* of you."

"We're going to survive this," Tekchin said.

"He's right," Tressa agreed. "We have Malcolm on our side."

"Of course," Moya said. "Absolutely. Why in Rel not?"

"You're starting to scare me now," Tekchin told her, though he didn't sound frightened.

The person who looked the least confident was the Keeper. The little bit of her face that Moya could see suggested the woman was about to be sick. "You all right, Brin?"

She hesitated. "Not really, but I don't see how it matters at the moment."

"Okay then." Moya nodded toward Tressa. "Whenever you're ready." She tested the tension on her bow, drawing it slightly, feeling the resistance. "Unlock this thing."

Tressa stepped forward into the dark. Moya heard the faint jingle of a thin chain.

"Here goes," Tressa warned.

They all waited, seeing nothing and hearing only the soft scrape of metal on stone. There was more scraping, and with each passing second, Moya knew it wasn't working. She couldn't say she was surprised. Moya had hoped, but she was used to disappointments, and what they were attempting was a long shot at best.

"Tetlin's Tit!" Tressa said.

"It's not your fault, Tressa," Moya told her, thinking how odd it was—how far they had come—that she was consoling Tressa for failure.

Then Tressa let out a hysterical laugh.

"Tressa?" Moya asked, concerned. *I hope she hasn't gone nutty.*

"I'm an idiot."

Moya considered making Tressa the butt of an obvious joke, but the giddiness in the woman's voice, the borderline crazy glee of her bubbly tone, made Moya hesitate.

"I'm holding it backward. Hang on."

An instant later, they were all blinded.

The walls of their prison dissolved, and light from the pure-white room hit them from every direction. After hours—or was it days—in the dark, the illumination was overwhelming. Moya was forced to squint so narrowly that for several seconds sight was impossible. This was most unfortunate because the first step in *the plan* was for her to blind Goll with an arrow. While she did that, the rest were supposed to rush down the stairs. The hope was that the men who had escorted them into the castle wouldn't be waiting in the vestibule. It was a slim hope, but not too thin to embrace.

With all of us encased in stone, why would they be stationed for an interception?

Moya wasn't optimistic enough to think the exit would be completely unguarded, and with her bow, she was going to take down anyone who got in their way. Meanwhile, the others would use the element of surprise to run out the exit. Tressa would hold open the door to Nifrel, allowing each of them to jump through. Then she would close the door and they would all hope that Goll and Drome had no way to pass between the two realms. While the gamble was plagued by too many hopeful assumptions, it had the benefit of simplicity. Over the years, Moya had learned that uncomplicated was good. Still, as straightforward as it was, she knew the plan would fail. All strategies did, to one degree or another—even the simple ones. The unexpected, the stupid, or a random piece of bad luck conspired at the junction of Planning and Preparation to bring down any strategy. That was why straightforward schemes were better than complex ones—fewer moving parts meant a decrease in the chances for something to break. But oftentimes, even simple plans went astray. Blinding the beast and running for the door to Nifrel sounded good in theory. But as it turned out, it was Moya's party that was blinded, and *Goll* was the one running—toward them.

Moya couldn't get a look. In those first few moments, she couldn't see anything clearly. The frustrating part was that her failure had been born from her own stupidity. The good news was that she could hear just fine, and she even felt the giant pounding across the marble floor. The jolting shook her whole body. In the event things didn't go smoothly, Tekchin had suggested an alternative approach where he distracted Goll while the others got away. He had sold her on the idea with the deceptive logic that they wouldn't need to do it unless she failed to blind the beast or the rest neglected to run. Both seemed more than unlikely to her. Tekchin, however, had witnessed more battles, and having adventured with the Galantians, he had more experience with overconfidence.

As Goll charged, Moya heard Tekchin strike his sword against something. By then, the room was visible, though little more than a whitewash of blurry images. Even so, she spotted what had to be Tekchin, trotting away and slapping his blade against the pillars.

Dinner bell!

Moya didn't know if Goll ate people, but giants did. Of course, no one in Rel appeared to eat at all, but Moya guessed that wouldn't keep Goll from trying. He didn't look like the finicky sort, or the kind to give up easily—or at all. It was because of his single eye. There was no way anything could look intelligent with just one.

Goll was halfway to Tekchin by the time Moya got her first clear view of the brute. He was huge, as large as or bigger than the dragon on the hill and taller than some trees. His arms and legs were like massive stone formations. Naked to the waist, Goll displayed a pale chest that was so white it matched the marble. The tent-sized cloth that wrapped his waist was fastened by a brooch that was the size of a spear. He bore no weapons. Moya was confident he didn't need any. The one big eye was his dominant feature. Like the yolk of an egg, it stood out on an otherwise plain face. Goll didn't have eyelashes, but he did have a singular furry brow that bowed in the center. With so little to work with, Moya could only guess at the giant's intended expression: irritation, rage, glee, maybe even hunger.

Goll heard Tekchin's dinner bell and charged his way.

Moya set her feet and pulled an arrow. By letting it fly, she announced to her lover that she could see again.

No one had ever mastered the kind of precision Moya commanded with a bow, and no one but she had a bow like Audrey. It had been named after her mother—both were tightly strung. Technically, Moya didn't have the weapon, either, but she had the memory of it, and the big bow sent Moya's arrow across the room faster than sight, piercing the exact center of Goll's eye. The force buried the arrow up to its feathers.

Goll shrieked. Maybe in pain, although up until then, Moya didn't think that existed in Rel. Perhaps it was just rage, fury, or fear. Moya didn't care. It was time to leave.

"Go!" Moya yelled, and her troop bolted like beetles from under a raised rock.

Tekchin went wide on the opposite side of the chamber as Moya directed everyone else toward the stairs.

Goll staggered but didn't fall, clutching at his eye.

Brin, who was way out front, reached the steps first, taking them three and four at a time. Gifford ranked second in the race, dragging Roan by the arm. Moya purposely lingered at the top of the stairs with another arrow nocked.

Goll stomped.

One foot was all it took. His massive boot slammed on the floor, and the entire chamber jumped. Pillars and marble slabs that formed the walls collapsed. Two of the statues holding up the ceiling tilted, and everyone fell as if the world had hiccuped. Through a snow of marble dust, Moya turned to see Goll wrench her arrow from his eye as if it were a splinter.

"Up!" Moya shouted. "Get up!" She grabbed Tressa and pushed her toward the steps.

Tekchin rolled to his feet and ran—not to the stairs, but at Goll.

"Tek!" Moya shouted. "This way."

The Galantian had only managed to take a few strides before Goll stomped another time.

The floor leapt once more, and everyone fell again. But that wasn't the biggest problem. The huge creature's acrobatics had created massive cracks in the floor, and they were growing, spreading out.

"Son of the Tetlin whore!" Moya cursed. "Everyone out! Now!"

The sound of her voice drew Goll's attention, and he took a long stride toward the stairs. This was bad news for the plan, but an invitation for Moya, who sent another arrow, closing Goll's eye once more. He stumbled, wavered, and fell. Goll might not have been a Typhon, but he was still massive. When his big body hit the marble, the floor gave way.

Accompanied by the cry of rock and scream of stone, Moya fell along with everything else, just one more bit of hail in a rocky storm. She landed well, and the lack of pain gave her the false impression that she was all right.

In her race down the steps and out of Drome's palace, Brin hadn't encountered any guards. She was the first out of the castle and halfway across the road to where the deserted gate stood. When she realized she was alone, she doubled back.

Gifford, Roan, Tressa, and Rain came out, and then everything collapsed. A massive cloud of dust and stone blew out of the front entrance as the interior of Drome's castle caved in.

"Moya! Tekchin!" Brin struggled to enter, but huge slabs of stone blocked the way.

"Brin?" Roan called. "What do we do?"

"I don't know—I—follow the plan, I guess. Get to the gate. Go! Tressa, unlock the door and hold it open. I'll get Moya and Tekchin."

Brin fanned her arms in an attempt to blow away the lingering dust cloud. Huge blocks of marble had fallen such that she was forced to crawl through the rubble.

"Moya! Tekchin! Where are you?"

"Brin!" Moya called out.

Scrambling over broken slabs and under toppled pillars, Brin found her lying on the ground. "Moya, get up. We need to—"

"I can't!"

Only then did Brin see that Moya's left leg was pinned from the knee down beneath a huge block of marble.

"And Tekchin . . ." With teary eyes, Moya looked toward a massive pile of stone where Goll and the bulk of the second story had come down. "He's under there."

Dust was suspended in clouds, and from overhead, heavier pebbles continued to fall, pattering like hail.

"Tek!" Moya screamed, her eyes frantic and wild, her cheeks smeared with tears and dirt.

Brin pushed on the stone that trapped Moya, but the block was twice her size.

"Stand back!" Rain appeared out of the dust-filled fog. He had his pickax in hand and struck at the stone.

"Tekchin!" Moya cried again in agony.

Something larger than hail struck nearby, and Brin noticed a spear. Then another whistled past, barely missing Rain.

"Tetlin's ass!" Moya shouted, slapping the floor where she lay. "He's coming. Brin, can you feel it? The weight is back. Brin, Rain, you've got to go. Leave us. Do it. Now!"

"No." Brin shook her head violently. "I can't do that."

"You have to."

Out of the dusty mist, Brin saw Drome's forces massing. They came from another section of the palace, struggling to find a route through the rubble.

"Leave!" Moya shouted.

"Moya, I can't leave you." Brin looked over at Rain, whose efforts had only managed to chip a small depression in the block.

The digger shook his head, a miserable expression on his face.

"Go, damn it," Moya growled through clenched teeth. "That's an order!"

Brin lingered as spears hit the wall and floor.

"Brin, please . . ." Moya cried. "Please. I'm begging you. Leave us. Go and save Suri. Please!"

Brin could hardly remember what had occurred after that. Later, it felt as if the events had happened to someone else while she watched from above. She knew she had grabbed hold of Rain, and together they abandoned Moya, leaving her trapped and helpless on the once black-and-white floor that in its ruin had turned a somber, indistinct gray.

"Go through!" Brin shouted to everyone waiting at the gate.

No one listened.

"What happened to Moya?" Gifford asked. "Where's Tekchin?"

Brin shook her head. "Not coming. Everyone go through now!"

Another boom sounded from the castle, and Brin felt heavier.

The master of the house is coming.

"We can't leave them, Brin!" Gifford declared.

Before he could think about it, the Keeper wrapped an arm around his elbow and pulled. "We have to! He's coming!"

"It's open!" Tressa announced.

Looking through the doorway to Nifrel, all Brin saw was darkness, but it hardly mattered; her eyes were too filled with tears to see.

She pulled on Gifford.

"Stop!" Drome shouted from somewhere—maybe everywhere.

With a leap, Brin hauled harder on Gifford and together they passed through the portal into the darkness beyond.

CHAPTER ELEVEN

The Hero

I can only imagine the fear that must have existed in the land of the Fhrey during those years when we besieged Avempartha. In Rhulyn, we were used to facing the possibility of dying every day, but to the Fhrey, Death was an unwanted stranger who had only recently moved in.

— THE BOOK OF BRIN

Mawyndulë never used to tire of the corridors and halls of the Talwara. He'd spent years inside, entertaining himself: He'd see how far he could slide across the polished floor or down the grand stairs' banister. He never got tired of trying to spit into the river from the map room's balcony or swinging from the curtains in the great room. Lately, however, none of those things interested him.

Maybe they never did. It's just all I had.

Serving in the Aquila, meeting Makareta, and going to war all managed to widen his world and tarnish the little pleasures of his youth. This last trip to Avempartha had utterly broken them. Those three days out and three back had been his first time on his own away from home. Treya had been with him, but if he counted her, he might as well include his blanket and the horse. That trip was his first taste of true independence, of freedom.

He'd found it scary, but exciting. While not as exciting as Makareta, his travels were better than sliding down hallways. And he'd also discovered something else—a sense of accomplishment. With this came a new restlessness, a sense that the Talwara, which had always felt so huge, was now stifling.

"You have truly solidified your status as a hero of the people," Imaly said as she came down the steps of the Airenthenon after the conclusion of that week's Aquila session.

Mawyndulë didn't go to the council meetings anymore. Too many bad memories in there. Instead, he had waited outside. He hadn't had a chance to speak to Imaly since coming back, and he was curious about what she thought of his excursion and prize. "Have I?"

"First, you protected the Aquila and the Airenthenon, and now this." Imaly descended the steps awkwardly—but then everything she did physically was ungraceful. "Come. Walk me home." She led the way down the steps.

"What do you mean—*this?*"

"News has gotten out that the Rhune you brought here holds the secret to our victory. Is it true?"

"That has yet to be seen," Mawyndulë said. "Vasek was put in charge of getting the knowledge of dragons out of her. It's been days, and so far, he has nothing. As a result, my father has taken to throwing things. If Vasek doesn't succeed soon, the Master of Secrets might become one more shattered wineglass."

"Why is Vasek interrogating her? Why isn't Synne, or you, forcing the truth out of this Rhune? Surely the Art is more adept at extracting information from unwilling subjects."

Mawyndulë nodded. "Normally it is, but this Rhune has a special collar on her that prevents the use of the Art."

Imaly looked confused. "Why not remove it? If an enemy warrior were taken prisoner, we wouldn't allow him to wear armor."

"Oh, it's not by choice that she wears it. Jerydd forced it on her. The collar also prevents her from using the Art."

"So, she really is a Rhune Miralyith?"

Mawyndulë shrugged. "There is some speculation to that effect. Jerydd certainly thinks so, but I never actually *saw* her *do* anything."

"Still, she could be dangerous, couldn't she? I mean, if the collar were removed." Imaly appeared outraged as she shook her head. "Your father ordered you to bring this monster into our city? What if someone unlocked that collar? How many would die before—"

Mawyndulë shook his head. "Don't worry. The collar can't be removed."

"Your father has many enemies. Some misguided fool might steal the key and—"

Again, Mawyndulë stopped her. "There is no key. The lock is sealed with the Art."

"It could still be cut off. A simple saw or chisel could do the trick."

"The whole collar and lock are protected."

Imaly frowned. "I thought this collar nullified magic."

"It does. The Orinfar markings are on the inside. This allows a weave to be placed on the outside. Sort of like varnishing the exterior of wood to protect it from harm. And it's pretty tight."

"So it can never be removed?"

"Only by a Miralyith, and all of them serve my father. It will never be taken off, not while she's alive. That's why Vasek is doing the dirty work. It all has to be done by hand."

Imaly considered this and nodded. "I see. Well, at least she poses no threat. Thank you for setting my mind at ease. I don't know what we would do without you."

The two walked a bit farther, passing by the crypts of the previous fanes. When they got to Fenelyus's tomb, Imaly said, "You know, many see you as the true inheritor of her legacy. They say the talent for leadership skipped a generation."

The weather had turned colder. Most of the trees had lost their leaves, their naked branches clapping hollow, woody applause as their clothes danced in the streets. Imaly lifted the hood of her robe.

Mawyndulë recalled Vidar's warnings about trusting Imaly, about her being dangerous, and he knew that was just so much dusty thinking. Since their first meeting, she had endeared herself to him, been the one true rock in the turbulent sea of his life. Hearing Imaly say words he'd recently thought or knew he was about to think, Mawyndulë realized that in all the world, Imaly was his only true friend. A shame she had to be so old and ugly.

Imaly began walking away, but in a quiet voice she said, "Your father is not a very good fane, Mawyndulë, but you will be. What's more, everyone else sees that as well."

Mawyndulë felt a rush of warmth. He wasn't used to such compliments, even though flattery had been part of his life since birth. People had praised his looks, his clothes, and his sheer luck at being born son of the fane. All of it was excessive, noisy, and false—just like the trees' applause. None of the approval had come in response to anything he'd achieved or from anyone whose opinion he respected. But Mawyndulë admired Imaly. Most people did. Even those who hated her—and she had plenty of enemies—held Imaly in high regard. That was something else he appreciated about her. She made her own current, moving against the tide until the water followed, and she never cared about the hostility forming in her wake. She was right; they were wrong, and doubt remained a stranger on her doorstep. He wanted to be like that. He would have to be when he was fane.

Pride rose to Mawyndulë's lips as his self-conscious smile became an open grin.

Imaly gestured at the streets around them. "Everyone knows what happened. They saw how your father floundered helplessly in water that was far too deep. He would have drowned and taken all of us with him. During the Battle of Grandford, you distinguished yourself, and he . . . well, he fled. The city knows how you captured the Rhune and brought her here. They know it was you who—"

"But it wasn't me at all. Jerydd was the one who actually caught her."

"Pishposh." Imaly waved a hand at him.

Pishposh?

He liked Imaly, but sometimes the things she came up with mystified him.

"Catching a Rhune is nothing. But you! You killed Arion," Imaly said. "I shudder to think what might have happened if you hadn't. Who knows how many dragons we'd be facing?" She grinned, and he noticed she didn't have the best of teeth.

"You knew that was me? Not many people do."

"Oh, you'd be surprised—word travels. I'm the Curator of the Aquila, so I hear it all, and the people have been talking about you in the most complimentary of terms. I can't tell you how good that is to see in these trying times. Do you know what the people want? What they need? I'll tell you: heroes to believe in. Don't try selling Jerydd and Lothian. No one wants an old bureaucrat or an impotent coward. They want to be led by a dashing young prince who saved the Airenthenon and the Aquila during the Gray Cloak Rebellion. The same one who defied his father to capture a Rhune with the secret that might save us all from destruction."

"I didn't disobey my father. He sent me."

"Details don't matter. The story is better if you ventured out on your own, and that's what the people will think. That's what they'll remember."

"But it's not true."

"Mawyndulë, the best chronicles are never true, not completely. But make no mistake, it is our stories that define us both as individuals and as a civilization. Long after we're dead, people remember. And those memories form the building blocks of who we are, what we value, what we believe in, what we stand for, and what we fight against. Truth comes from how we view ourselves and how others see us. Our stories are the most important things we have. The better the tales, the greater the legacy we leave, and the more worthy a world we create."

They walked across the plaza to the old residences, which Mawyndulë now realized had more interesting lines and character due to their age.

"You'll see," Imaly went on. "You turned the tide in this war. That's what people think and what they need to believe. It was you—not your father—who braved the frontier and returned with our salvation. You are the legacy of Fenelyus, the one coming to our rescue in our most desperate hour."

Imaly paused in front of her house, which long ago had been the humble residence of the first fane. "I knew Fenelyus well. She and I didn't always agree. We often fought about policy. I wrestled with her over the totality of power that the Miralyith wielded, and I reminded her that in our society, authority was meant to be shared. I was against the forming of the Miralyith as a new tribe because Gylindora Fane had decreed there be six, *not seven.* Your tribe has great power—there was a time when I was certain the Miralyith would destroy our civilization. And oh, how we fought about that! I swear we nearly came to blows over the subject. But then I met you—a Miralyith I could believe in. You give me hope, Mawyndulë. I want to thank you for that." She leaned down and kissed him on the cheek.

Before he'd met her, such an action would have made him want to vomit, but now he felt a tear well up. He was honored, honored by her.

Maybe she saw his eyes water, because she quickly continued the conversation. "Do you want to know something? Fenelyus actually threw a cup at me once. Can you imagine!" Imaly smiled warmly at the memory.

Mawyndulë couldn't conceive how Imaly could recall the event so fondly. Arion had done the same to him, and it was just one in a long list of reasons he hated her. But Imaly was unusual in ways he was still trying to decipher.

"That cup smashed against the wall in the Airenthenon. A chip struck me in the cheek here." She pointed to a faint red mark and smiled again, further bewildering Mawyndulë. "The old fane, who had raised the world's highest mountain, formed Avempartha, and single-handedly came within a hairsbreadth of wiping out the entire Dherg race, threw a teacup at me!" Imaly laughed. "But for all our wars, for all our disagreements, I understood there was a greatness in her. Fenelyus was special. You could hear it in her voice, recognize it in the way she walked, and see it in her eyes. She was regal."

Imaly reached out and placed both hands on his shoulders. "I see the same in you. You have her eyes, but I fear—*I know*—that the greatness of Fenelyus did, indeed, skip a generation." Imaly lowered her voice to a whisper. "Let us pray to Ferrol that we can endure the wait. I know this will sound awful, but in some ways, I almost wish the Gray Cloak Rebellion had succeeded. Makareta and the others might not have been as foolish as we thought. I often wonder what happened to her."

"Me, too," Mawyndulë replied with his own whisper. "I sometimes imagine spotting her in a crowd."

"What would you do if that happened?"

This was a question he'd asked himself before. In the past, he always knew the answer, but now Mawyndulë shook his head. "I don't know."

Mawyndulë left Imaly in front of her house and began to wander. With his father in such a foul mood, he had no desire to return to the palace, but he had nowhere else to go—or so he thought.

Perhaps it was Imaly's comments that caused him to take the river road back, or it might have just been an accident, but Mawyndulë found himself strolling along the Shinara. He stopped as he spotted the Rose Bridge and remembered the overgrown memories that gathered beneath it. Under the heavy gray sky, everything looked so dead: trees reduced to skeletons, fallen leaves rusting brown, the grass a brittle yellow. He tried to picture the place as it had been so long ago in the bloom of early summer, all of it so rich and full, so deep and green: people laughing, singing, drinking, making plans, and building dreams. He remembered the taste of the wine, the sound of the music, the feel of her hand—all of it gone. Mawyndulë felt the pang of that loss as a tightness in his chest, a fist squeezing his heart.

He considered going down, but the bank of the river looked wet and muddy and there were thorns.

It's not the same anymore. Nothing is.

Staring at the place was like visiting a grave. A cold wind pushed him. He shivered against it and sighed.

Time to go back to my room, he thought but continued to stare at the spot where Makareta had hugged him. He tried to recall how she used to look—always smiling, her lips rosy from the wine. He thought of how good her embrace had felt, how she smelled, and the warmth of her body. But the memories were so thin that the effort left him cold and sad. He endured the bitterness in search of the last drop of sweetness.

I loved her.

The revelation added to his suffering, lending righteousness to his pain. He was a martyr. In this, he found the drop of sweetness he'd looked for—self-pity. He was alone with his pain, with his grief, and that made him noble, even more courageous, and worthy of admiration. He could have been whole with Makareta. He knew this as certainly as he had ever known anything. She was the one person who could have completed him, his only chance at happiness, and their future together was gone before it fully started.

I've got to stop coming here. It's too painful.

A cold wind picked up.

She said she thought I would make a better fane. So did Imaly.

Mawyndulë pulled up his hood.

Your father is not a very good fane, Mawyndulë, but you will be. What's more, everyone else sees that as well . . . Let us pray to Ferrol that we can endure the wait.

He found the hood's string and pulled it tight.

Maybe Makareta wasn't a traitor.

The wind blew harder, coming down the open corridor of the river.

He heard his father's words, *Granted, I had my doubts when you were caught up in that Gray Cloak Rebellion. I mean, what were my options there? Either my son is a conspirator or an idiot.*

A freezing rain began to fall, making the surface of the Shinara jump and the trees rattle.

Maybe Makareta was right after all.

CHAPTER TWELVE

Astray in a Gloomy Wood

Drome and Ferrol were twins in the same way that day is related to night and good is the counterpart to evil. The underworld realms they ruled were mirrors reflecting their light—or lack thereof.

— THE BOOK OF BRIN

The crow sat on a patch of dead grass watching them. At least Brin thought it was a crow. The bird was big, black, and she'd known them to stand their ground over a carcass, but there was no carrion to be seen, no reason for the bird to be there. Still, the crow was less than six feet away, glaring at them with all the disdain of a thousand-pound aurochs.

The noise of their entry should have been enough to scare it away. The portal popped loudly upon each person's arrival. They burst through the door into the darkness of Nifrel with shouts and gasps. Brin had come across the threshold crying.

Moya and Tekchin are gone!

Moya had been Brin's closest friend. After Audrey's death, Sarah had opened their home to the orphan, whom Brin's mother used to call *The Handful*. Moya became Brin's troublesome older sister. She was the bad influence, the foul-mouth, the mischief-maker, and Brin's undisputed idol. Moya had taught Brin to dance, provided her first taste of mead, led the pair on forbidden adventures into the forest, and shown Brin she could be the hero of her own stories. Moya had also lied for Brin, telling Sarah that she was the one who had broken the treadle on the loom. Sarah had made Moya sleep on an empty stomach for that—Brin didn't sleep at all. Moya had always protected her, and in all the years they lived in Dahl Rhen, no one ever picked on Brin. No one dared. She'd always been safe with Moya around. Upon reaching the bottom of the underworld and kneeling in the frightful, dark, and gloomy wood, Brin didn't feel safe anymore.

Wiping her eyes, Brin saw Gifford looking back at the threshold, his sword drawn, likely waiting for Drome or that big one-eyed giant to come through. Tressa stood with hands on hips, peering the other way into the gloomy wood of pale leafless trees that was Nifrel. Rain clutched his pick, unsure which way to face, and Roan sucked on her lower lip the way she used to after someone had touched her.

"I don't think they're coming," Gifford whispered. He moved closer to the portal, which from their current side was a smooth sheet of pale light. With his free hand, he reached out, and his fingers passed through the barrier.

With a violent cry, Gifford was jerked forward.

Rain and Brin grabbed him, pulling hard. Roan and Tressa joined in, and the combined effort was enough to free his arm.

"Someone on the other side grabbed my fingers," Gifford said while clutching his assaulted hand to his chest and glaring up at the brilliant opening. "Doesn't look like they can come through."

Brin nodded. "I hope you're right."

"What happened?" Gifford asked her.

Brin tried to talk but her throat closed.

"The castle came down on them," Rain answered for her. "Tekchin is gone, buried, and Moya was pinned by a block as big as a roundhouse. I tried, but I couldn't make much more than a dent. Moya ordered us to leave." The dwarf looked at Brin. "Practically had to threaten this one before she got moving."

Gifford nodded solemnly. "So it's just us now."

Brin sniffled. "Looks like it."

Together they turned from the door to view this new place, the second realm of Phyre.

Tree trunks creaked and groaned, and a handful of shriveled leaves clinging to bone-white wood rustled—the whisper of a thousand ghosts. Brin couldn't feel a wind, yet bare branches clicked and clacked—a hollow, mournful sound.

Not at all a wholesome place.

Gifford, who also peered into the dark wood, summed it up. "Makes the Swamp of Ith seem nice, doesn't it?"

"Is that the same bird that was in Rel?" Rain asked, returning his pickax to the sling on his back.

"I don't know, maybe," Brin replied.

"I think it is," the dwarf said. "Strange."

"Are you kidding?" Gifford looked at Rain. "In all this, you find the bird stands out as unusual?"

Rain shrugged. "Nothing else came through the entrance—why the bird?"

"We should get moving," Tressa said, still staring out into the darkness that lay ahead.

"What about Moya?" Roan asked, her face illuminated by the threshold, eyes bright with the light that flooded the tiny clearing. "Maybe if we . . . perhaps we could—"

"That's as far as she's going to go," Tressa said.

Brin stiffened. The cold indifference in Tressa's voice infuriated her, even more so because Brin felt guilty for abandoning her friend. Once again, Tressa had become the heartless hag who'd thrown her pages in the river. "What if it were you, Tressa?"

The older woman gave a miserable smirk. "If it were me lying back there, everyone would have already left." She focused on Brin with a naked honesty. "And you know it."

"That's not true," Gifford said.

Tressa frowned. "Thing is, I wouldn't mind. I'd expect it because this isn't about me. We all knew the risks. I certainly did, and if Moya didn't, then she was an idiot."

"How can you be so cold?" Brin asked.

"I'm cold," Roan said.

"What?" Brin looked at the woman, puzzled and a bit irritated. Filled to overflowing with self-hatred and doubt, she didn't appreciate the flippant remark. It only took a second for Brin to remember that Roan never made offhand comments.

"I mean, I *feel* cold," Roan clarified, following this up by rubbing her arms vigorously.

Tressa shook her head in disgust. "Seriously? What are you, eight? I'm cold, too. We're all cold. Deal with it. We've got—"

"No, she's right," Gifford said. He was looking around suspiciously, as if the darkness and the dead trees were plotting against them. "I haven't felt *anything* since dying. And the chill just started. I didn't feel it when we were in Rel."

Brin noticed it then. Not a true cold, not in the wintry sense, but she felt a distinct chill rise up her back and neck. It danced along her skin. Something was different, she could feel—

Snap, crack, rip. In the forest of bleached wood, something stirred, something big.

The chill grew frostier as Brin peered into the forest. The world of Nifrel was dark. Not black, like it had been at the bottom of Neith where she couldn't see her own hands, but dim and hazy. This new world settled for shades of gray that built up to an eventual ebony where the sky had always promised to be. Brin wasn't aware of any light that made it possible for her to see, but then what good was light when she didn't have eyes? The world was no longer something she saw but rather something she perceived.

"What *is* that?" she asked.

Crack!

Brin couldn't tell if it was a large branch that snapped or just a really close one.

Gifford drew his sword.

The crow finally moved. Flashing black wings, it flew to a low branch of a nearby tree. Even it no longer felt safe.

Struggling to penetrate the hazy silhouettes of the eaves, Brin finally saw movement, a giant hulking creature bristling with fur. "What is it?"

"I think," Gifford said. "I think it's a bear—a really *big* bear."

"Is that . . . ?" Tressa started, then faltered. "Could that be . . . ?"

Out of the shadows the beast lumbered, a great brown bear. It rose on its hind legs and roared so loudly that the trees shook.

"The Brown," Brin gasped. She'd never seen the bear that had killed Konniger and so many others, but she'd heard what it looked like: reddish, the color of dried blood, and huge from a steady diet of human meat. Maeve had been among its victims, and Suri would have died, too, if she hadn't—

"Fire!" Brin said. "If only we had fire."

Roan looked at Brin, and their little miracle worker's eyes brightened. Without a word, she rushed madly toward the bear.

"Roan!" everyone called out in panic.

She didn't go far. Stopping short of the trees, she snatched up a handful of fallen branches before running back.

"What are you doing?" Gifford shouted.

"Fire! It will be afraid of it." Roan dropped her armload of wood and tore open her pack.

Rain joined her on the ground, breaking the branches into manageable sticks.

"I could use larger pieces," Roan told them while fishing out raw wool and a bit of cloth from her side bag. She handed these to Rain before digging back into her pouch.

"Does that even work here?" Tressa asked.

In the trees, the growling menace drew closer. Brin could hear it lumbering with heavy feet through dead leaves.

Rain helped Gifford drag a fallen log while Roan began striking a rock with a jagged bit of metal. Sparks flashed. She stopped, put her head down, and blew into the pile Rain had fashioned. Light appeared—a wonderful warm yellow flame that raised a host of shadows, which danced across the pale wood. Their patch of ground became a place to defend, a clearing turned into a campsite, a wilderness transformed into civilization.

Seeing the flickering shadows dance among the trees, Gifford said, "Build it larger."

"Let's hope it's still afraid of fire." Tressa found a stout stick and raised it like a club. "Will this work or are we—you know—maybe it's *attracted* to the light."

"What? Do you think it's a giant growling moth-bear?" Gifford asked.

"Look around you. Is that really so crazy right now?"

Gifford didn't answer and went back to collecting more wood. "Don't happen to have a spear in your bag of tricks, do you, Roan? A spear would be handy."

She looked up. "I could make one."

Gifford smiled back. "Maybe next time."

"Here, use this." Roan lit the bristling end of a branch and handed it to Gifford. With his sword in his right hand and the torch in his left, he advanced on the beast.

"What are you up to, Giff?" Tressa asked in a manner that suggested he shouldn't be doing anything of the sort.

"Hoping to scare it away."

Gifford swung the flaming brand before him. The bear, still some distance off, snorted and shuffled back, retreating once again on all fours. "It's working." Gifford pressed his attack, advancing forward and thrusting with the torch. The Brown growled in anger, and as Gifford reached the row of trees, the bear turned and bolted back into the forest.

"Ha!" Gifford watched it run. "Look at that!"

"How very cruel." The words issued from the fire.

Roan and Rain leapt back from their creation as it grew beyond its meager fuel to a blazing bonfire. Everyone retreated to the edges of the light as the comforting yellow-orange glow drained to an eerie white-blue flicker. In the depths, a face appeared—a woman's face: sharp chipped cheeks, black razor lips, a knife-blade nose, and pinprick eyes that glared out at them.

"My bear was merely coming to welcome you, and that is how you greet it?" the lady in the fire said with mock offense and then smiled—those thin black lips curling tightly at the corners. "Might have also eaten you, I suppose. Can't help it. It's her nature, but still, it was quite rude of you."

"Who are you?" Tressa asked.

Brin was impressed the woman found the courage to speak. Her own voice was trapped somewhere deep beneath her throat. Maybe it was only an illusion, but the image in the fire was the scariest thing Brin had ever seen.

The flaming expression looked surprised, even a dash hurt. "Why, I'm the ruler of this place, my dear. I am Ferrol, third-born daughter of Eton and Elan, Empress of the Dark, God of the Fhrey, Lord of the Damned, Queen of the White Tower. You need to come see it; the place is lovely this time of year. The bone just glistens against the dark sky."

Drome had said they were twins, but Brin saw no similarity. Compared with his sister, the god of the dwarfs was a jolly old uncle with a quirky sense of humor.

"I thought I would be considerate and extend an invitation to visit. We can have a nice dinner or pretend to, at least. I'm easy to find. Can't miss me. I live in the giant tower in the center. All roads lead to me. Just be sure to bring that marvelous key with you."

If Brin's heart hadn't already stopped, it would have now. The blue fire's glow revealed the same reaction on the others' faces.

"Don't look so shocked. Did you think you could stroll in here and I wouldn't know about that little trinket *Turin* gave you?" Ferrol pronounced the name in a mocking voice. "It isn't his to give, you know? He stole it, much the way he steals everything. Misplaced loyalty, that's what we have here. You're working for the wrong person." The fiery eyes shifted toward Gifford. "Especially you. Tressa I can understand, but not you, poor boy. You're from *finer* stock. You should know better than to serve an evil god. Don't you have some sort of sense about these things? Can't you tell the difference? We're the good ones, the virtuous, the believers in freedom, kindness, compassion, and love. Turin is a tyrant. He murders, lies, cheats, steals, and has managed to imprison all who would oppose him. This is his little oubliette, his forgetting place where he banishes all his troublesome truths, embarrassments, and fears. But that key—which rightfully belongs to my father—will let us out. With it in my hand, I can undo eons of wrongful imprisonment. Bring it to me."

"We aren't here to bring you anything," Tressa said.

"And yet you will. In this place, I am supreme." Ferrol caused the fire to flare, the bluish glow draining the color from every face and making the pale trees glow. "There is nowhere you can go, no corner to hide in. And make no mistake—I am not my brother. He's well-meaning . . . but a fool. Bring me the key and I will forgive your crimes. Defy me and I will take it. And for my trouble I will cast you all into the Abyss to spend eternity with the Typhons."

Abyss and *Typhons.* Brin tried to make mental notes, but thinking while horrified was difficult.

"You wouldn't come to us begging if you were as powerful as all that," Gifford declared.

The fire-eyes flashed. "Come here, dear boy," Ferrol said. "Let me show you what you get for disobedience in my realm."

Gifford took an awkward step forward. Even when crippled, he'd moved with less effort, less struggle. Step by step he crept toward the flames, his face pinched with strain.

"In my brother's principality, there is no pain," Ferrol said. "There is only eternity, a bland, gray existence. But here in my realm, you will feel your mistakes. For what is to be gained if nothing is to be lost?"

The fire flared brighter, glowing white in the center, making Brin squint just to see.

"Stagger closer, crippled brat, and feel the—"

With a violent hiss and a belch of smoke, the face of Ferrol vanished along with the flames. Beside the red glowing embers stood Roan with a now-empty waterskin. "Bad fire," she said.

The Queen of the White Tower's visit got them moving. No one wanted to remain near the smoldering embers of that fire. As in Rel, there was a road. Instead of Drome's white brick, Ferrol had but a worn path snaking between gnarled trees and withered rock. Still, the route was unmistakable, and they simply began walking. No decisions had to be made, no choices deliberated on. Gifford took the lead with Roan at his side. The rest of them followed in a haphazard fashion that changed given the landscape and obstacles, but Brin found herself often at the rear, looking back. She couldn't help wondering about Moya.

Has Drome captured her? Will she be tortured? Is that possible in Rel?

After their fiery encounter with the queen, Brin suspected that the innate dullness of Drome's realm could be suspended if he so wished.

And what has happened to Tekchin? Will he remain buried for eternity?

Brin had felt confident that stepping into the pool was the worst thing she would ever need to face, but now she wasn't so sure. Once in Rel, Brin had been certain everything would succeed. The impossibility of dying twice and the divinity of Malcolm made their success a certainty. She saw herself on a grand adventure, one where she was reunited with old friends and family—not to mention having the unparalleled opportunity to learn the true nature of the world that would make *The Book of Brin* greater than anything she could have imagined. Since then, Brin had learned that there was something worse than death, and she'd come to suspect that Malcolm might not be trustworthy.

Are we working for an evil god? Are Drome and Ferrol right?

Brin had always liked Malcolm. He was kind, friendly, quiet, and a little awkward, which made him comfortable to be around. No one had ever said a negative word about him—until Muriel. She hated him. She was the Tetlin Witch but not at all like Brin had expected. Instead of an ugly, evil crone, she was a beautiful, kindhearted woman. Then there was Drome, whom Arion had regarded as good-natured. He had described Malcolm as an evil tyrant who ruled the world with *razor fingers and stone boots.*

Now it was Ferrol's turn to weigh in with a similar opinion.

You should know better than to serve an evil god. Don't you have some sort of sense about these things? Can't you tell the difference?

In contrast, Roan, the dwarfs, and Tressa worshiped Malcolm. Brin had no idea what exactly had happened in the smithy the night Raithe died. She couldn't understand why Tressa of all people had become so devoted to him. Konniger's wife wasn't known for being virtuous.

Is it possible Tressa is drawn to Malcolm because he is the god of evil? Has he been lying to all of us?

She considered telling the others—would have if Moya were still with them—but wandering a dark wood in Nifrel with a god and a bear stalking them, she sensed morale was already in short supply. She couldn't steal the one thread of hope they still clung to. The possibility that Malcolm was evil would shake Roan and Rain and would destroy Tressa. So, while Brin was no longer certain that continuing their quest was a good idea, she was aware of no other alternatives, and she felt it was best not to punch holes in a boat while well beyond the sight of land.

It looks as though you may have been right after all, Tesh. Great Elan, how I miss you.

She wondered what he was doing.

Has he made it back through the swamp by now? Did he kill Nyphron, accelerating his timetable out of grief? Was it the Galantian leader's death we heard chime? Maybe years have passed since we entered Phyre and Tesh has found someone else and forgotten about me.

The crow stayed with them.

Brin didn't always spot it. In the forest, it was difficult to see anything. A gloom, like a smoky fog, shrouded the world. And then there were the trees, thousands of dead-white sticks. Easy to see why The Brown made so much noise—the branches were weak, brittle things. Bones. Brin tried to press between two and both of them broke, crashing to the ground and shattering to splinters. This forest was not a living thing. Like the people who passed through it, this wood was dead.

"Where will *you* go?" Roan asked Gifford in her inexplicable way, sentences coming out without rhyme or reason.

"What do you mean?"

"When this is over, what realm of Phyre will you end up in? Ferrol said you were made of finer stock. And you are. I've never known a more courageous, more loving, or all-around better person than you. I think you're bound for Alysin."

"No." He scoffed. "You're just saying that because you see me that way. I'm positive I'll be in Rel. I doubt that hanging on to the back of Naraspur qualifies me for anything else. The two of us will have a place in that village near Brin's family. Won't that be nice?"

"What if I don't go to Rel?" Roan asked. The whisper grew smaller; the exhale of a mouse would have drowned her out. "What if I end up here?"

"Here?" Gifford followed this with a laugh. "Why would you—oh." He paused, the laughter cut short, his words dropping in tone. "No. No, you won't come here."

"This is where the bad people go, isn't it?"

"Roan, you're not bad."

"But I—"

Gifford stopped to look full at her. "You're not bad, Roan. You're not."

"How do you know? How does anyone?"

Brin listened for the answer, but Gifford didn't reply.

Pop! Pop! The sharp reports cracked and carried in that still and silent place. This was followed by a horrible blood-chilling scream.

"Was that the portal?" Brin asked shakily.

"Maybe we should walk faster," Gifford said.

"And get off this road," Tressa added.

"What if we get lost?" Gifford asked.

"We can't. We have no idea where we're going. And right now, I think it would be worse to be found."

They left the road and pushed into the forest. Brin expected it to be hard going, but the trees remained brittle, shattering at the slightest touch. This was good and bad. The walking was easy, but they left an unmistakable trail, which anyone chasing them could see. Not to mention all the noise. Brin didn't know if this place had an official name, but in her head, she called it the Dead Wood for obvious reasons, and if she ever managed to return to the world of the living, she would officially name it that in *The Book of Brin*.

She spotted the crow up ahead, waiting for them. It had landed on a tree branch without breaking it. The bird bothered Brin because it wasn't normal. The absurdity of that thought almost made her laugh—almost.

What's normal?

In this place, she hadn't a clue. Still, she was certain the bird was watching them. Whether that was common or not, she didn't like it. Its black, beady eyes reminded her of the face in the fire. Ahead, the trees were starting to thin. They were reaching the end of the Forest of Bones. The moment she thought of it, Brin decided she liked that name even better and made a mental note.

The sound of movement made them stop. Someone was coming up the trail from behind and making a lot of noise in the process. There were heavy footfalls, snapping of branches, grunting, and even muffled cries. Every one of them instinctively crouched, and they looked back down the crushed-wood tunnel they had created since leaving the main trail.

Tressa pressed a finger to her lips and eyed each of them with an intense glare. They waited, listening as the sounds stopped. Brin thought she heard faint voices. Then the movement began again, this time closer.

"We're in trouble," Tressa whispered. "It saw where we left the road, and it's coming."

"Go on," Gifford said and quietly drew his sword. "I'll stay here—slow it down, or at least try to. The rest of you should look for help."

No one moved.

"I mean it," he whispered with as stern a face as he could muster. "Go on!"

Roan replied with a shake of her head and a hug of his arm.

As they waited, Brin looked for a bright light but saw none. At least Drome hadn't come. But what monster had he sent to fetch them?

Before long, they saw a figure with two heads and three legs shambling toward them.

Brin prepared herself for the worst. She grabbed up as stout a stick as she could find among the brittle bones of the wood. Roan let go of Gifford as he took a step forward, placing two hands on his sword's handle. Rain unslung his pick and planted his feet. Then, as the creature cleared the shadow of the trees, Brin saw it wasn't one, but two. A man and woman struggled to walk—one providing support to the other.

Brin stared dumbfounded as the pair emerged from the gloom.

"Tesh?" she said, the word escaping with her breath.

"Moya!" Gifford shouted.

Either it was a trick of the afterlife or Tesh was there, helping Moya, who hopped along on one foot.

"Brin!" Tesh called. "Give me a hand!"

The Keeper raced forward, pushing through an emotional storm that was equal parts joy and grief. Moya had made it out, but not unscathed, and Tesh was there, but that meant he had died.

"Moya!" Brin gasped. "Your leg. What happened?"

The woman was biting back pain along with her lower lip. Sweat covered her face, and her body shuddered. Her left leg had been severed from just above the knee. Blood soaked the fabric of her leggings and stained her arm; an additional smear darkened one side of Moya's face. Stuck to it, glued to her cheek, was white chalky dust she'd picked up by resting on the floor of the palace.

"I couldn't budge the stone," Tesh apologized. He, too, was splattered with blood, but showed no wounds. "She was pinned, and the block was too heavy. This"—he pointed to the absence of Moya's leg—"was the only thing I could think to do. Wasn't bad in Rel. Moya didn't feel a thing. But the moment we crossed over, she collapsed, screaming in pain. I practically had to drag her."

Tesh's belt was wrapped around Moya's stump, but it wasn't enough. The limb still drizzled an intermittent stream of blood.

"Lay her down," Brin commanded. "We need more pressure."

"Padera always used a stick or ax handle to twist the belt tighter," Roan said.

"That's right," Brin added. "Here, use this." She passed Roan the stick she had picked up for defense.

Roan twisted the tourniquet tight, making Moya cry out.

"We could make a fire, scorch the stump to seal it," Tesh said.

Roan shook her head. "Not a good idea."

"What do we do?" Gifford asked.

"Find help," Moya growled through clenched teeth.

Tressa nodded. "There has to be someone in this accursed realm besides Ferrol who can do something."

"I'll go," Brin volunteered.

"Brin, be careful!" Tesh called to her as she ran off toward where the trees thinned.

Brin had always been a fast runner, but in the afterlife, she seemed to fly. She shattered limbs of the Dead Wood without care, and after a long while, she exited the trees and found herself on an open plain. Just beyond, she spotted an orange-and-red glow that filled the horizon like a predawn sun. In such a gray world, that tiny bit of color was a welcome sight, but it wasn't a sunrise. The glow rose from below the edge of a cliff, its light making everything else darker. Rocks and the remaining solitary trees became inky silhouettes against an incandescent gleam that stretched to the horizon. From far below, Brin heard a faint rush like the gentle blow of wind in leaves, only there was no breeze and not nearly enough leaves.

Slowing to a walk, she crept up to see what was at the bottom. Even before Brin was close enough, she had a good idea what it was. Unlike sunlight, this illumination writhed and flickered. The sound wasn't a wind, but a constant roar of voices. In another few steps, she saw it. Fire. The canyon floor was an inferno. Amid those flames she noted buildings— huge fortresses stood perched on nearly every hill, bluff, and pinnacle. The largest and most magnificent was a white tower that rose near the center of the valley. Taller than the rest and as brilliant as a full moon, the singular pale finger soared to what Brin guessed to be the roof of that world, a black-sooted ceiling where smoke stained the sky. Between the fortresses, she saw movement, and her mouth fell agape. Hundreds of thousands, maybe millions, of people crowded the valley floor. They were fighting.

What lay below was incomprehensible to Brin: a jumbled mass of figures, some male, others female, and plenty of beasts. What looked like aurochs, but far larger, pulled massive wooden towers. Giants attacked with burning blades. Hundreds of tattered banners fluttered above ranks of endless soldiers. Winged creatures of all sorts flew, diving and snatching helpless victims. Balls of fire raced across the field, leaving long tails of dark smoke. The accumulated cries, clashes, and roars mixed into one unwavering sound, a constant noise like a waterfall's crash on stone. All of it was so immense, so vast, yet so diminutive at this distance that if she unfocused her eyes, Brin could have been looking into the embers of a fire.

Spotting movement, Brin turned and gasped. Transfixed by the sight before her, she hadn't immediately noticed the figure of a woman draped in a black cloak walking toward her. Silent and shrouded as a shadow, she approached, arms folded. When she came near, Brin saw what was unmistakably the most beautiful being she'd ever beheld. Bright, cheerful eyes shone above a smile formed of perfect lips. Her eyes were blue, hair blond.

Not a woman at all. A Fhrey.

"We need help!" Brin called out, hoping in her desperation that this person wasn't evil or a servant of the Queen. "My friend is hurt—it's bad. She's in terrible pain."

"Where?" the Fhrey asked.

Brin didn't feel she had the luxury of time to explain. She took the Fhrey by the hand and led her back through the shattered path. Before getting all the way back, they came across the others coming their way.

Moya was between Tesh and Gifford as they struggled to carry her forward. Seeing Brin, they paused and set her down, Moya moaning in anguish.

All eyes fixed on the Fhrey stranger, then shifted nervously to Brin for answers. In her haste to save Moya, she had none to give. Brin had been tasked with finding assistance and had no idea if she'd succeeded. "Can you help her?" Brin asked.

The Fhrey lowered her hood, revealing a look of shock, but her focus wasn't on Moya. She stared at the dwarf. "Might your name be *Rain?*" Her tone was inscrutably uniform, her inflection guarded.

"Aye, I am," he declared.

"So, it is true." The Fhrey shook her head. "Astounding."

"Can you save me friend?" Rain gestured toward Moya.

The Fhrey glanced over and appeared puzzled. "From what, exactly?"

"Are you stupid?" Moya growled. "My leg's been cut off. I'm bleeding out!"

Moya appeared bent on insulting every person they met, but then again, losing Tekchin and half her leg would leave anyone in a bad mood.

"Can you help her, please?" Brin added.

The Fhrey smiled at her, as if amused. *"Please?* That's different." She glanced at Rain, then back at Brin, and finally, she looked at Moya. She shrugged. "How can I refuse such a gracious request?"

The Fhrey unclasped her cloak, and with a bit of wrist-born flourish, she snapped it out and let it settle across the lower part of Moya's body. "Now, just calm yourself. Relax. Everything will be fine."

Moya grunted, a tear of sweat dangling from the tip of her nose as she sucked in air and blew it out with a violent force.

"Your leg is fine. There's nothing—"

"My leg has been cut off, you stupid bitch!" Moya shuddered in pain. One hand was white-knuckled on Gifford's arm, the other crushing Brin's hand.

"No, it hasn't." The Fhrey lady, who now revealed a stunning green gown, spoke in a soothing, confident, even authoritative manner.

"You're culling nuts! My leg is—"

"Fine, whole, and without defect."

Brin would never put herself in the path of Moya's red-hot fury, but the beautiful lady in the green gown showed no sign of yielding. She didn't even flinch.

The Fhrey's tone grew even firmer, as if she were losing patience with a bratty child. "Now, stop putting up such a ridiculous fuss."

"My leg—" Moya began.

"Is right there." The Fhrey pointed.

At that moment, everyone looked down and gasped. Under the cloak, there appeared to be two complete legs.

Moya stared openmouthed.

"Go on," the Fhrey said with a whimsical grin. "Wiggle your foot."

Moya's mouth remained open as she watched her foot wag from side to side.

Then like a magic trick, the lady in green snatched back her garment. Beneath it were Moya's legs—both of them. The blood was gone, and even the material of her leggings was undamaged.

"How did you do that?" Moya asked as the pain and anguish drained from her face.

The Fhrey woman laughed. "You haven't been in Nifrel long, have you?"

"We only just came in," Tesh said.

They all stared at Moya, stunned. She stood up gingerly, testing the limb, then smiled. "It's fine."

Brin grabbed, hugged, and kissed her. Then she launched herself at Tesh. "Oh, Blessed Mari, how I've missed you!" Nearly tackling him, Brin buried Tesh in a rapid burst of kisses. When his arms found her, she felt the familiar vice of his embrace, and if she had breath, his kiss would have taken it away.

"Fine, fine," the Fhrey said and sighed. "Bodies restored, lovers apparently reunited, now may we address the important matter at hand?" She stared at Rain.

The dwarf braced himself. "What do you want with me?"

"Absolutely nothing. I merely came here to satisfy my curiosity and apparently lose a bet. But I know someone who has been searching for you for a long time. In point of fact, she's quite anxious to meet you."

"Ferrol?" Rain asked cautiously.

"Is that it? You work for the bitch-queen?" Tressa accused.

The crow reappeared just then, flying in and landing on a nearby branch that rocked with its weight. Brin was once again impressed that the limb managed to hold it. The crow must be as heavy as a passing glance.

"I hold no fidelity to the Queen of the White Tower," the Fhrey declared. "Speaking of which." She looked over at the crow. "Hello, Orin," she said to it, then looking at the rest of them she asked, "Have you met? *He* is the queen's servant. One of many. Orin is her eyes and ears." She tilted her head to peer at the crow. "Orin, I hope you understand. This isn't personal."

Spooked by her words, the bird pushed off the branch, but it only took two wingbeats before bursting into a cloud of black feathers with a loud *pop!* Everyone gasped. Brin took a step back as she watched the onetime bird's plumage spiral slowly to the ground, where it made a tiny pile.

The Fhrey laughed as she watched the feathers fall. "That never gets old."

She walked over and picked up the black feathers. Wadding the pile into a ball, she threw them into the air. Upon release, they became dead leaves that fell to an indifferent ground.

The conversation died along with the bird. Brin wondered if she was going to explode all of them as well. By the looks on most of the other faces, they were thinking the same thing. The exception was Moya.

The Keenig's Shield was getting her feet back under her—both physically and figuratively. She stepped between the Fhrey and the dwarf. "I don't care who you are or what you want. If you have a problem with Rain, then you have one with me as well."

"You can put your fur down. I have no quarrel with Rain. And oh, by the way, you're welcome." The Fhrey smiled sweetly at her.

Moya only glared. "If you don't work for Ferrol, I don't—who are you, and what is it you want with Rain?"

"My name is Fen, and I'm not here to cause trouble."

Moya gave a glance at the dead leaves, suggesting she might suspect differently. "Why *are* you here?"

"Because I wagered Beatrice that no Belgriclungreian by the name of Rain was up on this ridge near the Rel Gate. I came here to prove I was right." Fen adjusted her cloak on her shoulders. "Thank you for costing me a favor and granting Beatrice bragging rights."

"Beatrice?" Rain asked.

"She's been going on about you for centuries."

"Who is she?" Rain asked. "How did she know I was—"

"Long story, and one we don't have time for right now. Orin isn't Ferrol's only servant. It won't be long before the queen learns of your arrival and comes looking."

"She already knows," Roan muttered.

"I'm sorry? What was that?"

"We already met the queen," Gifford said.

"In a world of overachievers, I suppose you don't rule by being slow or stupid. But how is it that you are still here if—"

"Roan got rid of her," Gifford said proudly, taking her hand in his.

Fen took a step closer and studied Roan with a critical frown. "Not to be rude, but you don't look capable of defeating Ferrol."

"She was going to hurt Gifford," Roan said. "Make him burn himself in a fire I had made to scare away Grin the Brown, so I put the flames out."

A puzzled expression appeared on Fen's face. She looked at Roan, Gifford, the others, and then back at Moya.

"What is it?" Moya asked.

"*You* hopped through the forest in agony on one leg." She pointed at Roan. "And *she* made a fire and extinguished the queen." Fen shook her head. "You're a very odd group."

Fen led the way back through the forest toward where she and Brin first met. Despite her earlier apprehension, Moya followed the Fhrey, and everyone else followed Moya. The others gave the newly reunited couple some private space, so Brin and Tesh brought up the rear.

"Tesh," Brin said, taking hold of his arm with both of hers. "I can't believe you're here. I missed you so much. I wanted us to be together, but I was cruel and selfish. I'm sorry for so many things. But what happened? How did you get here?"

"I went into the pool." He hung his head.

"What's wrong?"

"I'm ashamed it took me so long."

"Why did it?"

"You know why." Tesh looked ahead at the others. "Have you told them?"

Brin shook her head.

"Why not?"

"We had to break into the afterlife; I met my family and discovered we were wanted by the local officials, whom Moya had insulted; then we had story time with a god, and got into a fight with a huge one-eyed brute; after that, we destroyed a palace before taking on Queen Ferrol and an undead bear." She shrugged. "Been kinda busy."

Tesh nodded.

They continued to walk, and Brin patiently waited. He would tell her, but Tesh, who was always quick in battle, was slow with words.

"What you said," Tesh began, quietly, "about me becoming like *them*. I couldn't understand why you would say such a hurtful thing and why you suddenly hated me. I got angry. After you went into the pool, Muriel was still there. She had been watching. I told her, 'I thought she loved me. How could she leave me like that? How could she do that to me?'

"Then she said, 'Perhaps, she could tell you don't really love her.'

"'How can you say that!' I shouted.

"Then she said, 'The love of your life just killed herself in the hopes of saving another, and all you can think about is how it affects you? I'm not an expert, but I don't think that love grows well in such bitter soil.'"

He sighed. "The witch left me then. Alone, I sat and stared at that terrible pool. I had nothing but that memory of you sinking and my own thoughts."

"Why didn't you leave? Go back to the Dragon Camp?"

"I wish I could say that I realized you were right and found a way to overcome my hatred, but that wasn't it. Honestly . . . I think it was the pain. I wanted it to stop. I kept replaying your last minutes, seeing the fear in your eyes as you went under. I've never experienced anything so unbearable. I couldn't live with that. The pool was there, and I wanted to die, so taking the plunge seemed obvious. It wasn't the best solution. It means I've failed at everything. I've disappointed my family, neglected my duty to my clan, and failed you because I couldn't convince you not to die. I'm sorry, Brin."

"Tesh, don't apologize. It's me that should be sorry. I got you into this. Gave you that terrible ultimatum. But, Mari help me—and I know it's totally wrong—but I'm so glad you're here. I missed you so much."

Tesh nodded, but the sad frown spoke volumes. Her words hadn't helped. Rather than saying more, she squeezed his hand, kissed it, and walked with her head leaning on his shoulder.

They left the trees and reached the cliff. Far below, the battle continued. Each stood in awe as they beheld the sight, in much the same way that Brin had.

"It's a war," Gifford said, his face lit by the orange glow.

Fen pointed. "King Mideon has the strongest rebel hold in Nifrel. That Belgriclungreian fortress down there is where we are heading. It will be your life raft in this storm."

Rain stepped to the edge of the drop. "King Mideon is down there?"

"Yes. And for Beatrice's sake, I am willing to escort you."

"Down there?" Tressa asked, shocked. "There's a battle—a huge one!"

Fen peered over the edge as if she hadn't noticed. She pushed out her lower lip and nodded in appraisal. "Atella is doing better than usual. Of course, he has Havar now." She added in a quiet, casual tone, as if speaking among friends at a sporting match, "Traded Rhist for him in the last negotiations with Mideon—which was a great deal when you think about it. Won't help, though; they still can't get past Orr. Mideon is the only one who has a chance of fighting the dragon, and he won't leave his citadel." She shook her head with a disgusted, hopeless expression. "As long as Ferrol has Orr, no one will ever breach even her outer walls. Atella doesn't care. He will beat on that same door for all eternity. But then, that is what makes him Atella, is it not? Been thousands of years, but for him, losing is somehow still a novelty."

"This happens every day?" Gifford asked.

Fen nodded. "Well, yes, but it's always the same day here, isn't it? Now then, given that Ferrol has shown an interest, this won't be easy. Your only hope is that she doesn't know I'm with you. She'll assume it's just the seven of you wandering in the woods. You can refuse my help, but if you wish to avoid Ferrol, you'll want to get down off this ledge, and I know the fastest way short of jumping, which you could do, but it'll hurt almost beyond imagination. And if you're all like this one"—she pointed at Moya—"it will take too long for you to put yourselves back together."

They stared at one another, as if Fen were speaking an unknown language.

"Well?" she asked. "Do you want my help?"

"I'm inclined to say yes," Gifford said.

"I'm not," Tressa countered, folding her arms. "We don't know the first thing about her."

"She helped Moya," Brin said.

"That doesn't tell me who she is or what she's up to."

"You want to know about *me?*" Fen looked surprised, as if she were of no importance. "Well, you already know I'm Fhrey—or was when I was alive. That should be obvious. I have my own tower of sorts down there. You can barely see it from here. I visit the Bulwark often; that's Mideon's fortress. I'm one of the few Fhrey he allows in without armed guards. We have what you might call a friendship of sorts—a mutual history, at least. Ironic, as in life we were mortal enemies. Our newfound cooperation is something I take great pride in."

Rain gasped and took two steps back.

"What's wrong?" Moya asked him.

"I know who she is." Rain pointed an accusatory finger at the Fhrey. "The Dark Sorceress of the Ylfe. She killed tens of thousands of my people."

"I did not! That's absurd." Fen shook her head, then in a sad voice added, "I killed hundreds of thousands."

"Hundreds of thousands?" Tesh said, stunned.

"I know who she is now, too," Brin said. "Arion used to tell me tales . . . for my book. She practically worshiped her."

"Arion?" Fen asked surprised. "Arion Cenzlyor? You know my Arion?"

"She was a friend of ours, who was—"

"Was?"

"Yes," Brin said. "She died during the first battle of our war with the Fhrey. That was many years ago."

"Oh?" Fen said. "I wonder why I haven't heard of her arrival."

"She's in Rel."

"Really? What is she—oh, I suppose that makes sense. Despite all her talent, she always was a simple soul."

"And who do you think this Fhrey is?" Moya asked Brin.

"You know I'm standing right here," Fen said sardonically, folding her arms in mock insult.

Brin held out her hands to the Fhrey. "This is Fane Fenelyus Mira, Arion's beloved mentor. She was the ruler of the Fhrey before Lothian and the first Miralyith. She single-handedly created Mount Mador and the tower of Avempartha."

Fen smiled. "I think you'll find things are a bit less formal here."

"I say we trust her." Brin looked to Moya. "My official opinion as Keeper."

Moya licked her lips, then glanced down at her pair of legs. "Good enough for me." She looked at Fenelyus. "And thanks for the help, by the way. So, what do we do?"

Fenelyus smiled. "We travel fast. Starting right now, we are in a race." She looked at the raging conflict below and then at Rain. "For once, I get to have some fun. At last, there might be a battle I'm able to win. Follow me."

CHAPTER THIRTEEN

Point of No Return

Artists can create things of great beauty. Suri often described becoming an Artist was like turning into a butterfly. So I have to wonder if Suri's greatest creation was herself.

— THE BOOK OF BRIN

"This isn't a good idea," Makareta told Imaly as they reached Vasek's door.

Imaly spotted the familiar look of distress on the girl's face. Makareta had been a wide-eyed, skittish rabbit when Imaly had first taken her in. Over the intervening six years, the young Miralyith had calmed; depression was followed by a melancholy acceptance that had replaced panic. Now, the rabbit was back—but she was no harmless bunny.

"I'll kill him if I have to."

"You'll do no such thing," Imaly replied, trying to keep her voice low and even. Despite her outward calm, the Curator was terrified and not merely because she was about to introduce an outlaw she'd been harboring to the chief enforcer of laws. This was the moment of truth. She was about to cross the line, and there would be no turning back. "Just keep your hood up. It's winter and cold, and no one will think that's unusual. You leave Vasek to me. Don't say a word or do anything. He's expecting us."

"Don't you mean you?"

192 • *Michael J. Sullivan*

"No, I mean us. I told him I'd be bringing a Miralyith."

"But not me specifically, right?"

"It'll be fine."

"Says you." Makareta began flexing her fingers, stretching them.

Imaly sighed. "Look, Mak, this whole thing is tenuous enough as it is. Now, are you going to cooperate, or should we just go back home? You agreed to come, but your attitude isn't making it easy."

Makareta said nothing, and Imaly took that as consent. She rapped lightly on the door to the Master of Secrets' little home. He opened up an instant later and waved them in.

He offered no greeting. Vasek was just as austere with his conversation as with his furnishings. "So, who is this?" he asked after closing the door behind them. "What's with all the mystery?"

Imaly had anticipated the question. This was the first of many life-threatening obstacles she would need to leap over before the day was done. Imaly had weighed her options, and insane as it sounded, she had decided to tell the truth. Lying to Vasek was too costly a gamble. If he wasn't on her side, then none of it would work.

"We are alone?" Imaly asked.

Vasek nodded. "Except for the Rhune in my bedchamber."

"Pull back the hood," Imaly instructed, and with obvious trepidation, Makareta complied.

A gasp, a stagger, a shout of alarm—Imaly wouldn't have been surprised by any of these reactions, but Vasek merely nodded.

"I wondered what had become of the would-be assassin." He studied Makareta intensely but addressed Imaly, "Has she been with you all this time?"

The Miralyith glared right back. "None of your business."

Vasek's eyes narrowed, his lips pulled tight.

"Mak!" Imaly snapped, then pulled off her winter cloak. The garment was making her sweat.

Yeah, sure, it's the cloak that's doing that.

"Makareta is right. How she came to be here is none of your concern. I told you I was bringing a Miralyith, and here she is. After we leave, you can forget you ever saw her."

Vasek continued to stare hard at Makareta. "I will do my best."

"Let's hope that's enough."

"Imaly," Vasek spoke to her in a slow, serious, decidedly ominous tone, "do you know how dangerous this is? If the Rhune really does possess the Art, then this might be the trap Nyphron planned all along: unleashing her in the heart of Estramnadon could destroy us all."

"Makareta is a Miralyith—and a powerful one at that. I'm certain she can handle any unforeseen consequences. Besides, I'm out of options. Destruction is the destination we're already heading to; which route we take is immaterial. If you have a better suggestion, let's hear it."

Vasek didn't, and he stepped aside.

Imaly turned to the girl. "Mak, are you ready?"

Makareta nodded, her eyes still on Vasek.

"All right, then. Let's do this, and may Ferrol protect us all."

Suri was dozing on Vasek's bed when the door opened. Two female Fhrey entered. Imaly came in first. The second one she didn't recognize.

"Suri, this is Makareta," Imaly said. "She is a Miralyith."

The two stared at each other.

"Try saying hello, Mak," Imaly urged.

"Hello," Makareta said stiffly.

"Hello," Suri replied. "Nice to meet you."

Makareta's eyes widened, and Imaly wiped a hand across her exasperated face. "Why are you so surprised? I told you she's a Miralyith—or at least the Rhune version. Suri was a student of Arion Cenzlyor, just like you. And we believe she can conjure dragons—something that remains beyond the ability of the fane himself. But you're shocked she has mastered the Fhrey language?"

"It's just . . ." Makareta looked at Imaly and frowned. "Sorry."

"Don't tell me, tell her. She's the one you insulted."

Suri had trouble reading this new Miralyith. She wasn't anything like Arion, Jerydd, Lothian, or Mawyndulë. She didn't sound mean or cruel, but she hadn't said much. Without the Art, Suri had little to judge by.

Makareta looked back at Suri. "I didn't mean . . ." She tilted her head toward Imaly. "She doesn't tell me anything, but expects me to know everything." The young Fhrey's expression shifted back to curiosity as her sight settled on the collar. "So, normally you can weave? You can touch the chords, but that is stopping you?"

Suri nodded.

Makareta studied the metal band, then glanced at Imaly. "There's a seal-weave on it. No way you could have cut through it. The spell is oddly complex though. It's only on the outside, like it's painted on."

"Orinfar markings are on the underside," Suri said.

"That explains it." Makareta nodded. Then a look of sympathy arose. "What's it like having that on?"

"Like being blind, deaf, and numb," Suri said. Then she added, "And it's hard to swallow."

"Can you get it off?" Imaly asked.

"Easily. Once I remove the weave, I can open the lock and the collar will separate."

"What about the Orinfar?" Imaly asked. "Is there a weave to get rid of them?"

Makareta shook her head. "No. The Orinfar both blocks and is impervious to the Art." She turned to Suri and pointed at the collar. "May I?"

Suri nodded.

Makareta came over and examined the collar. "Just bronze; the markings are probably etched. That also explains why it's on so snugly, to make tampering difficult. But once the collar is off and open, it won't be too hard to neutralize the Orinfar. We don't have to get rid of all of the symbols, just deface a few. Vasek likely has a chisel or something. It should only take a few minutes to make the necessary adjustments. Then I can put it back on and restore the seal, and no one will be able to tell the difference. Except . . ."

"Except what?" Imaly asked.

Makareta nodded and made a circular motion with her hand at Suri. "Right now—artistically speaking—there's a dead space where she is. A void created by the Orinfar. Once we negate the markings, that will disappear."

"That's not good," Imaly said. "No one can know that we—"

Makareta held up a hand. "With the right blocking weave, she can create the same kind of void. With it, Lothian, or any other Miralyith for that matter, won't be able to sense her Artistic abilities. I can teach her how, if Arion hasn't already."

Imaly took a breath that appeared part relief and part concern. "Suri, I meant what I said during our last conversation, every word of it. I'm going to take the same leap of faith that you have. I'm putting my life in your hands for the sake of peace. I'm going to trust you." She took a deep breath. "Mak is going to remove that collar. When she does, do you promise you won't harm me, Mak, or anyone else in Estramnadon?"

Suri considered this, then replied, "So long as you uphold your side of the bargain . . . yes."

"And you will tell Lothian the secret to making dragons?"

"I will, but only if you also promise to"—she hesitated. The tension on Imaly's face and the fact that she had avoided detailing their agreement suggested Makareta might not be in her confidence—"do your part before the fane is able to advance his army across the Nidwalden River. I won't allow my people to be attacked."

Even with the removal of the collar, the deal was still one-sided. Suri would have to give up her part of the trade first, putting her at a disadvantage. But Suri knew something that neither Imaly nor the fane did. Gilarabrywns had a limited range. She guessed the first few dragons would be created in the city. Even if they were made on the riverbank near the tower, none of those creations would be able to travel beyond the Harwood. The Dragon Camp wouldn't be within range, and any troops in the area could retreat to there. If Imaly failed to deliver what she had promised, Suri would have time to correct the situation. After all . . . she'd have the Art again.

CHAPTER FOURTEEN

Descent Into Darkness

In the raging bonfire that is Ferrol's realm, faith, love, and hope are three delicate snowflakes looking for a safe place to land, but no such refuge exists.

— THE BOOK OF BRIN

The tiny path they took was filled with switchbacks and lined with sudden drops. Jagged rocks, bony roots, tangles of branches, and dim light required vigilance. Much of the trip was illuminated indirectly by the distant but ample fires of the war in the valley. Tesh had never seen such a sight before. Standing on the wall above the gate of Alon Rhist, he'd witnessed the Battle of Grandford when more than a thousand elves and giants clashed with the combined Rhulyn and Gula armies. In the collective memory, that battle had grown in size and significance until he, too, remembered it as if every living thing had engaged in a contest of wills to determine the fate of the world. But the Battle of Grandford was a tussle among village children compared with what was happening in that valley.

From the trail, he couldn't see the war anymore because the trail—if the two-foot-wide ledge could be called such—wound back around crags and squeezed through niches along the face of a gargantuan stone cliff. Only the glow of the many fires bathing the rock proved the battle continued. This was a good thing. The sight of so many fiery plumes rising hundreds of feet, massive apparatuses of war, and a sky so filled with flying beasts that they could have been schools of fish could only serve to distract him. That battle was warfare on a scale impossible to imagine, absurd to believe even while being near it. Given the width of the trail and the length of the drop, it was best his view was blocked.

Fenelyus led them, strolling the treacherous path as if they walked along a beach around a tranquil lake. She often turned and answered questions while still walking—*backward*. Tesh kept a hand on the wall and shuffled rather than stepped. The whole process was difficult as he discovered the stone was exceedingly rough and pockmarked with holes. Touching the rock was not only unpleasant but painful.

For the first time, Brin and Rain were at the head of their march while he and Tressa lagged at the back. As in the Swamp of Ith, Tesh once more regretted letting Brin get so far ahead, but there was no fixing it, no way for him to catch up. He didn't dare pass Tressa, who was having her own struggles to put one foot in front of the other. When he could spare a glance, Tesh was surprised to see Brin walking with arms swinging at her sides. Rain appeared equally at ease, and Tesh let out a gasp when both of them went so far as to leap a gap in the trail.

Tesh couldn't understand his fear. He'd fought Sebek, hunted deadly Fhrey archers, and drowned himself in a pool of slime. He thought nothing could have been worse than that. Even so, this ledge terrified him.

How is this possible? I'm dead. What am I scared of?

For him, Phyre had turned out to be a place of confusion—nothing was as he had been led to believe. Great warriors were supposed to go to Alysin, a beautiful land of green fields. Instead, he had entered a dull, gray world where he'd seen the ghosts of his parents. After proudly telling them he'd avenged their death by waging a war against Nyphron's Galantians, he had expected his father's thanks. He hadn't gotten that, and Tesh was confused by his father's reply, "If I had one wish, it would have been that you had died with the rest of us that day. If that were the case, we'd still have you. Now, she will."

Tesh had asked whom his father meant, who *she* was, but his mother had begun crying just then and ran off along the white brick road. With tears in his eyes, and without another word, his father had followed her.

None of that makes sense, but at least I found Brin.

Learning from multiple people that she had traveled deeper into Rel along the white brick road, he'd set out and arrived at the gate to Nifrel in the aftermath of a calamity. An incredible stone fortress had been destroyed by an attack of some kind. Rubble spilled out of the entrance. Fearing Brin was inside, he'd cautiously entered. He'd found no one except Moya, whose leg had been trapped by a giant slab of marble. She'd explained that Tekchin was buried beneath the other stones, and the rest of them had escaped through the portal into Nifrel. Years of battle had hardened Tesh to the necessity of severing limbs. Seeing no other option, he'd drawn his sword. When his stroke freed her, Moya hadn't made a sound. Maybe she'd been in shock. But whatever the reason, Tesh had found the lack of a scream welcome since he didn't want to alert anyone to their presence. He'd scooped her up and carried her out of the ruined castle and through the portal. It was only after they'd reached the other side that the screaming had begun.

"You've got to be kidding," Tressa said, stopping when she reached the missing section of the path.

"It's not that *far,*" Gifford told her while looking back from the other side and putting an added emphasis on the last word as he continued to delight in his ability to pronounce the *rrr* sound properly.

Tressa got on her knees, then on her stomach to look over the edge. "There's no bottom. There's no culling bottom!"

"Don't look down," Roan offered. She, too, had stopped and peered over Gifford's shoulder, offering support.

"Are you crazy? You want me to jump with my eyes closed? How in Mari's name am I supposed to cross . . . to cross . . . I can't do this."

"Of course you can," Gifford said dismissively, even bewildered. He had a smile on his face as if he found Tressa's protests to be some sort of joke.

"No, she's right. That's insane," Tesh agreed. "There has to be another way."

"Thank you!" Tressa said.

Gifford glanced at Roan, shocked. "But . . . it's just a *tiny* gap. You can practically step across. Here . . ."

To Tesh's horror, Gifford hopped back. "See? And don't forget, I'm a cripple."

Pivoting in place, he hopped over again then turned around and beckoned them with his hands. "Now you."

Tressa and Tesh gaped at each other. If there had ever been any doubt to the legend that Gifford was a man of bewildering bravery, it was erased at that moment. He also was clearly a bit crazed. Tesh's stomach had crawled up into his throat at the mere anticipation. Tressa had backed into him, and he honestly wasn't sure which of them he felt trembling.

"It's easier than it looks," Roan said. Her tone was far more serious, more sympathetic, but obviously she was as crazy as her husband.

"Nothing to lose. Nothing to lose. Nothing to lose," Tressa recited, in a manner completely at odds with the sentiment. She continued to repeat the three words as she backed up on uncertain legs. Then she shifted to, "Malcolm give me strength."

She ran forward and jumped.

Tesh held his breath as she flew through the air and landed safely on the far side, where Gifford wrapped his arms around her. The woman shook and cried. Gifford looked at him. "C'mon, Tesh, you don't bat an eye when elves shoot arrows your way. What's a little hop across a crack in a stone?"

A crack? Is he serious?

Gifford wasn't brave—not in the least—the man was insane.

But Tressa jumped it. She's not very athletic, but she made it across. So why is this hard for me?

"What's wrong?" Moya called back from the front.

"Waiting on Tesh to jump the crevice," Gifford said.

"You mean that little gap?" Brin asked.

Little gap? Has everyone lost their minds?

Gifford once more did the impossible and stepped *around* Tressa who, now that she was turned loose, hugged the cliff wall.

Gifford reached out his arms. "I'll catch you, just like I did with Tressa."

Tesh shook his head. "If I come over, if I make the jump, I might knock you off."

Gifford smirked. "I'm pretty sure that's impossible."

"I weigh more than you. It's a real risk."

Gifford tried to suppress a laugh but failed. "I'll take that chance."

Tesh took a deep breath and felt the air shudder as it went in.

Why am I so scared? I've never been terrified of heights before.

He hadn't been afraid of anything to the degree he was now—not fighting Sebek or stepping into that miserable pool; even saying goodbye to Brin hadn't been this hard. Tesh tried to take a step forward but couldn't. His feet refused.

"Tesh?" Brin called. She came back, and also walked *around* the others. "What's wrong?"

"It's . . . it's too far. I don't think . . . I don't see how I can . . ."

She looked at the path, confusion filling her face. "Is that what's causing the holdup? It's just a crack."

Brin walked past Gifford. She stepped right to the very edge of the other side. The toes of her shoes dangled off the precipice. She stared at him with a worried expression, then she reached out. "Take my hand."

Her hand? She's a mile away!

Even if he could touch her, he wouldn't. "No, I'll just pull you down, too."

She looked at him as if *he* were the insane one. "You won't."

"I will." He looked down at the darkness below, at depths that he knew went on forever.

"Tesh? Do you trust me?" Her voice drew his sight to her face. "Do you?"

He wanted to and always had in the past, but he still remembered the revulsion in her eyes when she had told him, "You aren't freeing the world of a monster. You're taking its place." It had hurt a lot less at the time, but now the pain was back. The sting of that moment rekindled, not in his body but someplace deeper.

Brin's eyes grew intense. She had a way of doing that, of being a frivolous, lovesick woman one minute, then transforming into another person: a wiser, stronger one. Her face softened, kindness and understanding bleeding in. "Tesh, you died—you killed yourself to follow me." She glanced down at the yawning chasm that her toes dangled over. "Are you seriously going to stop now?"

He was shaking.

"Take my hand, Tesh. I promise it will be okay."

"You can't know that."

"Just trust me."

It took every ounce of will he had to lift his hand and to slide his feet closer to the edge. It was so far down and she such a long distance away. Then, as if by magic, he felt her hand take his and she pulled. He was off-balance, starting to fall, and cried out.

An instant later, he was in Brin's arms. She was holding him, those tiny hands clutching tight, making him feel safe.

"See?" she whispered. "That wasn't so bad, was it?"

She gave him a moment to catch his breath—breath that didn't exist but he felt he needed—then she pulled him forward with her. As she did, he dared a backward glance. He looked for the crevice but didn't see one. There was only a small gap in the stone of a wide, worn trail.

The rest of the trip down was easier. The ledge, luxurious in its width on the far side of the crevice, lacked obstacles. Tesh continued to follow just behind Brin, who frequently looked back to make sure he was still with her. Something had made crossing that gap seem impossible. Some sort of enchantment, he guessed, and he didn't need to look far for the source. Rain had called her the Dark Sorceress, and she was a Fhrey—an elf.

He hadn't trusted Fenelyus when Moya consented to her help, and neither had Tressa.

Is it a coincidence that the two of us who voted against following her are the ones who've had so much trouble?

Joining with Fenelyus had been a mistake. He knew it then, and he was even more convinced the longer they were together. With every step he took, he felt heavier, and just walking was becoming difficult.

More magic?

They reached the valley floor, arriving in a darkened corner. They were once again in a forest, this one of dead pines. Gray needles lingered on limbs, creating the illusion of a hazy mist between the trees. Tesh thought he'd once had a dream about a place like this; as most dreams were, it was a foggy patch in his memory. In this forest, some needles had fallen to the ground, creating a soft carpet and an eerie silence. They were outside the influence of the firelight. Tesh could still see, but he was unsure how. Dim as on a cloudy night, the faces with him were ghostly, the trees shadows, and the path lost. No moon or stars provided guidance.

Also the way of dreams, isn't it?

Now that they were free of the ledge, they all clustered behind Fenelyus, chasing after her like puppies hoping for treats. Tressa was the holdout, hanging out in the back of the line. Prior to the meeting in Gifford and Roan's tent, Tesh hadn't met Tressa. He'd only known *of* her. *Bitch, murderer,* and *traitor* were the words most often laid at her feet. He didn't know why. Hadn't much cared—he liked Tressa. They were both fighters. Even before their shared fear at the gap, he'd known they were a pair. Self-destructive perhaps, but they would both go down swinging.

"Can I ask a question about the crow?" Gifford asked the Fhrey. "You used the Art to get rid of Orin, but since dying, I've found no source to pull from, no way to reach the chords."

"You are an Artist?" Fenelyus asked.

"I wouldn't go that far, but I have done a few things, and I know that you need power, and there isn't any here."

"I didn't use the Art. It just looked like I did. You're new to Nifrel and don't yet understand how things work. I suspect you're confused about many aspects of the afterlife. For example, what is the difference between the realms of Phyre?" Fenelyus asked.

"Ah . . ." Gifford faltered.

"Rel is where most people go," Brin said. "Alysin is where heroes reside, and Nifrel is . . ." She stopped and looked at Fenelyus, embarrassed.

"Where the evil ones end up? It's okay, that's what all new arrivals think." Fenelyus pursed her lips and tilted her head. "And what you said is correct—in a manner of speaking—but you have to understand that good and evil are relative terms. No one is truly good and, likewise, neither are they evil. The truth of the matter is that Rel is for those who, in life, found contentment in little things—or would have if life had been kinder. Arion—while powerful—cared little for employing that strength. She needed nothing and could find contentment in silence. That is why she remains in Rel. Those who are here are the ones who are never satisfied, no matter how much they attain. That's why I love Arion so. She had aptitude and talent but none of the addictive need for more."

"So, Nifrel is for the greedy?" Gifford asked.

"Still too simple. Greed is but a symptom, like conceit and vanity. They are the result—fruit born of the same tree: the tree of ambition. People sent to Nifrel are the ones who thrive on challenge, on competition, on conflict. In life, we were leaders—bad *and* good—because we couldn't stop striving for greatness. It's part of who we are. So, here in Nifrel we have—I suppose you could say—an overabundance of determination to succeed. That translates to a sort of magic. The effect is similar to lucid dreaming."

"I don't know what that is," Gifford said.

"Have you ever realized you were dreaming while still in a dream? It's when you figure out that you are sleeping and everything you're experiencing is just in your mind."

Gifford shrugged. "I don't think so."

"Well, some people who do are able to take control. They can affect the events, do magic. But it's not real—not the Art—not lasting. It's merely a dream."

Gifford still looked confused.

"Think of it this way. If you are strong enough while in Phyre, you can alter the illusion we all share. That's because the world around us is subject to the will of others."

"So, does that mean we can perform magic here?" Brin asked.

"You already are. You're wearing some sort of drape with a brooch. You have long hair and are quite pretty. Some of you have weapons, but they, like your bodies and clothes, were left on the surface of Elan. All you have, all you appear to be is manifested by your will, your sense of self. But I know it's not easy thinking of that as magic. After all, you only see what you've always seen. What most of you have yet to comprehend is that your abilities go beyond your own appearances and what you carry. You perceive what I did to Orin as something mystical, but that woman over there"—she pointed at Roan—"said she created a fire."

Gifford glanced at his wife. "But that wasn't magic."

Fenelyus chuckled.

"What am I missing?"

"This isn't Elan," the Fhrey said. "Well, it is, but not the living part. Do you think those were real trees you walked through? Did you believe they are made of wood? What you see is a vision created by Ferrol. This is her creation. We exist inside her dream, if you will."

"More of a twisted nightmare, if you ask me," Moya said.

"She does have a peculiar decorating sensibility. But I can assure you that making a fire here is as impossible as doing so in someone else's dream."

"But . . ." Roan started. Her expression turned fearful, as if she were guilty of a crime. "I didn't mean to mess with her trees. I didn't even know they belonged to her. I just did what I always do."

Fenelyus nodded. "That's mostly how it works. That's how everything does. We could fly, I suppose, if we could believe strongly enough in that idea. Our wills are tied to our confidence. We can do what we know we can. You knew you could build a fire, and so you did. I am confident in my ability to alter the world because I did it so often when I was alive that it comes naturally. It's not the Art, not really, but the results are the same."

Fenelyus focused on Brin with a curious stare. "And you . . ." Fenelyus let out a little laugh that grated on Tesh. "I can hardly imagine what *you* could accomplish here. It's obvious you're not like the rest of us. Somehow you muscled your way in, which is odd since everyone else wants out."

Brin looked hurt, though Tesh didn't know why.

The land continued to slope downhill, and Tesh realized that they still hadn't reached the valley's floor, but they were close. He could see the fiery light of the false dawn once more.

"What you have to realize is that there are two parts to every person," the Fhrey explained. "The living body born of Elan, and the spirit that comes from Eton. The body needs Elan to exist, and she reclaims it after a time, freeing the spirit. Our bodiless souls are forced to dwell here, deep beneath Elan in Eton's prison. No light seeps in. No life is allowed. We are all that exist here, but we are not without power. We are, after all, children of Eton. Our will, our determination, our very force of personality and sense of self lend us strength."

They walked down a gully where it appeared as if rainwater had washed the hillside away. If Tesh could believe the Fhrey, none of it was real. The hillside and the valley were the manifestation of someone else's imagination, someone's nightmare. He studied the ground and rocks. It all looked real to him.

"What about Alysin?" Tesh asked. "Who goes there?"

"The best of both worlds, I suppose," Fenelyus said. "Those with great ability but no ambition. The ones who never sought fame, or glory, but when they saw others in need, they took action. You'd know them as heroes. I suspect Arion could go there if she wished."

"And the Sacred Grove? What do you have to do to get there?" Brin asked.

"The Grove isn't part of Phyre. It's in the world of the living, so you can't get there." Fenelyus fixed Brin with a look that caused the Keeper to shrink back. "Why do you ask?"

"I just—I ah . . ."

"Brin is our Keeper of Ways," Moya interjected. "She's curious about everything."

Fenelyus studied the two for a moment longer, and Tesh was too far away to tell if it was curiosity or suspicion on her face. "I've had but a glimpse of the Grove, but I can tell you it truly is sacred. It's the birthplace of all life, yet only two reside there: Alurya and her guardian, the only one who earned the right—the greatest of all heroes." She turned away from them, walking faster than before.

❧

Snow was falling by the time they left the forest and entered the open valley, what Fenelyus called the Plain of Kilcorth. It was a mean snow. Small, icy pellets the size of sand fell at an angle as if driven by wind, even though there was none. In that skyless place, Tesh didn't know where the snow came from. He suspected the others didn't have a clue, either.

Fenelyus kept looking up, perplexed.

"Is this not normal?" Moya asked as she marched through the gathering drifts of granulated white. She had her shoulders up, trying to protect the back of her neck.

Tesh was doing the same thing. He could feel it, the harsh prick of snow, the burning pain when a grain caught against his skin, but he wasn't cold. This wasn't really winter when the cold cut to his bones. This was merely cruel and bitter.

"I've never seen weather in Nifrel," Fenelyus said.

"The queen is making it, right?" Moya asked.

Fenelyus pulled her hood up and tucked in an errant lock of golden hair. "She's trying to slow us down. Needs time to get her forces into position. You arrived at a bad time—for her. You're quite lucky."

"Not luck," Tressa said, though Tesh didn't think anyone heard. Tressa walked just behind him. Stooped over, her mouth pulled into a frown, she seemed to be in considerable pain, and her voice was no more than a muttered breath, but Tesh didn't think she was speaking to any of them.

"Ferrol is scrambling to head us off," Fenelyus said. "We must be moving faster than she likes."

The great warring hordes should have been somewhere in front of them, but in the heavy snowfall, Tesh couldn't see them. He didn't hear much, either. Even the sounds of their own feet were dampened by the fresh blanket of snow that was building on the ground. The black slate they walked over was filled with cracks—fissures scarring the terrain. These jagged mouths opened into bottomless expanses. The little ones they hopped. The larger ones they went around or used a makeshift series of bridges. The Plain of Kilcorth was littered with haphazard crossings. Some were fine causeways that were wide enough for an army to traverse. Other spans were nothing more than an oblong stone that teetered when stepped on.

"If the queen controls everything," Moya asked, "why doesn't she just—I don't know—summon us to her tower, or trap us in stone—something like that?"

"She doesn't control everything," Fenelyus replied. "Yes, Ferrol is the strongest force in Nifrel, but no single being wields absolute power. Distance and opposing wills limit her. Down here, arrogance and greed are a reasonably reliable indicator of power, and in that arena, few can compete with King Mideon. When he was alive, that little bastard was the wealthiest, most powerful ruler in the world. He started a war between his people and mine because I wouldn't give him access to a tree whose fruit granted everlasting life. Didn't matter that such fruit didn't exist. He sacrificed hundreds of thousands of his own people in its pursuit. And he wasn't planning on sharing immortality. He just wanted it for himself. That kind of arrogance is powerful down here. Mideon has managed to wrench from Ferrol a sizable piece of land that has become his realm, but he's still no match for the queen. All of us combined might not be enough to subdue her. After all, Ferrol is an Aesira, one of the five and third born of Eton's teeth."

The snow made everything slippery, and Tesh felt heavier than ever. Just as on the climb down, he found he had more trouble than most of the others. To his amazement, Brin practically hopped and skipped. Gifford wasn't quite so nimble, but neither he nor Rain displayed any sign of effort. Roan walked slowly while holding on to Gifford's hand. Tressa had it the worst. For her, each step appeared to be a struggle.

They came to a cairn, and Fenelyus called a halt. Slapping the pile of stones, she brushed up a cloud of snow. "This is Eon Ver, which means things are about to get interesting."

"How so?" Tesh asked. He was bent over, trying to catch an imaginary breath.

Fenelyus grinned, and in that guarded face, he saw the flicker of eager glee that must have won her entrance to the dark realm. "Between here and the Gray Gate of Mideon's Castle is a choke point with three bridges. Ferrol is waiting until we step out. That's when she'll hit us."

"Can we go another way?" Moya asked.

"Nifrel is one great battlefield. Fighting is what we do, and it's been happening since the dawn of time in every way you can imagine. Common belief is that there are no new tactics, no strategies that haven't been tried. It's all been done over and over again. That's one of the great disappointments of this place. Everything has been refined to the point that there are only a few sensible maneuvers, only a handful of moves and ways to counter. Everyone knows them, which takes all the fun out of leading with your gut. There's no going around. This is the best crossing available to us, and the moment we step out there, we'll be set upon."

"And from your experience is it likely we'll reach Mideon's castle?" Tesh asked.

"No," Fenelyus said. "To be honest, we don't stand much of a chance. In this scenario, we should get close, but we'll still fall short."

"Way to encourage the troops," Moya told her. "For a minute, I was starting to get my hopes up."

Fenelyus smiled, but it wasn't a warm thing, not a happy expression. Her look was a mix of amusement and irritation, as if to say, *Cute. Now be quiet. Your elder is speaking.* Like all of them, snow had settled on Fenelyus, frosting the Fhrey and making her appear all the more mystical and impressive. If nothing else, this place was all about mood and image.

"We have two advantages, one being that I hate to lose." Fenelyus winked. That same eager glee shining out.

"But Ferrol is your *god*," Brin said, mystified. "How can you openly defy her?"

Fenelyus laughed. "I think you will find that in Nifrel we are all gods. At least we see ourselves that way. If we didn't, we wouldn't belong here." The Fhrey glanced at Brin in a way that bothered Tesh.

"What's the other advantage?" Moya asked.

Fenelyus looked up at the flurry of flakes and shrugged. "The snow."

"Huh?"

"It's never done this before."

Moya lifted her hands palms up and looked at the others "So?"

"Ferrol knows more than we do. She always has. Aesiras appear to share that particular trait. So I have to ask—as you already have—why the snow? If I know there's only a slim chance of reaching the Bulwark, Ferrol certainly should, too, yet she felt it necessary to send snow to slow us down. Why?" She eyed Moya as if she knew the answer. Then she glanced at the others. "Any of you have any special abilities I'm not seeing?"

Moya bobbed her head at Tesh. "He's pretty good with those swords."

"How good?"

Moya frowned, and in an embarrassed whisper, she said, "Maybe the best ever."

Fenelyus studied Tesh for a long moment then shook her head. "When he was alive, perhaps, but he's dead now."

"What's that mean?" Tesh asked.

"You can't fight. You're weighted."

"What are you talking about?"

"Everyone in here is burdened with something. I am, Mideon is, even Ferrol." She nodded toward Tressa. "Her load is crippling." She took a step toward the woman and offered a sympathetic frown. "You're carrying some serious issues, dear lady, and Ferrol isn't making it easy on you."

Tressa looked up with a strained face and nodded.

Fenelyus turned back to Tesh. "You've got a heavy burden, too. So much so that you'll be slow and unable to fight."

"I still don't understand," Brin said. "What causes the weight?"

"Guilt, regret, fear." She ticked these off on her fingers. "If you spend a life *doing* rather than *not doing,* you'll make mistakes along the way. Those errors don't die with the body. Just like love, they're rooted in the spirit, and so they go with you."

Pointing at Moya, Tesh declared, "She's good with that bow."

"The what?" Fenelyus asked. She turned her head and studied the stick with the string attached to it. "What? You're good at starting fires?"

Moya laughed.

"It throws little spears called arrows," Gifford explained. "They travel really fast and very far."

"Yeah, except . . ." Moya frowned. "I'm out of *little spears.*"

"Out?" Fenelyus looked puzzled as she eyed the bow. "What do you mean, *out?*"

Moya held up the shoulder bag. "Only six left."

The Fhrey narrowed her eyes further and shook her head. "So?"

Moya spread her hands apart in a show of exasperation. "Sooo . . . what do you want me to shoot at the enemy? My dazzling smile?"

"Create more."

"That would take days even if I had decent wood, which I don't. How do you expect me—"

"What *are* you talking about?" Fenelyus's voice rose in irritation. Then in a scolding tone she said, "Make what you need. You made the bow, now create more of the little spears. How hard is that?"

"For one thing, I didn't make this bow. People keep saying that, but Roan created it years ago out of the heartwood of Magda."

"No," Fenelyus countered. *"That* contraption is still up in Elan. This one is all you, dear."

"But I . . ." Moya huffed in frustration. "If I did, I certainly don't remember doing so. And if that's true, how am I supposed to make arrows?"

"Do you remember growing a new leg?" Fenelyus asked.

"I didn't—you did that."

"I did nothing of the sort. I merely cast my cloak and made it appear as if a bulge in the shape of a leg was beneath. Your sense of self did the rest. You spent the majority of your existence with two legs. You wanted to believe that I had the power to restore you, and that desire was so great that you accepted that I had done so, but it was you who imagined that you had a leg again."

Moya narrowed her eyes. "That's not possible."

"You're in Nifrel now. Few are the things we count impossible. When I drew back my cloak, you had two legs because you believed you did. Your faith is what made it real. Confidence, conviction, certainty, these are the tools and weapons of this place. You made that bow out of reflex, without thinking about it, the same way you conjured your body and clothes. All you need to do is see that container full of tiny spears, and it will be."

Moya looked at the bag and the bow thoughtfully.

"Do you have an idea what we'll be fighting?" Tesh asked. He hadn't liked how the Fhrey had spoken of his combat abilities, but he also couldn't deny that ever since entering Nifrel, he had felt strangely heavy. That sensation had doubled once they descended from the plain. Moya was a slim woman, and normally he could have carried her, might have even jogged while doing so to catch up. But he hadn't even tried. He hadn't drawn either of his swords since entering Nifrel, and now he wondered if he would be able to lift and swing them.

"Bankors," Fenelyus replied.

"Ah . . . okay," Tesh floundered. "What are they and how many will there be?"

"Probably a swarm." Fenelyus made a fleeting wave with her hand.

"A swarm? So, these are little things?" Gifford asked.

"Little? No, I wouldn't say that. Picture a bobcat with a twelve-foot wingspan, bigger fangs, and longer claws." The Fhrey noticed the unanimous looks of shock. "The claws and fangs aren't a problem—well, not really. They can be painful for certain and take you out of the fight if they ravage you, but the real danger is that they will pick you up then drop you into the Abyss."

"The what?" Moya asked.

Fenelyus pointed at one of the many crevices around them. She stomped her foot. "This isn't real. Most of it was put here by the queen. It's like the flooring in a house. You can break it, change it, and do whatever you want because it is only an idea. Beneath it, however, is a hole, a very deep one that forms the bottom of Phyre. We call it the Abyss, and once you fall, you don't come back—not ever."

"What's down there?" Brin asked.

The ex-fane shrugged, but the look on her face was grave. "No one knows. Rumor says that's where Eton imprisoned the Typhons, and it's where Trilos fell. But no one has any proof. Like I said, no one comes back." She allowed herself a long sigh. Straightening up, she pointed ahead. "I suppose there's no sense in granting Ferrol any more time."

The snow had neither let up nor grown heavier. The icy grains continued to hurtle down, slamming to the ground, where they bounced and built up. Drifts formed, which Tesh couldn't understand, since there was no wind. Then he noticed that they were forming in front of crevasses, hiding traps. Tesh didn't need any more fears of falling, and he realized Fenelyus was right. There was no way he could fight. He would be as helpless as Sebek had been when Tesh butchered the Galantian in his sickbed.

Fenelyus instructed, "Everyone stay close and be ready to run. And, Moya, don't shoot your spears until the blue light fades."

"What blue light?"

Fenelyus didn't answer. Instead, she took three steps forward and extended her arms.

A moment later, noise emanated from overhead. It started as a buzzing, became a beating, and finally a growl. Looking up, Tesh saw that the sky, which had never been bright, had darkened further.

"Oh, great Grand Mother!" Brin gasped.

"Mother of Tet!" Moya shouted.

A moving cloud—discernible only by the gaps, of which there were few—circled above them. Within that veil, there were so many flying beasts that they blocked the fall of snow.

Thousands.

A host of two-hundred-pound locusts with fangs dove. Locked in disbelief and horror, the party watched as the multitude descended. Tesh had expected feathered wings, but the bankors' consisted of thin leathery skin stretched over bone. Their faces weren't at all catlike. They looked more like bats with flattened noses and saber-sharp teeth. Most of all, Tesh was disturbed by the tiny red dots that were their eyes, which glowed ominously.

Down they poured.

Moya raised her bow, and Tesh saw that she had an arrow nocked, but she held it, waiting. Gifford drew his blade, and Tesh pulled out his swords that, just as he feared, felt heavier than ever before.

We can't survive this.

Darkness grew as the swarm continued to speed downward.

"Where are these lights?" Moya hissed in frustration and fear.

Brin and Roan thrust arms upward to fend off the impact. Tressa fell to her knees. Tesh aimed both sword points up.

Then with a grunt, Fenelyus spread her hands.

A sound like thunder rolled as the bankors impacted a dome of shimmering blue light. As they hit, the beasts burst into pebbles, dust, and stone. So many of the bankors hit the shield that the sound turned from a rapid drumroll to a horrific roar, a constant drone with no break.

Fenelyus shook, her arms wavering and jerking. Sweat glistened on her brow. Her teeth locked as she groaned. Gasping in false breaths, she pressed her lips so tightly that they went white, and her face turned red. "Get ready," she growled.

Brin pressed herself against Tesh. She was so close that she'd be in his way, but he didn't care. It felt good and lightened the weight.

What difference can it possibly make?

The downpour lessened to an intermittent staccato, then Fenelyus collapsed to her knees. The bankors that had pulled up or held back now swerved and came in. The ones already on the ground hopped awkwardly on two feet, their big wings hindering their movement. With a flutter like a tent flap in a high wind, they attacked. Clearly not their preferred method of assault, because they, too, were slow. Tesh stabbed and slashed, happy to discover that a single solid hit caused the creatures to burst into dirt clouds.

"There!" Brin shouted, pointing at a leaping beast.

He crossed swords, turning a bat-faced monster into rubble.

Tesh's pride was short-lived, as to his left Gifford cleaved through three at a time.

"By all the gods—Moya!" Brin gasped.

Thinking she was in trouble, Tesh gave a glance and witnessed a stunning sight. With the shimmering blue dome gone, Moya was shooting her bow. The famous archer was hitting her targets as always but with one incredible difference. She wasn't pulling arrows or nocking them. She merely plucked the string. Each time she did, a new arrow flew. Her speed, already famously quick, became impossible to believe. Moya panned from left to right feverishly strumming Audrey like a stringed instrument. Then as they watched, she began firing two and three arrows at once.

A pile of loose rubble, the residue of Fenelyus's dome and Moya's attack, built up around them. The storm of bankors faltered, slowed, then stopped. Those remaining on the ground flew away.

"We won?" Gifford asked, shocked but elated. He was grinning and hugging Roan with one arm as the other still held his blade triumphantly.

Fenelyus struggled to her feet, shook her head, and pointed at the sky. "Two swarms?" She shook her head.

Far above, another, identical set of bankors started their downward trek.

"There's no call for that, Ferrol!" the Fhrey shouted at the sky. "You're just making me angry, now. Mideon did that once; now there is a new mountain in Elan and a hundred thousand fewer Belgriclungreians!"

Fenelyus let forth a scream that made Tesh and everyone else flinch. In that instant, her whole body burst into a brilliant white light that was too bright to look at. Through squinting eyes, he saw Fenelyus was a white-hot fireball, and from her blazing form, lightning arced. Countless tiny threads stretched out as pulsating tentacles of blinding light. Where they touched bankors, the beasts' bodies were blown apart, making it rain. Their smoldering residue melted the snow around them.

Moya went back to shooting, dropping to one knee for better support, as she, too, sprayed the falling sky.

In less time than the first, the second wave was dispersed, and once more, snow fell.

Fenelyus was panting hard and looking as weary as Tressa. "Move!"

She led them through the snow, a haphazard, undisciplined group. Fenelyus, who was visibly weakened, walked slowly. Even so, Tesh continued to fall farther behind.

Worse than that, Tressa was hardly moving. She staggered as if she might fall.

"Gifford!" Roan shouted. "Help Tressa!"

What limitations the crippled man had had in life were reversed in Phyre. Tesh was seeing the real Gifford, the invisible man who had been trapped inside the impaired body. Tesh never would have imagined it, but knew he should have. The potter had been a phenomenal artist and a bona fide hero, managing all of it as a cripple, and as such, he had to have an abundance of willpower. With grace and strength, he caught hold of Tressa, lifted her gently, and carried her forward with ease.

This left Tesh at the back of their line, and with each step, he faltered.

Who is the cripple now?

Ghostly outlines the size of mountains became visible through the curtain of falling snow. Easily the biggest thing Tesh had ever seen, the citadel of King Mideon was a monster of a fortress with a multitude of overlapping towers the shape of overturned drinking steins and topped with shallow domes. Two massive pillars, which were still no more than hazy shadows, indicated a gate—a tall gray one. Between their party and the entrance lay a wide fissure, a zigzagging rift torn through the ground. Spanning the gap, the final bridge provided access to the castle.

Those in front were running hard, dodging and leaping cracks, getting close. The castle and its open gate gave Tesh hope that at least Brin would make it through. Tesh knew he wouldn't. Cursing his weakness and clenching his fists, he dug deep for strength. He'd found it before. In fights he was sure he'd lost, he pushed beyond his boundaries and realized new strength. He was reaching again, struggling to find that hidden granule of reserve.

Nothing.

"Tesh!" Brin stopped and called.

"Don't! Keep running. I'll make it," he lied.

She turned toward him.

"We had a deal, remember? You run!"

"But—"

A moment later, it didn't matter, as all of them were knocked off their feet. Fenelyus was hit the hardest and was blown into the air by the force of an explosion of snow and rock. Directly in front of her, a mammoth creature burst out of the ground. The size of Suri's dragon, it looked similar, except this thing was longer—more snake-like, if a snake were a hundred feet long. And while it had no legs, it did have arms. Horns and spikes ran the length of its back. It wailed a hideous screech that ripped at the world with a voice to match the torn landscape around them.

Everyone found their feet, except Fenelyus, who lay unmoving before the monster.

"What is that?" Gifford asked.

"A digger," Rain said, but not in reply. The little guy had said the words out of fascination.

"Fen?" Moya shouted at the Fhrey as she aimed her bow at the beast. Their guide lay unmoving on the snow.

The creature rose up the way a snake does before it strikes, but it didn't attack. Instead, it screeched again and again.

"What's it doing?" Gifford asked. He was still holding Tressa, his eyes shifting repeatedly toward the bridge. Perhaps he was wondering if he could make a run around the snake.

"Not doing anything," Moya replied. She kept her bow up but hadn't shot yet. "Just making an awful racket."

"How come?"

"That's why," Tesh shouted, pointing behind them.

The snow had stopped. The hazy curtain was gone. A deep rhythmic booming sounded as three converging armies marched across the vast plain. Men, Fhrey, Dherg, giants, goblins, and a handful of other things he had no names for marched in perfect rows perhaps a hundred wide. He didn't know how many deep. They carried spears and shields and wore helms with a variety of symbols and plumes. Standards hung lifeless from poles along with jangling bells. Huge drums mounted on massive beasts beat a relentless cadence.

"For the love of Elan!" Moya raised Audrey, took aim at the giant serpent blocking their way, and let a barrage of dark arrows fly. They followed one upon the other so quickly that she had loosed twenty before the first one landed. She aimed for the eyes and hit her target with six. Four punctured its snout. The thing brushed them away with a swipe of a hand and roared its screech again.

"Son of a Tetlin whore!" Moya cursed.

"Rain! Stop!" Gifford shouted as the dwarf ran forward toward the great worm.

He didn't halt. With the serpent screeching in front and the pounding of the drums from behind, Tesh didn't think he had heard.

The serpent's eyes focused on the dwarf with greedy interest. When only a few yards away, Rain finally stopped. He pulled out his pick, and Tesh thought the dwarf planned to fight. The great worm looked to be of similar mind as it tensed, but they were both wrong. Instead, Rain drove his pick into the stone of the shelf. He struck the ground several times. His swings were mind-bogglingly fast, and each stroke sent up a burst of broken stone and dust. Then he stopped. When he did, the serpent stopped screeching, the muscles that had stood out so prominently relaxed, and the great worm lowered its head, studying the dwarf.

Moya looked back and forth between the armies and the serpent, who miraculously wasn't eating Rain. She lowered her bow and ran to Fenelyus. Shaking her, she shouted, "Wake up! Wake up!"

The Fhrey's head lifted.

"We've got armies behind us and a giant snake-thing in front. Could really use that lightning again because my arrows aren't doing Tet."

Fenelyus shook her head weakly. "Bankors are figments, not souls." She pointed at the serpent in front of them. "That ariface is real, as are the soldiers behind us. They won't vanish any more than I just did."

Rain continued to stand within an arm's length of the giant worm, staring up at it.

In a blink, Brin appeared at Tesh's side, and he felt her take his hand. She was trembling. "I'm scared," she whispered.

"Aren't you the same girl that jumped into a pool of slime?"

Brin tried to smile, but it came out as an overwrought frown. "I was scared then, too."

Tesh took hold of her by the shoulders. "Listen, you made me a promise. You said you'd run, that you'd leave me if you had to, remember?"

"There's no place for me to go, Tesh."

He glanced back at Rain, who was inching closer to the snake.

Tesh pointed at the armies. They were close enough that he could see the eyes of those in the front rows. "We don't stand a chance against them, but there's a possibility that you might manage to run past that snake."

Brin was shaking her head. "But, Tesh—"

"Shut up and listen to me. I can't make it. You understand?" His voice was desperate, cracking under pressure. "You must have noticed how slow I am."

"Tesh—"

"I can't run at all, Brin. But you . . ."

"Tesh, I can't—"

"You *can* run, damn it! You've always been fast, but not like now . . . I've watched you. You've been holding back. Whatever is dragging me down is somehow speeding you up. You're not even tired, are you? I can see it in your eyes. I'm exhausted, can barely stay on my feet, but you look fresh as a newborn fawn. I don't think any of the rest of us are going to make it. Do you understand what that means? Brin, you have to take the key from Tressa and run for that bridge."

"But I—"

"Take it and run as fast as you can."

"But—"

"You run for that bridge, and you don't stop until you get through the gray gate on the far side."

"But, Tesh!"

"I want your promise!"

"Tesh!" Brin grabbed his face and turned it so that he could see the bridge. The snake was gone, leaving the route clear.

"Everyone!" Brin shouted. "Run for the bridge!" The high pitch of her voice carried, and Moya was the first to react. She pulled Fenelyus up. "Go! Go! Go!"

"With Elan as my witness and Eton as my judge . . ." Fenelyus muttered, stunned.

She wasn't the only one to see they still had a chance. Horns sounded, and with a thundering roar, thousands of soldiers gave up their orderly march and charged.

With Tressa still in his arms, Gifford sprinted forward with Roan at his side. Half dragging a groggy Fenelyus, Moya chased them. Brin pulled on Tesh, and he tried to run, but all he managed was a slow walk. His feet were heavy and as awkward as swinging buckets of water. There was no hope.

Tesh jerked his hand back. "You promised!"

"Tesh, we can do this."

"*You* can. I can't. My feet don't work anymore. Go!"

"But, Tesh!"

He could see the buckles on the belts of the charging line, hear the jingle of their gear. Some had spears, others javelins.

"Brin, you don't need me! Run!"

She didn't move. "You're wrong. I do!"

"No, you didn't come here for me. That's not why you died. Go save Suri. It's okay. I can't die, I already have."

The first javelin flew. He saw it fly at Brin's back. Tesh shoved her aside.

Pain burst across his chest. He didn't have a body, but it felt like it. His legs gave out and he fell to his knees.

Brin grabbed his arms. She pulled, trying to drag him.

"Go!" He coughed blood and pushed Brin away. "Pl—please. You prom—"

In terror and tears, Brin looked at him one last time; then finally, mercifully, she did as he asked.

She ran.

For a moment, Tesh was scared a second javelin might hit her, but as he watched, as he saw her run, his breath caught in his chest. Nothing could catch her. He was right; she'd been holding back. The girl was a bolt of light.

CHAPTER FIFTEEN

Dragon Secrets and Mouse Slippers

Poor indeed are the infallible, for facing failure teaches us how to prosper.

— THE BOOK OF BRIN

Suri's second meeting with the fane was not in the throne room. Instead, she was escorted under dual guards to a smaller chamber in the palace. A long table of polished wood dominated the space. She was instructed to sit in the chair at the far end. This delighted Suri as it was the seat nearest a tall window. She sat in the chair, but sideways so she could look out. She hadn't had much chance to see Erivan, and the view was beautiful. From her position several stories above Estramnadon, she could see across the plaza to the far hill that was crowned by a white, domed building. Trees dotted the landscape. Most of them had lost their foliage, and what remained was yellow and brown. Without the leaves, the sunlight was able to reach the ground. It glistened off homes, shops, and dew-slick streets.

Although she still wore the collar, the Orinfar markings had been negated. Suri was free and once again connected to the world of the Art. On the first try, she had mastered the blocking shield that Makareta had demonstrated and she had received a concerned look of astonishment from the young Miralyith. If the fane attempted to betray Suri again, she would surprise him as well.

Lothian entered quite a while later, yet it seemed far too soon for Suri. He walked in with the two bodyguards she had seen before, the big and the little. The fane moved to the chair at the opposite end of the long table, which seemed a bit absurd given there were many closer seats. While still in the process of sitting, he asked, "Are you prepared to tell me the secret of dragons?"

"Yes," Suri replied.

The Fhrey ruler shooed out his escorts and sat down. He waited until they were alone, then leaned to one side and propped an elbow on the chair's arm. He appeared calm, but his eyes were as bright as full moons. Thoughtfully, he rubbed his lower lip. The fane and the mystic watched each other in silence. The glass of the window let in light but not sound: no wind, no songs of birds, no murmuring voices. The eye of the world was on her, waiting to see what would happen.

Suri thought about Arion.

Is this what you expected? Is this the moment you saw?

"Before I tell you how to make dragons, I must ask that I be granted Ferrol's Protection in return." Suri expected the fane to explode, to demand that she not make requests, but he didn't.

Imaly had stressed that she must obtain this concession *before* telling him anything, and she also cautioned Suri to be specific about the term. This two-word demand was something the Curator had drilled into her, insisting it was *Ferrol's Protection* and not the *Protection of Ferrol,* as the latter was something completely different. Ferrol's Protection was the decree by their god that Fhrey cannot kill Fhrey; the other had to do with the horn and the choosing of a new leader.

The fane was quiet for a moment, and then he said, "I thought you only wanted peace?"

Suri frowned. "I was made to understand that's not going to happen."

"I see. And who told you to ask for Ferrol's Protection?"

Imaly hadn't specifically asked Suri not to reveal how she learned about the law, but given the situation, Suri felt it was best not to name names—at least not anyone the fane could take action against.

"Arion explained many things about your culture."

Lothian accepted this without question, almost as if he had expected the answer. "If I were to grant that, it would make you an honorary member of the Fhrey, but I should mention that Ferrol's Protection only prevents *other Fhrey* from killing you. The edict doesn't apply to me."

"I'm told that even you can't kill someone without cause."

"I can. I'm the fane; I can do what I want, but it's true that it wouldn't be prudent to kill anyone who enjoys Ferrol's Protection." Lothian shifted forward. "Very well, I will grant your request. However, there will be other restrictions placed upon you. First, you will never be allowed to leave Estramnadon. Second, you will be placed in the custody of someone who will be responsible for watching you at all times. And in case you dreamed of getting your powers back, you should know that the collar has been magically sealed, and as such, it can never be removed."

"Are you *sure* you want this secret? Because you're not making it very enticing."

"You will have your life, a good deal of freedom, and you'll be allowed to live out the rest of your days in our glorious city. Would you prefer death? Because I see that as the only other alternative for you. Do you still want Ferrol's Protection?"

"Yes." Suri nodded.

"All right then." Lothian extended a hand and waved at her. "I bestow upon you Ferrol's Protection and decree that no Fhrey will be allowed to kill you under the law, except—as previously explained—myself." He showed her an apathetic smirk. "It doesn't matter to me. After you give me what I want, I'll have no interest in you whatsoever. When this meeting is over, we'll never see each other again."

Suri wondered if she ought to ask for anything else, but she felt it wasn't wise to push. She'd gotten what Imaly had told her to ask for, and Suri didn't know enough to bargain for anything further.

"So, tell me. How can I conjure a dragon?"

Suri nodded and began, "Well, first off, it's not actually a dragon."

৵

After the meeting with the fane, Suri was returned to Vasek's custody, and he took her to where Imaly was waiting. From there, they escorted her to the Curator's home. The trip between the palace and the house through the free air had been rapid and utterly lost to Suri, who was covered up in a bulky cloak with a large hood—the same outerwear that Makareta had worn when she had visited Vasek's house. She saw almost nothing as they rushed her through the streets while carefully avoiding any potentially curious Fhrey. Within minutes, they were at the door to a small home with glass windows blinded by closed drapes.

Suri entered the little house and was pleasantly surprised. Nicer by far than Vasek's stark accommodations, this place was a home. The door had a carved relief in the shape of a tree. Support beams were similarly adorned. One showed a series of branches with animals hiding among the leaves. Another was made to appear as a series of fanciful smiling creatures standing on one another's heads. All were worn smooth by hands and time. Shelves were filled with curiosities: cups, plates, candles, statuettes. The furniture looked comfortable, and Suri had the sense she was entering a place where every corner held a story, each inch a tale.

"I know you don't want to hear this," Imaly told her, "but it really would be best if you stayed here and didn't go outside."

At such times as this, Suri wished she could growl the way Minna used to. Instead, she conveyed her message by grinding her teeth.

Imaly's hands went up, warding off the expected explosion. "I'm not saying you *can't,* only that it wouldn't be *wise.* And I don't mean forever. Things will change. They must. And soon."

Suri was about to reply and level a few rules of her own when movement toward the back of the house stopped her. She stiffened as another Fhrey emerged from a darkened room, then recognized Makareta. Free of her hood and cloak, she didn't look like other Miralyith. Her head was wrapped in a multicolored scarf. It tried but failed to hide little sandy tufts of hair that peeked out. She wore an old smock that was wrinkled and stained. Her hands were dirty, covered in what looked to be dried mud, and she had a smudge of the same substance on her nose. This was unusual for a Miralyith to be sure, but what interested Suri the most were Makareta's slippers. Adorned with embroidery, the portions that covered her toes were made to look like mouse faces complete with whiskers. Just seeing those slippers and before a single word was said, Suri decided she liked Makareta.

"Oh, there you are, Mak. Come on over. This goes for you as well. Let me start by saying that the two of you *must* peacefully coexist," Imaly explained with all the authority of a parent. "I will not tolerate any magical foolishness. Cross me, Mak, and out you'll go. And you . . ." She turned to Suri. "We have an agreement. I'll hold up my end of the bargain, and I expect no less from you."

Suri wasn't certain what sort of *magical foolishness* Imaly anticipated, or why she was concerned that Suri and Makareta wouldn't get along. Perhaps Imaly thought Artists were territorial like squirrels, badgers, or eagles. She thought it was odd that while Imaly lived in a forest, the old Fhrey appeared ignorant to its ways. Only males were territorial; females rarely engaged in aggressive behaviors.

Imaly's expression softened. "The three of us need to work collectively. As strange as it may seem, we're one odd little family now because we each share the same danger—and the same goal. If nothing else, that makes us related." She shook her head. "Two Miralyith, a Rhune and an outlaw—I do pick up the strays, don't I?"

Makareta continued to stare at Suri with a baffled expression.

Imaly waited a moment longer, looking from one to the other. Then taking a deep breath and letting her shoulders relax, she said, "I need a drink. Play nice and don't destroy the house."

Once Imaly had departed through one of the archways, Suri turned to Makareta. "What is an *out-law?*"

Makareta looked at the floor. "When someone breaks the rules, they are supposed to be punished. If you run away, you're putting yourself outside the rules, outside the law. That makes you an *outlaw*. Most of the time, an outlaw is considered a bad person."

"You don't seem bad," Suri said. Of all the Fhrey she'd encountered, aside from Arion, Makareta appeared the most normal. She was dirty and wore mouse faces on her feet. "What did you do wrong?"

Makareta still looked at the ground. "I—I killed another Fhrey."

"Just one?"

Makareta looked up, disturbed. "That's all it takes."

"What would happen if you were caught? What is the punishment?"

"I would be killed—slowly, painfully, publicly. And then . . . after that, I don't know." Makareta's face turned sour. Her nose wrinkled up, her mouth squeezing tight. She looked down again.

Suri did, too. "I like your slippers."

This broke Makareta's malaise. The Fhrey wiggled her toes and smiled. "Imaly thinks they're stupid. She's afraid I've lost my mind."

"I think they're nice."

Makareta smiled. Then looked at Suri's bare feet, followed by the rest of her. "Do you—is that how Rhune—are these your normal clothes?"

Suri shook her head. "I came here wearing a nice asica. They took it. This was a present from Vasek." Suri pulled on the simple tunic.

"Oh." Makareta frowned. "Doesn't really fit, does it? I would . . ." Makareta made a subtle movement with her hands that Suri understood to be the suggestion of a reclaim weave, something that if completed might alter her garment. "But . . ." Makareta glanced in the direction that Imaly had gone and whispered, "I'm not allowed to use the Art—*at all*. Taking off your collar was the first thing I've done in years. She's afraid there are Miralyith watching the house or something. Terrified that they will smell the residue and investigate." She shrugged. "It's not entirely impossible, but seems an extreme precaution."

Suri felt her then. The Miralyith's power was warm, strong, and vibrant. She also sensed frustration, and on top of all of that—glistening like morning dew—was a coating of sadness, mixed with equal parts of fear and regret.

Makareta grimaced at Suri's dress, then beckoned for her to follow. "I don't have much, either, but we can find something better than that. Maybe we can make you a pair of slippers, too. That way Imaly can think we're both crazy."

Makareta's room was small and cramped. A mat lay on the floor, and she rolled it up the moment they entered, stashing it behind a cluster of clay pots. There was a mattress against one wall, a wardrobe in the corner, and a little table where a bowl of water sat and a pile of clay glistened. There were also a dozen little wooden tools, some small and pointed, others broad and flat. What Suri had first seen as a pile of mud, she realized was a sculpture in progress. Only partially formed, two vague figures were emerging.

There were other sculptures in the room. Most were tiny things, but all of them were beautiful. She spotted a perfectly depicted heron and a stag. On a high shelf, a very delicate clay tree appeared to grow. Of the dozen figurines on the shelves, one that rested on the windowsill halted Suri. Sunlight bathed the perfect figure of a wolf.

As a child, I found the courage to sleep in sealed rols because my head lay on Minna. She was my sunlit window.

Suri felt her stomach tighten. Her teeth locked together.

"Are you all right?" Makareta asked.

"No," Suri replied.

The Fhrey waited, expecting more, but Suri didn't say anything else.

Makareta nodded. "I understand." The Fhrey looked at the sculpture in progress and wiped a rising tear from her eye. "Life is awful, isn't it? And it just keeps getting worse." Makareta threw herself onto the mattress. "Have you ever lost anyone you loved?"

"Yes," Suri said.

"Were you responsible for them leaving?"

"Yes . . . yes, I was."

Makareta looked up, revealing more tears building. A hand went to her chest. "Me, too. I feel hollow, empty."

Suri nodded and looked at the wolf on the windowsill. "Part of me is gone, destroyed forever. Maybe the best part."

Makareta stared at her, nodding, biting her lip. "Yes—exactly. My soul is missing, and I don't know what to do about that. Imaly wants me to keep busy." She gestured with irritation at the menagerie of clay animals. "But I have a hard time finding reasons to breathe, much less sculpt. I used to like it, but not anymore. It all feels so pointless now."

Suri sat beside her, and both looked at the window that revealed Imaly's private garden. "The face of a leaf is no place for a butterfly."

"How's that?"

"A caterpillar spends all its time crawling on leaves and eating, but such things no longer satisfy butterflies. The mistake, I think, is to focus on what was lost rather than what has been gained."

"Nothing has been gained."

"Loss always provides something—losing twenty legs to gain two wings—the past for the future."

"What if the future holds nothing? What if there is no future?"

Suri looked at Makareta and smiled. "Then it's up to us to make one."

Makareta thought a moment, then nodded. "I like you, Suri."

"I like you, too, but I knew that the moment I saw the slippers."

Makareta looked down, then jumped up. "Clothes. Almost forgot." She moved to a wooden wardrobe. Opening the doors, she revealed an assortment of garments, all made of the same shimmering material as those Arion had worn.

"Which one do you like?" Makareta asked.

Suri approached the wardrobe. She reached out and touched the blue one. She'd never seen material that color before, and this asica rippled like water.

Makareta grinned. "Good choice."

She pulled it free and slipped it over Suri's head. The garment was too large. Makareta had to wrap the belt, rather than cinch it. But the bigger problem was the length. Makareta went over to the table and shuffled

230 • *Michael J. Sullivan*

through some small containers. She bent down and started pinning the fabric.

"We'll have to cut and sew the hem, and then it will be the perfect length."

While Makareta was on her knees, Suri studied the unfinished sculpture. "What is it?" She pointed to the clay.

Makareta pulled a few pins from her mouth and said, "Nothing at the moment."

"Looks like it could be two people holding one another." Suri could almost see it. A male and female intertwined in each other's arms.

"It's a dream, a fantasy that can never happen. I don't care so much about everyone else, but . . ." She wiped her eyes with the heel of her hand. "I wish I could explain to him. You know? Tell him why I did it. Maybe then . . ." She sighed in defeat. "He thinks I'm dead, and I can never let him know otherwise. I can never ask forgiveness."

"I'm not so sure of that," Imaly said. She was standing in the doorway, arms folded. Her eyes focused on the sculpture, and she nodded. "Maybe you *should* explain things. Yes, I think that's an excellent idea." Then, catching a glimpse of Suri, she frowned. "For Ferrol's sake, is that *my* good asica?"

CHAPTER SIXTEEN

In the Hall of the Dwarven King

I did not know much about dwarfs: their society, traditions, or culture. There is a reason for that. His name is Gronbach. Mideon did nothing to change my opinion of what the Fhrey referred to as vile moles.

— THE BOOK OF BRIN

Running faster than she ever had, Brin could hardly see. Everything was a blur, and not just because of her tears. She was going faster than was possible, at least with legs. The serpent was gone, and the route to the bridge was clear. Everyone else was already crossing the stone span— everyone except Tesh.

Brin shot across the remaining distance. The closer she got to the castle, the higher the walls revealed themselves to be. This place wasn't bound by the limitations of the living world. That stark reality announced itself while the roar of the army behind her was blotted out by explosions from in front. Out of dark recesses all along the fortress, deafening bursts emanated. Sparks erupted one by one in perfect synchronization from left to right as balls of fire shot out of holes in a bone-rattling succession of explosions. The flaming projectiles streaked overhead, trailing lines of smoke. When the sequence finished, the bombardment started all over again. This stunning series of rapid explosions wasn't the most astounding thing Brin had witnessed, for in her last few strides, she could have sworn that a part of the impossibly high wall got up and moved.

Brin entered the slender gray gate that emitted a sliver of warm yellow light into which the others had already disappeared. Gifford, Tressa, and Roan lay in the courtyard, collapsed from exhaustion or fear, probably both. Fenelyus was nowhere to be seen as men, women, Fhrey, Belgriclungreians, and Grenmorians rushed past. Most headed up steps to stone parapets to peer out narrow windows at the war raging outside. Brin didn't care about the battle. She stood just inside the gate, taking deep, unnecessary breaths that nonetheless felt crucial, as if the in-and-out movement of her chest was keeping her anchored. Everything was a blur of sight and a drone of sound. The only thing Brin could think about was the sight of a javelin punching through Tesh's body. Over and over she saw that with perfect clarity, right down to the teardrops of blood sprayed on his chin.

"Where's Tesh?" Moya asked, rushing to her.

The Keeper didn't answer. She couldn't.

"Brin?" Moya took her hands, her tone slipping into dread as the gate closed.

Brin didn't even try to speak. She shook her head, and the look on her face seemed to be enough for Moya. She felt a hand squeeze hers.

Finally, the words burst out in a gush, joined by a flood of tears. "He stepped in front of a javelin. That's the second time he's died for me."

Moya grabbed her in a hug just as Brin felt the strength of her legs give way. Moya's arms tightened, holding her up—keeping them both vertical. "He can't die again; he's already dead. Remember that. It's not over for him . . . or Tekchin."

"Tressa, are you all right?" Gifford asked. After he set her down, she hadn't moved.

Overhead, the uninterrupted pounding continued, hammering in rapid succession and only slightly muffled. Gifford and Roan were at Tressa's side. He had hold of one hand and she the other.

Tressa brought her head up and nodded. "Better now. Less weight. Felt like I was being crushed out there. Kept getting worse, like the air was filling up, getting heavier." She let go of them and slid her palms across the ground around her. "Look at that, grass."

"Stars, too," Roan said, pointing up.

Everyone tilted their heads to see the sky that normally held little interest, but in that place, its existence was a marvel.

"Not real," Tressa said, still exploring the grass with her fingers. "Feels good, though."

A dwarf approached. Although clearly an adult, he was the smallest Belgriclungreian whom Gifford had ever seen. A dwarf's dwarf, no bigger than a five-year-old, he had awkwardly short arms and stubby legs, but his head was oversized, so much so that it looked certain to topple him over. He'd emerged out of the maelstrom of activity that whirled around them.

He spotted Rain, who was dusting off his clothes. Gifford wasn't sure what had become of the great worm that Fenelyus had called an ariface. He only knew that Rain had started digging and the beast had done likewise. The two had disappeared for a time. Then Rain had entered the gate just behind Brin, looking as if he'd been plowing a dusty field.

The dwarf's dwarf addressed Rain directly, "What are your names so that I may properly introduce you to His Majesty?"

"Ah . . ." Rain looked to Moya.

"Go ahead," she told him. "You're the one with the clout here."

Rain presented each of them, and in return, the little dwarf introduced himself. Gifford didn't catch all of it—something long and complicated, making him wonder at the Belgriclungreian's propensity for creating words that were a great deal longer than necessary.

"His Majesty King Mideon wishes to see you immediately."

"Fine," Rain said.

"Excellent," the dwarf's dwarf responded and beckoned for them to follow.

"You all right?" Moya asked Brin.

234 • *Michael J. Sullivan*

"No," the Keeper replied, her voice straining to get the word out. "But I can walk. I wasn't the one hit by the javelin—just feels that way."

Moya nodded—not a casual or indifferent tilt, but a knowing bob. She had hold of Brin's hand, and she appeared determined not to let go.

Only then did Gifford realize Tesh wasn't among them.

As they left the courtyard, Brin looked back at the gate, perhaps hoping to see him there. Gifford did, too. He tried to imagine Tesh limping through the big doors, miraculously following them the way he had at the entryway to Nifrel. But the doors remained shut. No one was there.

The castle of King Mideon was a cavern, wondrous and massive, but a cave nonetheless. Scale dominated the experience. Passing through doors, chambers, and halls, Gifford couldn't understand the need for ceilings so high that lantern light couldn't reveal them, nor rooms so vast that massive doors on the far side appeared to be elaborate mouse holes. They walked on and on, seemingly without end, crossing polished floors, climbing steps, and passing through corridors lined with statues of ironically giant dwarfs. Before long, Gifford was hopelessly lost.

When they finally stopped, it was in a dimly lit anteroom. The dwarf's dwarf indicated they should wait, then he slipped through another impossibly huge pair of stone doors. He failed to close them completely, and a long slant of light escaped, cutting a brilliant shaft across the dark of the anteroom.

"What did you do to that big snake?" Roan whispered to Rain as they waited.

"Nothing," the dwarf replied. "We're both diggers."

"What's that mean?" Tressa asked. "You two in some sort of club?" Her recovery seemed to be complete. The woman was back to her old feisty self.

Rain nodded. "Something like that. Really rare to meet another digger—a real one, not merely one who digs. Doesn't matter who, or even what they are, there's a familiarity, a brotherhood if you will. Hard to explain. I suppose it would be like meeting another bird if you could fly.

I would think there's a shared language of flight the way there is for those who dig."

"I suppose it's like the story about Rhen and the Lion," Gifford said. "In his travels before building the dahl, Chieftain Rhen once granted a lion a hero's funeral because he respected how bravely it fought. Isn't that right, Brin?"

She didn't answer. She and Moya remained together, still clutching hands.

"So, what? You're like brothers with this thing now, Rain?" Tressa asked, but before he could answer, the big double doors opened.

The sight was overwhelming. The hall of the dwarven king was revealed in all its sumptuous splendor. From its impossibly high ceiling of gilded adornments and brooding statues of enormous size, to the cornucopia of precious metals and various gems that decorated nearly every surface, the room proclaimed that Mideon didn't shy away from opulence. His favorite color seemed to be gold, his favorite texture, shiny. The king was also fond of fire. Scattered throughout the hall, burning pools of flammable liquids threw up plumes of flame, making all of the surfaces dance with light.

Mideon sat on a raised throne made in the design of a sunburst. The chair was so enormous that Gifford had trouble finding the monarch on it. He actually saw the ax first. Mideon held the handle of the largest weapon the potter had ever seen. The double-bladed head rested on the floor. Gifford was fairly certain that no man, Fhrey, or Belgriclungreian could possibly budge it.

Mideon himself was huge—a good twelve feet high.

This is a Belgriclungreian?

Gifford was puzzled for a moment, then he realized that Mideon likely saw himself differently in death than he had been in life. In the king's own mind, he was a giant. His braided beard was three times as long as he was tall. He wore a shirt woven out of—what else—shiny gold. And on his back, a mantle was draped. It moved of its own accord, a massive red cloak trimmed in fur.

He wasn't alone. Gifford spotted Fenelyus and many others sitting on shimmering bleachers. Next to Arion's tutor was a person who stood out from the rest, a beautiful Belgriclungreian with long white hair. As they entered, she watched them with an eager smile.

"Welcome to the Hall of Mideon." The dwarf's dwarf said with a deep bow.

"Thanks," Moya told him, and she led their procession of clacking feet across the polished floor. They stood in a single row before the throne. Behind them, fires crackled, and the light lent everything an ominous atmosphere. "Hello."

"Hello?" the king said and laughed. *"Hello!* Did you hear her?"

The room was filled with politely suppressed chuckles. The dwarf's dwarf cringed with sympathetic embarrassment.

His head still bobbing from laughter, the king said, "Not the sort given to courtly extravagance, are you?"

"Doubt it," Moya replied. "Even if I knew what that was."

"Ha-ha!" The king exploded in laughter again. He slapped his thigh as if Moya were grand entertainment.

She didn't laugh, nor did she look amused. Gifford had grown to know that expression. Like a pot set on a flame, she was starting to steam.

"Most people who stand before this throne kneel and address me as *Exalted One!*" the king admonished her. "Or, they say, 'Hail and well met, Your Grand and Wondrous Royal Majesty.' You might do well to reconsider your approach, little girl."

"Uh-huh." Moya nodded. She set a hand on a shifted hip and delivered her reply with an irreverent smirk. "You know, if you're so fond of getting your ass kissed, maybe you shouldn't sit in such a high chair."

The room went silent. No one laughed, and a few sucked in air.

King Mideon glared at Moya, his bushy brows tilting down, shadowing his eyes. A thick lower lip rose in a judgmental frown. He leaned forward on the handle of his great ax to study them better, and then he took a moment to scratch his bearded chin. "Hmmm," he mused. He shot a glance at the white-haired female. "Maybe you're right."

"I always am," she replied, hotly.

The king continued to stare, his gaze shifting from one to the next. "And you're sure these are the ones, Fen?"

"They were in the forest heights not far from the Rel Gate. Right where Beatrice predicted."

The white-haired Belgriclungreian lady slipped off her perch. She was not gigantic, but she made an impression nonetheless. Her eyes were so deep and bright that they glowed like moonlight reflecting off a still pond. Her hair was just as luminous. Not white with age, but her locks were silken and the color of stars. She circled around, walking directly to Rain. Standing before him, she put both hands over her mouth and looked to be on the verge of tears.

"This is him then, Beatrice?" the king asked.

"Yes," she said with an overabundance of admiration. "This is the Great Rain."

"I'm not great," Rain said, barely audible in the vast hall.

"Don't argue with my daughter, lad," Mideon told him. "Beatrice has the gift. If she tells you something, listen to her. Believe her. I wish I had done that when she told me not to war with the Fhrey." Mideon glanced toward Fenelyus. "What a waste of time and effort that was."

"Speaking of wasting time," Moya said. "Is no one concerned about the attack outside? In case you didn't notice, there's a rather big army trying to get in."

"You're a feisty one, aren't you?" Mideon licked his lips. "I like that."

"Beatrice," Fenelyus said, "shouldn't you explain?"

"What do you mean?" she asked, distracted. Her eyes were still locked on Rain.

"Why did we have to run such a heavy-handed gauntlet? What would make the queen upend her entire realm to hunt this group? Why is a siege army outside your father's walls? There's something important going on." Fenelyus pointed at Brin. "Look at that one. She stands out like blood on snow."

"Beatrice?" The king looked to his white-haired daughter.

"What?" she replied innocently, never taking her eyes off Rain.

"Don't give me.*that!* You know everything."

"Not always."

"You know about *this*. You've spoken about this day for so long that I can't recall a time when you didn't."

"You never cared before." Beatrice spoke with a petulant disregard as she continued to fawn over Rain.

"Before now, it was just a story. But the time has arrived, and your ramblings have come to pass. You know what's going on—tell us!" He slapped the arm of his grand chair and the sound echoed.

"Yes," she told him. "I know."

Gifford considered the little white-haired beauty. She was slight, elegant, radiant, and entirely taken with Rain, whom she stared at as if he were a window through which she could see for miles.

What does she know?

"Well?" the king pressed.

"Well, what?"

"Tell us!"

Beatrice huffed and finally turned to face her father. "No, I'm not going to." She looked up at the rest of those assembled in the hall. "I won't tell any of you what's going on, except to say that Fenelyus, as usual, is correct." She took a moment to present a complimentary nod to the Fhrey. "Something *is* going on . . . something most important."

"*How* important?" Fenelyus asked.

Beatrice paused. She clasped the palms of her hands together, then said, "I could say everything depends on the group you see before you—the future of Elan, all of our souls, and even the outcome of the Golrok. And if I did say that, you wouldn't believe me. You'd think I was overstating the matter. But honestly, that wouldn't be the half of it. You're going to have to trust me because I'll say no more, other than to insist that these people are given safe passage."

Gifford heard every word Beatrice said, and—individually—he understood most of them, but taken together they made no sense. Then he figured it out.

She doesn't know anything. She's making it all up. But why?

"Passage to where?" Mideon asked.

"Alysin," his daughter replied.

The room erupted in laughter. All those gathered on the benches guffawed or snickered, but Fenelyus, Beatrice, and the king were not among them.

Neither was Gifford. With that one word, he was forced to reconsider his assessment. *She knows at least that much.*

"The door to paradise is locked to all except to the greatest of heroes," said a bald, muscular man who sat with his feet up on an overturned barrel. "And these don't look up to the task."

"I'm not asking you to unlock it for them," Beatrice said. "I'm only requesting that you help them reach it. Ferrol will do everything she can to prevent them from crossing the bridge and reaching the gate. We must ensure she doesn't succeed."

The bald man shook his head. "Fools are always certain they are left in the wrong realm. *Oh, no! I'm supposed to be in the warriors' paradise,* they say, not realizing they already are. If none of us can pass, then there is no way *they* can."

"May I ask your name?" Moya inquired, and she did so far more politely than Gifford would have expected. But then she added, "I like to know who's insulting me, in case it comes up later."

The bald man's brows rose up in shock. "You don't know me?"

"Should I?"

"The name's Atella."

Gifford saw Brin falter and take an unconscious step backward.

Moya saw it, too, and whispered out of the side of her mouth. "Brin? Talk to me."

This time, the Keeper spoke. "Atella is a myth, or was thought to be. A hero from an age long ago. The greatest of all warriors, he couldn't be killed or even defeated on the field of battle—except by the one he loved most."

Moya narrowed her eyes. "Your lover killed you?"

"Was an accident. She didn't mean it. I fell to the ground, and in the confusion, she trampled me."

"How does one die from being stepped on?"

"Her name was Yolan Og, a beautiful elephant," Atella said.

"What's an elephant?" Moya asked.

"I have no idea," Brin replied. "I mean, the old stories described it as a giant beast, but the description made no sense—long nose, short tail, wrinkly skin, and huge ears."

"She sounds lovely," Moya added.

"Now who's throwing insults? And for the record, I didn't. If I want to offend you, believe me, there will be no question. I'm not a subtle man. What I said was a fact. There is no sense in fighting our way to the door because no one can open it."

Beatrice stepped back. Sweeping her arms, she gestured at all of them. *"They* can."

"How?" Mideon asked, leaning farther forward. He looked each of them over. "You're not saying these are heroes, are you?"

"I'm not *saying* anything." Beatrice turned around and smiled mischievously at her father. "Like I said, you're just going to have to trust me."

Mideon raised and slammed the head of his great ax against the floor, shaking the room. "You can't tell your own father?"

"Truthfully? Next to Ferrol, you're the *last* person I would tell."

The king straightened up. "You cut me, daughter."

Beatrice slammed hands on both hips and glared. "You killed hundreds of thousands of our people and destroyed Neith for a fruit salad!"

Mideon looked angry. "Why are you—you've never acted like this before."

"All the more reason to listen then, isn't it? Didn't you just tell Rain that you wished you had? So heed your own counsel, Father. And as for all of you"—she whirled around to the figures on the shimmering bleachers, spraying a fan of that amazing hair, her eyes brighter than before and her voice ominous—"you need to do whatever you can to ensure that these six make it to Alysin, and the sooner the better. Believe this of me if you've ever accepted anything in life or death. I do not speak of matters that I do not know. I'm saying this on behalf of Alurya, of Elan, and Eton, and the Chaos that bore them. Heed me, all! Help these heroes before you suffer the consequences. Consequences that I assure you will be dire."

The king continued to glare at his daughter, who glared back in equal measure.

Fenelyus broke the contest. "She was right about Rain being on the ridge." She looked at the lady dwarf. "I guess I owe you a favor, Beatrice. Let's hope it's a sensible one."

The white-haired dwarf smiled. "You will consider it little more than a trifle."

Fenelyus focused on the king. "Whatever is going on, Mideon, Ferrol is committed. When was the last time she attacked you at home? There is a siege army outside your walls. She'll bring everything she has to bear, and she won't stop. Your walls are strong, but she'll break them. That much is evident." She raised a finger, and in the silence, they could all hear the faint booms of Mideon's defenses still firing. "If these six remain within your walls, the queen will destroy the Bulwark. Your grand fortress will be rubble under her feet. This group is not worth the cost of holding onto."

"But why does Ferrol care so much?" the king asked. "What's so special about these people?"

"They are going to change the world," Beatrice said. "What once was broken can finally be made whole."

Okay, this part is certainly made up, Gifford marveled at Beatrice. *I could never pull off such a charade, especially in front of so many. What lies this person weaves! They won't believe her. They can't. No one could possibly mistake us for heroes. Moya, maybe, but—*

"Will the future be better?" Fenelyus asked.

"Yes, I'm sure of it." Beatrice took a step toward the throne and spoke to the king. "I'm your daughter. I have only ever acted in your best interest. You can trust me. You know that I can see the future. How many times have I proven it? How many times have you ignored me and suffered? After the war with the Fhrey, you cried into my robes. You begged for forgiveness and said, 'Never again.' Well, here we are, Father. Here we are once more. If you won't listen to me, listen to yourself. Or have you descended so low that you can't even do that?"

The hall was silent as Mideon brooded. He made an arched bridge with the fingers of both hands and rested his chin on them, watching the fires. Then he looked around and finally turned to Fenelyus. "It is a nice castle, isn't it?"

The onetime fane nodded with a pleasant smile. "The strongest in Nifrel. Be a shame if it fell."

"I was thinking that very same thing."

"I don't give a bankor's buttocks about the Bulwark," Atella shouted and stood up. Then he smiled. "But cutting a path through the queen's army to Paradise's Door would be a joyous fight."

"Certainly would have the benefit of being different," an unnamed man said. He wore what Gifford could have sworn was a Rhen-patterned cloth. "The queen won't expect an attack, and her forces are already committed. We could cut a hole, find a weak spot, and push . . ."

"You going to help?" Mideon asked Fenelyus.

The Fhrey's eyes twinkled as she fought back a smile. "I suppose I could have my arm twisted."

"If everyone is united"—Mideon nodded—"it might work."

Beatrice threw her hands up. "It *will* work. Honestly, old man! It's like we've never met before."

CHAPTER SEVENTEEN

The Drink

Everyone speculated on Persephone's marriage to Nyphron. From the outside, it appeared hard, cold, and difficult to swallow, but so is an oyster, and in some of them pearls are found.

— THE BOOK OF BRIN

"Is she in there?" The sound of Nyphron's voice entered through the thin canvas walls of the tent.

Persephone had just put Nolyn down for the night, tucking him into the little cot that had been made by Frost and Flood. Persephone had thanked them for the beautifully crafted bed, which the two had humbly excused as nothing more than an act of boredom.

The tent flap drew back, revealing the flaming brazier just outside. Nyphron entered, wearing a thick cloak over his armor, the helmet tucked in the crook of his arm along with a bottle.

"There you are," he said, smiling at her.

"Shhh!" She placed a finger to her lips. "I just got Nolyn to sleep." She cast a glance behind her at the cot, then taking Nyphron's hand, she led him back outside.

Habet was the only one there. Down on his knees, he attended the fire with intense care. Now that the weather had grown cold, his task was no longer trivial. The air was crisp, the fire warm, and overhead the stars shone brightly.

"Where are the guards?" Nyphron asked. "There should be one on either side of this entrance."

"I don't need any. When the weather was warm, I put up with them for your sake, but I won't ask men to stand for hours in the cold when the nearest threat is miles away." Persephone sat beside Habet on one of the big cushions. There were several around the pit because the fire had often been a meeting place. "So, to what do I owe the honor of your visit?"

Nyphron appeared surprised by the question. "Does a husband need a reason to see his wife?"

"Apparently. You rarely do so."

"I've been busy," he said while taking a seat beside her.

"Really? I envy you. I wish I had something worthwhile to spend my hours on."

"I would think the boy would be running you ragged."

Persephone shook her head. "Justine sees to most of his needs, and he's getting older now. He doesn't need me as much. No one seems to." She gave him a lingering look, but subtle hints were lost on her husband, who had never been a perceptive person.

She let it go. Persephone had long since accepted their arrangement. She wasn't a blushing bride longing for a husband who cherished her. Those days were long behind her. She had spent the spring and summer of her life with Reglan, had a momentary autumn revival with Raithe, but now winter had come. She knew exactly what to expect from Nyphron— less a marriage and more a trade agreement.

"What's with the bottle?" She pointed.

Nyphron looked to it as if shocked to find it in his arms. "Oh, right." He placed the tall, dark container on the ground before them. The firelight made it sparkle and glow with a golden hue, as if filled with honey. "This is erivitie, a liquor made from a special blend of berries picked within a secret grove deep inside the Erivan forests. They are harvested at midnight and only during a full moon on Summersrule. That's when the fruit is at its ripest. It's highly sought after in Estramnadon and utterly impossible to obtain on this side of the Nidwalden."

"And yet you have a whole bottle?"

"Half, actually. I've had this for several years. I was hoping you'd share a bit with me."

Persephone's eyes widened, and she gave a glance to Habet, expecting he would recognize the oddity of her husband's statement. The keeper of the flame only smiled as he always did. "You know, I'm not much of a drinker. The quality of that liquor would be wasted on me."

"Special occasion," he said.

"Really? What is it?"

"It's your birthday."

"No, it's not."

Nyphron appeared taken aback by this denial, and he, too, looked toward Habet for support, receiving the same pleasant but unhelpful smile. He thought again. "Our anniversary then."

"No, not that, either."

"Really? Hmm. Then it's *my* birthday."

She stared at him dubiously until Nyphron shrugged. "Could be, I honestly have no idea. I'm actually stunned you remember yours. Talk about an insignificant event."

"Excuse me?" Persephone straightened up in protest, and she shot another look at Habet, this one soaked with indignation. The fire tender was busy poking logs, captivated by the sparks rising into the night sky.

"Nothing personal," Nyphron said. "Everyone's birth is inconsequential. It's what you do afterward that's important."

Persephone studied him. The leader of the Galantians, commander of the Forces of the West, sat with arms balanced on bent knees, hands hanging. In a melancholy-filled pause, his eyes focused on the illuminated bottle.

Nyphron wasn't one to ruminate or brood. Reflection was as awkward for him as walking backward. The past was pointless. Only the future held value, so pondering what had happened was a waste of time. Knowing this, Persephone struggled to understand his newfound desire to commemorate an occasion. The only time she'd ever known him to was—

"Oh," she said as realization dawned. "This is your farewell bottle, isn't it?"

Nyphron nodded. "I bought it in Estramnadon when my father went to fight Lothian in the challenge for the Forest Throne. I had planned to celebrate his victory. Instead, he died, and I cracked it with the intent of drinking the whole thing. Turns out I only managed one swallow, which was dedicated to him." His fingers found a stone, and he threw it into the fire. It set off a burst of sparks and drew a delighted clapping from Habet. "Since then, it has become something of a tradition. Next came Medak, then Sebek, Grygor, Vorath, Eres, and Anwir."

Persephone's eyes narrowed on him. "Why is the bottle out now? And why share it with me?"

"You were right about not having much to do these days. And we both hate sitting and waiting." Nyphron took a slow breath and faced her. "The men you sent to the swamp to search for Moya and Tekchin's party—I went with them. We just got back."

"And?"

"Naraspur was tied near the edge of the swamp. We set up camp there and began our search. It's not a big place, and we were quite thorough. All we found was a campsite on a spit of sand with a few items of theirs. Persephone, I—"

"They drowned," she said. "All of them. They're dead."

"You knew?"

She nodded. "Malcolm told me some time ago, but I had to be sure."

"Malcolm," Nyphron spoke the word as if it were a curse. "So, you've talked to him, too? He's maddening. Without warning, the man disappears for years, then he returns to remind me I owe him a favor, but he still won't tell me what he wants. What did he say to you?"

Persephone pushed out her lower lip as she looked up at the stars. "That my friends had died, but there was a chance they could come back." She looked at him and rolled her shoulders. "Sounds crazy, doesn't it?"

Nyphron stared at her for a long moment. Then he reached for the bottle.

"Not even a comment?" Persephone asked.

Nyphron shook his head. "At this point? No. And it doesn't change anything. Tekchin is dead. They all are now, my Galantians and yours."

"I don't have Galantians."

Nyphron gripped the cork and tugged it out with a deep, resonating *pop!* "Sure you do. Moya, Suri, Roan, Arion, Brin, Gifford, and Padera are your elite band of adventurers, your friends."

"Suri isn't dead . . . not that we know of." Persephone looked at the glistening bottle. "Maybe I will have that drink."

Nyphron handed her the container.

"To the heroes I loved." Persephone put the rim to her lips. The liquid was warm and sweet and unlike anything she'd ever tasted. It ran down her throat like sunlight on a cloudy day. "Good that this is rare, or I might develop a fondness for it."

Nyphron took the bottle, then lifted it high over his head. "Farewell, Tekchin. Until we meet again, my friend, in the green fields of Alysin." Then he, too, drank deeply.

Together, they stared at the fire, silently watching the flames jump and dance. Sparks blew toward the stars before fading all too soon in the vast, cold darkness.

"Those are them," Persephone finally said. She pointed at individual sparks. "That's Moya, and there's Gifford, Roan, and Brin. Their souls are flying to the stars. Suri *is* probably in there, too. We'll *all* be ash soon."

"You were right about not being much of a drinker," Nyphron said.

"What? Why do you say that?" She looked at him and noticed that when her head shifted, the world rocked a bit.

He smiled at her with an amused expression. "Erivitie is extraordinarily strong and known to hit with shocking quickness, especially if you haven't eaten."

"I ate today. I think. But it was only a biscuit." Persephone moved her head again, marveling at the way the firelight blurred. "How about you? I suppose being an expert at drinking, you don't feel anything at all."

"Wouldn't say that. There's another reason there's so much still in that bottle. One pull makes you dizzy, two makes you crawl."

"And three?"

"Don't know. Anyone who's ever tried hasn't lived."

"Did you just make a joke?"

"Apparently not a very good one if you had to ask."

They resumed watching the fire in silence. Persephone had never before realized how fascinating blazes could be, how complex, how magical. More sparks flew, and she couldn't help wondering if more souls were taking flight.

"What do you think of Malcolm?" she asked.

"I try not to."

"Why?"

"He annoys me."

"I find him a comfort. Sometimes when I'm up at . . . when I'm feeling blue, he comes to me. He thinks you don't spend enough time with your son."

"Good example."

"You know, after he told me all my friends were dead, Malcolm mentioned he was sending them help. That same night Padera died. Do you think that was a coincidence?"

"You suspect he killed her?"

Persephone rubbed her face. It felt hot, and she wasn't sure if it was flushed with the fire's heat or the liquor. "I don't know. I'm not sure of anything anymore."

"Watch this." Nyphron tipped the bottle. Catching a drop of liquid on the tip of his finger, he flicked it into the fire. Instantly, a bright blue flame exploded.

Habet's smile turned into a huge grin, and he clapped his approval.

"And we drank that?" Persephone said, shocked.

"It helps that we were sitting at the time."

She leaned back, hoping to cool the heat of her skin. "Why don't you visit your son more? Are you . . . are you repulsed by him? Because he's half Rhune? Do you wish—"

"I don't have time."

"Oh yes, you are *so* busy—we both are. We've been stalemated in this conflict for years and are incredibly preoccupied with sitting, waiting, and staring at fires, while those we love die or disappear because of the orders we dole out or quests we sanction."

Nyphron also leaned back on his elbows. "I hate waiting. Never used to do it. My whole life has been rushing from one skirmish to another. Now . . . I honestly don't know how long it has been since I've drawn my sword. If I tried to use it, I'd likely develop blisters."

"Maybe you should spend more time with Nolyn."

"No." He shook his head. "That's not how you raise a proper son."

Persephone had wanted him to admit he should spend more time with Nolyn. Perhaps even an apology for relegating everything to her would be in order, but beyond even those desires, she had hoped he would promise to do more. His answer irritated her. "How would you know?"

"I'm sure it's hard to believe, but I was once a son, and I hardly ever saw my father before the age of ten. That was when I was sent to the garrison to start my training. Nolyn should begin soon. Then neither one of us will see him much. He'll begin his life as a warrior, a hard, grueling existence."

"That sounds like an awful way to raise a child."

"You think you could do better?"

"Absolutely."

Nyphron shook his head. "Then I fear for Nolyn."

Persephone rotated to her side to get a better look at him. The motion revealed just how soupy the world had become, and in the glow of that liquor and flame, she noticed just how handsome the last Galantian was. "Why?"

"You're basically saying that the way I was raised wasn't good enough. That you expect greater things for our son. But look at me. I'm still in my first millennium, and I've very nearly taken over the world. How much more could you possibly want?"

"Are you drunk?" she asked.

"I didn't even have a biscuit."

Nyphron looked back at the tent. She wondered if the drink had made her more appealing in his eyes, too.

"You really should have some protection. Let's not forget about the raow."

Guess not.

"Now that Moya is . . ." He stopped himself, and she appreciated that he didn't finish that thought. "Anyway, you need a new Shield."

"I have Habet here," she declared. Reaching out, she touched his hand, which generated a grin and a nod.

"The war will come back to us. It won't be long now. The advantage is shifting once more. You can feel it, can't you? We've enjoyed too many years behind the lines, but that will soon change. Lothian won't wait on the weather. As soon as he gets his dragons, he'll strike. The keenig needs a proper Shield—and my wife will have the best. With Tekchin gone, Sikar is second only to me in ability. I'll inform him he'll have the privilege from now on."

"Sikar doesn't like me. Doesn't like humans in general, I think."

"I don't see how that matters."

"It probably would help to have a bodyguard who *wants* to protect me."

"Sikar is a consummate soldier. He'll do as ordered."

"Okay, okay. Fine," she said, her head still floating. "How long do the effects of erivitie last?"

"Should wear off by next week."

She turned abruptly, and if she hadn't already been reclining, she would have fallen. When her eyes were able to focus, she saw Nyphron grinning.

"We're quite a pair, you and I. Look at us drinking to our losses and making light of the future. In a way, it's exactly how the last of the Fhrey and the Rhune Galantians ought to behave. It's like we're heroes in a story that a Keeper of Ways would tell, except . . ." Persephone looked back into the flames, tears came, and somewhere in that confusing moment, she felt Nyphron's arms surround her, holding back the dark.

CHAPTER EIGHTEEN

The Great Rain

As I write this, I have no idea if the prophecies are true: Rain's, Malcolm's, Suri's, everyone's. I hope they are—if for no other reason than it makes a better story.

— THE BOOK OF BRIN

"Why did you say I was great?" Rain asked once they were outside the Hall of Mideon. He looked beyond bewildered and appeared pained, as if the honorific had been a cruel insult.

Beatrice had come out with them, just her. The king's daughter had made it clear she wanted time alone with the visitors. Everyone in the hall had treated Beatrice with unquestioning reverence. Her beauty, white hair, youthful face, and diminutive stature had dressed her in the appearance of purity so perfect that Gifford wondered if it were all just an act.

Even in the world of the living, appearances can be deceiving, and in Nifrel, a dwarf can make himself into a giant.

Beatrice looked at Rain and then at the others. "When we're alone," she promised. She reached out as if to touch his arm, then stopped. She looked at her own hand and retrieved it awkwardly. "You've all had a long journey. While the others prepare, let's get your people settled, and then you and I can talk."

She set off across the antechamber, but the dwarf never took a step. Beatrice turned. "Rain?"

"These are me friends," he said. "I won't have secrets."

"But—"

"Wouldn't have made it this far if not for them."

Beatrice didn't look happy. She stared back at him for a long moment, but Rain was like stone. Given that he'd recently bested a tornado-sized serpent, Gifford didn't have high hopes that Beatrice would get her way.

It didn't take the white-haired dwarf long to figure out that Rain couldn't be budged. "Fine, but let's get out of the hall before we talk. There are certain *key* elements in this discussion that we wouldn't want others to overhear. We can go to my chambers."

Gifford stared at Beatrice, stunned. *She knows!*

Rain nodded. Nothing else was said as the Belgriclungreian princess escorted them deeper into the recesses of the Bulwark.

A warren. That's what came to Gifford's mind as they snaked their way through corridors and down flights of stairs. The Belgriclungreians' fondness for burrowing was well known, even to him, and apparently, it didn't end with death. They were moving through an insanely elaborate rabbit hole, one that he imagined looked a bit like Neith, based on the tales Roan had told.

Beatrice led them to a stone wall. She tapped it with the gem of a ring, and the outline of a door appeared. She shoved, and it opened. Inside was not just one room, but many. Lower ceilings, smaller fireplaces, and plenty of rugs, pillows, and wall hangings gave the apartment a warm coziness that the rest of the castle lacked.

"Make yourselves comfortable," Beatrice told them. "Would anyone like tea? Cake, perhaps?"

She saw the confusion but had anticipated it because she quickly added, "Just because we don't *need* to doesn't stop us from *enjoying* eating and drinking. Nifrel is all about sensations: pain and pleasure. I would've thought you'd have figured that out by now."

Beatrice walked into another room and emerged with a tray of steaming cups and a large plate of tiny cakes.

"Beautiful ceramics," Gifford said while taking a cup. He showed it to Roan, who nodded her agreement.

He took a cake and found it moist and sweet, with just a hint of cinnamon. Beatrice continued moving through the room offering refreshment to each of them. Even Brin took a cup and a cake, a sign she was coming around, if only a little. When the princess got to Rain, he took nothing, and she set the tray down on a low table within easy reach of anyone who wanted more.

Rain's face remained chiseled. "Will you answer my question now?" he asked.

She nodded. "But only if you answer one for me first."

Gifford thought it was going to be about Tressa's key, but instead, the princess said, "Why have you come?" Rain didn't answer, and Beatrice added, "Your friends deserve the whole story, don't you think?"

Rain glanced at Gifford and Moya, then nodded. "All me life I've been haunted by a dream about a woman—one I never saw, only heard. It's the reason I became a digger. I felt . . . no . . . I *knew* she was buried deep under the ground. It's why I went to Neith with Frost and Flood, and why I returned there with Persephone. I've been looking for her without knowing why. When I reached the Agave, I knew I'd gotten to the bottom of the world, but she wasn't there. She was deeper still. I knew it then. The one who haunted me wasn't trapped, she was dead—she was in the underworld."

Rain stared hard at the princess.

Beatrice nodded. "Yes, I called to you. I needed you to come."

"Why?" Rain asked.

Beatrice smiled, walked to the door, and tapped it again with her ring. The outline vanished, and the opening became a wall. They were sealed in, trapped with the perfect white-haired princess.

෨

"What I'm about to tell you is for you alone, Rain." Beatrice gave a glance at the others. "And for your close friends, apparently."

The princess took a seat near the fire. For Brin, this was the closest thing she'd experienced to the dahl's lodge since she was a girl. Food, a fire, and a wonderful story coming—if Tesh were sitting beside her, she would have called this paradise.

"As you've likely surmised, I know that one of you carries Eton's key."

"You don't know which one?" Moya asked.

"No," Beatrice replied. "I see the future—I always have—but it's not that precise. Like stars at night, only the big ones, the brightest, are clear. The little things, the tiny details, are lost in the background, crowded out by the brilliance of the rest."

"The stars." Roan spoke up. "We saw them when we passed through the wall. They're yours, aren't they?"

"Yes." She smiled. "My tiny contribution to my father's world."

"I like them," Roan added.

Beatrice nodded. "Thank you. I miss the real thing. I used to look to them for guidance. They are a constant, you know? Everything changes except the stars. You can plot your way by their positions."

Brin had heard of people traveling by way of stars, but she suspected Beatrice might mean something else entirely.

"I also know why you are here. At least why you *think* you are. In that respect, it is quite likely that I know more than you do." Beatrice poured a bit of tea. As she did, she said, "People have lied to you."

With a hard swallow, Brin braced for the rest, but Beatrice left it there. Instead, she added what looked to be honey to her drink.

Brin admitted to herself that she had no idea what to think about this strange white-haired dwarf with the sparkling eyes and childish face. The princess was the sort of odd, magical individual—like Suri—who had always fascinated Brin.

Perhaps it is only a façade, but the faces we choose to show others say much about who we are because we picked them. What sort of person selects that exterior?

Beatrice finished stirring her tea and lifted the cup with both hands. She held it beneath her chin, the steam rising before her face. "You can be certain that some lied with good intentions, others not so much, but everything will be revealed before the end. What won't be, what will remain hidden, is that the end will not be where you think it is. There will be much more that has to happen. Your part might seem like that's all there is, but in many ways, it's just the beginning. You—*we*—are but the faded mythology of a world to come. Many of our names will be forgotten, lost in the dust of time, but what you do now will shape the world until the Golrok, when everything is at last decided. That's what it comes down to, what all this is ultimately for. There is a set of scales, and each soul will choose their side. How the balance tilts at the end, when all is over, means everything. Either way spells disaster of one sort or another. The hope is that the scale never tips, that it stays balanced. But ensuring that outcome will take courage the likes of which the world has never seen." Beatrice looked at Brin. "And it will also need help from the most unlikely of people."

"I don't understand what this has to do with me," Rain said.

"Really?" Moya popped a bit of cake into her mouth. "Because I don't understand what this has to do with *any* of us. Do you think you could be a little *more* vague, Betty?"

Brin thought the princess might take offense, but that didn't appear to be her nature. Instead, she nodded. "I know, and I'm sorry about that. I must sound like such a tease, right?" She held up a hand and shook it. "Hey, look! I know the future, but will I tell you anything of real value? No!" She took a sip of her drink and instantly pulled it back. "Hot," she said, rubbing her lips. "Ha! I know the future, but I can't tell when my own tea is too hot to drink."

"And why won't you tell us anything important?" Moya asked.

"Look," Beatrice said, "the gods gave me a gift, or maybe a curse, or possibly I'm an accident, I don't know. But I can look behind the veil. I see everything, the future and the past like a map—like the stars—points connected across a vast darkness. I've had this ability since I was born. I tried using it. Who wouldn't, right? But my efforts to take advantage of what I knew never worked because acting altered the map. It's like trying to grab a bit of dust in liquid. It's hovering there; you can see it, but the moment your hand enters the pool, you disturb the water, and the dust moves away. Over the years, I've learned it's counterproductive to reach in and grab. Subtlety is required. Telling someone the truth doesn't work. Instead, people need to be directed, coaxed in the right direction. And the easiest way to do that is to keep them ignorant. Then it is possible to move the dust into the right place at the right time. That's why I can't explain what I know. If I did, then what I know would change—understand?"

"Sounds like a weak excuse," Moya said.

"I can see that, but it is the truth and the nature of all seers." Beatrice ventured another, more tentative sip that bore better results. "The good news is—in the case of Rain—I can tell him exactly what is going to happen because I'm the one who is supposed to let him know." She straightened up, clutched her cup, and grinned widely as she focused on the Belgriclungreian. "Rain, you will survive this quest. You will return to the world of the living. When you do, you will go to Belgreig and to a little town called Muldain, just a tiny fishing village—a place that time has forgotten. At the end of the seaside lane, you'll find a small whitewashed stone cottage, a very humble home with tattered curtains and a rotting boat out front. Inside, you'll find a great treasure: an eight-year-old girl named Amica."

Beatrice paused to drink. When she lowered her cup, she continued to stare silently at Rain.

"And then what?" he asked.

Beatrice's eyes sparkled brightly. "You marry her."

Rain's brows shot up. This was the most emotion Brin had ever seen the dwarf exhibit. Even drunk and singing, he never showed more than a smile. "Marry an eight-year-old?"

"Not straightaway, of course." Beatrice scowled. "But eventually—when she grows a bit."

"Why?"

"Amica is my . . ." She paused and thought a moment. Throwing up fingers, she counted. "Great-great-great-granddaughter. Yes, I think that is right."

"She's your—wait . . ." Shock filled his face. "I thought the line of Mideon is dead."

"No, it's not." Beatrice shook her head slowly, her eyes eating up his reaction to the news. "And you will reestablish it. Rain, you will be king. You will unite the clans and make the Belgriclungreians great once more. You, my long-awaited hero, will establish an alliance with the First Empyre and make us proud once again."

"You're going to be king?" Moya pushed out her lower lip and nodded in approval. "Congratulations."

"Hopefully, you'll be better than that monster Gronbach," Brin said.

Rain shook his head. "No one will believe me."

"Oh, yes they will," Beatrice assured him. "Especially when you return with Lorillion."

"Mideon's sword?"

Beatrice nodded. "The very same."

"But it's gone."

"That's right. And where did everyone say it went? Grave robbers?"

"O' course not. It was proven that the tomb hadn't been breached."

"But they buried him with it, so where did it go?"

Rain looked a bit embarrassed. "Folks said that old King Mideon was so greedy he found a way to take it with him when he died."

"And they were right." Beatrice moved to a bare section of her wall and once more touched it with her gem. A drawer appeared. She pulled it out and lifted a sword from it. "*This* is Lorillion—not the *idea* of the sword, but the *actual* sword."

Rain took a step closer to look. "How is that possible?"

"What do you know about Lorillion, Rain?"

"What everyone does. That it was forged by the master, Andvari Berling, from a bit of star that had fallen from the sky."

"That's right. It was a one-of-a-kind creation."

"That doesn't explain how it got here."

"Yes, it does," Roan murmured, and everyone looked her way.

"How so?" the princess asked, a grin on her face.

"That of Elan stays in Elan," Roan said. "That of Eton goes to Phyre; that of both can be touched by the living and the dead. That sword is like the key. It can exist in both worlds."

Beatrice nodded. "Very good, my dear, very good, indeed. Andvari— the greatest craftsman the world has ever known—made Lorillion from equal parts metal from Elan and the remains of one of Eton's falling stars. This is the real sword of Mideon, and Rain will take it with him when he leaves." Beatrice put it back and made the drawer disappear.

"Aren't you going to give it to him?" Moya asked.

"Not yet." She looked guilty. "My father doesn't know I have it, so it'd be awkward if he spotted Rain wearing it."

"Won't he be angry when he finds it gone?"

Beatrice laughed. "He doesn't use it. My father prefers his big ax. I took his sword centuries ago, and he still hasn't noticed." She looked toward the dwarf. "You can retrieve it before heading out. And when you return to Elan with it, everyone will know you are the rightful king."

"Won't they just think he's the rightful grave robber?" Moya asked. "Just because some folks said the tomb wasn't opened, doesn't mean there won't be a lot who think they lied."

"Yes, but there was a famous prophecy from hundreds of years ago that told about a great hero, a legendary digger of the first order who would enter the underworld and retrieve the Sword of Mideon and return it to Elan. It was also predicted that the hero would marry the long-lost descendant of Mideon and restore the royal line of Belgreig kings."

"That's a pretty specific prediction," Moya said.

"I know. I was the one who made it. I had it chiseled on the wall in Drumindor."

"You wrote it down?" Brin asked, shocked. "You understand writing? You can read?"

Beatrice shook her head. "I ordered the court artists to create the story in an engraved mural. Rhunes aren't the only race which has Keepers. This tale has been passed down for centuries. Many Belgriclungreians know it, and many wonder whether they are the worthy one. When Rain stands beneath the portrayal of the triumphant hero holding Lorillion aloft in Drumindor's Great Hall, there will be no doubt. He will prove the truth of his words and mine."

"But even if they believe, there will be those who refuse to accept me based only on a sword and a prophecy."

Beatrice nodded. "Which is why you are not returning with Mideon's socks. You will have to fight to unite the realm, but you do so knowing that you will succeed and become the First Lord of Drumindor. Then you marry Amica and have a child who will succeed you, and the blood of Mideon will be restored. This will usher in a Silver Age for the Belgriclungreian people. For the next one thousand eight hundred and sixty-nine years, the Lords of Drumindor will rule with dignity and honor, and your name will be remembered. And attached to it will be a signifier *The Great*. And you will be the only king in our history to hold that honor."

Rain thought about this, and in a most un-Rain-like manner, he looked worried, even a little scared. "Is this—is Amica—is she pretty?"

"Truth be told, she's an ugly little thing with a bad temper, but love is overrated."

≈

If Brin were still alive, she would have been sleeping.

The thought brushed against her with a sympathetic touch as she looked at the warmth of the fire and the soft cushions on the floor. After such a long trip, after running, after . . . *everything*, Brin would have curled up in blankets, hidden her face from the world, and let herself drift into the comforting refuge of sleep. Like the sun, the real stars, and a heartbeat, this simple comfort was gone. Brin missed being alive. For the first time since entering the pool, she wondered if she'd made the right choice.

If I hadn't come, would Tesh and I be alone in our tent, mourning the death of Padera and wondering what became of Moya and the others? Would I be just as miserable? Probably. But I'd have Tesh and could still find refuge and consolation in sleep.

Beatrice had left to check on her father's progress. That's what she had said, but Brin felt the princess was granting them a respite. Even shades needed time to pause, to think, and gather themselves. They had been constantly moving ever since the night they spent in the Swamp, and Brin recalled that she hadn't slept well.

But now she found that having time to think wasn't such a good idea. Sitting off by herself in a corner of the princess's parlor, Brin realized that as exhausted as she was—as see-through thin as her soul felt—the constant movement had been a blessing. With no time to dwell, no opportunity to think, she'd been granted an unseen gift. Now that she was sitting in a warm, softly lit room, thinking was all she was able to do. And all she thought about was Tesh.

"You okay?" Moya approached and sat beside her. In a strange way, she reminded Brin of Darby, the dog of her childhood. Whenever Brin had been sad, Darby would come over and curl up alongside her. The shepherd would lay his head on her ankle, and Brin would tell him everything. Getting it all out made the hurt easier to bear.

"Not so good," Brin admitted.

Moya pulled her knees up and held Audrey across them like a bridge that ran too far. The longbow spread out on either side like wings.

"Moya? How did it feel?" Brin asked. "When your leg was crushed and cut off, I mean. I know you weren't in pain in Rel, but when you crossed over . . . was it . . . did it . . . was it bad?" Brin asked this with a pleading hope that somewhere in Moya's response she could find solace that maybe Tesh wasn't suffering.

Moya let her head rock back and rest against the blond-paneled wall. The whole of the princess's room was decorated in lacquered wood, the color of creamy butter, soft and simple. Not a princess's parlor at all, not even a woman's chamber; it was a child's room. Brin wondered if it was always like this, or if Beatrice had changed it for them.

Moya frowned. "I know what you want me to tell you, Brin. But I'm not sure which would be better, the truth or a lie. I'll go with the truth because I know you are strong enough to take it. You may not feel like you are, but I know it to be true. Just as Rel has no feeling, I think that here in Nifrel everything is greater, more intense. Those cinnamon cakes were amazing. No food has ever tasted that good. Pain is the same way."

She looked at Brin with heartfelt openness. "But hey, it's not all doom and gloom. My leg is fine now. Tesh will figure it out. He knows he can heal himself. And of course, we can't die again, remember? He'll be waiting for you when we come back through—"

"I'm not continuing." Brin decided as she said the words. "I've got to go look for him. Not on the way back, but now."

"You can't, Brin. There's a war outside. It's still going on. You know that."

Although the deep pounding of the wall's defenses was muffled and faint, Brin could still hear it. The explosions never paused.

"When it stops, I'll go out and look. They can't fight forever."

Moya stared at her, shocked. "Brin, this is Nifrel. Of course they can, and probably will—and besides, we have to go to Alysin."

"How, Moya? How can I? I can't leave him . . . he died for me, not once but twice. He went into the pool." Brin took a bitter breath and put a hand to her lips to hide their quivering. "He said . . . he said he did it just to stop the pain, but I don't think so. He was so bent on revenge, but he gave that up—he gave it up for me."

"So, Meeks *was* telling the truth?" Moya's face hardened.

Brin nodded.

"How did you find out?"

"Tesh told me. He admitted it when trying to stop me from going into the pool. Tesh killed them all—murdered the Galantians one by one out of revenge." Her eyes lowered, and her voice grew quiet. "I think that's why he wanted to go to the swamp—why he didn't want me to come. I think if he'd had the chance, he would have tried to kill Tekchin."

Brin took her friend's hands. "Please, Moya, don't hate him. He had a reason. It wasn't just any Fhrey that destroyed Dureya and Nadak. It was Nyphron and the Galantians. I know you love Tekchin, but he was part of that. Tesh saw them—*all of them*. They slaughtered the whole village, old men, women, and children. Tekchin has blood on his hands, too. They both do."

"Nyphron said he was the only one who *refused* to obey the fane's order, that he and the Galantians were the only Instarya that didn't slaughter Rhunes."

"There was no order, Moya," Brin said. "Only Dureya and Nadak were ever attacked. They were sacrificed to convince the rest of us that we had to fight. The fane never wanted this war. Nyphron did."

"Are you saying Nyphron *started* the war?" Moya rocked where she sat.

Brin looked into Moya's eyes. "I . . . I think so, yes. He wants revenge against the fane, but his god prohibits Fhrey from killing Fhrey, so he made us do it. He put the blood on our hands so his could remain clean."

Moya stopped rocking and stared at Brin. "And Tesh knew this and didn't tell anyone? He never told Persephone? If he had spoken up instead of seeking his personal revenge, she might have—" Moya shook her head. Her eyes roamed the room as her mind worked to absorb more than she likely wanted to know. "Oh, Brin . . . they married and had a child!"

Brin closed her eyes, and tears ran down her cheeks. Moya was right. Since learning about what Tesh had done, she hadn't had the time to consider the implications. Now that she saw it, the horror left her overwhelmed and lost.

Brin felt arms pulling her close, reeling her back. "Shhh, shhh, Brin, it's all right. It's okay." Moya's hands stroked her hair as the two rocked together, the motion soothing away the impact. "Don't . . . don't do this to yourself. You couldn't have known."

"My mother was right—the world is broken. It's like an avalanche, and it gets bigger as each rock is set into motion. Lothian brutally murdered Nyphron's father, so Nyphron warred against him. Before Tekchin met you, he thought Rhunes were the same as animals, so he thought nothing about following the orders of his friend. Tesh thought it was his responsibility to avenge his family, and now Persephone has had a child with a man that was responsible for thousands of her people's deaths. Where does it all stop? If we manage to return to Persephone . . . do we tell her the truth? Or will that just make matters worse? Will it be another rock that sets a huge boulder rolling?"

"It would put her in an impossible position," Moya said, "She couldn't ignore the transgressions, but Nyphron has proven he's too dangerous to imprison or exile. So what can she do? Execute the father of her child? Would his absence ignite a power struggle between the clans? And how can we win this war without his military leadership? Oh, I don't know what . . . " Her voice trailed off as her own tears began to flow.

They hugged and rocked, rocked and hugged. For how long, Brin didn't know. When at last she could think again, she pushed back, wiped her eyes, and said, "I still love him, Moya. Mari forgive me, but I do. Despite what he did, I can't help myself."

Moya sadly nodded. "I feel the same way about Tek." She cupped Brin's face and leaned in, until forehead touched forehead. "Tesh and Tekchin are clearly not the sharpest teeth in a hound's mouth, but then neither are the women who love them."

Beatrice's bed frame was made of stone shaped to look like a grand sled. Upon it were a comfortable mattress, half a dozen brightly colored pillows, two dolls, and a stuffed dragon. The bedspread was a quilt of bright yellow with a flock of bluebirds stitched in the upper right-hand corner and a mountaintop in the lower left.

Why does she have a bed at all? Gifford thought. *Do people in Nifrel sleep?*

When Brin had started crying and Moya went over to sit beside her, Gifford and Roan had silently urged the others into the bedroom to grant them privacy. Each remained awkwardly just inside the door. No one dared sit on the bed.

Shelves decorated the walls and were filled with pretty ornaments—glass balls containing liquid and miniature scenes: a little mountain, a house, or dwarfs strolling through a forest. Gifford had picked one up, and artificial snow swirled, then settled. "Anyone else notice how . . . well, childish everything here is?" Gifford gestured at the bedchamber. "For a seer who commands the respect of so many important people in Mideon's Hall, it just seems odd that her bedroom would be—"

"A nursery?" Tressa suggested. She finally took a seat on the chest at the end of the bed, which had a pretty tasseled cushion.

Roan likewise sat down, but on the floor. She put a lock of hair in her mouth and chewed.

"A bit older than that, but it does seem girlish, doesn't it?" Gifford said. "Maybe she died young."

"She did," Rain told them. "The legend says she looked like a child when Mideon gave her hand in marriage. The war was going badly, and he needed an alliance. Many people believe he sold her for weapons."

"Couldn't have been too young," Tressa said. "She was old enough to have a daughter."

"Some would say that's debatable," Rain replied. "Seeing as how she died while giving birth."

"How long we gonna stay in here?" Tressa grumbled. "It's a bit cramped for all of us. Rain doesn't even have enough room to properly pace, and his *step-step-turn* thing is starting to grate on me."

Rain stopped walking and frowned. "Helps me think."

"Really? Well, it's driving me insane."

Roan muttered, still chewing on her hair. "Moya is here."

The others looked around, puzzled. Moya was still with Brin. Gifford could hear them whispering and occasionally weeping.

"She's not, Roan. She's in the other room."

"Yes—yes she is." Roan shook her head slowly as her hand crept to her mouth. "Poor Brin."

Gifford looked at the others and wondered if anyone else understood. They didn't. "What's wrong, Roan?"

"Moya and Tesh," Roan said. "They followed us into Nifrel."

"But that's a good thing, isn't it?"

She shook her head. "They didn't have the key."

Understanding reached each face.

"How did they do that?" Gifford asked.

"Because they belong here," Roan said. "Everyone rides the river to the Rel Gate. Those destined for Nifrel walk the White Brick Road to here, and they can pass through the door."

"The bad ones do," Tressa said, sadly. "Moya I can understand, but I would have thought that Tesh—"

"Nifrel isn't for bad people," Gifford recalled what Fenelyus had told them. "It isn't punishment. It's for ambitious, brave, and courageous people. Which is good because that means Tekchin will be able to cross over, too. He'll be able to find us."

Roan nodded. "Yes, he will, and that's good for now, and I'm happy for Moya. But eventually, when this is over and we really die—you know, come to Phyre forever—Brin's place will be in Rel."

"But that's good, too, right?" Gifford asked. "She'll be with her family."

Roan looked at the door, toward the sound of crying. "But she won't be with Tesh. You and I, Moya and Tekchin—we'll be together for all of eternity, but Brin . . . she'll never see him again."

The full weight of the revelation landed, and in turn, each looked at the door and the sound of the weeping women beyond.

"Yeah, okay, that's messed up," Tressa said.

CHAPTER NINETEEN

Sacrifices

I had imagined that if Suri told the fane the secret before we reached her, there would be so many dragons in the sky over Rhulyn that they would blot out the sun. But I had not been in the smithy, so I did not understand.

— THE BOOK OF BRIN

"It's to be a lottery." Imaly shouted the words. Such a thing wouldn't have been necessary in the intimate chamber of the Airenthenon, but that hall couldn't accommodate the gathered multitude. Instead, Imaly spoke from the Airenthenon's steps, casting her words to the crowd that gathered below in Florella Plaza. Mawyndulë wasn't sure if they could hear her. The silence that followed answered that question.

Mawyndulë stood on a step above the members of the Aquila, who were gathered on a lower landing. Vidar was there, but no junior councilor stood beside him. So few Miralyith remained in the city that none could be spared to take the position. The only available Miralyith was Mawyndulë, and Vidar refused to have him. The prince looked down at his ex-mentor's gray head.

Another political blunder, you fool. When this crisis is over, I'll be certain to remind my father to replace you.

"There will be exceptions." Imaly plowed ahead through the drifts of morbid silence. "The prince will obviously be excluded, as well as the *senior* members of the Aquila."

This caused a low rumble, not words but gasps, groans, and whimpers that came from the juniors who hadn't been in the meeting the day before. No one liked the decision, but none of them was willing to fight for their own survival. Mawyndulë was surprised. The Aquila was famous for its insolence toward fane edicts. That morning they were silent.

Dire times. Dire measures.

Those were the words his father had used when he personally explained to the senior members of the Aquila that sacrifices would need to be made. That was yesterday, but today, every citizen of Estramnadon had been invited, and the entire plaza was filled to capacity as the people came to discover their fate. The fane had learned how to make dragons, but there would be a price. For every creature created, a life would be taken—a Fhrey life. Everyone had come to learn who the first victim would be.

"Likewise," Imaly said, "the palace staff will not be included, nor will"—Imaly hesitated—"any member of the Miralyith."

The gathered crowd roared with outrage. Fists shook and feet stomped. Imaly made no attempt to rein them in. She simply waited. One word shouted from the back row pierced the din. It had come from a Gwydry. "Why?" he asked. "It's not fair for the fane to exempt his own tribe."

"It's because the Miralyith are indispensable in this war," Vidar said with all the impunity of someone privileged with a double pardon. "Without them guarding the river, none of us would survive. And make no mistake, the Rhunes are salivating for our blood. They are savages, uncivilized barbarians who will defile our children and revel in our humiliation. And slowly, monstrously, they will butcher every last one of us. They will carve us like venison, cook us alive over bonfires, and toast their victory with goblets stolen from the fane's table, filled with the blood of our sons and daughters. If you were freezing to death in a wooden home, would you begin by burning the walls or start with the furniture?"

Mawyndulë frowned in curious surprise. Vidar had actually made sense. Although comparing them to furniture was a bit insensitive.

"As a member of the Aquila and leader of the Nilyndd, I am not impartial," Imaly said. "There aren't many here who can claim to be fair-minded. Fewer still, perhaps, who can be trusted with such an onerous task. That is why I nominate Mawyndulë, prince of Erivan and son of Fane Lothian, to draw the name. I believe he is the only person we can truly put our faith in."

This brought a snort from Vidar, which didn't sound the least bit respectful, much less a sign of agreement.

Just keep digging that grave, old Fhrey.

Imaly extended her arm to Mawyndulë. "Will you help us?"

He climbed the remaining steps slowly. Applause followed from every councilor. Vidar was the last to join, and his token appreciation was far from enthusiastic. The clapping didn't end with the Aquila. Across the plaza, everyone in attendance was demonstrating approval.

He reached the top step, and a large vase the size of a barrel was brought forth. "The names of the eligible citizens of Estramnadon have been placed in this urn. His Highness will now choose one."

Mawyndulë faced the great ceramic crock: around the base were geometric patterns and circling the neck, a single flying goose. He knew it well. The vase had been in the Talwara vestibule for years. As a child, he'd often hidden toys within it. Using the Art, his father had filled it with tiny stones engraved with the names of all those eligible. Looking inside, he found thousands of pebbles. At first, he marveled at his father's ability to keep track of all the names. Then he wondered about how few there were.

Is this all who remain in the city?

There were likely thousands more in the towns and villages, those living deeper in the trees, those farther east.

Or maybe this is all there is.

The thought staggered him.

What if these stones represent all the remaining Fhrey, excluding the few paltry Miralyith and members of the Aquila?

It wasn't impossible, but it was terrifying.

How close are we to vanishing?

With that singular thought, he plunged his hand into the pot and scooped around, swirling the markers as best he could. Even tiny stones were heavy en masse. Then, keeping his head up and looking toward the frescoes of Gylindora and Caratacus, he grasped a pebble and pulled his arm free.

Refusing to look at it, Mawyndulë handed the pebble to Imaly. She took the stone in solemn reverence as if he'd just pulled the heart from an innocent child.

Maybe I have.

Imaly held it up between her fingers, showing it to the audience. "Does anyone find fault in this decision?"

Heads shook, but no words were uttered.

"The name I now read will be regarded as a great hero, one who will give their life to save us all." Imaly brought the stone close to her face and focused on it. She nodded once with a frown. "Amidea, of the Gwydry."

A scream came from the crowd. Heads jerked. Everyone turned around to witness the commotion. Guards were already present—palace guards.

Amidea was middle-aged, somewhere in her fifteen hundreds, a lithe worker with braided hair and terrified eyes. She screamed over and over again and kicked her legs in protest as the lion-helmeted soldiers drew her away with hooked arms. One of her braids came undone as she thrashed. By the time they had hauled her from the plaza, she had gone limp, her toes dragging on the marble.

The gathered crowd was silent once more, but the mood was clearly lighter than before. Relief reigned. The hand of Death had plucked someone else.

⚘

Imaly hated herself, but she couldn't help feeling relieved. The lottery could have picked anyone, and she knew a lot of people. She didn't know Amidea. She was Gwydry—a worker bee—who didn't buzz in the same hive as the Curator of the Aquila. The Gwydry were on the bottom, but it wasn't supposed to be that way. Gylindora had imagined a world where everyone was equal, but she might as well have imagined a reality where oil and water mixed and cream didn't rise to the top.

Maybe Amidea was a wonderful person, kind, loving, and always available to help her neighbors. But Imaly didn't want to think of her that way. Instead, she conjured the notion that Amidea was a terrible person. Perhaps that was the reason Ferrol had singled her out. Perhaps Amidea secretly kicked dogs and tortured squirrels. That would make it okay, make it acceptable.

I'm so full of crap, she thought while trudging home through the light snow, which was struggling to survive for more than a few seconds after hitting the ground. Imaly had made a life arguing in public, oftentimes creating sense where there was none. She used logic even when building arguments on sand, and her expertise made her points appear solid. Swaying opinion was a talent she had always excelled at. The problem was, she knew all her tricks—there was no way to fool herself.

This is all because of me. I did it. I got Suri to teach Lothian about making dragons even though I knew innocents would die. I thought it was the right decision, but seeing them drag Amidea out kicking and screaming like that is more than . . .

There was blood on her hands now. She'd have a lot more before this was finished.

"Who will it be?" Makareta asked when Imaly entered her overcrowded home.

Once upon a time, she could count on the restorative balm of solitude. Now she lived with a headstrong premillennial and a Rhune Miralyith.

Life is absurd.

"A Gwydry," the Curator said as she hung her cloak on a peg near the door. She missed her mark, and the garment fell. Imaly stared at the hook as if it had joined the rest of the world in tormenting her. She left the cloak on the floor and walked toward the hearth where a dwindling fire burned. The house was cold. Makareta couldn't be bothered to add more wood.

For Ferrol's sake, no! That would require doing something useful with her hands.

"What's their name?" Makareta asked. She sounded worried, as if it might have been her who had been picked, an odd tone, since she was already living under a death sentence.

Imaly raised a brow. "You care about a Gwydry?"

Suri appeared then, wearing Imaly's blue asica, which had been tailored to fit. She crept out from the direction of the nook. The Rhune preferred the big windows that opened to the outdoors. Despite Imaly's initial fears of two powerful rival Artists of different cultures trapped together, the two had gotten on like sisters; each acted as a calming influence on the other.

"Who is it?" Makareta insisted.

"Amidea."

Makareta thought a moment, then shook her head. "I don't know her."

"I wouldn't think you would." Imaly rubbed her arms, trying to scrub off the chill.

Suri overheard their conversation. Her brows, which were covered in queer markings, drew together in concern. "Does the *fane* know the person who is going to be sacrificed?"

Imaly took a log from the bin and added it to the fire. "Wouldn't think so. I mean, he may know *of* her. I did. I've certainly seen her face before, might have even heard her name. After a few centuries, you get to know almost everyone, but if you don't see them often, it's easy to forget. Still, I highly doubt the fane *knows* Amidea. I can't imagine—I mean, how hard would it be to execute someone that you actually know?"

"Suri?" Makareta said with enough concern to make Imaly turn.

The Rhune bolted for the door. Finding the latch, she threw it wide and rushed out.

"Suri!" Imaly shouted. "What are you doing?"

❧

Suri ran as fast as she could.

Snow was falling, so it must have been cold, but she didn't feel it. The world was bright in a colorless, hazy way, but she hardly noticed. She ran for the palace—the one place she knew how to get to. Suri assumed that was where she would find the fane. If she had stopped to think, Suri might have realized the fane wouldn't wish to create a dragon inside a building. What she was confident about was that the fane would perform the act immediately. Making the victim wait was cruel. Suri didn't hold Lothian in high regard, but she didn't think he would stoop that low.

She never made it to the palace.

A Fhrey dressed in blue and gold caught her before she reached the plaza. A number of armor-clad soldiers were out, and it was one of them who stopped her. Perhaps they would beat her, take out their frustrations on the only Rhune they could touch. This was why Imaly had warned her not to go out, but Suri had to try.

With a rough solid grip, the soldier held Suri by the wrist, but he didn't otherwise hurt her.

"Let me go!" she shouted, and to her surprise, he did.

"Can't come this way." The Fhrey shoved her back a step. "By order of the fane, the plaza is closed."

She watched as the guard grimaced and rubbed his hand on his thigh.

It's the new clothes. He's only now realizing who I am, what he grabbed.

From behind the guard and in the direction of the plaza, a horrible scream rose. The guard turned to look, and Suri darted past him. She jumped the evergreen hedge and the stone benches and made it all the way to the bricks before the Fhrey caught her again. But it was too late for the guard and for Amidea.

The fane stood in the empty plaza. His cream-colored asica was stained with bloody handprints near the neckline and around the wrists. He wiped the blood from his face with the sleeves, doing a poor job. There was a surprisingly large, dark-red pool. A body lay in its center, a sword on her chest.

"You lied!" the fane shouted when he saw her.

The guard, who had previously grabbed her, caught up. He began to pull her away but stopped when he saw the gory scene.

"No, I didn't," Suri said as calmly as she could, but in the presence of that dead body, she was struggling. "You didn't listen!"

"There's no dragon! No gilarabrywn! Nothing happened. *Nothing!* I did everything you said and I almost felt it, but I couldn't move the deep chords."

Suri jerked hard and tore her wrist free of the guard, who made no further attempt to stop her. Looking at the body, Suri took only a single step forward. The Fhrey lay prone, her arms and legs spread out. She didn't wear an asica, just a simple pullover shirt and a vest with pretty needle-worked flowers. "Who was she?"

"What?" Lothian asked.

"The one you killed." She pointed. "Her. Who was she?"

He shook his head. "What difference does that make?"

"It makes *all* the difference. I told you, but you didn't listen. Did you even know her name?"

The fane looked back at the dead body and shook his head. "Amidea, I think."

"You think? So, you didn't love her?"

The fane looked lost.

"I told you, it needed to be a sacrifice!"

"It was! I killed one of my people!"

Suri shook her head. "How much of a hardship could it be if you barely knew her name?"

"How dare you—"

"I'm sure it was unpleasant, but the power that's needed to make a gilarabrywn is greater than the total output of Avempartha. You don't get that from discomfort or regret. I told you it had to be *heartbreaking*. You can't get that from killing a stranger. You don't get that from sacrificing an acquaintance. Doing it right . . ." Her voice cracked and her hand flew to her mouth as her throat tightened. Her lips quivered and her sight grew foggy as tears gathered on the sills of her eyes. "It has to *kill* both—all of them and a little of you. You are sacrificing part of yourself in the making. You won't ever be whole again because you had to cut off part of what you were to make it. It's the loss that matters. The sacrifice is just as much you as it is them. To make the weave work, to give it the required power, you have to kill someone that matters *to you*. Someone you love—someone you would otherwise die for. It has to hurt worse than anything you've ever experienced, and it has to be so painful that you'll never want to feel that way again."

The fane continued to stare at her, but the hateful glare was gone. The distrust, the suspicion, the anger faded. His gaze shifted across the plaza then down to his bloodstained hands. Slowly he began to nod. "Yes . . . yes . . ." He continued to bob his head. "That *would* do it. The death, the pain, the anguish—of course."

There was no joy in his discovery, no victory to cheer.

The snow increased, flakes falling on a windless afternoon. The world where the fane and Suri stood became a silent place.

The fane focused on Suri. For the first time, he looked at her as if she was a person. "There aren't that many people I care about that I can afford to lose."

Suri nodded. "Now you know why you only face one."

CHAPTER TWENTY

In the Presence of Legends

Tesh had always been brave, determined, and invincible in battle. But he had never gone against a god before. Of the five, Ferrol— third-born daughter of Eton and Elan, Empress of the Dark, God of the Fhrey, Lord of the Damned, and Queen of the White Tower— was the last god anyone would want to face, and that included Tesh.

— THE BOOK OF BRIN

"The victory will come at a price."

Outside, the trumpets blew again, and Tesh imagined that the Fhrey were fighting in the lower courtyard. "We can have this talk later, can't we?"

"No, we can't. Tesh, when—if anything happens to me, you'll be the last Dureyan. You should make sure that our people don't die with you. You like Brin, don't you?"

"I really don't think now is the time—look, I need to get down to the—"

"Now is the perfect time because I don't want you anywhere near the fighting."

"What? You can't be serious! You stopped me last time—and I can help!"

"You can help more by living through this night."

"What do you want me to do? Cower somewhere?" Tesh exploded. "You're being stupid. I can—"

278 • *Michael J. Sullivan*

"I want you to go to the Kype and protect Brin."

Tesh remembered his dream and lost some of his anger.

"And when this battle is over," Raithe said, "I want you to start a family, raise children, and live a good and happy life—someplace safe and green, like on a high bank overlooking the Urum River. I want you to do what I never could."

Why is he telling me all this now?

Tesh noticed the others watching them, Suri and Malcolm especially. The tattooed girl had tears glistening on her cheeks. "Why are you—?"

"You have talents, and you've learned to use them, but don't let that be your whole life. Dureyans have always been known as warriors, but you need to change that. Promise me you'll do something good, that you'll make your life worth something more than killing."

"What's this about?"

"Promise me."

"But I don't understand why—"

"Promise me."

When Tesh opened his eyes, he didn't know where he was or where he'd been. A reality, clearer and more real than the one he found himself in, was slipping away. He'd been talking with Raithe. A memory. Yes, that's all it was.

But why that one? Of all my years and experiences, why that strange conversation? Maybe because I never saw Raithe again.

He didn't have time to ponder because he wasn't alone.

Tesh lay on a hard, white floor. He was cold, downright freezing—a strange but familiar feeling. He'd only experienced it once before—on the morning after he'd witnessed his family being butchered. Back then, Nyphron and his Galantians had moved to the houses and dragged out those who, like Tesh, were cowering in the shadows, hoping to go unnoticed. The only difference between him and the others was that his hiding place was better. He'd watched as the few survivors had been found and murdered. They screamed with animal-like panic until a sword or spear silenced them. After that, they weren't animals, nor people, nor his friends. All that remained were piles of flesh and bloody clothing.

When the Galantians left, Tesh had been too frightened to move. He stayed hidden, mostly buried in the dirt beneath his home. He woke to sunlight, smoke, and a terrible cold that owned his whole body. No cold before or since had ever matched it—until he woke on the white floor in the throne room of the Queen of the White Tower.

"That didn't take too long," Ferrol said. At least Tesh assumed it was her, and that she wasn't talking to him. There were others in the room. Tesh didn't look around, didn't need to. He sensed a group watching him, five, six, ten maybe, not a multitude, but plenty. None of them was his friends. He sensed that, too.

A harsh white light poured down so powerfully that he felt it. Looking up was impossible. The light was centered on him, stealing colors and leaving those around him in shadow. He could see *her*—some of her. The queen was sitting just a few inches away. A pair of unforgiving boots whose toes came to long spear points were eye-level with him. Her long leather-clad legs had a black polished sheen, or maybe that was still the boots. He couldn't tell. She had them crossed, the top leg bobbing on the other, rocking with impatience.

"Feeling better?" the queen asked. "Perhaps not." Now, she was talking to him. He knew this although he still couldn't see her face. Everything above the queen's knees was hidden behind that painful illumination. "This is where you are supposed to be. You know that—must have felt it the moment you entered. That girl was confusing you. She doesn't belong, and yet she is here, so there has been deceit and underhandedness. Let me be the first to extend some sympathy. I know it can't be easy to discover that the one you love doesn't feel the same way."

Tesh resolved not to speak. She was goading him, and he was weak and off-balance. He felt it best to keep his shield up and his head down.

"She just left you there, ran away, saved herself. I'm sure that's what you told her to do, but it didn't take much convincing, did it? If she *really* loved you—the way you love her—she would have stayed. You wouldn't have left her, would you? Even if she begged, you'd have stayed. But she ran off. Why is that, do you think? We both know the answer, don't we? Because there can be only one reason."

Her voice, like the light, fell on him with a physical sensation. The words stung like cold pinpricks of ice; they hit him from above, from out of the impenetrable glow.

"Havar of Mari stood his ground in the face of the countless Uber Ran that poured out of Erebus. He stood alone on the field before the golden gate. When everyone else fled, he remained rather than abandon his dog, which had been mortally wounded, beyond help. We pleaded with him to run, to fight with us another day, but still he stayed. And he died. The great Havar gave up his life because he loved that stupid dog—because *he loved it.*"

The overhead light shifted. Tesh heard movement, and when the queen spoke again, her voice was closer. "Brin doesn't love you. Maybe she did once. Then she learned what you were, what you are, and what you did. Those things drove a wedge. Convinced her that your allotted place wasn't with her—it's with me. You are one of my kind, Tesh. You don't live in a dream. You see the world for what it is—a fight. All of us have been thrown into this arena and were given weapons to survive if we can. Loyalty has to be earned and cruelties repaid. That's how war is conducted, and it doesn't end when you die. Life is merely the process of qualifying for entrance. Living decides whose team you join. You belong on mine. She doesn't. Your feelings for her were misplaced. If the two of you had lived, she would have left you just as easily as she did on the battlefield. She could never love a murderer."

Those last words were more than chilling, more than mere pinpricks of ice. They were like a stabbing icicle. The truth did that. He cringed, gasped, and clawed the floor in real pain—the white floor that wasn't stone but bleached bone.

"Tell me, Tesh," the queen asked in a soft near-whisper that came close to his ear. "Where is the key?"

He shivered.

"We searched you. Didn't find it. Is it Moya? Brin? Does she have it? Gifford maybe?"

She waited.

Tesh stayed silent.

The queen moved away, taking the light with her. "You're here now, Tesh." She spoke louder. "You'll be here for eternity. There is no changing that. You might as well meet your new family."

With the light dimmed, Tesh could see—not far, but enough to view the faces of those around him. Many were unknown—the Galantians were not. The only face that surprised Tesh was Tekchin's, who stood with the others circling him. Most of them he'd killed, all taken by surprise, caught when weak or off-balance. He didn't regret any of it. Nor would he make any apologies. They got what they deserved. Their slaughter of his village hadn't been a fair fight, either.

Sebek watched him with particular intensity. The Fhrey was no longer injured, and his swords, Lightning and Thunder, were undamaged and once more at his sides.

"Tesh," the queen said, "you aren't going to be with Brin, no matter how things turn out. She won't stay here. But you will. You understand that, don't you? And it's important to know that I'm not speaking of a year, a decade, a lifetime, or even a century. No, I refer to all of eternity. This is where you will be—this is your home now, and I am your ruler. I can make things very pleasant for you. My realm might lack frills, might seem dark, cold, and unappealing at first glance, but there is pleasure here— *great* pleasure. My world holds delights beyond the imagination, granted to you by the miserable life you led. In your brief years under the sun, you ate slop; I will feed you banquets of exotic beasts and birds. You drank muddy water; I will satisfy your thirst with wines, beers, and liquors the likes of which you've never dreamed possible. I'll see you have servants, your own kingdom, a castle built to your liking. In life, you had but one woman. I will grant you thousands to use and discard as you please. Each day will be filled with the joy of battle followed by nights of drunken pleasures. This will be your eternity *if . . .* you help me find that key."

Tesh could see her. She was the light, and looking at the queen hurt. Her features were sharp and beautiful. As he watched, her razor-thin lips frowned, and he felt as if something squeezed his heart.

"Should you choose to deny me this small thing, your future will be less than pleasant. Sebek has requested that you be given to him, asked that you be shackled as his slave for that same unending amount of time. Apparently, he has plans for the two of you, plots he hasn't even shared with me. But I can guess. Knowing him as I do, you won't experience a dull moment."

The queen came closer, and as she did, the oppressive light returned, crushing him. "Tell me, Tesh. Where is the key?"

There was no resisting her, no gritting his teeth and enduring the pain. This wasn't a matter of his spirit standing fast against the tortures of the body. He had none. This was a bare-knuckled war of wills, and in a contest with Ferrol, Tesh came up short.

Reduced to a puddle before her, he blurted out, "Tressa . . . Tressa has it . . . It's on a chain around her neck."

"He's lying," one of those around him said—a human with a thick black beard and a bearskin cloak. "And I could have told you that's what he'd say. They all hate my wife. Despise her. No way they'd let her have the thing, but of course, she's the first one he'd give up."

"Is that true, Tesh?" The light bore down hard, causing him to make noises he never thought he could. "Are you being tricky? Are you capable of resisting me? Did you lie?"

Tesh couldn't have answered if he wanted to. At a certain point, when pain became too great to bear, he had always passed out. That wasn't happening this time. The pain kept increasing, and he knew it would never stop. There would be no unconsciousness, not even a release through death. He cried and screamed, but the pain was always there. Nothing would make it go away, not ever.

❧

Seven sets of staircases had brought them to the bowels of the Bulwark, a fearful place of fire and darkness that Brin wouldn't have had the courage to descend into if it hadn't been for the fact that Beatrice was leading. Great gear wheels rotated, shrieking with the voice of stone on stone. Massive vats of glowing molten metal spilled from gargantuan kettles bursting yellow light. A chorus of hammers beat a continual ringing rhythm while chains jangled a melody that steam whistled to.

The daughter of King Mideon, a pale-white ghost against a fiery-red world, swept through the maze of columns and arches until she came to a small, battered desk tucked into a back corner. Far from the belching brilliance, a small lantern hung overhead, illuminating a dwarf with a long gray beard and rolled-up sleeves who sat on a tall stool. He was bent over the work area. Brin thought he might be laboring on something very detailed, as his head was quite close to the surface. Then she heard the snore.

"Est Berling?" Beatrice said respectfully.

The head came up slowly. The dwarf on the stool grunted, then coughed long and hard, as though he had a couple of stubborn mice nesting in his throat. He wore a pair of little glass windows held on his nose by thin brackets of metal. He peered at the group through these while mashing his lips together. He pointed at their guide. "Beatrice, right?"

She frowned, and the dwarf on the stool smiled.

"This is Alberich Berling," Beatrice said with a slight flourish and a nod of her head. "Est Berling, these are the ones I spoke of."

He tilted the pair of windows down the bridge of his big nose and looked over the top. "The ones you want armor for?"

"Yes. If it wouldn't be too much of an inconvenience."

"He's . . ." Rain started, then just stared at the dwarf for a moment with a look of disbelief. "You're—you're *the* Alberich Berling? Of Clan Brundenlin?"

The dwarf on the stool raised a very expressive single eyebrow and smirked. "Aye. I'm not aware of another, are you?"

"Oh, no! Certainly not," Rain said.

"Well, there you are then." The dwarf studied Rain and scowled. "Is this 'ere what passes for clothes now?"

Brin scrutinized Rain's outfit looking for issues but saw none.

Apparently, neither did Rain, who looked down at himself. "Aye, I made them meself, I did."

Alberich reached out and took hold of Rain's hands, spreading his fingers. "Odd."

"What?"

"Don't understand it. Ye have ten fingers like everyone else, and this is what you make?" He let go of Rain's hands, shook his head in disgust, and turned away after gesturing again at Rain's clothes.

"Est Berling, can you outfit them?" Beatrice asked.

"Aye. O' course, I can. I'm Alberich Berling, aren't I?"

"It needs to be done quickly. My father is already taking steps to launch a counterassault. These six will be going out with the first wave."

"Seriously?" Again, Alberich peered at them over the top of his little glass windows. "Don't look like warrior types."

"They aren't, hence the need for armor—your best."

"Best?" That single eyebrow shot up again, and he took the windows off his nose to glare. "I'm Alberich Berling, child. We've established this, yes?"

Beatrice nodded. "Sorry."

Moya looked at Brin expectantly. She wanted information, but Brin had none to give. Brin was the Keeper for the Rhune clans. She knew nothing about dwarfs. "Pardon me?" she said. "Should we"—she motioned to herself, Moya, Gifford, and Tressa—"should we know who Alberich Berling is?"

This time both bushy brows were hiked up.

"He's a craftsman, I believe," Roan said. "Frost and Flood spoke of him often."

Alberich dropped his windows into his lap.

Beatrice covered her face in embarrassment.

Rain was shaking his head as if trying to dry his hair. "Alberich Berling is no *craftsman*. Alberich Berling is *the* Master of Trades." Rain looked at them for a spark of recognition and saw none. "He's *legendary.*"

Still nothing.

"He's the inventor of gemlocks, and he crafted the Drakon Hart. Throughout antiquity only his father, Andvari, is said to have been his equal, and Andvari Berling designed and helped build Drumindor, the greatest fortress the world has ever known."

"I apprenticed on Drumindor," Alberich said. He fished up his wire-rimmed windows and set them back in place.

"Oh!" Gifford smiled as if a light had been lit inside his head. "He's like Roan."

Rain opened his mouth as if to protest, then he stopped and looked confused, his eyes shifting back and forth between the dwarf and Roan.

"Who is this—*Roan?*" Alberich asked.

"She is," Gifford said proudly, laying a hand on his wife's shoulder.

"Beh," Alberich said dismissively, and he walked away into the darkness beyond the lantern's light.

They all watched him go.

Before anyone could answer, Alberich returned with a measuring ribbon. "You there—*Roan*—come 'ere."

Roan looked nervously at Gifford, then crept slowly forward.

"We'll start with you, shall we?" Alberich said. "Can't have the Rhune version of *me* getting skewered by some pathetic bit of bronze spear, can we? Now, stand with your arms straight out, like you're a flying bird, and don't move."

"Armor?" Gifford spoke to Beatrice. "I—I guess I don't understand. How can—I mean, none of this exists, right? Not really. Even our own appearance is invented. What good is armor that isn't real?"

"Not real?" Alberich shouted. Getting up, he walked into the shadows again. They heard clanking, and this time when he returned, he brandished a great sword that glimmered with a bluish light all along the edges.

Roan gasped at the sight.

The dwarf's angry expression caused Gifford to draw his own weapon. Moya took a step back and raised Audrey, but the dwarf either didn't see her or didn't care. His eyes were on Gifford and his sword.

"Ha!" Alberich Berling shouted at him. "You see!"

"No—not really. I mean, I see you coming at me with a sword," Gifford said while holding his weapon with both hands.

Berling sighed, shook his head, and gave Beatrice a frown. "It's as if they just arrived."

"They did," Beatrice replied.

"Oh." Berling looked to be chewing on something as he frowned again before facing Gifford. He waved the glowing blade, and Gifford took a step back. "Why are you scared of me wee sword, boy?"

"Wee?" Gifford said. "That is in no way *little.*"

"Beh! 'Tis *nothing,* you say. Doesn't exist, you say. A figgyment, yes? Not real? So, why are you nervous of a figgyment?"

"I—I don't know."

"You don't know a lot of things, I think." Alberich set the sword on the desk, and he resumed measuring Roan, who hadn't moved an inch. "Everything is *eshim,* 'ere."

"Everything is—what is everything?" Gifford asked. *"Eshim?* What is *eshim?"*

"Eshim is *eshim,"* Alberich said, slapping his own chest. "You don't have that word in Rhunic?"

They all shook their heads.

Alberich scowled. "Stupid language you have, then. *Eshim* is—is *heart,* is *understanding,* is *belief.*"

"Confidence?" Moya asked. She had strung Audrey but no arrow had appeared.

Alberich shrugged. "Sort of, only more so. More from 'ere." Again, he hit his chest. "Understand?"

Brin nodded along with the rest, but honestly, she wasn't sure.

"You pulled your sword because it gave you more eshim—made you feel stronger, safer, bolder, aye? The armor I will make will do better than a sword. My armor will give a boost to your *eshim* that will make you strong."

"So, the armor isn't metal; it's reassurance?" Gifford asked.

"It helps increase your sense of willpower," Beatrice said. "Makes it harder for others to impose their will on you."

"I guess that makes sense," Gifford said. He started to slide his sword back into its scabbard.

"Wait, wait, wait." Alberich held out a hand, opening and closing it. "Let me see this thing you have 'ere."

Gifford hesitated. Beatrice mouthed, *Give it to him!* and Moya nodded. He handed it over.

The dwarf brought it closer to the light, rapped on it with his knuckles, then licked it. He swished his lips back and forth contemplating the taste. "This is formed from your *eshim,* but you didn't make it. This is a memory. You used it in life. From whence came the original?"

Gifford glanced at Roan. "She made it."

"Roan," Alberich said, eyeing her with a new intensity.

Roan still had her arms out, but they were starting to droop.

"She calls it *steel,*" Gifford said.

Alberich looked at Beatrice with suspicious eyes. The princess showed no reaction but held his gaze. Her awestruck respect for Est Berling had vanished, and her face became an unassailable wall. The glaring continued for several awkward minutes until finally Alberich slammed the flat of the blade hard on the desk, making them all jump. Roan had had enough of standing out with her arms up, and she retreated to Gifford, who grabbed her.

"The impression the original made on you is strong," Alberich said, looking at the blade. "Must have been good metal." To Roan, he said, "Good . . . *steel*, Roan." He laughed a bit like a madman. "Ha-ha! She *is* me!" He handed the sword back to Gifford. "And for you, for all o' you, I will make my *best* armor. Aye, the very best."

With the measurements completed, Beatrice offered to show them the view from the top of the Bulwark, but Tressa, Roan, and Rain remained in Alberich's workshop to watch "the show," as they called it. That Roan and Rain wanted to observe a master craftsman was understandable, but Tressa was the surprise. Despite feeling better within Mideon's walls, it was obvious the woman still wasn't up for a lengthy climb. As a result, only Moya, Brin, and Gifford followed Beatrice up the long stairway to the high tower. Upon reaching the pinnacle, they were rewarded with a view that Brin wanted to memorize because she knew she'd never see anything like it again. Below were the colossal walls of the Bulwark, made small by the height of the tower. Flashes of firelight sparked all along the fortification in perfect timing as the defenses of Mideon's fortress continued to send forth flaming missiles that flew out and exploded in the midst of the attacking armies surrounding the fortress.

An ant war.

That's how it looked—if ants fired flaming projectiles.

Brin saw ladders and rams. Great creatures with giant hammers beat against the Bulwark's walls while rocks, spears, and boiling liquid were thrown down from the ramparts. So high were they that the sound of war was muffled—made small. The thunderous explosions were *pops,* the drums *taps,* and the cries of pain and cheers of victory a soft hum.

"Out there is the White Tower," Beatrice said, pointing at a singular column. At such a distance, Brin could have hidden it with her outstretched hand. "The home of the Queen of Nifrel."

The tower looked like a tree with a massive root system but not a single branch. From its base, hundreds of tangled white lines spread for miles in all directions. This vast white web of roads, walls, outposts, and fortresses seemed to be made from the same pale dull material: stone or possibly the salt and sun-bleached wood that drifted onto the beaches of Tirre. The network of white created a large circle, but other fortresses infringed on it, most notably the Bulwark itself.

The fortresses, towers, outposts, and roads were not, however, the dominant feature of the land. Nor were the mountains, hills, valleys, or plateaus, of which there were many. The most abundant characteristic of the landscape was the fissures. Dark zigzagging scars broke the land with unnerving cracks that reminded Brin of a dry lakebed. They ran everywhere, necessitating numerous bridges, which required battlements and towers to control each of them.

"Over there"—Beatrice pointed to the far left where the largest of the cracks formed a great canyon that was spanned by a lone and narrow bridge—"is the Mouth of the Abyss. And that bridge leads to the Alysin Door. As you can see, it's on the top of that slender pinnacle of rock that rises out of the center of Nifrel. Some call it the Needle; others refer to it as the Tongue of the Abyss. Most just call it the Alysin Pillar."

"How far away is that?" Gifford asked.

To Brin, it looked like it was days away.

"In Phyre, distances are deceiving. Although, it might feel like an eternity to reach it."

Moya looked down at the raging siege. "How can we get past the armies?"

"This is King Mideon's castle, a *Belgriclungreian* citadel." Beatrice smiled. "You may be aware that we have a bit of an obsession when it comes to digging. Beneath this fortress is a labyrinth of tunnels—roadways to all corners of this realm. The queen knows many of our routes, but not all. You'll be going by the *flyway,* one of our most secret paths. It will pop you out over there by that roundish hill."

"That's more than halfway," Moya said excitedly. "We could run for it from there."

"You'd think that, wouldn't you?" Beatrice shook her head and frowned. "But you don't know the queen like we do. She is the oldest in this realm—well, the oldest up here, at least. Her older brother Trilos and their uncles, the Typhons, are supposed to be below us in the Abyss, but no one has heard from them in eons. So up here, Ferrol reigns. She's one of the Five, and their powers are beyond imagining."

"What *are* the Five?" Brin asked.

"The Aesira." Beatrice looked confused when she failed to see recognition. "You don't know about them? But you were sent here by—" She stopped and again looked puzzled. Then a smile came to her face. "He didn't tell you anything, did he?"

"He?" Moya asked.

Beatrice narrowed her eyes in thought, considering her words. "The one who sent you."

"You mean Malcolm."

Beatrice showed no sign of recognition, and after thinking for a moment, she shrugged. "Okay, but I'm right, aren't I? He hardly explained anything to you."

"Explain what, exactly?"

Beatrice grinned sheepishly. "I have to wonder why he didn't. Maybe there's a reason." She looked away, her face straining in thought.

"Maybe he forgot," Moya said, a dash irritated. "Perhaps he didn't have time. What's *your* excuse?"

"I've already explained that, and I don't think he *forgot,*" Beatrice replied.

"So, are you going to tell us?" Brin pressed.

Beatrice squeezed her lips together, trying to decide. "Shouldn't matter—he must have known how this would turn out. There's no way you can get through all three realms and not learn the truth." She muttered this mostly to herself, then nodded. "I'll tell you what I know, which isn't close to everything, but obviously far more than you know now. But to do that, I'll need tea." She headed back toward the stairs.

Moya and Gifford followed, but Brin lingered at the window, looking out at the war and the scarred land. Blackened, cracked, and barren—this was Nifrel, exactly as she might have envisioned it if her imagination had been clever enough.

Are you out there, Tesh? If I think about you really hard, can you hear me? Can you somehow feel me?

She placed her hands against the stone of Mideon's walls, leaned out, closed her eyes, and focused on him.

I know you're here. I know you still exist. I want to thank you for saving me and for dying in the first place. I never told you how much that meant. I should have. I should have said a lot of things. I write words, but I never think to say them. I wish I knew where you are. I don't know what I'd do—or if I could do anything for you. It would just mean so much to know you are all right.

Just before she opened her eyes, in that momentary flash of light before she could focus, she thought she saw him crying out in pain.

Tesh never lost consciousness, but he discovered there was a maximum threshold to pain, a point of diminished return where it just didn't matter anymore. Neither did time, which he was certain had stopped at a really inopportune moment. He also discovered that without a mouth, throat, or lungs, he could scream forever.

Forever mercifully came to an end. The pain stopped, time resumed, and Tesh lay on the white bone floor of Nifrel's throne room, an exposed nerve waiting for what came next.

"I don't know, maybe," someone said. The voice reached him from far away.

"Only six left, how hard can that be?"

"What would *you* do?"

"Besieged like they are? I'd use the tunnels."

"Which one? That's the problem with Belgriclungreians, they have a network down there. A nest of rats is what they are."

"Can we cave them in? The surface layer here is of your making, right? The real rock is below. If the Dherg can dig, then we can collapse."

"Such a thing would—I honestly don't know what it would do—and I don't think the situation is that dire." This was the queen's voice. Tesh had no trouble recognizing it but guessed he'd have a great deal of difficulty trying to forget. "I'd rather not reshuffle this deck to such an extreme degree. As you said, there's only six left, and we know where they're going."

"A trap, then? Before, or perhaps on, the bridge itself? We know they have to cross it. There's no way to tunnel the gap, and their forces will need to converge. It's not very wide."

"Before, then. I don't want them getting that close. I don't want to risk losing my prize to the depths." This was the queen again; her words felt once more like pinpricks of ice. "We'll take them on the slate between the monoliths."

Tesh opened his eyes. The light—her light—was away from him, off in the distance. A circle of dark figures was revealed by the pale pool of illumination—not a warm or life-giving brilliance, but an empty, cold light, the soul-warping gleam of glittering gems.

"I'll have the Grenmorians make a line. Alon Rhist can lead the Galantians in a flank attack."

"We'll need to worry about Fenelyus. She'll be in it this time."

"We have Gryndal to counter her."

"Inerus can make the push, lock them up, and drive the ambush. When they reach the narrows, they'll have to reduce the width of their ranks. That'll make their defenses vulnerable."

"That ought to be more than enough."

"I'm not interested in what *ought to be*," the queen said. "I won't lose that key. Now, if we only knew which one carried it, that would be a help. And that fool Mideon will make it harder. He's making plans in the Bulwark—but what kind?"

Tesh felt her look at him. It hurt enough to make him wince.

"Are you sure he's not telling the truth?" she asked Konniger.

"Tressa and I are a pair, so much alike," he said. "Would you give *me* the key?"

"Very well, he's not going to give it up. Put him in the hole."

"But you promised me," Sebek said.

The queen laughed. So did a few of the others. "You can never trust what I say, child. Only what I do. Throw him in the pit. We have our own planning to do."

Tesh heard footsteps approach and saw the unmistakable outline of Sebek coming his way.

Tucked safely in Beatrice's chambers with tea in hand, the princess sat on a soft stool in front of them. She looked very much like a child, a young girl huddled before a hearth, gripping the white cup with both hands, the base resting on her knees. A sparkle was in her eye, the hint of a smile on her lips. Both made Brin feel certain this was going to be a good story. She hoped so. She needed one.

"What do you know about how the world began?" the princess asked.

Roan, Tressa, and Rain hadn't yet returned from the workshop. Moya and Gifford looked at Brin.

"Brin is our Keeper of Ways," Moya explained. "She holds the stories of our people's past."

Beatrice looked at Brin expectantly.

Brin felt embarrassed. "Actually, I'm a little confused on a few points."

Moya seemed surprised.

"Well, you see, there is what Maeve told me about Chaos, Eton, and Elan. And then there's what I learned in Neith—but now after listening to Drome . . . I just don't know anymore."

"What did this Maeve tell you?" Beatrice asked.

"Chaos existed as a void." Brin said, repeating the words Maeve had taught her. "Then from her came Eton the sky and Elan the world. From the union of Eton and Elan came their first children: Light, Water, and Time. From the union of Light and Time came their sons, the Sun and the Moon. From Time and Water came their daughter, the Sea. From the Sun and the Moon came their children, Day and Night. The Sea's children are the Four Winds, and they each had one child: Winter, Summer, Spring, and Fall." Brin hesitated. "Then in the Agave, I read about Ferrol, Drome, and Mari on tablets, and I know I made some mistakes. For instance, I thought Erebus was a person, but Drome said it was a place, a city."

"You *read?*"

"Yes, I created markings that represent sounds."

"And you found tablets in the Agave? Ones with marks you could understand?"

Brin smiled sheepishly. "Yes, but the one who sent us here, the guy we know as Malcolm but whom others have referred to as Turin, told me that the person who wrote those tablets did so using the symbols I invented. That seems impossible because the tablets were created long before I was born."

"The name Turin and the word impossible have no business being together," Beatrice assured her.

"Okay. Well anyway, it was easy for me to understand them."

The princess nodded, then her eyes widened. "Oh! So, you're *that* one. Okay. That makes sense, I suppose."

That one?

"Well, you were doing well up through the seasons," Beatrice said. "I'm actually impressed. It's quite an accomplishment that you kept it that straight through so many generations. I don't think your people ever had the whole story. Let's back up just a bit." Beatrice set her cup on a little table near the stool so her hands were free.

A good sign. All the best storytellers use their hands.

"First, you need to understand that Eton is infinite—in other words, he goes on forever. When you look at the sky, you can see this. Elan is not. She ends, sort of. She's a circle. So, everything that comes from her also expires. But everything that comes from Eton is immortal. Eton and Elan gave birth to a daughter named Alurya. She was beautiful, and Elan loved her above all else—even Eton. The two were inseparable, and Eton grew jealous of Alurya. But like all things of Elan, Alurya was destined to die. When she did, Elan was so heartbroken she refused to speak to her husband. She wouldn't talk to anyone. This was a time of great depression, when the North Wind and his son Winter kept watch over Elan as she wept.

"After seeing Elan's sorrow, Eton relented and granted immortality, allowing Elan to breathe life into Alurya once more. But each year, Alurya had to die for the span of three months. During this time, Eton would have time alone with Elan. Alurya went on to become the mother of life, of the plants and animals."

"I never heard that before," Brin said.

"That's because this is where the story turns dark," Beatrice replied. "People like to forget terrible things."

She took a sip from her cup, set it back down, and started again. "Once more, Eton united with Elan, and from this union came the three Typhons." Beatrice paused as if waiting for them to react. No one did, so she went on. "These triplets were named Erl, Toth, and Gar."

"Not Goll?" Brin asked, and the others nodded their approval of the question.

"No, Goll isn't a Typhon. Goll is Gar's son—but that's another story, one that leads to the birth of the Grenmorians. Our tale goes elsewhere. You see, once again, Elan loved her sons too much for Eton's liking. Worse yet, Elan spoiled the Typhons, which made Eton hate them. He despised his new sons so much that he pushed them back into Elan's womb and imprisoned them there." Beatrice extended her hands palms-up and indicated the walls around them. "In *here*—inside Elan, in the place known as Phyre."

Beatrice took another sip, wiped her lips, and went on, "Elan was bereft once more, but this time Eton wouldn't relent. He also refused to join with her again, for he didn't want to see the creation of more immortals. Furious and lonely, Elan plotted against her husband. While Eton slept, Elan stole five of his teeth and sowed them in her soil. From them, the Aesira were born: Turin, Trilos, Ferrol, Drome, and Mari. When Eton learned of the Aesira, he was angry, and Elan pleaded with him not to send her new children to the Abyss. Luckily for them—and us—he didn't. Not at first. Eton found that the Five were not at all like the Typhons. Perhaps advised by their mother, the Aesira showed Eton respect and thoughtfulness, but this only got them so far. Eton still wouldn't budge on his vow that no other immortals would come between him and his wife. A deal was reached. Elan expanded Phyre, making a pleasant home for her children. What was made of Elan would live happily with her until their time was over, and what was made of Eton was sent to dwell in Phyre, a prison with a lock and a key that he kept. Such was the plan, but as with all intentions, this one went astray. The problem began when Turin, the eldest of the Aesira, took ill. His time to die, his time to move on to Phyre, had come and—"

The door to Beatrice's chambers opened, and Mideon entered, followed by a parade of people carrying armloads of armor, including Roan, Tressa, and Rain, whom Brin hardly recognized. They were bedecked from helm to boot in leaf-style bronze so polished it glowed. None of it appeared sensible. Tesh had taught Brin that armor needed to be smooth and clear of lines and creases to avoid giving a sword's point a place to catch, but these suits were beyond extravagant. Roan's helm was adorned with a long crimson feather that came from no bird Brin had ever seen. It extended several feet above Roan's head. Rain's chest was covered in overlapping scales in teardrop shapes. Both Roan's and Rain's boots came up to their knees and looked as if gold-colored ivy reached up out of the ground, wrapping their legs. Both of them were bigger. The normally tiny Roan was two feet taller, and that didn't include the helm or the feather. Even her hands—now encased in brilliant metal gauntlets—seemed twice the size of Brin's. The shy woman with a tendency to chew on her hair and talk to herself had been transformed into a hero of epic proportions.

But that's the point, isn't it? The armor doesn't protect the flesh. There is none. The armor builds the spirit. Its purpose is to scream, "I am here, but don't even think of messing with me!"

Alberich Berling, Brin realized as she gaped at them, was truly a genius and a master.

CHAPTER TWENTY-ONE

Wars Within a War

*All too often, that which we are most certain of is that which we
are the most wrong about; and that which we are wrong about can
change everything.*

— THE BOOK OF BRIN

"Holy mother of Ferrol!" Imaly exclaimed. She threw her cloak at the
stone bench and missed. It crumpled into a pile on the floor.

"This is no time to blaspheme the name of our lord," Volhoric said.
He paused for a moment, staring at the discarded cloak with a grimace so
disgusting that he might have been viewing a corpse.

"I wasn't," she said. "I was blaspheming Ferrol's mother."

"Ferrol doesn't have one," the High Priest snapped back.

Imaly made a show of dusting off her hands. "No harm done, then."

She went to the sarcophagus of Gylindora Fane, leaned over, and bowed
her head. Volhoric likely thought she was praying to her great ancestor
or some other such nonsense. Imaly just needed to catch her breath. She
wasn't as young as she used to be, and old Gylindora just happened to be
there.

*Good ole Great-Grandmama, lending support in my time of need. Maybe
I am praying to her.*

Nanagal came in next, looking pale, his hands nested together, the left squeezing the right. "I thought he was going to kill us right then and there."

Imaly had stressed the importance of not marching directly from the palace to the crypt. Chances of an observer reporting them were unlikely. Still, she didn't want a line of ducks waddling into the old tomb. The idea of meeting there was to avoid attention, and all of them gathering at once in broad daylight would be impossible to miss. Imaly had been forced to pick her co-conspirators based on their positions of influence, not their skill at subterfuge. She wondered if she would come to regret that, but she took solace in the notion that if she did, everyone else would, too.

Nanagal removed, neatly folded, and carefully laid his cloak on the bench. "Is anyone else sweating? My clothes are soaked. Another hour in that room with the fane and I swear I would have melted into my shoes. I kept thinking of Zephyron, you know?"

Imaly didn't nod, but she had most certainly been thinking of Lothian's prior challenger, not to mention the Gray Cloaks who'd had the misfortune of surviving their uprising.

"I doubt any serious effort went into cleaning that spot in the Carfreign Arena," Nanagal said. "I think Lothian wants it to remain. Wants us—wants everyone—to see it."

Hermon arrived next. He paused for a second near the entrance, halfway between the light of day and the darkness inside. He stared at them as if waiting for permission to enter.

"Get in here, you damn fool," Volhoric growled, beckoning the leader of the Gwydry with his arms and making the loose sleeves of his asica flap.

Hermon rushed forward, nodded to each of them, then pulled off his cloak and moved to the bench. He picked up Imaly's discarded garment and put it neatly on top of Nanagal's before adding his own to the pile.

"He's utterly insane now, isn't he?" Nanagal said, his eyes shifting from one to the next, even landing on Gylindora's vault, including the old fane in their number. "And I'm not sure I like meeting here anymore. It's too obvious. If Vasek finds us, what explanation can we offer?"

"That's not a problem," Imaly said. "Besides, we need to be able to speak openly, and this is the best place for that."

Imaly liked to believe that Gylindora would have been on their side, wanted to think Caratacus would have agreed, but there was no way of knowing. In a way, the original fane and her wizard sidekick were at fault for this mess. They had constructed the system the Aquila were trapped beneath.

"We have to do it," Volhoric said then. His words sounded like the conclusion to a private argument he'd been holding with himself. "We have to." This last bit had the tone of pleading, and he said it while looking at Imaly.

As if it's all up to me. Is that right, you old bastard? Will you say it was all my doing when Synne and Sile come for you? Will you proclaim, "It was all her fault! She corrupted us!"

The tomb of Gylindora wasn't too far off Florella Plaza. They all had to walk past the withering remains of those once majestic trees. Like the black spot in the Carfreign, the severed stumps had been left as a fitting memorial to all those who had died in the Gray Cloak Rebellion.

That's how Lothian had framed it in his speech to the Aquila so many years ago. *Let us never forget the brave and loyal defenders of Erivan who lost their lives to the evils of defying the truth of Ferrol.*

The truth of Ferrol had been a thinly veiled synonym for the rule of the Miralyith. The stumps in the plaza weren't a memorial to the defenders of the faith, but rather a reminder for any who might think of challenging Lothian again. He'd gruesomely executed the Gray Cloak survivors.

All but one, Imaly thought.

"Lothian doesn't really expect us to supply him with a list of names, does he?" Osla asked. "I don't know many Miralyith—and none so well as to be able to point out which people in their lives they love dearly."

"At least it is restricted to the Miralyith," Hermon said. "In a way, that feels like justice."

"Does it?" Imaly retorted. "No Miralyith will die. Only those of us whom the Miralyith love. That's how it works. And what if they don't love any single person enough? Will they be required to kill more than one? And how many? A handful? A score? Will it take a hundred acquaintances to generate the needed power to create one drag—"

"Why isn't it a problem if Vasek finds us?" Nanagal asked.

"What's that?" Imaly struggled to see the leader of the crafter's tribe, as he was in the shadows, outside the ring of light where the eternal flame burned upon the altar.

"Vasek," he explained, "you said if he finds us it wouldn't be an issue. He's Lothian's eyes and ears, so I think that would be a very big problem. Are you keeping secrets from us, Imaly?" Nanagal asked with surprising bluntness.

"Of course I am. I keep secrets from everyone. Sometimes, when I forget where I put my shoes, I suspect I'm keeping secrets from myself. That's the way this has to be done, for the protection of everyone. You have to trust me—and you do. Otherwise, none of you would be here." She stared each of them down. "I have a plan that could save us, but it requires the death of Lothian."

"As we feared, it has come down to breaking Ferrol's Law," Volhoric said.

"Yes."

A silence followed.

"Who will do it?" Volhoric asked.

"Leave that to me," Imaly replied.

"One of your many secrets?" Nanagal asked.

"The list is long, my dear."

"And what of his son?" Volhoric asked. "Mawyndulë will inherit the throne should Lothian die. We would be trading one Miralyith for another."

"My plan accounts for the prince as well. As Conservator of the Horn of *Gylindora Fane*"—Imaly put extra emphasis on the name she shared, to leverage every advantage she had—"I need you, Volhoric, to play your part. I must know that you'll present the horn and hand it over when I request it."

The High Priest nodded and said, "I swear it."

If all went according to plan, this would be their final meeting before she jumped off the cliff, dragging everyone else with her. Imaly gestured toward the others. "And all of you must do your parts. Each must agree to grant me the right to challenge."

"No one can hope to beat a Miralyith in combat," Hermon stated. "Least of all—and no disrespect intended—an elderly female Nilyndd."

"That's assuming there will be a challenge, which won't be the case." Imaly saw the bewilderment on their faces but told herself not to explain. The less they knew, the better. Conspiracies worked best when they were a conspiracy of one. "The wonderful part is that none of you will have broken a single law."

"What about you?" Nanagal asked. "Will you be able to say the same?"

"A few moral ones, certainly." Imaly turned and placed both hands on the stone that contained the first fane's remains. "In return, I hope to ensure the survival of our people, our culture, and our legacy. I think that's a fair trade."

"And if things do not go according to plan?" Hermon asked.

Imaly turned back. "Then we'll live under the heel of an insane fane who will force his people to kill their loved ones. Let's pray it doesn't come to that. So, do you agree or not?"

Each nodded in turn.

"Good. Now, as duly appointed Curator of the Aquila, I hereby call this quorum to session. All those in favor of granting me, Imaly Fane, granddaughter of Gylindora Fane, the Right of Challenge in the event of Fane Lothian's death and the end of the Sixth Uli Vermar, please indicate so by responding 'aye.'"

As he often did, Mawyndulë watched his goldfish swim back and forth in the bowl at the side of his bed. He'd never named it, referring to it as *fish* when he referenced it at all. The only person he ever discussed the fish with was Treya, his personal servant. He'd remind her to feed the fish or clean the bowl. Truth was, he didn't feel right naming the goldfish. Who was he to give something else a name? He was glad now that he hadn't. A name would have suggested a degree of value, a hint of fondness. These days, such attachments were dangerous.

The knock was a formality and shockingly short. An instant later, the door burst open. Synne entered quickly, locking eyes with him. Aggressive, cold, deadly, she was an unsheathed weapon. Behind her, Sile entered, his massive hands shoving Treya into the room.

Treya looked as scared as that time she had dropped the fishbowl. She had just finished cleaning it, and the sides had been wet, causing it to slip and burst against the floor. Water and glass had exploded, the fish skipping across the tile, flopping and slapping. Back then, Treya must have expected to die; she'd had that kind of look on her face. She displayed the same expression now.

Vasek came in last. The Master of Secrets appeared to be there as a witness, and he slipped to the side, standing between Mawyndulë's wardrobe and the washbasin. Of the three invaders, Vasek alone appeared regretful. But then, Mawyndulë had always believed that except for Imaly, Vasek must be the smartest Fhrey in Estramnadon. No matter what happened next, Vasek knew that Mawyndulë would never forgive the intrusion. That expression of remorse, false or not, might save him when Mawyndulë sat on the Forest Throne.

"What is the meaning of this?" Mawyndulë asked with conviction. He knew why they were there, and he was willing to play his part in the charade. He stood up to make a better showing.

"Your servant was found stealing from the fane," Synne said, in a furious tone, passionate enough to be insulting.

She actually thinks I'm clueless.

"Claims she's innocent," Synne added.

"I didn't do it," Treya told him. "I don't know how it got in my bag!"

Treya wasn't acting. She didn't know anything about the alleged offense, and she was so terrified that tears welled.

"What was it?" He was careful to phrase his response so as to not presume a crime had occurred.

No point in making this easy.

"Your father's gold candlestick from the reception hall," Synne responded rapidly. Her language was no different from her use of the Art. One was often a reflection of the other. Personalities came out in both.

Candlestick? Seriously? Is that the best you could come up with?

Mawyndulë struggled not to roll his eyes.

Do they expect me to believe she's got some sort of illegal merchant operation out in the plaza? Or maybe I'm supposed to think she'll set it out on her little nightstand and gawk at the grandeur? It would make more sense to accuse her of stealing the candles themselves; at least they can be lit and would be of some worth to her.

"Please, Your Highness, please *Mawyn,* tell them I would never do such a thing." While Treya had been his servant since Mawyndulë was an infant, she didn't look old. Neither did she look young. She was lost in that nondescript nether space of time between the two, but at that moment, she looked ancient. As Sile's massive fingers gripped her with judgmental tightness, Treya's eyes revealed lines of worry he'd never seen before. That she used his name—that she used a shortened familiar—showed the depth of her fear. Treya was clueless about the game, but not about the stakes. "Please tell them that I've been a loyal servant. That I've never disappointed you."

Mawyndulë thought of the shattered goldfish bowl, and his eyes unconsciously tracked to the tile on which it had fallen.

"We caught her leaving with the candlestick in her bag," Synne said. "The fane has decreed that she is to be put to death . . . unless you intercede on her behalf."

"Oh, holy Ferrol!" Treya wailed.

Mawyndulë showed no surprise or concern. He did frown in disappointment at Treya's outburst, then looked squarely at Synne and asked, "Why would I do that?"

This caught all of them off guard, and Mawyndulë struggled to forbid his lips from smiling. He had a secret place in his heart for making a fool of Synne. She thought herself so quick, so clever.

"Why what?" Synne asked, losing a good deal of her intimidation to puzzlement.

Mawyndulë shook his head in a show of ambivalence as he plopped down on his bed and hooked fingers behind his head. "Honestly, Synne. I thought you were quicker than this. Let me explain it in small words for you. Why have you come to me about this? If she is guilty and my father has ordered her execution, why haven't you obeyed? Why come to me?"

Vasek stepped forward then. "I suspect your father is concerned that since Treya raised you, her execution might be upsetting. As he doesn't wish to make his son unhappy, he is willing to mitigate the sentence should this be the case."

Doesn't want to make me unhappy? Vasek might not be as smart as I thought.

"It is not." Mawyndulë turned to his side and set his attention back to his goldfish, tapping the glass.

Treya's lips were quivering, tears running down her cheeks. "For the love of Ferrol, Mawyn, I'm your—" She stopped herself, hands covering her mouth, eyes bulging, pleading.

"Are you sure?" Vasek asked him.

Mawyndulë shot him an appalled look. "Usually, you hear people when they speak, Vasek. Apparently, Synne is growing slow and you deaf."

"But Treya is . . ." Synne made an uncharacteristic verbal stumble. She hesitated, eyes shifting between Treya and Mawyndulë. "She's the closest person you have to a mother."

"Are you *trying* to insult me, Synne? Treya is a servant—a Gwydry. We have others, I trust? After you melt off her flesh, or whatever you plan to do, be sure to find me a suitable replacement—one that doesn't *steal*. Can you manage that?"

Synne glared. She looked downright irritated.

Treya broke down in sobs.

Mawyndulë responded by looking back at the fish and reached out once more to tap the glass with his finger.

The four remained in the room for another round of heartbeats.

"Is there something else?" he asked with irritation.

"No, Your Highness," Synne said.

They withdrew, taking a sobbing Treya with them. When the door closed, Mawyndulë fell on his back. He felt exhausted. More than drained, he felt sick. He hadn't liked seeing Treya like that. He wanted to believe he'd just saved her life, but they could still kill her. Vasek might insist on it just to cover up the lie. Then he could claim ignorance of the sham, a poor assertion for a Master of Secrets.

Despite Mawyndulë's best efforts, it was possible she would still die and do so thinking he didn't care. That would be regrettable, but it was better than the alternative. He didn't know if he thought well enough of Treya to provide the adequate power to touch the deep chords required to make a dragon, but he didn't want to find out.

They won't kill her, he assured himself. *There would be no point. She's safe. She's safe.*

He told himself that over and over as he lay on his bed, crumpling up the covers in tight fists.

Synne was right, Treya was like a . . .

Mawyndulë sat up.

Why did they assume I would be upset? Why try this with me? And why use her?

Mawyndulë looked to where Treya had stood. He remembered her covering her mouth with her hands, stifling words that never came out.

Mawyndulë saw him sitting on the bench in the Garden across from the Door. The same person he'd spoken to years ago was back, or maybe he'd never left. Mawyndulë wouldn't know; the prince couldn't remember the last time he had been in that part of the Garden. It might have been years. Mawyndulë was almost certain this was the same fellow. There couldn't be two like him in Estramnadon. Only priests braved cold weather to sit and contemplate the Door, and priests were always clean. The fellow on the bench had wild, unkempt hair and a dirty cloak. Not a winter wrap, either, but a thin summer cape.

Fresh from his run-in with Synne and Vasek, Mawyndulë had chosen to take a walk. That way, if they killed Treya, he wouldn't hear the screams. He didn't usually go out in the cold. Took him ages just to find his heavy cloak, and after stepping outside and being hit by that first blast of wind, he decided to make his outing a quick circuit through the Garden, past the Airenthenon, around Florella Plaza, and then back to the palace. The trip would take him less than an hour, but even that seemed too adventurous.

He was having second thoughts, slowing down as he passed the Door, thinking that perhaps he could stomach the screams better than he could weather the cold, when the dirty fellow on the bench spoke.

"They won't kill her."

"Excuse me?" Mawyndulë asked. He did stop then, annoyed that this person felt it appropriate to speak to—

"Your father isn't a coward, you know."

"I'm sorry?" He wasn't, but Mawyndulë had no idea what this fellow in the disgusting clothes was talking about. It had sounded like an insult, and Mawyndulë's mood ramped up from annoyed to irritated and was now rolling quickly toward anger. "Who the—"

"It isn't that your father is trying to avoid the burden of killing the people he loves—that's not it at all. It's just that Lothian doesn't really love anyone. You shouldn't feel bad. It's not your fault. It's his deficiency, not yours. As for companions, a long—but not immortal—life span makes it so that Fhrey drop in and out of one another's lives. Not unlike dandelion tufts on a passing breeze. Passion is short-lived. After a while, you see affection for what it is—or what you *believe* it to be—a weakness. Losing people is painful. For you, they don't have to die. You just lose interest and move on.

That sort of thing becomes old fast. Less invested is less lost—and there is always a loss. Such deficits stack up over centuries. Scabs and calluses form, numbing you to the simple joys you once knew. After a few thousand years, you start to wonder if you were ever really happy. Probably not, you assume while safe in a cocoon, feeling nothing and afraid of everything. Of course, *you're* still young, still passionate, but you'll learn—learn far better than anyone."

Despite himself, Mawyndulë approached the stranger on the snowy bench. "You spoke to me once before. I remember the conversation now. You spouted some nonsense about hate and revenge. Who are you?" Mawyndulë said, folding his arms in a clear show of disapproval.

The fellow before him either didn't notice or didn't care about the prince's reproof. Apparently, he didn't care about a lot of things, like the fact that winter had arrived or that bathing was a virtue.

"You don't want to know," the fellow continued. "You don't actually care. You really just want me to leave you alone. You merely came out here for a walk, just wanted to get clear of the palace for a while. That's how life works. As you walk through it, you can't see the big moments coming at you. Don't notice them until they've gone by. We always see them from the back, never from the front, which presents a distorted perspective. Everything looks different from behind in that wonderful reflective afterglow. Afterward, things consistently appear bigger, more obvious, and we think, *How could I not have seen that?* But the moments that change our lives are indistinguishable from everything else because they aren't significant—until they are. Do you understand?"

"No!" Mawyndulë shouted at him. "But you're right about not wanting to talk to you." He had turned and started walking away when something hit him in the back. He spun to see the fellow on the bench grinning. Something was on the ground. It was small and red and lying on top of the thin coating of snow at his feet.

A strawberry?

Mawyndulë bent down and plucked it up. The fruit was fresh, ripe, and perfect.

"Jerydd taught you how to eavesdrop from long distances using the Art. You'll need that ability in the future, but that's not all you'll require. It'd be in your best interest to learn about Troth."

Mawyndulë looked over the top of the strawberry at him. "You're very strange."

The person on the bench smiled. "Troth is the chord of creation."

"There is no such thing," Mawyndulë declared. This was a topic he knew about. This queer little creature on the bench was presuming to know about the Art and was—as most laymen were—wrong. "There is no chord of creation."

"Of course there is. How do you think everything was made?"

"It can't be reached with the Art."

"How do you think Jerydd made his strawberry? Where do you think this one came from?"

Mawyndulë stared at him.

How does he know about Jerydd and his mysterious fruit? How did he know I would be taking a walk? And about Treya and my father? There is no way he could know any of that. Who is he?

"Troth is massive—so big it doesn't feel like a chord at all. That's why most—like you and your teachers—don't know it exists. Wouldn't matter if you did; the power it takes to pluck it is overwhelming. Jerydd needed the full force of Avempartha just to make that single tiny strawberry. An autonomous creature like the one your father is struggling to produce is even harder to achieve."

Mawyndulë looked down at the berry in his fingers. "But you made this without . . ." He looked around at the dead and snowy world.

"It'd be best if you took me out of such contexts. Doing otherwise will only confuse you. I'm different, and I don't play by the rules. My presence is a perfect example. That I intend to teach you how to make a real strawberry is another."

Mawyndulë looked back at the fruit. "Why?"

"Because twice is not enough." He pointed at the Door. "I need footprints to track, and my prey is a crafty one. I'm hoping three times will be the key." He laughed. "Get it? The key?"

"You're making no sense at all."

The fellow on the bench smiled, this time with amusement that bordered on sinister. "It will be clear when you look back on it, when you see *this* moment from behind. All the pieces are in position, or will soon be. Still, you need to be armed for the future because you're going to need all the help you can get. Now listen closely."

Mawyndulë had escaped the Garden. That's how he looked at it, how he *saw it from behind.*

The guy on the bench had blathered on and on about Troth and creation, while Mawyndulë had retreated with smiles and nods until he finally waved farewell and hurried off.

What was that all about?

Mawyndulë made a mental note to report him to Vasek. As he left the Garden through the gate, a wave of relief washed over him. The stranger on the bench was disturbing.

Both times!

He did appear to know about the Art, but his ideas were queer. Not thinking about where he was going, Mawyndulë ended up exiting on the river side of the Garden. He should have headed back to the palace. His feet were cold, and if Treya were going to be killed, the execution would be over by now.

Who—or what—was he?

While still trying to make sense of his trip through the Garden, Mawyndulë was working his way along the river, approaching the infamous bridge, which was now covered in snow. That's when he saw her. At first, the prince was certain he was wrong. What he was seeing had to be an illusion, a trick of light, maybe a vision, some sort of manifested memory, even a ghost. But no, it was Makareta. She was there, not under the bridge but at the end of the walkway between two leafless birch trees. She wore black and white in the fashion of an Umalyn. Even with the dark hood pulled up, he recognized her. In the shadow of that cowl, a pair of frightened eyes looked out at him.

Lost in shock and disbelief, he stared.

"I've been afraid to show myself to you—afraid you'd—but now . . ." Her eyes fluttered with concern.

Same voice. All the muscles in Mawyndulë's stomach were squeezing. The cold of his feet was forgotten. "How—how are you alive?"

"I got away. Stayed hidden."

"Where?"

"Here." She made a vague motion at everything and nothing.

"You stayed hidden here in Estramnadon for seven years?"

The dark hood barely moved as her head nodded.

Is Vasek that terrible at his job? How has no one seen her? How did she get any food? How did she survive?

Makareta didn't look any different.

Well, maybe a little, he conceded.

That happy smile she used to wear was gone, and her eyes seemed older—worn out—exhausted. She was still pretty. The pout and the sad, frightened eyes she now wore suited her, made her more vulnerable, more appealing. He thought this even as he remembered that she had betrayed him, that she was a murderer. But that second thought was only an idea, like plans for tomorrow, and she was right there in front of him.

"I had to see you," she said.

"Why?"

"To say I was sorry. To make sure you knew that I never meant—" She took a deep breath. "You see, I planned to explain things later on, but that time never came. And I thought that if I . . ." Her hands came up toward her face, only going half the distance. The sleeves of the robe were so long that all he saw were the tips of her fingers. Makareta nervously looked around at the empty landscape and adjusted her hood, pulling it forward to cover more of her face. "Can we go somewhere and sit? Will you give me a chance to explain?"

"You used me to try to kill my father. What explanation could you possibly give?"

"That if we had succeeded, you'd be fane. And if that had happened, the Miralyith wouldn't be exiled on the banks of the Nidwalden, and we wouldn't be in a pointless war with the Rhunes."

Mawyndulë glanced over his shoulder toward the palace. He wasn't sure what to do. He'd told himself that if he ever saw her again, he'd kill her. He could. When she murdered other Fhrey, her own action ejected her from their society. By Ferrol's Law, Makareta was no longer Fhrey and no longer under his protection.

He had played out the scenario thousands of times. He'd make a flippant remark and casually set her on fire, or do what Gryndal had done to those Rhunes in the burned-out village. He would snap his fingers and she would blow apart. He'd pictured those scenes many times, but in none of them had she looked so sad, so vulnerable, so enticing. In his daydreams, she always presented him with a vicious, maniacal grin.

He'd always thought that seeing her would be frightening. Just as he could kill her, she could do the same to him. Having murdered once, any added body count wouldn't make the state of her soul any worse off. He ought to be tense, terrified, but he didn't feel any of those things. She wasn't threatening in any way. He stared at her, and she looked back. It felt as if he were peering into her soul through a door she'd purposely left open.

"Yes, we can sit," he said.

She nodded, pivoting on her left heel, and led him to a flat rock near the bridge, close to the scene of the crime. She dusted it off with the too-long sleeves that flopped about in a ridiculous manner. She cleared a patch big enough for both of them. Then she sat down.

Her disguise was a good one. Umalyn priests dressed just that way and were often seen near the Garden. No one but he would have recognized her, and he did only because she wanted him to.

Mawyndulë took a step and sat beside her.

"You can kill me," she said, shocking him with the invitation. "I won't even put up a shield, but I hope you'll let me speak before you do. I know you must hate me. Probably see no reason to listen, but . . . well . . ." She shook her head. "I know you won't believe this, but my feelings toward you were always sincere, and, yes, I really believe you'll make a better fane than your father."

She bowed her head, slapped her lap with her sleeves, and emitted a frustrated huff. "All of this sounds so contrived! Anything I say now will come off like begging, and I suppose I am, but you should be able to accept this much." She looked up at him. "By coming to you now, I'm literally putting my life in your hands. You don't even have to kill me yourself. All you have to do is tell your father that I'm still alive. If you do that, I'm dead. It's that easy for you to kill me."

"Maybe not. If you've evaded the search for this long—"

"No one has been looking. Not for a long time, at least. Everyone thinks I'm dead or gone to some faraway place."

"And so you risked your life just to apologize to me?"

"No—that's part of it—a big part, but there's something else."

Mawyndulë waited, but Makareta didn't say anything for a long while. She sat with her head bowed, her knees clamped together, shivering slightly. He could see the fine material of the robes quiver.

"What is it?" he finally asked.

She sucked in a breath, and he thought she might be crying, but her face was lost in the hood. "This is hard for me. I'm—I'm really scared."

"Of what?"

"Of you."

"Really?"

"I'm afraid you won't believe, and that you'll hate me."

"What you really fear is that I'll kill you—or have someone else do it."

She shook her head. "I did—I was—not now. I think if you were going to do that, you already would have. No, I'm scared because—Mawyn, *I've killed Fhrey.*" She drew back the hood, and he could see tears in her eyes. "When I die, I don't know what will happen. Maybe I'll just disappear or dissolve, but one thing I know for certain is I'll be unable to enter Phyre. No one will mourn me. No one cares—no one at all." The tears slipped down her cheeks. "You have no idea what it feels like. I'm facing oblivion, and I'm all alone. I just want to know someone somewhere cares. And right now, you're the only one who I think might. But if what I have to tell you doesn't change your mind, then I'm truly lost. So please, try to listen with an open mind and heart, and if when I'm finished you want to hand me over to your father, so be it."

He reached out and touched her trembling hands. He didn't know why. He hadn't thought about it, but he was glad he had. They still felt the same—better, even. In the past, Makareta had been a wild thing he was trying to impress; now she came to him in defeat, in surrender. He realized that no matter what she said, he could never hand her over to his father. He was stunned to discover the truth, but not surprised. He wouldn't give even his goldfish to Lothian.

"I'm listening," he told her, and he meant it.

Makareta nodded, took a shaky breath, and began. "Seven years ago, I fell in with a group of foolish kids who had an insane idea of assassinating the fane. We were going to save Erivan for the Miralyith. I was wrong. Erivan isn't just the Miralyith. There are seven tribes, and they all deserve a voice. They all deserve respect. That's how Ferrol meant it to be, but your father is standing in the way. And he's made a mess of this war. The most recent rumor is that he intends to force Miralyith to kill their loved ones to make dragons."

"Yes, that's true."

"If Lothian remains fane much longer, even if he manages to defeat the Rhunes, there won't be an Erivan left to save. He's destroying all that's good about our society in order to win a war that *he* started. He's lost the heart of the people. No one has faith in him anymore. You're in the palace, so maybe you don't hear, but I'm out here in the shadows, listening. I can tell you that our people are undecided about who is the greater threat, the Rhunes or your father. That lottery he ran was horrible. What an awful way to choose a sacrifice, and it was for nothing—he botched the weave, and now he'll try again and hope for success."

"He didn't understand how it worked. Now he does."

"And you believe that?"

Mawyndulë nodded. "Not because he told me, but because it makes sense. The weave requires enormous power, the sort of burst you can get from anguish, fear, and the release at death, but it has to be doubled by the anguish of killing a loved one. All that energy needs to be channeled, funneled into the weave. My father didn't know the Gwydry, so he couldn't generate enough power."

Makareta nodded thoughtfully, and as she did, he saw concern followed by resolve.

"What?" he asked.

"Years ago, I was wrong to try to kill the fane, but times have changed. I can see that now."

"What are you saying? Are you—"

"Mawyn, how badly does your father want to make dragons?"

"It's all he thinks about."

"What's stopping him? Why aren't there ten dragons out there?"

Mawyndulë considered this for a moment. He had thought it was because his father was a coward, that he didn't want to be the one to perform the sacrifices. Except . . .

Your father isn't a coward, you know . . . It's just that Lothian doesn't really love anyone. You shouldn't feel bad. It's not your fault. It's his deficiency, not yours.

Mawyndulë wasn't prone to believing strangers on a bench, but it *felt* true. His father couldn't make a dragon because he couldn't touch Troth.

"I suppose my father—I guess he just can't—I don't think he cares that much about anyone."

"See, I think you're wrong. I think he does," Makareta said. "The only question is . . . what happens when he realizes that he isn't too old to have another heir?"

The thought had never crossed Mawyndulë's mind, and he still struggled to grasp what she was suggesting. When the pieces finally fell into place, he shook his head. "You have me confused with my brother Pyridian, the son my father loved. Killing me wouldn't be a big enough sacrifice."

"Neither was Amidea, and she's dead. I don't trust your father, and I don't think you are safe with him around." She paused, and then with trepidation she added. "Mawyn, I'm going to try to kill your father again. For you and for all our people, and this time I'm *asking* for your help."

CHAPTER TWENTY-TWO

The Hole

Endless, pointless, careless, needless—Nifrel should not be a name for one of the realms of the afterlife. Instead, it should be the word we use to define conflict for conflict's sake.

— THE BOOK OF BRIN

Brin walked between Tressa and Moya as the army traveled through the dark tunnel. Thousands of heads bobbed in the dim light, and twice that many feet struck the floor, a sound that echoed and was as ominous as a drumroll. Brin had seen Rhunes, Fhrey, and even a few Grenmorians among the many Belgriclungreians. Each of them carried weapons and were dressed in elaborate armor as if they were going to some grand celebration. Brin felt safe, even though she knew she shouldn't. She'd seen what happened to even the most impressive of armies when they reached the field of battle. She knew what was out there, what they were marching toward. All the tall warriors in the world couldn't protect her from that. Brin knew this, yet as she traveled through the underground, she *did* feel confident.

It's probably the armor.

All six of them wore metal now. Brin had expected that the pile of glittering bronze Roan had handed her would be heavy and restrictive, but once she got it on, she felt lighter and freer than ever before. More than that, she felt stronger—and she glowed. They all did to some degree, but Brin was the brightest.

"How do you do that?" Moya asked, squinting slightly as she looked over. "It's not the armor, is it?"

"No," Roan said from behind. "Not really."

All six of them were bunched together in the center of the marching column. Beatrice had insisted they be protected above all else, and her father had agreed.

"The armor only enhances and amplifies," Roan explained. "The light is the visual representation of your spirit."

Moya nodded toward the Keeper. "So, what's with all the light? Are you saying Brin has a dazzling spirit or something?"

"Innocence," Beatrice called back. She walked in front of them between Rain and a man who wore a sword slung on his back. "She shines so brightly because innocence is not something found in Nifrel. It's how Fen knew Brin didn't belong. Even before the armor, you must have noticed the way she glowed. The girl is pure light."

"I'm not *that* innocent," Brin said, defending herself. "I've seen some stuff. I've *done* some things."

"Kill anyone?" Beatrice asked.

"Ah . . ." Brin almost laughed, but stopped herself when she realized Beatrice wasn't joking. "No."

"Just about everyone here has. In Nifrel—well, we all have memories we want to forget—shadows that stifle the light."

"Wait a minute." Moya shielded her eyes as she spoke. "That light is really bright. Exactly how *innocent* are you, Brin?"

"About as unsullied as they come, I would think," Beatrice replied.

"Brin . . . ?" Moya said. "You and Tesh—you, ah . . . the two of you have been seeing each other for years. It isn't possible that you and he have never . . . you know?"

Brin didn't answer.

Moya's eyes widened. "Seriously?"

Brin looked uncomfortable.

"And Tesh was okay with that?"

Brin frowned and shook her head. "Wasn't me. It was him. He insisted we wait so we wouldn't have children before the end of the war. He didn't want to leave me a widow with little ones to care for."

"War never got in my way when it came to having a family," said the man walking next to Beatrice with the sword lashed to his back. "War is like snow in winter. Yeah, it makes everything harder, but it's always gonna be there. Can't stop living just because of a few flakes."

Brin thought he looked familiar. He wore no armor and was dressed in poor wool and badly stitched leather with a leigh mor wrapped over one shoulder. The pattern was Dureyan. He had a thumb hooked in his belt; the other hand held a spear like a walking stick. And then there was that sword on his back. She was certain she'd seen it before. "Excuse me, do I know you?"

"Don't think so. I'm certain I'd remember a pretty thing like you. I'm Herkimer of Dureya," the man said over his shoulder as he marched.

"You're Raithe's father!" Brin exclaimed.

"Indeed, I am. Did you know him? His brothers are here, too." The man lifted his chin, trying to see over the heads of the others in the moving column. "Somewhere."

"Where's Raithe?" Brin asked.

Herkimer shrugged. "Still alive, I suppose. Up there killing Gula and preserving the family name."

"Actually, he died several years ago," Moya said. "And the Gula and Rhulyn Rhunes are united now. They all serve under Keenig Persephone."

This brought a puzzled look to the man's face, not sorrow but confusion. "Strange. I guess maybe he went to Rel then. He always was an odd boy. Head full of dreams. Used to say he wanted to *do* something important with his life—as if the fighting his brothers and I were doing in the Gula Valley wasn't good enough. Looks like he never amounted to anything. That's too bad."

Brin looked back at Roan, whose workshop had hosted the sacrifice. Of course, Roan wouldn't say anything, and Tressa, who looked exhausted, didn't seem as if she had heard. Brin held her tongue.

That isn't why Raithe did it. That isn't what he would want.

The tunnel was mostly uniform, but from time to time, it widened in natural places where the cut passage broke into existing caverns. Dull, shattered rock with uneven floors announced the shifts. At such times, they could have walked as many as twenty abreast, but they never did. The three-wide march was a disciplined one. In these natural caverns, Brin noticed that the stone under their feet was different from the rest. The gray stone was harder, colder. How she knew this was a mystery, but she felt the change—the gray rock wasn't eshim, it was *real.*

Tressa, who'd been strangely silent since they left the Bulwark, stumbled. Brin turned. "You okay?"

The woman shook her head, causing the plume of feathers on her helm to whip from side to side. Despite the armor, Tressa didn't look heroic. She looked withered.

"Tressa, is it because of . . . what you're carrying?" In a place where ideas and feelings had substance, such a powerful thing—such a responsibility—must be a burden.

"No," Tressa replied. Both her hands crossed over her chest, palms to the key hidden beneath. Her armor didn't glow, not so much as a glint or reflection. Tressa's was so dull the metal looked worn. "That's not a burden at all. If anything, it's lifting me up," she said with a strained voice. "I swear, right now it's all that's keeping me on my feet."

"What's wrong, then?"

"I don't know. I just feel . . . I feel so *heavy.* Didn't bother me so much in the fortress, but outside . . ."

The column slowed to a crawl. Brin couldn't see over the heads and shoulders of all those ahead of her.

"What's up?" Moya asked Beatrice when they came to a complete stop and stood within the forest of metal-clad men and dwarfs.

Beatrice looked back, bright eyes flashing within that frame of white hair. "We've reached the first crevice. With so many people crossing, it will take some time." She sighed. "Just have to wait our turn."

"So, we're beyond the castle walls now?" Moya looked up.

"Oh, yes, but there's no going under the crevices. They go all the way down to the Abyss, and much of the stone here can't be dug."

"The Abyss," Brin said. "Where the Typhons are?"

"Exactly."

"You never finished your story."

"You're right, I didn't." Beatrice thought a moment. "And it seems we have some time." She motioned for them to gather close. "Where did I leave off?"

"Turin's time to die had come," Brin said.

"Oh, yes." Beatrice thought a moment then began her tale once more. "So at that time, everyone—all the peoples of the world—lived in one place, a great city named Erebus." She winked at Brin.

"So Drome was telling the truth. It really *was* a city." Brin grinned.

"That's right."

"I suppose that works, too. I mean, people *come from* a city, but—where did those first people come from?" Brin asked.

"Descendants of the Aesira, that's what we all are. People had longer lives then and many, many children."

"In this city—in Erebus—were there Fhrey, and men, and—"

"No, there were no races. Everyone was pretty much the same at that time—except the Grenmorians, who, as I said, are another story, and they didn't live in Erebus." She waited a moment to make certain no more questions were coming, then went on. "So anyway, everyone lived in this great city, and they were happy, but no one had ever died before. Turin was the oldest, so he would be the first. He didn't know what to expect, but he knew he would be alone, and he was terrified. He begged Eton to reconsider but was refused, and Elan wouldn't chance going against her husband again. No one was willing to help him. No one except his closest friend—Alurya. Using the gift of immortality granted to her by Eton, she grew fruit that held the essence of eternal life and offered it to Turin. He plucked two, devoured one, and saved the other in case he needed it."

The line of soldiers shuffled forward, and they followed suit. As they did, Brin noticed a light coming from above. Faint and starless, what the realm of Nifrel considered a sky outlined the crevice they approached.

"This was the start of it all," Beatrice said as they moved forward. "By eating the fruit, Turin made his Elan-half—his body—immortal. With no fear of death, he grew arrogant. He saw himself as superior to his brothers and sisters and began to rule over them and their families. Having successfully defied Eton's edict, he saw himself as a god and changed his name, calling himself Rex Uberlin. He became a tyrant. Then when his brother Trilos fell in love with Turin's daughter Muriel, Turin—who was every bit as selfish as his father—separated the two and ordered that they never see each other again. Trilos and Muriel defied him and plotted to run away together. Turin discovered their plans, and in a fit of rage, he killed his brother, making Trilos the first ever to die.

"Outraged at the murder of Trilos, Ferrol took her people and left Erebus. She set out into the western wilderness, into the forests. Soon after, Drome did the same, taking his descendants and leading them to a dome-shaped mountain in the southwest where they built their new city. Mari followed suit, escaping to a river valley and settling on its banks.

"Distraught over killing Trilos, Turin let them go, maybe thinking they would come back. When they didn't, when he heard that they mocked him from their new cities, Turin followed his invention of murder with the creation of war."

The line of warriors moved to single file then, as they found themselves inching out onto a narrow ledge. The story came to an abrupt end as they became too strung out. Wouldn't have mattered; Brin couldn't have concentrated on the story anymore. They had their backs to a sheer cliff as they shuffled sideways. In front of them, the world dropped away into darkness. Across the narrow split, the far wall of the canyon could barely be seen. Brin heard a *zzrrupt!* sound and saw movement as if a bird had taken flight. Her mouth dropped open when she realized what it was.

Twelve ropes were stretched across the chasm. The far side was lower than the near side. As she watched, Herkimer tied his spear on his body. Then he laid a leather strap over the next available line and wrapped both ends around his fists.

He's not going to—

Before she finished the thought, Herkimer jumped off the ledge and dangled from that tiny strap, his feet kicking out in front of him. The Dureyan slid as fast as a diving hawk across the gap between the two cliff walls.

"Oh Grand Mother of All!" Brin declared.

"Not as scary as it looks," Beatrice called back as she stepped up and without a second's hesitation, she followed Herkimer's example.

Zzrrupt!

"I can't do that," Tressa said.

"Have to," a dwarf at one of the ropes' anchor points said while waving her over. "Only way across."

"Why isn't there a bridge?" Moya asked, sounding less than pleased as well.

The dwarf pointed up. "Queen's forces would spot it—smash it. You're lucky. They're usually dropping rocks on us at this point. Guess they haven't seen us yet."

A dwarf stationed at a different line handed Moya a strap. She looked with wide eyes at Brin and shrugged. "Can't die when you're already dead, right?"

"Falling into the Abyss is worse than dying," the dwarf said.

"Oh, shut up, will you?" Moya snarled. Then, mimicking the others, she shoved off.

Zzrrupt!

Brin held her breath as Moya rapidly diminished in size.

"Here." The dwarf handed Brin a strap. She took it mindlessly. The thing was about three feet long, no more than an inch in width, and as thick as a belt.

"Like this?" she asked as she dropped it over the line. "How many times do I wrap it around my hands?"

The dwarf looked at her, irritated. "What hands? Now go, you're holding up the line."

Brin scowled. "You know, I've never really liked dwarfs."

"What's a dwarf? Never mind. Go!" he shouted.

At least he didn't shove her. Thinking he might, Brin summoned the courage to jump.

To her surprise, the trip was incredibly easy. She expected to dangle helplessly, stretched by the weight of her body, but she found she hardly weighed a thing. Her arms never even extended as she zipped down the rope with ease. And then she was there, the trip over in a flash.

"Told you," Beatrice said. "Easier than it looks. Of course, I think you'll find that in *here*—for *you*—most things will be."

From what Tesh saw, none of the realms of Nifrel were pretty or pleasant. Not the sort of place anyone would choose to be. In that respect, it had the odd virtue of feeling like home. Nifrel and Dureya were surprisingly alike: dreary, dismal, barren, filled with disagreeable people, and in a constant state of warfare. And like Dureya, some parts were nicer than others. The hole they dropped him in was by far the least pleasant place he'd been.

It really was just a hole: two stories deep, with sheer sides of damp stone and a puddle of something at the bottom. Not water, the liquid was something else—something slick, thick, and oily. It glowed a bit. Not much, but the bottom of the hole generated a faint blue light, which was good because otherwise Tesh would have been trapped in total darkness since the top of the hole had been sealed shut by a rock.

No ladder or rope for him—just a good solid shove. He bounced off one wall and crumpled at the bottom. He didn't have a body to bruise, but it hurt anyway, just as falling on stone should. That might be part of it; things happened in Nifrel as he expected. This led Tesh to wonder if what he felt was real or merely what he imagined. Perhaps he anticipated pain, believed in it, and that belief became his reality. A lot of times nightmares worked the same way. When he was running from something, he would think how awful it would be if the door ahead were bolted closed. The moment he pulled on it, he knew it would be true, and sure enough, it was. That was Nifrel in a nutshell, and he imagined that's what Fenelyus had been trying to explain.

Then a new thought arose. What if it wasn't merely Nifrel or Phyre? What if it was the spirit? When the soul suffered pain, whether in Elan or Phyre, it translated it into familiar, understandable terms. As Brin entered that loathsome mud puddle in the Swamp of Ith—when he watched her die—he'd felt a pain in his chest and stomach like swords gutting him. Such wounds had nothing to do with the flesh, but that was how his spirit understood the pain, and it was his soul that had been wounded. Here in Nifrel, he didn't breathe, but he felt short of breath while trembling at the bottom of that greasy black pit where only the glow of the liquid allowed him to see.

Maybe the mind and the spirit were linked in ways the body couldn't share. If what he thought became real, how was that different from what Suri could do with the Art?

He shuffled to get his feet underneath his body.

The pit was narrow. He could touch both sides at once. Lengthwise, it was wider, and, stretching out, his hand touched a shoulder.

I'm not alone!

Through the gloom, Tesh could see that his cellmate was bald, and he had bushy brows, a craggy nose, and a beard that was braided like rope—a dwarf certainly, and none too attractive. He sat with knees up, his arms hugging them. Wide-set, deep-sunk eyes watched Tesh with alarmed intensity as if Tesh were a fanged monster. The dwarf didn't move. He sat still as stone, easy enough when breathing wasn't a requirement, which was why Tesh hadn't noticed him sooner. Even his eyes didn't move.

They watched each other for a long while. Tesh had no idea how long.

"Who are you?" the dwarf finally said, his voice the sound of rough rocks rubbed together.

"Tesh of Clan Dureya." For some reason, pointing out his clan felt important even though his people had died years ago.

Start a family. Raise children. Live a good and happy life—someplace safe and pretty. At the time Raithe had said those words, they meant nothing. Years later, when Tesh was fighting in the Harwood, little had changed. Sitting in that hole beside the ugly dwarf, they were everything.

"What'd you do?" the dwarf asked.

"What do you mean?"

The bearded knee-hugger cast a quick glance toward the top of the hole. "To get tossed down 'ere."

Tesh considered this. He was there because the queen didn't believe him about Tressa; because he followed the woman he loved into a muddy pool; because he was born Dureyan. "Nothing," Tesh said.

"Aye, me, too." The dwarf nodded with a contrived grin. "Nothing at all." He tightened his grip on his legs as if trying to squeeze himself as far away from Tesh as possible. The dwarf watched Tesh through surreptitious peeks from the corners of his eyes.

Tesh didn't move beyond what it took to get comfortable, or as comfortable as he could get in a wet pit.

The dwarf was breathing again, but too quickly to be normal. "Well?"

"Well, what?" Tesh asked, but the dwarf didn't answer.

Tesh laid his head back on the stone.

Tesh, you aren't going to be with Brin, no matter how things turn out. The queen had intended this to be hurtful, as some sort of revelation.

Had he thought of it at the time—had he been capable of thinking—he might have told her, "No kidding. Let me introduce myself; my name is Tesh. I'm Dureyan."

Tesh had hoped he might have a future with Brin in the same way he wished winters to become a passing fancy. Such hopes were nice to dream about; everyone needed something to look forward to. But believing in them was the mistake. Once that happened, dreams grew teeth, and if you didn't feed them, they would bite. Tesh had only one dream he'd endowed with fangs. He'd come inches from achieving it, but now it gnawed on his bones. Ferrol didn't know about that dream or she didn't care. She thought his disappointment of losing Brin would hurt more, but she was stabbing a numb leg. Tesh knew he'd never had a future with Brin. This was why he'd kept her at a distance, why he'd spent so much time away. Brin liked him too much, and she deserved better.

"So you're not going to do anything to me?" the dwarf asked.

Tesh looked over, puzzled. "Like what?"

The dwarf shrugged. "Beat me, stab me, gouge me eyes out?"

"Why would I do any of that?"

The dwarf squinted at him and shifted his lips so that his mustache and beard did a little dance. "You're new 'ere, aren't ya? How long ya been in Nifrel?"

"I don't know." Tesh looked up. "How do you tell time?"

"When was it ya died?"

"Just about winter."

"Ah, no, ya crazy badger." The dwarf rolled his eyes, scowling so that the hair under his lower lip bristled like the back of an angry woodchuck. "Rhunes," he muttered. "Ya have no sense of history."

"Whose story?"

The dwarf turned his head and looked at Tesh with full-faced disbelief.

"How long have *you* been here?" Tesh asked.

"Don't know." The dwarf relaxed his grip on his knees and let his back settle against the wall. "Was hoping you could tell me. Several centuries, I'm guessing."

"You've been in Nifrel for that long or you've been sitting here for that amount of time?"

"Aye." The dwarf nodded. That single word was spoken casually and followed by a tension-releasing sigh. The dwarf let his little legs extend out as far as they would go, which was almost straight. "Ya might want to get comfortable, too, lad. Ya ain't going anywhere, either."

"Why's that?"

"Ferrol doesn't let anyone near me unless she trusts them, or they are beyond all hope, and you don't look like the trustworthy type."

"I don't understand. Do you have a disease or something?"

"Worse. Knowledge. Can't let me run loose, and she doesn't want ta lose me to the Abyss—that's how aff 'er hide she is."

"How what?"

"You know, doo-lally." He made a swirling motion with his finger while pointing at his own ear.

"Crazy?"

"Aye, she is that. No one has ever come back from the Abyss, but that's too great a risk. Might need me someday. This hole is her solution to the folk she doesn't want to erase, but also doesn't want running around and causing trouble. A way to bury us forever, but in a place where she can check on. There's only this one hole that's deep enough and made o' real stone, with a mouth small enough to be covered by those flat rocks they laid over top—they're real too. So, we're stuck together, I guess. The good news is she's not done with ya, but that's also the bad news."

Tesh rotated and put his back to the stone to better face his hole-mate. "Who *are* you?"

"Wondering when you'd ask. Name is Andvari Berling. You should be impressed, should have your mouth hanging open right now, but being a Rhune, you have no idea what that means, do ya?"

Tesh shook his head.

"Doesn't matter." Andvari noticed the bottom of his beard was starting to unravel and worked at rebraiding it.

"So, what is it that *you* know that's so important?" Tesh asked.

"Nothing world shattering. In a way, that's the worst part. Maybe if I knew something tremendous, something that could upend the order of things—but I don't."

"What is it then?"

"Have you heard of the Golrok?"

"Nope, sounds like a Grenmorian."

Andvari shook his head. "It's not a who. It's a what. Mideon's daughter has the gift of future sight and told everyone about it before she learned there be some things best kept to 'erself. The story goes that one day the door to Alysin will open, and everyone will march out of Nifrel for one great final battle that will determine the fate of the world. The queen thought she would tilt the scales in 'er favor by destroying the bridge after she and 'er forces leave, but before anyone else could, giving 'er a head start. So she built 'er fortress as close to the bridge as she could. Then she made preparations to destroy it."

"Arranged? Can't she just make it go away? Isn't all of this her creation? A reflection of her will and all that?"

"Most of what we see, sure, but it's like carpet and drapes. Phyre is a real place, carved out of the center of Elan, out of the bedrock of the old lady. It's a container, you see. Everything else in 'ere is sand in a sandbox, filled with expressions of ourselves—eshim, we call it. The ground, the trees, the buildings are all inventions. But the bedrock—that's real. It can't be altered by force of will. The genuine stone, the rock that is Elan, is what keeps all of us 'ere. We can't affect it, not with spirit hands. The bridge to the Alysin Door is an actual bridge, made from the bedrock of Elan. For all 'er strength, the queen is powerless to change it any more than she can affect the door itself. We are all just spirits 'ere, shades bouncing around in the stone prison of Elan's womb."

"So, how did she do it? How did she arrange to destroy the bridge?"

"*She* didn't. I did." Andvari looked sick as he said it. "Didn't want to, but you must know how she is. There's no defying 'er, not when she's got that light on ya, and it bears down hard. All of the five are incredibly powerful, but she's the worst. Ferrol is an example of what hate can do to a person. She was beautiful once, inside and out, but hatred ruined 'er. Revenge is all that's left. All she exists for. Such a thing consumes a spirit, makes it into something bottomless, like the Abyss, I suppose."

"How did you do it? You're a shade, too, right?"

"Aye, yer right." Andvari smiled, a glint of pride in his eyes. "What you don't know about me is that I know a little something about stones and minerals, metals, and crystals. I can build things."

"Can you build a ladder?"

"I could, but wouldn't do ya no good. As I said, that lid above our heads is real stone, razor-thin flecks of mica that in life weigh no more than wet oak leaves. But as shades, we can't touch them and can't pass through."

"Someone moved them."

"Aye, two people if ya gonna be precise. If ya join wills, ya can join power."

"There are two of us now. So, couldn't we—"

"Nope, because there are two rocks, one atop the other. If you're up there, you can move them one at a time. Down 'ere, we'd have to move two at once, and that's if we could do it at all. Hard to move stone without hands." Andvari reached up and clapped the wall. "This 'ere is real. This muck we're standing in is, too, but it is possible with great effort to affect things in minor ways." He put his hand into the pool and swirled it around. Nothing happened. Then he took a deep breath and, biting his lip, cupped a hand and lowered it into the oily liquid. Lifting it, Tesh saw that a tiny bit was carried up before slipping through his fingers. Afterward, the dwarf slung his shoulders as if exhausted. "It's not easy, but it can be done. That's how they slid those rocks over us."

"How'd you do that?"

"Willpower and a lot of concentration. Ever heard anyone say they achieved something through *willing it to be so?* Well, there's a lot more to that than just a saying. The Fhrey have wizards who can tap into the power of Elan and make things happen, but spirits can do it, too. Most of us are weak little flickering flames when compared with the power of the whole living world, but our spirits are of Eton, and there's no one who can say Eton is weak. So up there, two or three can work together to slide those rocks, or maybe it's just the queen 'erself that does it."

"Okay, sure." Tesh looked down at the muck, remembering the tiny drop of liquid. "But there's no way you could destroy a bridge of solid stone that way."

"O' course not." The dwarf shook his head. "But as I just told ya, I know rocks and minerals. Some of those when struck can make a spark."

"I've seen that before," Tesh said.

"Right." The dwarf raised a finger and pointed at him. "And others will actually burn, and when they do, they give off a gas. If trapped inside stone, that gas can become strong enough to blow rock apart." Andvari frowned and sat back down, pulling his knees up once more and hugging them. "Took a very long time, but I scraped up the materials I needed and poured them into cracks in the bridge. There's a pin of metal mounted on a plate of flint at the center. Hitting it with enough single-minded determination will cause a spark that will destroy that bloody bridge. The queen is well equipped to manage that."

"So, she dropped you in here so no one else will ever know about her plan."

"Aye, agin yer right. This pit is me grave, where I will dwell for eternity because she must win 'er fight. She must have 'er revenge."

"Revenge *is* a powerful motivator," Tesh agreed.

Andvari nodded. "Makes otherwise sensible people do foolish things."

The sliding of stone overhead made both of them look up. The rocks were cleared away, and Sebek's face peered over the edge, plastered with a sinister grin.

Brin still had the piece of leather strap in her hand. She'd used it three times so far and wondered if there would be a fourth. The ends were damp as if from sweat, which was impossible. She couldn't be sweating. She didn't have hands. As she thought about it, she realized she probably didn't have a piece of leather, either. She was holding the *idea* of a strap of hide.

I'm so glad I didn't think of that before.

The thought of jumping out over that gorge suspended only by a thin idea might have been too much of a leap. She turned the leather over in her fingers. It was all so real. Her hands, her fingers, the strap—smooth on one side, rough on the other. Her mind was making it all up, drawing from lost memories to build this new world. Like a potluck dinner, everyone brought a dish, and together they created a banquet for the senses.

"Don't need that anymore," Beatrice said pointing at the strap. "We're here."

The column of warriors had entered a large cavern. Orders were barked, and everyone appeared to know right where to go. All except the six, who stood like abandoned sheep.

The king and Fenelyus approached. "This won't be easy." Mideon said this more to his daughter than to them. "Ferrol's forces didn't even throw rocks at the jumps."

"I know," Beatrice replied.

"They know we're coming, took the easy route of just waiting for us at the bridge. They'll be dug in with everything and then some."

"Yes," Beatrice said. "Even more than that."

King Mideon frowned at his daughter, and Brin didn't know how Beatrice could take such a look. The king was like a thunderhead or a raging sea.

How was it that Moya was able to stand up to him?

"This is no joke, child. We'll be fighting on the edge up there. People are lost this way—lost forever. You go over that edge, and the Typhons will have ya. Are ya certain this is worth it?"

Beatrice looked past her father and beyond the horde of assembling soldiers, who adjusted armor and shields. She stared at the darkness of the cavern wall. Her eyes shifted as if seeing something none of them could.

Then she nodded. "This will be the second most important thing any of us will ever do."

"Second?"

"Consider it a dress rehearsal for the Golrok."

The king set his fists on his hips, that frown of disappointment hovering over all of them. "You're not filling me with a lot of hope here, child."

"All we need to do is see them safely to the bridge."

"That will be difficult enough."

"What do *we* do?" Moya asked.

The king stretched out a hand and gestured all the way around. "Everyone here, you see them? All these people—each one is a hero, a champion, a legend—their whole purpose is to surround and protect the six of you. Look! Look over there!" He pointed to the man they had seen in the throne room. "That there is Atella the Great—unmatched in battle. He will guard our left flank. Havar, who stormed the walls of Erebus and nearly tore them down, will guard our right. Gath of Odeon, Bran of Pines, and Melen the Hammer will be your personal protectors. Fane Fenelyus, first wielder of the Art, will provide extra support when we need it. And I, as always, will lead the charge. The rest of them"—he nodded slightly as he surveyed the chamber—"will fight and once again die."

"But what about us?" Gifford asked. "What should we do?"

"Stay in the middle, stick close to Gath, Melen, and Bran," the king said.

"And when you get close to the bridge and see that the way is clear," Beatrice said, "run for it. Race across the span. Sprint for the door on the far side."

"Still don't know what good it will do," Mideon said.

"Just have to—"

"Trust you?" the king bellowed. Even in that place, smothered beneath the din of a thousand boisterous heroes prepping for battle, his voice boomed loud enough to draw looks. "I don't do that well. It's not my talent." Mideon turned around, and his voice grew in volume. "Form up! Caldern, see if you can hold that front corner a little better this time. Engels, remember you can duck."

This brought a roar of laughter and shouts of excitement.

Mideon headed off, and the whole room was alive with movement.

"We're going to be okay, right?" Moya asked Beatrice.

The princess hesitated.

Moya stared at her. "What aren't you telling us?"

"Look . . . ah . . ." Beatrice sighed.

"What do you mean, *look?* You can see the future. You know what's going to happen. Or was that all a lie?" Moya glared at the white-haired dwarf, who, at that moment, appeared more like a guilty child.

"I told you the truth—just not all of it. Listen, I can guarantee that Rain will survive, and he'll go on to be great, but this isn't going to be easy for any of you."

The Belgriclungreian seer's eyes dimmed just then. Her mouth turned down and tears gathered and glistened. She refused to look back at any of them. Instead, she looked at her own feet and bit her lower lip as if in pain.

"Sure hasn't been a skip through a field of flowers so far," Tressa said. Her voice was strained and tired.

Beatrice raised her head. She wiped her eyes and sniffled. "In a moment, once we go up those steps and return to the valley floor, things are going to become . . . bad . . . very bad. Then . . . they'll get worse, and finally . . . well . . ." She let out a little laugh that sounded a bit insane. "You'll find out."

"Yes, please don't spoil it, whatever you do." Tressa scoffed.

"The point is," Beatrice said, "there will come a time when you'll believe that everything I told you was wrong. That I'm insane. When that happens, just remember this: It's not important to have faith in me, because I have faith in you."

Beatrice gave Rain a hug, which he suffered awkwardly, but the princess didn't seem to mind. "The Great Rain," she said with an amazed shake of her head. "I've finally been able to meet you."

"Come on, *Great,* "Moya said, "the king is calling us."

They followed the rush of men who flowed like a river up a set of stairs that took many branches and spilled out onto the flinty plain through numerous holes at once. Coming up, Brin saw the sky had turned red, and all around them was a forest of spears.

"We have unfinished business, you and I," Sebek told Tesh. His face was only an outline against the light from above, but his voice was unmistakable.

A moment later, a rope snaked down, dangling the length of the hole and coiling around three times at the bottom. Tesh thought Sebek might climb down, but the onetime Galantian's face disappeared from the edge. The rope remained.

Tesh looked at Andvari, who looked back, surprised.

"Turning out to be an exciting day for me," the dwarf said.

"Me, too." Tesh looked at the dangling rope, then shouted up, "Why should I bother to give you the satisfaction?"

"Beat me, and you can escape," Sebek replied from somewhere beyond the lip.

Tesh coughed out a bitter laugh. "From Ferrol's castle? You really give me no credit at all, do you?"

"Almost everyone has gone to the battle at the bridge. Place is nearly empty. Even if it weren't, if you can best me, you can best anyone."

Tesh continued to look at the rope, unconvinced. Even if Sebek was telling the truth, Tesh couldn't beat him. After years in the Harwood, even if he were fresh, even if they were in Elan, Tesh didn't have the skill to take Sebek. He never had. And in Nifrel, Tesh wasn't confident he could beat Tressa in an arm-wrestling match. Tesh wasn't at all certain he could summon the strength to climb the rope. His arms were deadweights. His legs dragged. And he was tired, so very tired. If he were breathing, he'd say the air was bad, because he felt sick.

"You just going to sit down there?" Sebek called out, his tone rich with that same jeering scorn Tesh remembered hating from his youth. "Even if I'm lying, there's still a chance you could get away. Slim, but possible. You really want to stay down there forever?"

"What would you do?" Tesh asked Andvari.

The dwarf looked down at himself. "I've been here so long that I don't think I can remember how to walk. But if someone lowered a rope for me, I wouldn't be asking anyone for advice."

Tesh took hold of the line, then looked back. "If I beat him, I'll throw the rope back for you."

Andvari's face brightened. *"Can* you beat him?"

"No."

The light in the dwarf's face faded. "Way to get an old Belgriclungreian's hopes up. What did you do in life? Pull the wings off flies?"

"No, I was a warrior. I killed the guy that's waiting up there for me. He was my teacher, and I only managed to best him because he was wounded and helpless."

"So. What yer saying is, I shouldn't expect to see a rope anytime soon."

"Not really."

Concern about being able to climb was removed when Sebek pulled him up. Tesh expected that Sebek would be right at the top, ready to cut his head off, but he wasn't. The Fhrey was at the far end of the chamber, limbering up, stretching nonexistent muscles.

This was the first time Tesh had the chance to take in his surroundings: large round room, white bone floor with a fancy floral design, circular colonnade, and a ring of fluted pillars. Everything was made of bone. In some places, it was polished so smooth and perfect, it could have been pools of cream. No torches or lanterns lent their glow; the light came from the bone itself. It, too, was white, with the indifferent luster you'd expect to leak from cold stone.

Sebek wasn't alone. He couldn't be, according to Andvari, as it would have taken at least two people to move the twin sheets of mica. Tekchin stood beside Sebek, holding Tesh's swords. He looked the same as the last time they'd met, and for an instant, Tesh let himself hope.

"Here!" Tekchin shouted and tossed his swords. The pair of Roan-made steel blades clattered on the polished bone. When they hit, the noise was hollow.

"Couldn't get Eres or Vorath to come?" Sebek asked Tekchin.

"All of them went with the queen. They'd rather fight than watch, I guess."

Sebek nodded. "The old lady is planning a grand party. Hate to miss it myself."

"Do you really think this will take that long?" Tekchin asked. He looked across the open floor at Tesh. On his face was a smirk of contempt.

In that look, Tesh understood that Tekchin knew the truth.

Of course he does. They're all here. The Galantians—his best friends— have told him everything—told him how they died. How I killed them.

"Better not. Need to get done before the queen bitch returns. I don't envy your girlfriend, boy," Sebek shouted at Tesh. "The queen aims to bring the hammer down hard."

Sebek drew Lightning and Thunder. "Remember these? Go on, boy. Pick up your toys. It's time we settled this debate."

"What debate?" Tesh asked, stepping forward. He knew he was about to endure an incredible beating. He refused to even glance toward Tekchin. The swords he picked up were, indeed, his, or at least his memory of them. The real things were at the bottom of some miserable muddy pond along with his hands.

Funny. I'll spend eternity with Andvari in that disgusting hole, but if given the choice of drowning in that puddle again . . . I wouldn't change a thing. I should remember that. I might not think so in a century or two.

Tesh picked up the blades. He couldn't help feeling better the moment he held them. Looking across at Sebek, everything seemed so familiar. Still, his arms felt heavy.

Didn't I do this already?

"Can't expect enemies to be courteous and only attack when you're prepared," Sebek said, stepping forward with a great smile on his face. "Sometimes they catch you off guard in awkward places where you can't retreat."

Yes—but that was when I was on a bridge and Brin had saved me. She can't do that this time.

"So, you saw me kill your parents that day," Sebek said. "Your mother—she had some sort of shawl, didn't she? A miserable ratty cape that was dyed the color of clay, or was it just filth? I remember because I wiped Lightning on it after I cut her head off. Did you see that? I kicked it out of the way, I think. Did you see it roll? I seem to recall it wobbled with her long hair dragging behind."

Tesh felt his fists tighten on the sword grips, his feet striding forward without being told.

Sebek's grin grew. "I'm lying, of course. Honestly, Tesh, I really don't remember. How could I? I killed hundreds just like her. But you know what I think? I think even *you* don't remember. Not really. Such an important thing to you, but it's been so long, and you've colored that day to suit your aims, to justify your life since then. I bet you aren't sure anymore, are you? *Did* Mommy have a shawl? Did I kick her head? Did she even have long hair, or was it short? Was it tied up that day? Tell me, Tesh, what good is revenge when neither one of us can even remember what it's for?"

Sebek performed practice swings, just as fast as ever.

Tesh didn't bother. He didn't want Sebek to know how weak he was.

"Now *you*, I remember. Every detail of your visit to my sickbed. Of how you—"

Tekchin shoved his long, thin blade through Sebek's back. The tip poked out of the Fhrey's chest. Sebek froze, hovered, then collapsed.

Tekchin kicked Thunder and Lightning away. "I was going to let you fight him for a while, for laughs, you know? But he was talking way too much. What a *brideeth eyn mer*. Help me drag his ass to the pit. I don't want to be near him when he wakes up."

"How long does it usually take?"

"To wake up?" Tekchin shrugged. "No idea."

Tesh looked down at Sebek lying on his face. "If we cut his head off, will it take longer?"

Tekchin shrugged.

They grabbed Sebek's arms, spinning his body around. "Let's just get him in the hole. Won't matter then."

Together, they lugged Sebek to where the marble floor faded into the rough dull rock of reality. The effort exhausted Tesh.

"You all right?" Tekchin asked.

Tesh shook his head. "I thought—" Tesh paused. "Why'd you do it?"

Tekchin smirked. "Certainly not for you, but I have a woman, and she has this friend she thinks of as a little sister, who cares about you, and . . . well, you did step in the pool."

"Didn't the queen—didn't Ferrol interrogate you?"

Tekchin shook his head. "The queen only knows the rumor that Gelston had spread. He wanted people to think better of Tressa, I guess, and he proclaimed that she and others would bring the key into Phyre. Orin had reported seeing seven in Drome's palace—he said one was a warrior. When you were spotted in Nifrel, she assumed the warrior in Drome's palace was you. I walked into Nifrel alone. No one even asked how I got here. I bumped into Eres and his brother Medak up by the gate. They were searching for Tressa and the others. They assumed you killed me."

Together, they rolled Sebek over the edge and heard a cry from below.

"Andvari!" Tesh called. "You all right?"

"Aye, but you nearly crushed me!"

Tesh found the coiled rope and kicked it over the edge.

"What are you doing?" Tekchin asked.

"Grab onto that, Andvari," he shouted down, then looked back at Tekchin. "I promised the dwarf I'd get him out if I survived."

"Seriously? We don't have time for this. We need to get out of here."

"He doesn't deserve to be left down there. You know, if you're in such a hurry, you might consider helping."

Tekchin rolled his eyes, but he also took a grip on the rope and together they pulled.

The dwarf was light, and they hoisted him out to the marble where he flopped like a caught fish.

"Can you walk?" Tesh asked.

"Who knows," the dwarf said, pushing to his feet.

"Skip walking," Tekchin said. "Time to run."

The dwarf looked miserable, but Tesh couldn't help smiling. He could have shown more empathy given that he'd felt the same way.

"Yeah—all right," Andvari said. "Centuries in here and I keep forgetting: not real legs. Aye, I can walk."

"Ready?" Tesh asked.

Andvari pursed his lips. "Ya realize there's little chance of us getting away. This is her world, after all."

"Not only that," Tekchin added, "but the queen will be in a really bad mood if she loses this battle. And she'll take it out on us."

The dwarf forced a tight smile. "That, too."

"You could just stay in the hole," Tesh said.

"No, this is better." The dwarf jogged forward, following Tekchin. "At least it's different."

"Yeah"—Tekchin chuckled—"this will definitely be different."

CHAPTER TWENTY-THREE

The Sword of Words

The Killian boys always made me smile. I thought they were handsome and gallant. They flirted with Moya but never noticed me. Still, I loved them. After years of fighting, all save Brigham were dead, each, along with their father, lost to the war. Whenever I see Brigham Killian these days, I cannot smile . . . I cry.

— THE BOOK OF BRIN

Brigham, the last living son of Gavin Killian, dipped the linen rag in the oil bowl, then applied it to the sword. He rubbed the metal carefully for two reasons. First, the blade, which was known as the Sword of Words, was a precious relic and deserving of special care, and second, it was incredibly sharp. He'd already nicked himself once, and he didn't want to do that again.

This was the first sword, the one Persephone had brought back with her from the dwarven lands, the one she had used to cleave Shegon's blade in half, establishing her claim as keenig. It was also wielded on the plains of Dureya in the Battle of Grandford by the already legendary hero Raithe, son of Herkimer. But perhaps the Sword of Words' greatest claim—from which it drew its name—was its magical nature. Enchanted by Suri the Mystic, it had once been used to kill a dragon. The markings were still on the blade. Brigham could feel them as he rubbed the oil into the metal—little grooves and lines along the flat, otherwise flawless surface.

This is a dragon-slaying blade, he thought. *Perhaps the only one.*

"Doing a good job with that sword, er ya?" Atkins asked. The big, bearded redhead crouched down between Edgar and Vargus on Falcon Ridge's *Sittin' Log,* as it was cleverly named—the bark having been worn off by the rumps of hundreds of men over the years. Brigham sat alone on his side of the campfire, perhaps due to how he held the sharp relic horizontally across his lap. Vargus had only recently established the little rock-ringed cook fire and was still cautiously adding small branches to feed the fledgling flames. The sun was going down, and the evening meal would be delayed.

The Techylors were just now returning to the Harwood after a week of beer, hot food prepared by others, and a well-needed rest. They had been waiting for Tesh to return from the swamp, using that as a valid excuse for lingering at the Dragon Camp. Tesh was only supposed to be gone for a few days, but after nearly a week, Persephone sent a troop to look. Nyphron went with them, but before setting out, the Galantian leader had ordered Tesh's men back to the tower. No one argued with Nyphron.

With the fading light, Edgar had decided to spend the night up on Falcon Ridge. All of them were tired and in no hurry to reach the legion camp where everyone would be begging for news and handouts of whatever they had brought back with them. The other Techylors would also want to know what had happened to Tesh—their leader, the founder of their band, and the commander of the First Legion. The men from the Dragon Camp didn't have an answer.

"You better take good care of that sword," Edgar said. "If Tesh finds out his only inheritance has been mistreated, he'll demand you spar with him."

Tesh was known for being a vicious instructor. He had learned combat from Sebek, who had a reputation for cruelty. Tesh felt the only way to teach others to match his skill was to put them through the same training. Just as with Sebek, no one wanted to face off with Tesh.

"Where do you think he is?" Brigham asked.

Atkins laughed. "He's off with his woman. If I were him, I'd be in no hurry to return to the likes of us, either. Although, Avempartha is pretty at sunset."

Brigham looked up to make a retort, but his eye caught sight of the tower in the distance. It was always amazing at sunrise or sunset.

The others turned to look. They were still several miles away—as the bird flew—up on the ridge, looking down at the falls where the last rays of sun made the water sparkle and the tower shimmer. From up there, they could see the bulk of the legion camp—a village of white tents in a clearing—and the tower beyond. Avempartha was beautiful, but the falls were the most impressive natural wonder Brigham had ever seen. The tower was simply the snow on the mountaintop, the welcoming smile on a beautiful woman.

Vargus placed another set of sticks on the smoking fire. "Hillman was asking when he could finish his training in the Vorath Discipline. It's all he has left, and he's anxious to be a full Techylor."

"Why don't you teach him?" Edgar asked.

"Didn't think I could," Vargus said. "Only just got the title myself a few months ago."

"You're a Techylor—you can train a Techylor. That's how it works."

Brigham saw Vargus smile and didn't envy Hillman.

Mopping up the excess oil that had gathered around the guard, Brigham noticed Atkins still looking at the tower. Then Edgar stood up and he, too, stared. "What the Tet is that?"

Brigham, still holding the rag and the sword, also got to his feet. Peering into the golden mists of the falls, he saw something move—something big.

"Is that . . ." Atkins stopped himself and put up a hand to shade his eyes.

Within the cloud that billowed up from the cataract, Brigham saw it swoop. Then two great dark wings flapped, and behind them, a long serpent's tail swiped. A moment later, fire engulfed the tents. A stream of

344 • *Michael J. Sullivan*

flame swept left to right, turning the riverbank into an inferno and setting the forest on fire. Massive trees cracked and split as they went up like dry blades of grass. The creature in the sky dove like a raptor, picking up men and tents. Banking, it dropped them off the cliff, where bodies tumbled through the air like chaff in a stiff wind.

Brigham hastily shifted his grip on the sword, cutting himself for the second time on the oily blade.

"Grab what you can!" Edgar ordered.

"What are we doing?" Atkins asked as he picked up his pack.

"We're moving. Going back to the Dragon Camp."

"What?" Brigham was shocked. "That thing is killing everyone. They need help!"

"They're dead men!" Edgar shouted. "Nothing can kill a dragon."

This is a dragon-slaying blade.

Brigham looked down at the sword in his hands. "With this, I might—"

"Grab your things, boys! That's an order! We are going back to report this to the keenig." Another wave of flame blanketed the riverbank, creating a wall of fire and a thunderhead of dark smoke that churned and rolled upward. "Persephone needs to know that the elves have dragons."

CHAPTER TWENTY-FOUR

Queen of the White Tower

The most important battle of the Great War did not disturb a single blade of grass, nor spill even a drop of blood, and it did not leave any footprints on the face of Elan. The clash of legends that changed the course of human events went unnoticed far beneath the feet of those whose lives it forever altered.

— THE BOOK OF BRIN

Gifford didn't know what to expect as he came up those stone steps. He was still enthralled at how he was able to trot like everyone else, as if he were dancing. Gifford had always wanted to dance. He used to have fantasies where he twirled with Roan around a moonlit clearing in the middle of the Crescent Forest. Just the two of them spinning like fireflies, summer mist shrouding them from the rest of the world. With stars overhead, bright, clear, and sparkling, he would hold her in his arms, strong and sure, and she would let him kiss her. He imagined such a moment as perfect, but there was no such thing.

Gifford *had* kissed Roan. He hadn't been strong or sure, they hadn't danced, and there were no stars or fireflies. The kiss, like all things in Gifford's life, had been clumsy, but even with all its awkwardness, he wouldn't have traded the moment for all the moonlit glades in the world. Still, he hoped for a chance to have that dance. Then he reached the top of the stairs.

At first, Gifford couldn't tell what he was seeing. They were on a flinty field of chipped rock. With the snow gone, it was a sheet of gray slate. Not far to his right, the White Tower of Ferrol was close enough to be frightening. Off to his left was the castle of King Mideon, made small by its distance. Straight ahead, a great stone bridge extended over vast emptiness. The long tongue was connected to a tiny pillar of stone, a weird twig-finger of rock. On top of it was what looked to be a small cave.

All of this Gifford understood easily, which was good, as it gave him his bearings. What he didn't understand was everything else.

The body of a long-horned bull crossed his sight as it flew through the air, tumbling as it went. Gifford couldn't begin to guess who or what had thrown the furious animal, but it slammed into a host of charging dwarfs, knocking them down.

A dark-skinned, bald, and very husky man dressed in little more than studded straps of leather wielded a fiery sword. He used this burning blade to hew through a contingent of Fhrey who tried to scatter away from him.

A giant—maybe the same one who'd tossed the bull—was throwing rocks the size of roundhouses into the most congested areas, igniting screams. Gifford couldn't tell whose side the giant was on because the races were all mixed up. He couldn't see a dividing line and soon realized there wasn't one. The giant hurling rocks certainly didn't care. That's when Gifford took Roan's hand with his left and drew his sword with his right.

Even with his perfect feet and straight back, Gifford knew little about combat. He'd never had a lesson in wielding a sword.

Why waste time teaching a cripple?

All he knew was what he'd seen others do—swing the sharp edge at people. He'd done that while trying to save Roan in the Battle of Grandford and failed. As it turned out, swinging a sword was harder than it looked.

Gifford had long envied *normal* people, the ones who could walk without leaving a drag mark, or talk without spraying faces. They could do most things so effortlessly that they took it all for granted. He knew that if he were like them, there would be nothing he would fear, nothing he couldn't accomplish. Standing on two perfect feet on that field of battle made up of flying bulls and screaming men, he understood he'd been wrong. He was still Gifford the Cripple, and it didn't matter if his feet worked or not. He could finally say Roan's name, but he still couldn't protect her—not from men, dwarfs, Fhrey with swords, and certainly not from giants heaving bulls.

"Galantians attacking on the right!" shouted Melen, who could see over most of their heads.

"Techylors, counter!" King Mideon ordered, and sixteen men in green cloaks, all who wielded dual swords, rushed toward the opening breach.

Gath did nothing except display his palm to the six of them, commanding everyone to stay where they were. He wasn't huge. That was the thing that surprised Gifford. Gath of Odeon was reputed to be the greatest hero of their culture. He was the first keenig, who united the tribes and convinced them to cross the sea to the unknown world that lay beyond. Many were the tales of how he and his fellow heroes fought sea monsters, dragons, and goblins before finally settling in Rhulyn. Hearing the tales over and over, Gifford imagined he must be a giant, rugged and handsome. This Gath of Odeon reminded him of a shaggy dog. Wearing only a skirt of leather, Gath had wild, dark hair growing from his head, shoulders, arms, and legs. The mane was so thick, snarled, and matted that he appeared more beast than man. When agitated, he bared his teeth, and when angry, he growled.

Gath was snarling just then as he surveyed the chaos of the battle. All around them rushed a churning crash of violence held back by a wall of men and dwarfs. A handful got through, only to be crushed by one of Melen's hammers or laid out by Bran's ax. These three legends protected them from the very few that breached Mideon's defenses. Fenelyus stood by as well, her eyes looking beyond the nuisance runners. What they watched for, Gifford had no idea, and he was certain he didn't want to know.

Only Beatrice, who stood with them in the center, in that quiet core, appeared unconcerned. Gifford checked her several times, feeling better with each glance.

She knows it will be okay. She's already seen it.

"Okay, everyone forward, but don't pass me!" Gath ordered.

Like dutiful children, they all shuffled behind the first keenig, keeping their heads down as ordered. Before long, they were too far away to see the steps. Retreat was no longer an option. They swam in deep waters, the banks no longer visible, their futures cast among perils vast and veiled.

"Can't die when you're already dead," Moya told them. "Remember that."

It should have helped but didn't. Gifford felt the need to breathe and to take steps to move, but he was also afraid to be hit, scared to have his head chopped off or see the same happen to Roan. Maybe they would just get up and dust themselves off afterward, but the idea of dying terrified him nonetheless. The concern wasn't unlike how some people were afraid of bees. A sting might hurt, but it wasn't the end of the world, yet many folks panicked whenever they heard a buzz.

And how exactly does a body go about putting a head back on?

Gath stopped them again, and a moment later, King Mideon appeared with a solemn expression. He faced Fenelyus. "She's got the Breakwaters guarding the approach."

"How many?"

"All of them."

"All?" the fane asked, stunned. "Has she left the rest of her realm open? Why would she do such a thing? Why take such an insane gamble?"

"A shame we didn't know," Gath said. "We could be ransacking the White Tower right now."

"Can you do something about the giants?" Mideon asked.

Fenelyus nodded. "Draw your forces back."

The king gave the order, trumpets sounded, banners waved, and troops retreated. As they did, Gifford saw that the way ahead was blocked by a dozen giants with locked arms. These were not normal Grenmorians, but something more rudimentary. Just as roundhouses were simpler versions of Fhrey homes, these giants were primitive even among a race not known for sophistication. They seemed to be unfinished—blunt faces, mouths that hung agape, and dull eyes that constantly looked to one another for reassurance. They were also big and solid and scary, standing with shoulders lined up, making a wall twenty feet high.

Fenelyus moved forward. As she did, a section of the floor rose, giving her height. At the same time, she grew in size and brilliance. Her cloak became a vast cape of shadows and her hands as bright as torches. They left streaks in the darkness as she moved them in a rotating pattern. Between them, a great ball of purple light took shape and expanded. Then without fanfare, she rolled it forward. As it moved toward the Breakwaters, the ball swelled. Gifford watched in anticipation for a great impact, eager to see what would happen when the line of giants was struck, but well before it reached them, the great purple sphere of light winked out as if it had never existed.

Then from the right, a jolting blast of lightning streaked across the plain. The blast struck Fenelyus—or nearly so.

This was not the first time Gifford had witnessed a magic duel. He'd stood with the other residents of Dahl Rhen when Arion and Gryndal had fought. But in the realm of Nifrel, that which had been invisible in the real world was exposed. Just before the lightning reached Fenelyus, he saw a glowing blue shield block it. The shield was simpler and brighter than the armor Alberich had made, but it was every bit as effective.

Watching the two Miralyith was the key to understanding the true nature of the realm of Nifrel and perhaps all of Phyre. Power came from a spirit's strength of will, from desire, whether that was to obtain something or merely to exist. But the ability to wield power in meaningful ways was limited by familiarity. None of them needed to walk, to move, or swing a sword to fight. Alberich didn't need to hammer fictitious metal to make armor, and armor wasn't necessary. But these were the ways people understood how to achieve what they desired. Fenelyus worked closer to the raw power than the dwarf. She made her armor from sheer resolve. The Art of the living world and the force of will of Phyre had to be nearly the same in principle, except that in Phyre, using the Art would be like painting without the paint. All that was brought to the canvas was the idea.

A second bolt of lightning struck the shield Fenelyus held. Tracking it back, Gifford saw a familiar ring-pierced face. Gryndal stood on his own raised pedestal of stone and shot his white-hot streaks over the heads of the army. A shout went up and troops charged the former fane's position. Held fast, locked down in defense, she would be unable to defend herself.

"Get in there!" Mideon shouted at the Belgriclungreian leader, Caldern, who started forward with a troop of well-armored warriors.

"Wait," Fenelyus shouted. With one hand up, still holding the shield that illuminated the world around them, she squeezed her other hand over and over, molding something into existence. Gifford couldn't see what it was until she threw it.

A dark ball rocketed across the plain from pedestal to pedestal. Gryndal threw up his own shield of light, but the dark ball passed through, snuffing out the shield as it did. A burst of brilliant light blinded everyone watching. When the flash was over, Gryndal was gone, and so was his pedestal. What remained was a shallow crater.

By then, the armies were converging on the former fane.

With a grunt, Fenelyus swept her arms and threw everyone back with a force that, in the land of the living, might have been a powerful wind, but in Phyre, it was a spray of silver.

"Whoa," Roan whispered.

"Fen! The Breakwaters!" Mideon shouted.

With teeth clenched and eyes ablaze, Fenelyus thrust an outstretched hand and sent another purple ball of light. Once again, it picked up speed and size until it was huge. The bounding boulder rushed at the giants, who braced for impact, tightening their locked arms and leaning forward. When the sphere hit, it did nothing. The great boulder of light popped like a bubble. But at that moment, Fenelyus clapped her hands and the ground beneath three of the giants tilted sharply upward.

They fell back, sliding into the Abyss.

Hooked arm in arm, unwilling to let go, the chain of giants was dragged backward, toppling one by one over the edge. The armies stopped to watch the sight, for there was a terrible slowness to this strange inevitability. No one screamed, no crash of weapon defeated them. What brought that powerful wall down was the giants' inability to let go of one another's arms. Fenelyus had ingeniously and elegantly touched off a landslide, and everyone paused to watch the tragedy unfold.

When the last three giants were whipped off their feet with looks of disbelief in their dull eyes, there was a pause in the battle that Gifford wanted to think was a moment of silence to honor the Breakwaters.

It lasted less than a minute.

Then the clash returned, and Gath ordered them forward again.

The White Tower was as beautiful as a winter's night when it was so cold that ice cracked. No chairs, no cushions, no furs—everything was hard, white, and chilling. Sebek hadn't lied to Tesh regarding the tower being vacant. Stairs and corridors were silent, save for the sound of Andvari's, Tekchin's, and his own footfalls. And as he rushed as best he could to escape, Tesh saw no one but his own reflection. Nearly all the walls were polished to a mirror-like shine.

"Don't look at the walls!" Andvari shouted, but Tesh already had.

He saw himself—not as the hero of the Harwood, not as a Techylor, but as a Dureyan. Even less than that, he was a Dureyan boy, thin, dirty, and frightened.

Tesh stopped to stare at himself.

Am I really that pathetic? That small?

He did feel tiny. Ever since entering Phyre, he had felt like that—the way he was brought up to feel. What he saw in the mirror was how he still saw himself, that part he had struggled to erase but failed.

Maybe because that's how I am. I have no false body to disguise the truth. In Phyre, Gifford is an athlete, but this is what I am.

"Stop looking and run," Tekchin called back.

Tesh felt a hand on his arm and found Andvari pulling him away.

"This is an enchantment," the dwarf said. "Who you are lies at the intersection of how you see yourself and how others do. Where the two overlap is truth. You aren't seeing yourself. This is how the queen sees you. You're looking at yourself through *her* walls—her eyes. It's not the truth."

"But it isn't a lie, either."

"It is *a* truth. Her truth."

Tesh forced himself to look away and focus on running—no small feat, as he still felt the terrible weight. Reaching the main floor, they spotted two soldiers in black-and-white armor.

Not entirely deserted, after all.

Tesh slowed down and watched as Tekchin waved to the soldiers. One waved back. Neither of them looked at Tesh—at the dirty Dureyan boy.

"Better hurry. The party is about to end," the guard who had waved told Tekchin. "The queen has unleashed Orr."

Tekchin cursed as he bolted out the door. Tesh followed. No one stopped him; none looked his way; no one cared.

Back on the stony plain, Tekchin and Andvari no longer waited, and Tesh fell hopelessly behind. He knew where to go. Lightning bursts flashed at the front of a bridge beyond which lay nothing else.

Tesh was fearful that without Tekchin, the forces of the queen would recognize him for the escaped prisoner he was. None did. Even as he ran past hosts of men, he didn't receive even a second glance.

Maybe all they see is a starving boy in a ragged shirt. No threat here.

He came to a crack in the valley, one of the many crevices that weren't wide enough for a bridge. Others were jumping it with ease, but they weren't panting from exhaustion, or stooped over like an old crone. And this time he didn't have Brin to help him across.

With no choice, he made a running leap, hoping this would be another illusion, a mere crack in the rock. It wasn't. Still, he almost made it.

Most of him reached the far side. His left leg was the exception. His shinbone cracked against the sharp stone's edge. He heard it snap. Felt the bone break. Crying out in pain, he fell and rolled, thrashing on the flinty rock. His eyes watered, and his sight blurred. The pain ran up his leg and coursed through his whole body. He clutched at his shin and found the brittle bone where it punched through the skin.

As he lay on his side, shivering in agony and fear, he felt a downbeat of wind. Above him a great shadow passed, a long one with two vast wings and a massive tail.

The army of King Mideon was nearly to the pylons of the bridge, which appeared as twin spears jutting up from the end of the flinty plain. Those formations marked the start of the narrow crossing. A roar sounded. That Gifford could hear anything above the crash of combat was astounding. The battle had reached a tumultuous pitch. He felt it, as he had once perceived Elan through the Art, but Gifford didn't believe it took much insight to feel the urgency in the rapid claps of swords on shields and the staccato cries of desperate men. This was *the push*. Here was the final conflict. The two sides threw themselves into the effort—and the forces of Mideon were winning. Inch by inch they advanced. Gath coaxed Beatrice and the six of them closer to the bridge.

A monstrous creature with a small head, tiny eyes, fangs, and a spiked club charged, but it was brought down by half a dozen men wielding spears. A squad of dwarfs from the queen's forces advanced in chevron formation. Swinging shining hammers, they ripped through rings of defenders. Seeing them, Gifford understood how it was that the Belgriclungreians came so close to defeating the Fhrey. The dwarfs made small targets and shook off blows that would have crushed an average man. The last of their attack made it all the way to Gath who, along with Bran of Pines, put an end to them.

By then, they were close enough to the bridge that Gifford saw it wasn't merely narrow; the width was so small that their passage across would need to be single file. He thought of Tressa and worried whether she could manage it.

If she'd had so much trouble with a crack, how will she traverse a walkway across the Abyss?

Despite the horrific violence around him, Gifford couldn't help thinking the fight was anticlimactic. He'd expected more. They were nearly to their goal, and only a few opponents remained in their way. The dire warnings had braced him for a far more desperate struggle. He smiled at Roan. She smiled back. They were going to make it.

Then the dragon came.

Not a creation of Suri, nor a manifestation of the Art, this was the real thing—or at least a deceased version. Until that moment, Orr had been a story told by a lodge's firelight. The dragon was the embodiment of power and evil. A creature of the old world, Orr slew Gath of Odeon, and in turn the beast was slain by Gath's Shield, Bran of Pines, in the greatest epic tale the Keepers had to tell. "The Song of Gath" was the story always recounted on the night of Wintertide, and the tale of his death often brought tears to the old and nightmares to the young. As a boy, Gifford had imagined Orr as a monster so ugly that he could never fully picture it. To him, Orr was a mass of eyes and shadows. And while Gifford had no way to know what Orr had truly been in life, in death it was terrifying.

Larger than three gilarabrywns combined, its great, dark wings swept silently over the heads of the army. With all the effort of an afterthought, Orr swept fifty souls from the field, tossing them with catlike amusement before settling itself on the causeway. Possessed of fore- and hind legs, a barbed tail, and a mouth of teeth the size of trees, the beast rose and glared down at them with eyes alight and filled with joyful malevolence.

"The queen is insane!" Fenelyus shouted as she stared at the dragon. "She's emptied her house—but why?" Fenelyus whirled to look back at the six of them. Confusion gave way to suspicion as she focused her attention on Beatrice.

"Fen?" Mideon called excitedly.

"I can't fight Orr!" she shouted at him. "That thing is . . ." She never finished, but in her eyes, a story of frustration and fear bloomed, and Gifford guessed she spoke from experience. "You have to summon the golem."

The king's eyes darkened, his lips folding up in anger.

"It's the only way," Fenelyus told him.

"Golem?" Brin asked.

"It's old magic," Beatrice explained, "from the days when our people lived closer to the stone. Those of great power could call the ground up to fight for them. My father did it once near the end of the Great War. At Neith, he called up a golem of stone that withstood Fenelyus, allowing most of our people to escape to Drumindor. Doing so nearly killed him."

The dragon flapped its wings, knocking those closest to it to the ground, then laughed. Nothing about the horrific sound was reminiscent of laughter, but once more Gifford felt it. He sensed the glee in that sound, which was more akin to a hundred-foot-tall rabbit screaming in a snare.

"Do it!" Fenelyus shouted at Mideon. "Do it, or this is over!"

Orr took a mighty breath.

"Dammit!" Fenelyus braced herself, throwing out her arms.

Massive flames burst forth, washing over all of them.

Gifford gasped, staggered back, and fell. The world was gone, all of Nifrel lost as they were bathed in fire. He could see it brush up and over them, held only a few feet away as if by glass, the licking flames washing by in an oily smear of colors. Heat. He felt as if he were standing too near a bonfire, except this heat rolled in waves.

Fenelyus was screaming with effort, fingers splayed, hands shaking. At last, the dragon ran out of breath. The fire went out, and Fenelyus collapsed.

Again, the dragon laughed. "Such sweet fruit," Orr said in a voice that Gifford felt more than heard. "And oh! What a banquet."

Moya raised her bow. Beatrice touched her arm and shook her head. "Wait. Not yet."

That's when the ground rose up.

Deafening *cracks* and *pops* announced the shards of stone that grew from the stone floor of the valley. They coalesced and stood up. Dark rock in the general shape of a colossal man rose to face the dragon, who eyed it cautiously.

"Back! Get back!" Beatrice shouted, shooing them to give the golem a path to the dragon.

"Move that beast out of the way," King Mideon ordered, though his voice was hardly more than a whisper. "Clear the bridge."

Gifford never saw the initial clash, as he and nearly everyone else was scrambling to get clear, abandoning the field to the gigantic combatants. He didn't need to see it. The impact declared itself. The ground jumped, the dragon roared, and a clap loud as thunder echoed. Both Gifford and Roan, whose hand he still held, fell and sprawled on the ground that sprang and shook with all the bounce of a stretched tarp.

Beatrice huddled them together. "Here! Stay here." She turned to view the fighting behemoths. "Prepare to run."

Gifford looked back and saw the hulking brutes, two shadowy mountains grappling in the dim light. One staggered—

Brin was the first to scream, but not the only one, as the stone giant grabbed hold of the dragon and pulled, taking a step toward them. One massive stone foot slammed an arm's length away. The ground hopped, and they flew into the air, spilled once more off their feet.

"Now! Run!" Beatrice shouted. "Across the bridge! Go!"

Moya got them moving. She led off, running for the causeway. If she hadn't, Gifford didn't think any of them would have moved. The golem had managed to wrestle Orr off the bridge, leaving the way clear. Less a *way* and more a *window*. The dragon was none too happy about being pulled aside, and legs the size of columns danced across the path between them and the bridge.

Gifford held tightly to Roan. Too much so, he guessed, but Roan didn't complain, probably didn't feel it, any more than Gifford felt the ground he sprinted over. Despite the dancing giants, the war was back on as everyone saw the race to the finish. Dead Galantians fought with deceased Techylors. Iron-clad dwarf warriors clashed with bronze-covered Fhrey. And fur-wrapped spearmen fought leather-armored swordsmen. Spears flew, javelins rained, and feet charged. Shields clapped as the last of Mideon's defenses held back the engulfing wave.

As they came to the bridge, Gifford saw Gath go down. Not by Orr this time, but by sheer numbers. Bran fought valiantly at his side, then he, too, fell to multiple blows. Only Melen remained. The huge man shooed them forward, onto the span, as he took position at the start of the bridge to stop any would-be followers.

They had made it.

The king joined Melen at the mouth of the bridge, swinging his great ax and cleaving all comers. Fenelyus, back on her feet, took up position beside Atella. The four heroes formed a wall where the Breakwaters once stood as the golem continued to wrestle with the dragon.

Gifford saw that the span across the Abyss, the path to the door to Alysin, was clear. He could see a cave on the far side, a dark opening that he guessed was the door, the exit from Nifrel. Then, as Gifford took his first step forward, Roan was ripped from his hand—pulled straight up.

It's not broken. It's not broken, Tesh repeated in his head.

When that didn't work, he said it out loud. "My leg can't be broken. I don't have a leg!" No one heard, not even himself. He could feel the throbbing, shooting pain, which exploded from just below his knee. He shoved himself up, first on his elbows, then his palms; then Tesh crawled. He dragged his *not-broken* leg, the one that certainly felt fractured.

What does it matter? What does any of it matter?

He could see the battle from where he was, so tantalizingly close. The queen had built her tower on the high ground, a great mound of stone, which she also must have made. That whole plain of shale rock was her sculpture, her putty laid over the bedrock of the world. Not far below, he saw the dragon drop down before the bridge. He couldn't see Brin. He couldn't see any *single* person. Below were thousands clashing and mingling in shadows like a vast beast with many heads. Fronts formed and fell away, pushes and retreats, pockets and currents. The dragon changed all that. Those nearest it pulled back. Fighting continued on the outskirts, but the dragon commanded attention in the center. Didn't take long to discover why.

Fire exploded from its mouth, sweeping left to right, bathing all.

Is Brin in that? Is she—

He pushed up onto his one good leg to get a better view. His other not-broken leg made him wince, but he cared too little to give it attention.

What happens now? The queen will take the key, and then what? I'll continue to exist here, and Brin . . . will she go to Rel?

He didn't know how it worked. It might be that she would be escorted under armed guard; or perhaps she would just disappear, sucked from the realm and sent to her rightful reward. But no matter how it happened, the fact that she would be pulled away was a certainty.

I've lost her.

He felt pain—not in his leg, but a stabbing in his heart—so physical, so real, that he clutched at his chest. He expected to find a javelin or perhaps an arrow, but nothing was there, no weapon, no wound. And he was alone. Tesh understood then that shades were exposed nerves without the garment of bodies. Love, hate, fear, joy—these were the iron and steel of Nifrel and regret a form of suffocation.

You aren't fixing anything. You're breaking more things and calling it better! And you aren't freeing the world of a monster. You're taking its place, Brin had said.

And Raithe's words again, *I want you to start a family, raise children, and live a good and happy life—someplace safe and green.*

Brin would have jumped at the chance to go somewhere—back to Rhen, maybe—and start a family. He could have done it. They could have had a home somewhere. She might have been seated at the spinning wheel inside, and he could have been out front chopping wood for a fire instead of watching this one—watching this flame burn the one person who . . .

If I let you go, I'll never see you again.

Of course you will. If not in this life, then the next.

The pain in his chest ripped so hard he grunted, his hands making fists.

If I had one wish, it would have been that you had died with the rest of us that day. If that were the case, we'd still have you. Now she will.

It was as if his parents didn't even want him to seek justice for their deaths.

The fire went out.

Before the bridge and under a torrent of flame, the crowd had scattered. Some burned. The rest fled. The area before the bridge lay empty. At the center, before the dragon, stood a small group—no more than ten or twelve.

Is that her? Is she among them?

Hope welled up. The agony in his chest changed to a different sort of ache; the pain in his leg faded. Without applying thought, Tesh was moving, running down the slope, dodging spearmen, axmen, dwarfs, and elves. He hopped rocks, cracks, and crevices, his sight struggling to stay fixed on those at the feet of the dragon who had managed to survive the fire.

Has to be them—has to be her.

Tesh ran faster, charging downhill. The weight was still with him, but he'd switched it from one sore shoulder to the other fresh one. He entered the thick ranks of the queen's legions just as all the crowd took a step back and gasped. Not at him—a portion of the valley floor had just stood up.

Nothing was likely to impress Tesh anymore, and even as the stone giant grappled with the dragon, he focused on pushing through the crowd. Dodging his way through, exploiting the holes and gaps, or shoving when he had no choice. Tesh didn't want to attract attention, but he had to get through.

The rock giant took hold and jerked the dragon off the bridge, hauling it to the side. Tesh was close enough to see the small group struggling to reach the bridge. At that moment, his hopes died.

It's not them—not Brin.

What he saw were mighty heroes dressed in grand armor that glowed with power. These people were big, powerful, and impressive. Near the center was the brightest of them all, a beacon of brilliance in a suit of stunning armor.

"Now! Run!" someone in their number shouted. "Across the bridge! Go!"

Six of the heroes ran forward in a jostled line, madly winding their way through the legs of a dragon and a stone monster that kept the army at bay.

The brightest one of the six was also the fleetest, the fastest runner he'd ever seen, except for maybe—

Brin!

Tesh pressed forward.

Coming up behind the forces of the queen—who were now all standing still—he shouldered his way through their ranks, his eyes ever on the racing streak of armored light. Brin had reached the bridge ahead of everyone and kept going. She ran so fast that she got to the center of the span before looking back and finding she was alone. She stopped and waited for the rest to catch up.

Tesh lost sight of everything because he hit the densest portion of the front line. He was far from the tallest, and a forest of shoulders and heads blocked his view. He continued to shove through. Those around him spoke to one another by name, and he realized that to these warriors, who had fought in countless battles, Nifrel was a small village. They didn't know him, but at that moment, they didn't care.

Four defenders were effectively holding the entrance to the bridge: a giant dwarf with a crown and a massive ax, a wild man with a short sword and shield, another big man with a pair of hammers, and the Fhrey fane, Fenelyus. These four had already built up a hedge of slain bodies. No one was eager to challenge them, and that allowed Tesh to move ahead. Some—the closest—even helped push him forward into the fray that they wanted no part of.

When a sweep of the giant dwarf's ax cleared a row of three men, Tesh broke through. He took a place in the front line, shoulder to shoulder with the rest of Ferrol's bravest, struggling to find a means of taking down those guarding the entrance to the bridge.

Tesh hoped Fenelyus would recognize him, but the Fhrey wasn't looking his way. "Fenelyus!"

The man behind Tesh shoved forward, pushing him into the killing ring. He waited his turn to die again.

The dwarven king swung at Tesh.

With no retreat possible and his swords in his belt, Tesh cringed as the massive glowing ax whistled down on him.

"Fen!" the dwarf shouted in anger as his ax froze mid-stroke.

"Sorry," Fenelyus said, her hands outstretched, fingers pinched together. "This one is not the enemy. He's one of *them.*" She jerked her head in the direction of the bridge where all the others had gone.

Before Tesh could react or respond, the big man with the hammers grabbed and jerked him through their wall of defense, tossing him onto the bridge like a sack of wool. Tesh fell, skidding across the stone, and rolled to a stop just before falling into the Abyss.

"Good to have you aboard, boy," the king shouted after him, then resumed his attacks, cutting a charging Fhrey in half. The dwarf king laughed, but Tesh could see sweat on his brow and weakness in his eyes.

Looking back, Tesh spotted Tekchin trapped in the crowd.

"Hurry," Tesh shouted.

"Go on!" The Galantian waved. "I'll catch up!"

"That way!" a pretty, young white-haired dwarf woman shouted at Tesh. "Across the bridge. Hurry! We're almost out of time."

Those last words worried him even as he ran across the bridge.

Out of time for what?

The others didn't look like themselves, but aside from Tekchin, they were all there. Brin was out in front. Moya was near Gifford, who had hold of Roan's hand. Rain came next, and Tressa, as always, was in last place. The way across the bridge was clear, a vast and flat expanse of what Tesh noticed was natural stone rather than the slate or the rough rock they had found on the ridge. Beyond Brin, at the far end, he could see what looked to be the dark opening of a cave. The door had to be in there. Brin could have already reached it if she hadn't stopped.

We're going to make it!

No one saw the bankors until it was too late.

"Moya!" Brin heard Beatrice shout.

The Keeper stopped, turned, and discovered she'd outdistanced everyone else. That's when she saw the bankors grab Roan and Gifford. Beatrice was still at the start of the bridge. She hadn't stepped a toe onto the causeway even though the rest of the party were all running across as fast as they could.

"Now, Moya! Now!" Beatrice shouted.

Moya, who was almost up to Brin, had her back to the attack. She didn't see the bankors swooping in. Still, at the sound of the princess's voice, Moya fully drew back her bow even before twisting around. Then while still running forward, she shot and struck the bankor holding Gifford. The winged beast exploded.

Gifford dropped twelve feet to the surface of the bridge. A second arrow followed only an instant later and struck the bankor holding Roan. It was an incredible shot and an impossible feat to have missed Roan while still managing to hit the beast that had been pulling Moya's friend away. The bankor became a cloud of dirt and pebbles, but Roan had been higher and farther away. A long way up and too far out, she missed the bridge. With no need to breathe, Roan's scream remained long and constant as she fell into the Abyss. Eventually, it faded with distance, an eerie echoing sound.

"No!" Brin cried in shock.

Gifford got to his feet and ran full-out toward the side of the bridge. He would have gone over if Rain hadn't tackled him. Together, they fell near the edge.

Another bankor swooped down at Tressa, who lagged far behind the others. Moya was still staring over the side, no doubt trying to see Roan.

"Moya, Tressa is—" Brin shouted, pointing down the length of the bridge, but stopped when the bankor burst before even touching her.

Two shining swords were in the air, and holding them was—

"Tesh!" Brin screamed.

Before he could answer or even look, a loud *boom* shook the world.

A crash that sounded like nearby thunder made Tesh spin in time to see the golem explode. Chunks of rock flew in all directions, raining down, crushing many still engaged in the battle. In its wake lay a stillness beyond anything Tesh had experienced. The fighting stopped. No one moved or spoke. The bankors halted their assault and circled silently.

Out of the darkness came a light—a familiar one—and row by row the ranks of warriors knelt.

"The queen," Fenelyus said, amazed. "Ferrol herself comes to the battle." She turned to stare at Tesh with a look of astonishment on her face. "Who *are* you people?"

"They are mine," Ferrol said.

Tesh saw her clearly for the first time. Tall and lean, she appeared mantis-like, draped in her cloak and ethereal gown of white with hands cupped together before her. "You've had your fun. Playtime is over. I want my spoils, and I certainly hope, for everyone's sake, it wasn't on that unfortunate girl who fell."

The queen didn't hurry, didn't rush. She gracefully walked to the bridge's entrance where the dwarven king was down on one knee, but not out of reverence. The destruction of the golem had an effect on him, and he appeared mortally wounded.

"Evening, Mideon. Cute toy you made. What did it cost, I wonder? Not much, I hope. Move aside."

The king, the two warriors, and Fenelyus all shuffled away, granting the queen access to the bridge.

Ferrol glanced behind her. "Orr? Be so kind as to gobble up any who try to run."

The dragon flapped his huge wings and took flight. Everyone watched as he soared overhead and then landed on the spire just above the door's cave with all the grace of a hawk.

The queen stepped out onto the bare rock of the bridge. "I suggest you all come back before Orr decides you look too sweet to resist. For those of you new to our realm, let me explain that, just as those lost to the Abyss are never seen again so, too, is the fate of those eaten by him." She made a show of looking over the side and shaking her head. "It's a long way down. No one really knows if there even is a bottom."

She took another step. "All I want is the key. The one who has it can just walk back and hand it to me, and we're done. No one else has to fall; no one has to be eaten. Do you understand?"

She paused, but no one said a word. "Despite what you think, I'm not evil. I don't derive pleasure from hurting. I don't enjoy destroying beauty. I was once the most beloved leader of the most beautiful city in the world. I was a hero—the first to stand up against true evil. The first to resist, to believe there had to be a better way than submission to cruelty. I raised my hand to protect the weak and defy a monster. And I wasn't alone." She whirled around. "All of these people here are my descendants, mine and my brother Drome and sister Mari, who joined me in the great rebellion. You"—she pointed at them—"are my family, too, and I will treat you as such, for we still have a common enemy who walks upon Elan and keeps us caged. Bring me the key, and help us right a wrong that is eons old."

No one moved.

She waited, but not for long. Patience was not the queen's strong suit. "Bring them," she ordered, and the bankors flapped again.

Moya began firing the moment she saw the first one move, and she kept shooting with startling speed and accuracy. But even her skill and determination were no match for the swarm the queen had sent. They went for Rain, Brin, Moya, and Gifford. None came after Tressa or Tesh. She knew they didn't have the treasure she sought. Rain killed one, but two more were heading his way. The bankors had no trouble with Brin. Catching her, one lifted off.

Moya, who struggled to keep the beasts off herself, could only manage a quick shot that killed the bankor holding Brin. Tesh gasped as she fell near the edge of the bridge. Brin hit hard, skipped across the stone, and looked like she was going to go over. Miraculously, she managed to catch the lip even as her legs spilled off. All Tesh could see was her fingers.

"Tesh!" Brin screamed, her fingers slipping.

He dropped his swords and ran for her as fast as he could. He dove headfirst to grab her, but before he was close enough, her fingers disappeared. He heard the scream, that same long unending wail. He pulled himself to the edge and looked down. He could still hear her, the sound receding, but she was already lost to the blackness below.

Just like Roan, Brin was gone.

"No!" the queen shouted. "Get under the bridge! No one else falls!"

Tesh continued to stare into that unending dark, into that empty space that had swallowed Brin. His mind worked at grasping what had happened but refused at the same time. Two parts of himself warred for dominance while he lay there looking into the Abyss, into the impossible.

She's gone. How can that be?

By the time Tesh looked up, Moya and Rain had been taken by the bankors and the only ones left on the bridge besides himself were Tressa and Gifford.

Gifford destroyed five bankors before one managed to catch hold of his sword arm and lift off, flying toward the queen with its prize. He was out over the open when he switched his sword to his other hand and swung upward. The bankor holding him exploded, and Gifford fell. Another bankor swooped in to intercept. Gifford angled his head downward and held his sword straight out, making himself a human spear. The second winged creature burst into rubble as he passed through it.

"Catch him! Catch him!" the queen demanded.

Two more tried. They came close. Gifford cut through them. Then he, too, was gone.

"Tesh," Tressa whispered. She fell to her knees beside him. "Tesh, we can't let her have it." She glanced down the bridge at the dragon watching them. "I'm going to jump."

Tesh was still seeing the disappearance of Brin's little fingers.

If I let you go, I'll never see you again.

Of course you will. If not in this life, then the next.

Tressa moved, crawling toward the edge as if she dragged a boulder on her back.

"The bankors will just catch you." Tesh was surprised by the calm of his voice. He looked to the edge of the bridge where Brin had clung.

"Then help me, Tesh," Tressa begged. "Please."

"I can't," he said. Lying on the stone, he began to cry. Something sharp was jabbing into Tesh's cheek, and he pulled his head away.

From the darkness, they heard Moya scream. She screamed again and again, and finally . . .

"Tressa has the key!" the queen shouted, her voice carrying across the void. She whirled on Konniger. "And you said Tesh was lying!"

The bankors are coming, Tesh thought. *Best to go down fighting.*

His swords were too far to retrieve in time. *A rock maybe?* Tesh looked down and saw the thing that had jabbed into his cheek. A small pin of metal.

Tesh stared at it, stunned.

"They're coming," Tressa said. He saw her pull a dagger, the one he'd given her in the swamp. "Maybe if we just threw it down, or maybe if—"

"Give me that," Tesh ordered, pointing at the weapon.

Tressa didn't question him, sliding it across the stone. "Tesh, they're—"

"Tressa, she's not going to get it, but what I'm about to do might destroy the future of the world. You okay with that?"

Tressa looked at him confused for a moment, then shrugged. "Yeah."

Tesh smiled. "Me, too."

Taking the dagger in both hands, he aimed the blunt metal pommel at the pin.

Hitting it with enough single-minded determination will cause a spark.

The bankors were flying again, and for the first time, Orr began to move out across the bridge toward them. All along the edge of the Abyss, Tesh saw the heroes of old—who since their deaths had fought and died and fought again in an unending war. Tesh realized he didn't want that.

Promise me you'll do something good, that you'll make your life worth something more than killing.

Maybe it isn't too late.

Tesh remembered Brin, not the look of panic before she fell, but the girl he was in love with.

So, what is it you're writing?

I call this the Book of Brin. It's going to be the story of the whole world.

But it wasn't now. All that was lost. All of her was gone, not just away from him, not even to Rel, but vanished—gone forever.

If I let you go, I'll never see you again.

Of course you will. If not in this life, then the—

As tears ran down his cheeks and bankors dove, a queen screamed in realization, sending the dragon to leap in response, and with every ounce of strength in his being, Tesh brought the handle of the dagger down on that little metal pin.

A boom. Pain. Darkness. A sense of falling. Then, nothingness was followed by more of the same.

Afterword

Hey all, Robin again. For those that don't know, I'm Michael's wife, helper bee, and advocate for his readers. I want to thank people for writing and saying you've enjoyed my afterwords. It's one of the reasons I'm back! As before, Michael isn't going to see this until after the book is published, so we can talk privately. Or at least I can write, and you can read.

Am I the only one with a slightly revised version of Britney Spear's song in my head: *Oops! . . . He Did It Again?* Yep, it's another cliff-hanger, and it's remarkably similar to *Age of Legend*'s ending. Most of our would-be heroes are falling into the unknown, but this time we also have everyone else in dire straits, too. Fortunately, this is the last time we'll be left dangling because the next book (*Age of Empyre*) is the sixth and final installment. We're finally going to see how everything plays out. I'm so excited! Oh no, now *that* song is looping. I was better off with Britney.

Before I dive into my commentary, I'd like to address my current emotional state, which is quite melancholy. You see, my infatuation with Hadrian from the Riyria books is well-documented, and I didn't expect others to find their way into my heart, but they did. With only a single book left, I know I'm going to be depressed when I have to say goodbye to all my newfound friends from Legends. Plus, I can't count on Michael to give me more tales with them as he so generously did with the Riyria Chronicles. Why? In Riyria, Royce and Hadrian had been together for ten years at the start of *Theft of Swords*, so we could go back in time to see how they met. That's not the case with Legends. So while I'm dying (no pun intended) to find out how the final installment concludes, I know I'll be in mourning when I finish the last page.

But all that heartache is for another day. For now, let's turn our attention to this book, shall we? I see that Michael continues his sadistic tendencies, and he's even upped his game by leaving virtually everyone I love in some form of jeopardy. There's been a lot of ominous comments about the Abyss, and the fact that no one has ever returned from there doesn't bode well for Brin, Tesh, Gifford, Roan, and Tressa. And, of course, having Moya, Rain, and probably Tekchin in the clutches of Ferrol won't exactly be a walk in the park. With Suri and Persephone now facing Lothian and his dragons, it's not looking good for the home team.

Even with this stress, I'm glad there is danger in Elan's afterlife. When I started reading *Age of Death*, I thought, "Well, they're already dead, so it can't get worse." And while that idea was comforting, it also made me worry that the trip through the afterlife would be boring. I mean, it's the presence of risk that keeps me riveted, and I didn't think there would be any. Boy, was I wrong!

Michael actually touched on two of my greatest fears. The first being a life without purpose but without end. That's how I see Rel. Sure, the people there have no pain, but they also are free of want and have nothing to strive toward. For someone like me, who thrives on challenges, that certainly isn't a state I would like to find myself in. While I'm sure Arion's discussion about ceasing to exist was supposed to be frightening, I'd much prefer fading away then being stuck in all that monotony.

Then there is Nifrel, a place with plenty of challenges, but aside from a small victory here or there, it, too, is the same from one day to the next. I see it much like Sisyphus pushing his rock up the hill only to have it roll back down. But unlike in Rel, existence in Nifrel isn't free of pain. In the movies, when someone is tortured, they eventually die or pass out. But in Ferrol's realm, neither option is available, so the torment could literally go on forever. From a purely intellectual perspective, I know the concept of unending pain is engrained in Christian beliefs. Still, I've never personally feared such a fate. Yeah, I'm far from a saint, but I have tried to be a good person and help others, and I think I have some brownie points in my column. But now Michael plants the concept that it's not about "good" or "evil." His notion that ambitious people might prefer the struggle, even if nothing changes, gives me food for thought. For me, that's an even more frightening future than the blandness of Rel.

And now I have the Abyss to worry about! Because so many people have talked about that place with such foreboding, and because I know how Michael's mind works, I'm more than just a little concerned about what we might find down there.

The one bright spot is that Suri is no longer captive, and she has access to the Art once more. But even that bit of hope isn't without trepidation. I'm not sure what Imaly has in store for Suri, Makareta, and Mawyndulë, but I'm not hopeful that it will turn out well. The curator has her own agenda, and I don't think she cares about the casualties in her wake.

And of course, we know that Lothian finally figured out how to make gilarabrywns. So far, we've only seen one, but are more coming? That fact brings up all kinds of questions. Will Suri try to prevent additional ones from being made? Can she do anything about the one that was created? The only thing I'm confident about is she won't be making another to counteract it . . . unless her newfound friendship with Makareta deepens. Hmmm . . . I don't want to go there. Let's just be happy that Suri is in a significantly better place than she has been in recent books and call it a day.

Oh, and while I'm discussing gilarabrywns, I'll let you in on a little secret. They weren't supposed to show up in this book. Michael moved up their appearance from *Age of Empyre*, and I'm glad he did. It makes for higher drama now that all the pieces on the chessboard are at risk. Seriously, there isn't a character I care for, well except maybe Malcolm, who isn't in peril.

Speaking of Malcolm, I'm so glad he's back, even if I can't figure out if he's "good" or "evil." I must say I've waffled about him and his motives on many occasions throughout this series, something I've enjoyed quite a bit.

My current suspicion is that Michael is trying to make a point rather than just being coy. But either way, I always enjoy his scenes. For those who have read Riyria, did you get the same sense of déjà vu that I did regarding the timing of his reappearance? If you're not sure what I'm talking about, drop me a line, and I'll say more.

In any case, Nyphron's and Malcolm's scene was one of my favorites. Upon re-reading it, I noticed how deftly Michael inserted Malcolm's comment about Uberlin and his followers in a scene just before Drome's tirade about the same person. That's a nice bit of seed-planting by Michael.

Speaking of seeds, I'm glad to see that one which was sowed in *Age of Swords* finally sprouted. I'm referring to Rain's "mystery woman," who has been haunting his dreams for years. He became a digger and took two trips into the heart of Neith looking for her. And now he has finally found what he was looking for. I'm encouraged by Beatrice's foresight that Rain will live through whatever awaits him in the last book. Also, I wonder if the reestablishment of the dwarfs comes into play in Michael's Rise and Fall series, which takes place between Legends and Riyria.

I'm a soft touch for an emotional scene, and this book had plenty of them, but two stood out for me. The first was the drink shared by Nyphron and Persephone. Yes, we all know that their marriage is primarily strategic. Still, it was nice seeing them share a time of loss and vulnerability. I appreciated that even someone as stoic as Nyphron was able to provide a bit of comfort to Persephone. Michael hasn't given us insight into their union, and I think that was purposeful. But with this scene, we see that it is not all bad. Also, I think this chapter had a great Book of Brin entry that nicely encapsulated their relationship.

Speaking of touching, another favorite of mine was Tressa's reunion with Gelston. The fact that she kept coming back despite all his ill treatment really told me a great deal about a character that I had previously despised. I think that's one of Michael's strengths, taking a seemingly insignificant and reprehensible character and giving me new insight. For those who have read Riyria, you know that redemption is at the heart of those books, and I'm glad to see that the Legend of the First Empire follows in that tradition.

There are many other scenes I loved, but if I concentrated only on them, I'd run out of time and space to discuss what was the biggest aspect of enjoyment for me. Which is the revelations! All the pieces of the puzzle are coming together, and I can see the picture emerging. We are finally at the point where Michael can reveal some of the cards he's held in his hand for so long, and that is, by far, my favorite part of this book.

So, let's recap what we've learned. Everyone lived happily in Erebus until Turin (a.k.a. Malcolm, a.k.a. Uberlin) killed his brother Trilos and became a tyrant that warred against his sister Ferrol and brother Drome. I think that qualifies as "breaking the world." Now comes the real question . . . is Malcolm trying to fix things, or is he manipulating everyone to do his bidding for a goal that we aren't yet aware of?

Another new piece of the puzzle is that Trilos and Muriel were in love. And Turin tried to keep them apart. I guess that justifies Muriel's hatred for her father. But we know something that Muriel (and maybe Malcolm) does not. Trilos is currently hanging around the garden and stirring up trouble. So, I guess that whole death thing didn't stick, which makes me wonder . . . why hasn't Trilos and Muriel reunited? I think there is still more we need to find out, and I'm fairly certain Michael will tell us before everything is said and done.

As for things yet to be discovered, what's up with the message Malcolm passed to Brin via Padera? And why didn't he just tell Tressa when he gave her the assignment in the first place? I'm guessing Malcolm discovered something while he was out and about. Since the mysterious line about trees walking and stones talking didn't come up again in *Age of Death*, I'll be looking for it in the last book. In a way, I'm glad there is a little break between this and the final book. I like having a bit of a breather and time to ponder. Sometimes the anticipation of a great meal is as good as eating it.

Well, those are some of my thoughts and ramblings. I hope you enjoyed the story as much as I did. Since we are getting near the end of the series, we've received a lot of emails asking, "What's next." So before I go, I should touch on a few things.

First and foremost, we need to release the last book of this series, and yes, there will be a Kickstarter for it just like there was for *Age of Legend* and *Age of Death*. If you want to be notified when it launches you can sign up at https://michaeljsullivan.survey.fm/age-of-empyre-early-notification. The release date for *Age of Empyre* is May 5th, but early backers will receive the ebook near the end of February and the hardcovers just as soon as they come off the press. If you miss the Kickstarter, don't worry, we can always do a manual add for you after the fact. We had more than 400 people who did exactly that for *Age of Death*.

As for what comes after Legends? Well, for the last several years, Michael has been working on a new series, which is tentatively titled, The Rise and the Fall. This is a trilogy, and the current plan is they'll start releasing in the summer of 2021. As I write this (early December 2019), Michael is about three-quarters of the way through writing the second book.

Like Revelations and Legends, Michael is writing the entire series before publishing the first book, and no, I've not read any of it yet. That said, I do know a few things. First, there are no cliffhangers . . . hooray! As for where it fits in Elan's history, it starts about eight hundred years after the end of the Legend books and ends a thousand years before the start of the Riyria tales. I have heard Michael bring up a few names that will be recognizable by either Riyria or Legend readers, but I'll mention only one: Esrahaddon. That name won't mean anything to people who have read just the Legends books, but I suspect that Riyria fans will be excited to see the full backstory for this particular character.

I'm sure there are many Riyria fans who are wondering, "Will there be more Royce and Hadrian books?" The answer is, yes! The fifth Chronicle book, Drumindor, is planned, but we don't have any release date for it yet.

Okay, I have just one last thing to mention before I go. If you participated in the Kickstarter for *Age of Death*, then you've already received a Suri and Minna short story called "Pile of Bones." It takes place before the start of the Legends of the First Empire series, so you can read it without worrying about spoilers. Also, it'll be free on Audible.com for a number of months after its release. But if you missed the Kickstarter ebook, or the Audible version while it was free, drop us a line at michael@michaelsullivan-author.com and put "Send me a Pile of Bones" in the subject. If you do, I'll send you an ebook version of that story.

Well, I see that my time is up. In conclusion, I want to thank you for reading my little afterword. I'm a big fan of the series and it's nice to be able to share some of my thoughts with others. I hope you are doing the same!

Acknowledgments

When you buy a Michael J. Sullivan book, it's my name on the cover, so it would be understandable for you to assume that I'm the only one responsible for the story between the pages. Maybe for some authors, that is true, but for myself, it takes a lot of people to produce a work that I feel is worthy of your time. I would feel remiss if I didn't mention their names and bring to your attention their incredible contributions that made this book what it came to be. If you've previously read my other acknowledgments, you're going to see some familiar names.

Anyone who is even a little familiar with me knows that Robin is hugely responsible for the story you've just read. She is the consummate reader advocate who makes sure that the book is as good as it can be. Her fingerprints are throughout the pages as an alpha reader, line editor, first-pass copyeditor, organizer of the beta and gamma readers, and she even takes care of the ebook design and print book layout. She also runs the Kickstarters, and I'll have more to say on that in just a minute.

What you may not know is that during the final stages of *Age of Death*, my mother passed away. As it turned out, Robin was at my mother's, sister's, and brother's side when Mom passed. Having her there was nothing short of a miracle. Robin's main strength is bringing order to chaos, and I know that Mom's final days were significantly better with Robin ushering her passage. With Mom gone, our primary focus was on the well-being of my brother, who had been Mom's selfless caregiver for decades. Robin prudently kidnapped Pat and brought him to live with us in Virginia, an action that got my brother through the worst experience of his nearly seventy years of life.

Why is this important? Because Robin and I were spinning many plates at a critical time in the development of *Age of Death*. You see, while I thought the book was in good shape, Robin had a different opinion and no time to discuss her reservations. Initially, I wasn't concerned because her alpha feedback is usually easy to incorporate, and it takes no more than a day or two. When we finally got some time to go over the changes, it became evident that hundreds of hours of work would be required, and with our time divided between dealing with Mom's affairs and Pat's welfare, days slipped into weeks and weeks into months.

When we finally got the book to a state that both Robin and I were happy with, time was running short. The recording date, which had been scheduled nearly a year before, was quickly approaching. If we missed that date, it could mean slipping *Age of Death*'s release date by six or eight months, as Tim had many other projects already booked. Given we had already committed to a quick release (due to the cliffhanger nature of *Age of Legend*), we didn't want that to happen. Something had to give, and in this case, it was the beta. Rather than Robin's usual process, we had to do a "mini-beta." We want to thank Beverly Collie, Buffy Curtis, Jeffrey D. Carr, Louise Faering, Cathy Fox, Nathaniel and Sarah Kidd, Evelyn Keeley, John Koehler, Jonas Lodewyckx, Richard Martin, Jamie McCullough, and Jeffrey Schwarz. Not only did they give us great feedback under tight deadlines, but they did so while deviating from our standard procedures.

Another corner cut was how we did the copy editing. As we have done for years now, we enlisted the talents of Laura Jorstad and Linda Branam. Originally, Robin scheduled them serially such that Linda would receive the book after Laura had already gone over it. As time started to compress, we knew that wouldn't be possible. Linda's date was unmovable due to the timing of other jobs. Luckily, Laura was able to be more flexible, but that meant that each editor would receive the books at roughly the same time. The fact that we could still use them both was a positive, but on the negative side, that meant more work falling on Robin to collate their edits. To make matters worse, I was doing a last-pass review, and there were paragraphs added, deleted, and line edits performed. So, that meant Robin had to take input from three different people and combine them into one cohesive file. Not a small feat, especially with the recording deadline approaching.

Speaking of recording, Tim Gerard Reynolds returns once again to add his amazing talents to the narration of the audiobook. I'm sure everyone already knows how much we love Tim. We talk about him all the time! When Robin and I went to New Jersey for the first three days of recording, we met Frank Lopez, recording engineer extraordinaire. This is our first time working with Frank, and we certainly hope he can return for future books, as he was terrific. And, of course, I want to thank Kristin Lang (Senior Director, Acquisitions & Content Partnerships), who shepherds all of our titles through Audible. She is our point person with the entire Audible team, and the promotional plan that she and the marketing folks have put together will surely get this title noticed.

If you are a print reader (and you purchase your hardcover or paperback through the retail chain), then you can thank Shawn Speakman and his company Grim Oak Press. Together they make it possible to get my physical copies into bookstores. Shawn is a true innovator who is revolutionizing how writers and publishers work together. Here's hoping that what he's doing for me can be utilized by others in the future. I think it will be good for Shawn, fellow authors, and the publishing industry as a whole.

And speaking of printed books, let's not forget the more than 3,600 people who took a leap of faith and supported this book sight unseen, making printed versions a reality. These gracious men and women either backed the Kickstarter (3,107 people), placed a pre-order through the BackerKit online store (127 people), or wrote to Robin for a "manual add" (393 people). At the time I'm writing this (early-December 2019), they contributed more than \$142,000, which not only paid for the printing, but they also provided a nice-sized advance (something I wouldn't usually get now that I don't publish through traditional means). You can find the names of many of these people in the Kickstarter Backer section.

Wide distribution and Audible's marketing will certainly help to get the book noticed, but we all know that what people look at first is the book's cover. If my baby were ugly, few people would give it a chance. Thankfully, I don't have that problem because the cover was once again created by the incomparable Marc Simonetti—who continues to be a treasure of the fantasy community. I marvel at every creation he produces, and his coffee table art book, Coverama, remains one of the few things I'd grab up if my house caught fire. Thank you, Marc, for your continued hard work.

And while a beautiful cover will get people to pick up a book, typos can make someone toss it aside. Yes, Laura and Linda did the vast majority of that cleanup work, but even the most eagle-eyed can't find everything. Plus, there are the little boo-boos that Robin or I incorporated as we pulled everything together. So, I'd like to extend my thanks to two additional groups of people. First, I'd like to thank the early Kickstarter readers who reported typos as they gobbled up the story. And second, I'd like to thank my gamma readers who are my last line of defense on such matters. These are people who proofread the book just before it hits the press. Some of the gamma readers included Sundeep Agarwal, Dee Austring, Tim Cross, Mike DePalatis, Christopher Griffin, Audrey Hammer, Steve Kafkas, Mark Larsen, Alex Makar, Chris McGrath, Ganesh Olekar, Tracy Newman, Julian Portillo, Doug Schneider, and Jenn Strohschein.

Whew, I told you I had a lot of help. Each of these people has devoted their time, talent, and in the case of the Kickstarter backers, their hard-earned cash to make this release what it has come to be. Robin and I want to extend our heartfelt thanks to every one of them.

Just one last thing, and then I'm done. An acknowledgments section is about naming those who made a book possible, and for thanking them for their efforts. So, I can't leave without including you, dear readers, for picking up a copy of my books, writing reviews, and telling others, "You must read this!" You've helped this series soar to heights I never thought possible. For instance, did you know that both *Age of War* and *Age of Legend* hit the New York Times Bestseller list? And three books of this series became USA Today bestsellers. But even more gratifying than those prestigious accolades is that all books in this series have been nominated for Goodreads Choice Awards. That is particularly special to us because it's the only major book award decided by readers, and you are the only judge and jury that Robin and I care about. We appreciate your faith in us and the books, and in return, we're dedicated to making sure that each title we release is worthy of your time. In other words, we'll keep the books coming, and we hope they'll continue to meet with your approval.

Kickstarter Backers

Our eternal thanks go out to the following people (and to those who chose not to be recognized publicly), for being patrons of the arts and making the hardcover edition of this book possible by pre-ordering through our Kickstarter project.

— A —

Colin A. • Husain A. • M. C. Abajian • Terri Abbett • Holly Buell Abbott • Winston Percy Abbott • Chuck Abdella • Julian Abernethy • Shilpa Anna Abraham • Brian Abrams • Thérèse Abrams • Andrij Abyzov • Iris Achmon • Andy Adams • Colin Adams • Frederick Adams • Helen Adams • Matt "Bubba Moose" Adams • Rob Adams • Sam & Skylar Adams • Szilágyi Ádám • Iain Addienll • Michael & Heather Adelson • Anna Adler • Daniel Adler • Scott Adley • Lee A. Adolfson • Sandu Elena Adriana • adumbratus • Aerronn & Rae • Svetoslav Agafonkin • Kawika Aguilar • Emely Aguino • Eddy Aguirre • Matthew Aguirre • D. Ahlrich • James & Diana Aiken • Garrett Aikens • Geoff Akens • Leila Ako-Adjei • Samir Ako-Adjei • Alfonso Albarran • Dan Alber • Dan Albrent • Turned Alchemy • Andrew Alderman • Alex • Jason D. Alexander • Scott A. Alexander • Heather Aley • Kristel Alger • AliiKatt • Misha Ali • Seth Alister-Jones • Harrison Alldred • Caitlin & Liam Allen • Cody L. Allen • Julie Marie Allen • Laura Allen • Stuart Allen & Lorri Stone • Sami Almudaris • Nardeen

AlSaffar • Emilia Alston • Marcos Alvarado • Alyksandrei • Benjamin Ames • Amokima • Anamue • Jan Anderegg • Brian Anderson • Carol Beth Anderson • Chris Anderson • George Anderson • Julie Anderson • Kris Anderson • Matthew & Alex Anderson • Nathan Alan Anderson • Richard Anderson III • Sadie Anderson • Sean Anderson • Sean L. Anderson • Tyler Andor • Andrea • Becky Andreasen • David Andre • Dennis Andrews • Joey Andrews • Androsso • Jocelyn Andruko & Mitchell Farmer • Andy • Angela • Rachel Angle • Jaime Anglin • Jacek Aninowski • Chrissy Anjewierden • Catrina Ankarlo • Stephanie Annee • Lara Antonuk • Renam Antunes • Summer Applebaum • Ricardo Araujo • Maryrose Arcuria • David Arcuri • Tamara Arens • Sue Armitage • Mary-Helen Armour • Carl Mya Armstrong • Matt Armstrong • Cassie Arneson • Aubrie D. Arnold • Quint Ashburn • Ashton • Dagny Athena • Angela Atkinson • The Atkinson Family • Brent Auble • Jon Auerbach • Marco Auger • James R. Aurandt • Devan Ausiello • Stephanie Austin-Ellis • Matt Avella • Marcus Avery • Alice Aviles • Manpreet Kaur Awasthi • R. J. Aytes • Arya Azarshahy • Andrew Azzinaro

— B —

Alex B. • Ariane B. • Glen B. • Hamza B. • Marius B. • Maura B. • R. J. B. III • Richard B. • John Bachmann • Nathan Bacon • Woodcrow Bacon • Anurag Bagri • Jacob Bahr • Chris Bailey • Michael Bailey • Asher & Teagan Baima • Charlie & Sarah Baker • Gary Baker • Jeff Baker • Blake Baldwin • Don Baldwin • Joseph Baldwin • Rob Ballew • Tyler Ballew • Meghan Ball • Nic Baltas • Ben Balzarini • Bamesinator • Maciej Banasiak • Donovan Banh • Preston Bannard • Tony Baraconi • Callum Barber • Joshua Barber • Heather Barcomb • Caldwell Barefoot • Yasmine Barghouty • Logan Barker • David Barkman • Aaron & John Barlow • Bryan M. Barnard • David Barnard • David Barnett • Johnathan Barnett • Josh Barratt • Christopher Barr • Nolan Barrett • John &

Lori Barron • Jan Barthold • Michael Jonathan Basaldella • Emily Bass • David Bassler • Alyssa Bastug • Wes Batcheller • Dotsy Bates • Susan Bates • Aaron Batey • Berta Batzig • Marc Baudry • David Bean • Tyke Beard • Kuma Bear • Abby Beasley • Dana Beatty • Craig Beaumont • Mark D. Beaumont • Brian Becker • Felix, Niquela & Christian Becker • Nicole A. Becker • Brent Beckman • Anne Beckmann • Nate "The Kaiser" Beck • Maile Beckwith • Danielle Bednar • Cheryl Beebe-Skynar • Algernon Beechworth • Momtaj Begum • Alex Bekerian • The Belden Family • Chuck Bell • Douglas Bell • Jessica Bell • Emily Benger • Michelle Beninati • Henry Benn • Erin Benson • Shane Benson • Dirk Berger • Larry Berger • Justine Bergman • Scott Berman • Mary Catherine Bernadette • Ben Berndt • Clare Bernier • Evy Bernier • William & Sydney Berroteran • Alexis Briel Berry • Scott Berry • The Berrys • Meredith Bertschin • Taylor Besenski • Peter Bess • Nathan Best • Annette Bettencourt-Ouellette • Oliver Beuchat • Rati Bhargava • Deven & Krish Bhatia • Bhill • Maria Bianchi • Nate F. Bibens • Seth Biber • S. Bickersmith • Ralph Biddle • Bigbogie • Justin Biggs • Bill • Christian Billen • Adam T. Billups • Chris Bilodeau • Sarah Birchard • Rochelle Bird • Christopher Birkheimer • Jodi Bishop • Joshua Bishop • The Bitterman Family • Jessica Björklund • Ross Bjorklund • Airon Black • The Black Roth's • Samuel Robin Blackwell • Benjamin Blakeslee • Jacob Blank • Laly Blasco • Karin & Dietmar Bloech • Ben Blount • The Blount Family • Ser Ian Arthur Blum • Tylor Blythe • Liz Boatwright • Angelique M. Keppler Bochnak • Billie Bock • Jeff Bogzevitz • A. J. Bohne • Nicholas R. Boileau • Mircea Boistean • Matthew Boley • Lucas Bombardier • Nancy Bonanno • Jasen Boothe • Mark Booth • Tom Borealis • Borehams • Rikke Borgaard • Halli Borgfjord • Andy Bosher • Becky Bosshart • Riaan Botha • Nick, Sue & Arielle Botta • Elizabeth Bougie • Kris Boultbee • Andy Bowden • Chad Bowden • David Bowden • Jason Bowden • Elise "The Cat" BowerCraft • The Bowersox Family • Robert Bowling • Kayleigh Bowman • Leo Matthew Boxley • Carol Boyd • Chris Boyd • Christine Boyd • Justin Boyd • McKayla Boyd • Timothy "Doc" Boyd • Michael

Boye • Kevin Boyer • The Boz • Iain Brabant • Brad • Angela Bradley & Kevin Enax • David M. Bradley Jr. • Joe Bradley • Orin R. Brady • Sandy Brady • J. Leigh Bralick • Amanda Brandt • J. Branstrom • The Brass Family • Lauren Bratt • Amy Braun • Neil Breault • Milou Breedveld • James Stewart Breen • Ethan & Ben Breese • Liva Brekka • Alexander Brener • Steve Brenneman • Carmen Brenner • Hannah Bridge • Joaquin Bridges • Sarah Bridges • Ashley Britten • Svemir Brkic • Julien Brochet • Sébastien Brochet • Mary Brockmyre-Martin • Kelly Diana Brogdon • Frank Broussard • Rachel Brousseau • Chris Brown • Christina & Terry Brown • Curtis Allan Brown • Dustin, Amy, Owen, Molly & Baby Brown • Jordan Brownfield • Forrest Brown • Joe "BrownSloth" Brown • Kevin R. Brown • Michael Brown • Steven M. Brown • V. Brown • Rose Broyles • Jana Broz • Sara Brunson • Joanna Brzeska • Ryan Buchanan • Danielius Buckus • Amit Budhu • Laura Warren Buehler • The Bugge Family • Stephen Burchfield • Randy Burdick • Elwood Burgess • Micah B. Burke • Rob Burke • Robert E. Burke • Kylie Burkot • Jennifer Burns • Jeri Burns • Phil Burns • Meghan Burrell • Benjamin Burroughs • Cassandra L. Burton • Brandon Busby • Jenny Busby • S. Busby • Dave Bushnell • Nathan Bussey • Janet Butler • J. L. Butler • Laura Butler • Megan Butler • Kevin Butrick & Elena Tenchikova • Nicholas Buttram • Alexandru Butuza • Joris Buys • Guy Byars • David Bybee • Kenneth L. Bynon • Tanith Bynon • Nicole Bywater

— C —

Amy C. • Beverly C. • Carley C. • Erin C. • Nikaya C. • Courtney Cabaniss • John Gerald Cacas • Brandy C. Cacciamani • Josh Cain • Linda Rae Calamaio • Hilary Caldwell • Kristen Caldwell • Joshua Callahan • Callie & Cory • Tatiana & Chancie Calliham • Clay Calvert • Ross Cameron • Sarah Cameron • Dustin & Katie Campbell • Miki Campbell • Rob Campbell • Trevor Camp • Clinton Canady IV • Kevin Candiloro • Candy & Justin • Clay

Cannon • Sean Cannon • Eric Caraboolad • Jennifer Caracappa • Marnilo Cardenas • Alicia Cardillo • Alfredo R. Carella • Carolyn J. Carideo • The Carklin Clan • Steven & Elizabeth Carley • Victoria Carlini • Richard Carlock • Stephanie A. Carlson • Ty Carl • Dane Caro • Allison Marie Caron • Alex Carpenter • Jodi Carpenter • Joseph H. Carpenter, IV • Inés Carradice • Jasun Carr • Jeffrey D. Carr • Robin Carroll • Alex M. Carter • Brandon Carter • Carolyn Carter • Jennine S. Carter • Mark Allen Carter • Michael Caruso • Tricia Cascio • Beth Case • Brian Casey • Sarah Casey • Amanda Cassuto • Gonzalo Castro • Joseph Castro • Victor Cata • Tammie Causey • John Cave • Tim "Starmarc" Caves • Mícheál Ó. Ceallaigh • Michele Ceballos • Lawrence A. Cerniglia Jr. • David Lars Chamberlain • Laura Chamberlain • David Chanda • Monica Chandler • Paul & Shirley Chandler • Douglas Chan • Jaime Chan • Kevin Chan • Rawee Chanphakdee • Tony Chan • T. S. Chan • Bernardo Chapar • Maya Chapman • The Charles Twins • Jordan Charlton • Neville R. Charlton • Treana & Max Chartier • Owen & Bryce Chasteen • Anthony Chatfield • John R. Chauhan • Jesse Chavez • Brent Chelewski • Yu-Wen Chen • Reagan Chesnut • Kristopher Childress • Noel Chin • Chip-N1MIE • John Chipman • Leigh Chittum • Jennifer K. Choi • Chris • Hans Bredgaard Christensen • Dylan Christian • Megan Christiansen • Mikaela Christiansson • Christina • Derek Christman • Olivia Christopher • Christy, Jollin & Abby • Maria & Sara Christy • D. Chritchley • Michelle Chrpa • Shanna Chugg • Kevin Cinq-Mars • Jasmine Clancy • Brandi Clark • Chris Clark • David Clark • Georgia Clark • Jenelle Clark • Michael, Ella & Sophie Clark • David Clayton • CleanerSprout • Alex Clement • Joshua Cleveland • Francis & Charles Clifford • Greg Clinton • Michael Clougherty • Richard Clouston • Mike Cluff • CMHMZ • Peter Coates • Mike Cochran • Lisa Cockrell • Larry Coker • Ryan Colbeth • Mathew Colburn • Ab Colby • Jason S. Colby • Jenny Colby • Misti Colcleaser • Antonino Cole • Ashton Cole • Ryan Cole • Susan Collingwood • Justin Collins • Lawrence Collins • Richard Collins • Todd Collins • Todd

M. Colucci • DeWillo Elisabeth Colvin • Matthew & Robin Colwell • CompuChip • Conflux • Benjamin Conrad • Susan Contreras • Ed Cooke • Elise Cook • Richard Cooke • Christine A. Cooney • Jessica Cooperman • Michelle Cooper • W. Cooper • Anke Corbeil • Ashley Corbeille • Sarah Corbeil • Jonathan Cordell • Jorge Cordero Martínez • The Corey Press • Mark Corsi • Arletta Kelley Cortright • Kelley Cortright • Olivia Corvec • Rin Corvetti • Anthony Cossio • Adrian Crawley-Da Costa • Ricardo Costa • Tyson Y. Cote • Brandon A. Cottrell • Haiyden Cottrell • Rachel Anne Carlson Cottrell • Larry Couch • Damon J. Courtney • Stephanie L. Couturier • Donna Coviello • Paul Coward • Jonathan Cowles • C. J. Cox • David Cox • Leo Coyle • Brian Crabtree • Tim Crandall • Anya Crane • Jeffrey Crane • Jeremy Crane • Clayton Cravath • Belinda Crawford • Chris Creech • Ben Crew • Shawn Crimmins • R. P. Crisp • Nathan B. Crocker • Kevin Cronic • Michelle Crosby • P. L. Cross • Tim Cross • R. L. Crothers • Andrew Cruise • David Crumbley • Aaron "Crumpy" Crump • Cygnus Crux • Mark Cummings • G. L. Cunningham • Vincent Thomas Cunningham • Sam Curran • Glenn Curry • Lesley Curvers • Mary Cusick • Andrew Cutler • Nate Cutler • John Cutright

— D —

Brett D. • Dave D. • Karen D. • Lauren D. • Leolani D. • Mikee D. • Yung J. D. • Giuseppe D'Aristotile • Sapphire D'Chalons • Brian Dabbs • Katerina Dadakova • Rachel Daeger • Ahmed Daher • Daimadoshi • Sean & Katrina Dalton • Dani Daly • Elizabeth Daly • Leon Daly • Joel & Dianna Damir • Stephen Damon • Dominik Daniel • Danilo & Trine • Joshua Danish • Patricio Danos • Darek • Jennifer Dath • Daniel C. Daugherty • The Dave • Harry David • Chad Davidson • Boyd Davis • Colton M. Davis • J. Davis & Family • Joanna K. Davis • Leslie A. Davis • Lori Davis • Rocky A. Davis • Luke Davitt • David A. Dawson • Dino Dayao • Wendall Dayley • Justin Ć de Baca • P. H. A. de

Bekker • Bob, Merilin & Kirsi de Brabandere • Chris de Eyre • Marcel de Jong • Daniel de la Torre • Gerber de Lange • Jeffrey de Lange • Elodie de Peretti • Wendy de Peuter • Dénes Deák • Stuart Deakin • Joseph Dean • Deborah • Kyle Debuck • Rhel ná DecVandé • Emmeline DeGolier • Jean Dejace • Jennifer DeLeon • Marci DeLeon • Mark W. Dell'Orfano • Scott Dell'Osso • Brian Christopher Dell • Terry Dellino • Sheldon & Brittani Dement • Jessica Demers • Diane S. & P. J. Dempsey • Stephen Denney • Ollie Denning • Paul Dennison • Ryan Depuy • Max Dercum • A. Derda • James Michael Derieg • Deryk, Crystal, Sabryn & Seymoure • Joe Desiderio • Tim J. De Silva • RaeAnn Desmarais • Alexandre Dessureault • Prasana Devanand • Peter Devine & Gina Jiang • Robert DeVoll • Andrew DeVore • Emmanuel Dexet • Chris Dhanaraj • Patricia Diani • Paul Diaz • Tobias Dickbreder • Jeffrey Dick • Simon Dick • Anthony DiCostanzo • Ethan Dietz • Bret Dillingham • Dina • Crystal Dinh • Betsy Dion • Chad Ditter • Lewis Dix • dmsaelee • The Doan Family: Randy, Marla, Colin & Evan • Andrew Dobry • Michael W. Dodge • Christopher Kenneth Doelker • dogpoop • Andrew Doherty • Gregory Dollins • Miguel Domingo • Donna • Máire Donohue • Ben Donovan • Shannon Douglas • Kevin Dougwillo • Jacob Doukas • Zathras do Urden • Nate Dowd • Michael "Infael" Dowds • Alycia & Jesse Doyle • Mary Kate Doyle • Thomas J. Doyle, Jr. • Grandpa Dragon • Maxine Drake • Weston Dransfield • E. L. Drayton • T. J. Driver • Tara Drost • Tina Druce-Hoffman • A. F. Dudley • Maleh Duenas • Colm Duffy • Lisa M. Dugan • Lauren Duggar • Duke • Mengmeng Du • Michelle P. Dunaway • Christyn Dundorf • David Dunn • Alexander Dupuis • Eric Durfee • Vince Dutra • Lana Dvorkin

— E —

Michael-Scott Earle • Dain Eaton • Mary Eaton • Heather Eberhart • Blake Ebert • Brandy Eckman • Steven Ede • David Edmonds • Paul T.

Edmunds • J. D. Egbert • Nathan Eggleston • Gary L. Ehret • Josh Ehrich • Ehtasham • Lukas Eichler • Martin Eichman • Evan Eisenberg • Daniel Eisen • Rambo Eitner • Kjetil Vinjerui Ekre • Evan Elder•Alyssa Elery•Thomas Elfing•Elizabeth•Karen Elizabeth•Mohamed Elkammar • Elldaryck • Kyle G. Eller • Lindsey Ellertson • Ian Elliott•Jasmine M. Elliott•Matt Ellsworth•Lady Eloquence•Elo, Tasha & Jason • Bryan Elstad • Max Elwell • Elwen • Scott Ely • Sean Ely • Christian Emden • McJames Emem • Emil • Andrew Enano • Matt Enberg • Travis Enfield • Angie Engelbert • Alex Engelhardt • Kory Engle • MaryAnn Erickson • Pierce Erickson • J. L. K. Erso • Gabe Erwin • Jill S. Erwin • Angelina Escobar • Tarasa Escoubas • Joel Espina • Emmanuel Estipona • Etel • Antonino Ethan • David W. Etherington • Walker Etherton • Jason Eubank • Paula Evans • Joshua Ewer • Morgan B. Ewers

— F —

L. P. N. F. • Maja F. • Phil F. • Brian L. Fabbi • Iga Fabry-Byczkowska • Magdalena Fabrykowska-Mlotek • Rod Fage • Chad Fairchild • Victoria Fair • Shawn R. Fairweather • Anne Falbowski • Urs Falk • M. Falvey • Anthony Farana • Jackson A. Farnsworth • Mitch Farrell•Sonja & Daniel Farris•Emma Faubion•Mathue Faulkner•Michael Faulkner • Michael Fazio • Sherry S. Featherston • Jeremy Feath • Febin • Chuck Fecteau • Carol Feeney • Kevin Feeney • Sander Fekene•Horst Feldhaeuser•Angela L. Femrite•A. Fennell•Natalie Shannon Fennell • Bruce Fenton • Addisyn Rae Ferguson • Shani Ferguson • Paula Fernández • Jacob Ferrell • Robert Fiallo II • Randall Fickel • The Field Family • Patricia Field • Andrew D. Fields • Cari Fifield • Michelle Findlay-Olynyk • Finlynn • The Finnegan Family • Kathleen Finnegan • Shawn P. Finn • Dan Firth • G. Fisher • John Fisher • Brooke Fishman • Simon Fitz • Cameron Flagg • Tom Flaherty • Courtney Flamm • Vince Flaxfield • Matthew Fleck • Melissa Fleisch • Tristan Fletcher • Chris Floden • Manuel A. Flores • A. B. C. Flowe • Robert Flower • Travis

Floyd • The Fluhr Family • Ann Flumerfelt • Holly J. Flumerfelt • K. Flynn • Shawn A. Focht • Sharon Fodor • Sylvia L. Foil • Cooper & Isabelle Folwell • Ron E. Folwell • Gordon & Liza Forbes • Martin Forbes & Julia Charlow • Mark & Michelle Ford • Callum James Forrest • Forry • Jonas Forshell • Monica Elida Forssell • Hannah Forsyth • Jason Forsyth • Darryl Fortunato • Landon Foster • Marty Foster • Jeanine Fournier • Emily Foust • Cathy Fox • Jessica Fox • FoxyVixen • Richard Tyler Francisco • Elizabeth Francois • Frank • Constance Franklin • Miles Frank • Tyler Fredrickson • John Fredrik • Gavin Freeman • Spencer Freeman • Randall J. Freitas II • Kelly French • Jess Freund • Phil & Sarah Freund • Åsa Frid • Schuyler Frincke • Julien Froment • Jared Frost • Michael Frost • Frowldrees • Meg Fry • Miguela Fry • Will Fuentez • Tanner Fuhr • Daniel Fullem • Nicholas & Rachel Fuller • Yurii "Saodhar" Furtat • Arthur Fyles

— G —

R. C. G. • Choko G. • E. A. G. • Mariah G. • Noah G. • René G. • Grant Gabbert • Brian Gacki • Krishna Chaitanya Gagda • Denis Gagnon • Robert Gaissmaier • Kenzie & Cailyn Gaither • Patrick Galizio • Parker & Edward Galligan • Roumen Ganeff • Anna Ganey • Elora Garbutt • Guilherme Garcia • Jonathan Garcia • Amanda Rae Gardner • Christine Gardner • Kelly Gardner • Mikel & Kelly Gardner • Kat Garibaldi • Andrew Garinger • Garren • Greg & Tess Garrett • Peter Garvey • Cedric Gasser • Brian Gaudet • Cody Gaudet • Madeline Gaunt • James & Lexi Gauthier • Sarah Gaxiola • Kenneth Geary • Bryan Geddes • Gehn • Jason the Gentleman • Tamara Gentry & Cody Todd • Will Gerboth • Mathieu Gervais • Sheri L. Gestring • Courtney Getty • Leila Ghaznavi • Chand Svare Ghei • Hennie Giani • Ryan Gibson • Casey Giddens • Serena Giese • Alexander S. Gifford • Andrew Gilbert • Terra Gilbert • Ginger Gilbreath • Jeff Gilkison • Stuart Gillespie • Claire Gilligan • The Gilpins • Tom Gladney • Patrick Glancy • Kenn Gleason • Kenny

Glenn • Richard Glodowski • Ira Gluck • Jeramy Goble • Gargi Godbole & Omkar Kolangade • Kriti Godey • Carman Godfrey • Yamir Yusuf Godil • Wolfgang Goetz • Cary J. Goggin • Michael Goldman • Sarah Gomez • Gone To Khatovar • Emily Gonyer • Peggy Jo Gonzales • Gabriel Paz Gonzalez • Osvaldo Rivera Gonzalez • Gonzo • Melissa Goodall • John Goode • Olya & Joe Goodrick • Melissa Goodwin • Samantha E. Goodwin • Bhavik Gordhan • Dylan Gordon • Krista Goretzky • Cara Gorman • James L. Gorman Jr. • Justin & Lisamarie Gorman • Michael Gorman • Joshua Eli Gossett • Michael "TarnHead" Gouker • Lisa M. Gowin • J. Daniel Grabau • Alejandro Grados • Stacy Gradushy • Robin Graf • Travis F. Graham-Wyatt • Kris Graham • Robert Graham • Ryan Graham • Eliza J. Gramling • Kate Gramling • Sven Grams • Tisha Grana • Aaron Granofsky • Dion F. Graybeal • E. M. Gray • Gary Gray • Greg Gray • Todd Greco • Gail Goldner Green • Jason T. Green • Gemma Greet • James D. Gregory Jr. • Andrei Gribakov • Kirk Grier • Tyler Griesinger • Brian Griffin • Britt Griffin • Charlie Rose Griffin • Christopher Griffin • R. W. Griggs • Robert Grimes • Ben Grimsrud • Fitz Groenke • Kasper Grøftehauge • Pat Grogan • Grace Gronniger • L. Ethan Gros • Alex Grossman • Crystal Growe • Therese Guerette • Gilles Guerin • Andrew Guerra • Kelly Gumpert • Troy Gunnell • Katja Günther • Sheri Gurney • Michael Gurry • Marce & Allen Guthier • Mark Edward Guymon • Gabriel Estepan Guzman • Michael Guzzo • Noreen Gwilliam

— H —

Andrew H. • Carol H. • Clint H. • Phillip H. • Jon Haas • Tyler Hackett • Jason K. Hackworth • William C. Haddock • Jon Hagen • Justin & Stephanie Hagler • Derek Hahn • Gary Hake • Kenny Ha • Runar Håland • Dan Halen • Patrick Haley • Brody, Joanna, Elayna & Edwin Hall • E. Hall • Glenn A Hall • Nathan C. Hall, MD • Steven Halloway • Rebecca Hall • Chris Halmos • Tim Halsey • Esko

Halttunen • Bradley Hamilton • Lama Hamilton • Pamela Hamlet • Audrey Hammer • Steve Hammonds • Roanan Hammons • Nicole Ham • Samuel Hamrin • Cora Hancock • Daddy Hancock • Kristian Handberg • Gregory Richard Wayne Haney • Hannah • Jeffrey Hann • Andrew & JoLynn Hansen • Denise Hansen • Luke Penny Emma Hansen • Jim Hanson • Kimberly Hanson • Matthew Steven Hanson • Nichole Haratyk • Matthias Harder • Jordan Harding • Jacob Haronga • Brandon Harris • Damien Harris • David Harris • C. C. Harrison • Chad Harrison • Margaret Harrison • Jacqueline Hart • Yolanda & Kevin Hartley • Michelle Hartline • Nicholas Hart • Ryan M. Hart • Kenneth Harward • Justin Hase • Brandt Hasser • Doug Hastings • Rick Hauert • Chris Haught • Martin Haugland • The Haure Family • Sam Haurie • Natalie & Joseph Hawkins • Deb Hawley • Jennifer Hawton • Josh & Meaghan Haxton • Melissa L. Hayden • Benny Hayes • Matthew Hayes • Tim Hayes • Alexis Haymaker • Noah Webb Haynes • Trevor Hayward • Greg Hearn • Chris Heck • Espen Agøy Hegge • Matt Heiberger • Nathan W. Heinrich • Chris Heintz • Kyle V. Helliar • Peter Helmes • Cole Helms • Hema & Chris • David Hemmings • Kevin Hempe • Drew Henderson • Jocelyn Henderson • Björn Henke • Mattias Hennerfors • Leah Henry • Scott Henryson • John Henson • Chadrick Hess • Kenneth Hess • Lori Hewlett • Chris Heymanns • Douglas Hickel • Joe & Cassady Hild • Bryan, Joy, Alamea, Kai & Millie Hill • Dan Hill • Kay Hill • Mark Hill • Mark Hindess • Kenneth Hines • Daniel Hirsch • T. Hise • Kevin Hjelden • Daniel Engeberg Hjellestad • Zuzana Hlisnikovská • Hanh Hoang • Stephen Hobbs • Lisa Hobon • Carmen Ho • Greg Hoch • Rose Hochman • Ben Hockaday • John Hocking • Christina Hoffman • Douglas Hoffman • Garrett Hoffman • Jeff Hoffman • Sam Hogan • Andrew Hogg • Linda Hojlund • Steven J. Holden • Chris Holdren • Patrick Holland • Adam Holliday • Simon Hollingsworth • Andrew Hollins • Christophe Holmes • Corinna Holmes • Lena & William Holmes • Scott & Jacquelyne Holm • Tamara L. Holsclaw • Donald Holsworth • Christian Holt • Julia Holt • H. Holton • Kara

Holtzman • Allen Holub • Kristiina Hommik • Brendan Hong • Wai Chung Hon & Mark Sanasie • Danny Hood • Adam K. Hoover • Patrick Hoover • Andy Hopkins • Mike Hopkins • Sabine Horak • Alysa Hornick • Ira Horowitz • Brian Horstmann • Paul Horvath • Aleksander Hougenb • Thomas Houseman • Jeff Howanek • Lee Howard • Lowell "J. R." Howard • MaryAnne Howard • S. D. Howarth • Angela Marie Howe • Jamie Howe • Zach Howell • NC Howerton • Katherine Howett • Santiago Hoyos • Christopher Alan Huddleston • Caroline Hudson-Hale • Austin Hudson • Curtis A. Hudson • Mia Huffman's Clan • Dundi Thompson Hughes • Jon Hughes • Ron Hughes • Jonathan Hui & K. K. Miller • Caleb Hulbert • Leland Hulbert • Jeff & Anna Hullihen • Joseph & Isaac Hull • Carol & David Humm • Morgan Humrichouser • Nathan Hundley • Rebel Hunter • Rebecca Hunt • Richard Hurst • Hamzah Hussain • Johannes Huster • Jaqueline Huth • The Hwang Family • Jeremy Hylen

— I, J —

I (Sigrid) loves Niels-Peter, too • John Idlor • Curt Iiams • Paz Ilan • Marcus Ilgner • Matthew Infantino • Mike Ingram • Gino Inhin • iomniavlys • Andreas Irle • Michael Irmler • Torian Ironfist • Jeremy & Stacy Ironside • The Iron Viking • Isak • Marion Istrate • Paul A. G. Ivany • Ciro Izarra • Kyle J. • L. J. • L. Keith J. • Rima Jabbour • Jacinda & Kaitlyn • Aren Jackson • Aron Jackson • Douglas R. Jackson • Martin Jackson • P. & S. Jacob • Heather Jacolbia • Catherine Jacqué • Kati James • Jane • Victoria Jang • A. A. Jankiewicz • Gisele Jaquenod • Jared • Erik Jarvi • Anam Javed • Jaya • Matt Jefcoats • Jeff • Owen Jenkins • Jenn • Jason Jennelle • Jason Jennings • Kooper Jensen • Jhaelein • Chelsea Jobe • Tom Jobes • Jobobo • JoDash • David Johansen • Henrik Johansson • Raney John • Aaron D. Johnson • Amber L. Johnson • Casey & Marissa Johnson • Dennis Johnson • Eleanor Mallory Johnson • Emily Johnson • Fred W. Johnson • Jason C. Johnson • Jim Johnson • Kelly Johnson • Lynn Johnson • Ryan Johnson • Terry

Johnson • Tyler Johnson • David Johnston • Jokito Jo • Pepijn K. Joman • Jonas • Jonathan • Andrew Jones • Beau Jones • Dianne Jones • The Jones Family • Jason Jones • Jessica, Nathan & Noah Jones • Rebecca & Shawn Jones • R. Nickolas Jones • Stephen F. Jones Jr. • Jonna, Anthony & DonnaLucia of Aurora, IL • Sreenadh Jonnavithula • David Jordan • Tim Jordan • Jorge • Loretta Joslin • S. Josten • Kathrin Jost • Sunshyne Joubert • The Jovanovich Family • Kala Judd • William Jung • Juraj & Andy • Just a Paramedic • Matthew Justus

— K —

Mia M. K. • Marty Kagan • Joshua Kail • Greg Kajko • Naveed Kakal • A. M. Kalmus • Brandon Kamaka • Kanab • Brett Kane • John Kiwi Kane • Kanthai • Kapiness • The Karalash Family • Elvinas, Agne & Adele Karaliai • Eli Karasik • Eliza Karlowska • David Karlton • Roberth Karman • Dirk Karrenbauer • Richard B. Karsh, MD • Emerson Kasak • Karmen Kase • Sean Kashino • Anika Kastelic • Christopher "Lobo" Kaster • Kimberlee Katekaru • Kati • Jacob M. Katz • Maiko Katz • William T. Katz • Armin Kaweh • Kaya • Brynn K. • Debbie K. • Andrew Keane • Eoin Kearney • William G. Keaton • Liam Keegan • Mark Kelley • Sean V. Kelley • Erin Kello • Adam Kelly • Emily Kelsey • Brian Kelso • Sam Kemble • Stewart Kenedy • Diane Kenney • Robert Kenny • Kent • Ingrid Kepinski • J. T. Kercado • Mark Kerrigan • Patrick Kerr • Gijs Kerstens • E. M. Keswick • Freda K. • Nelli Khamraeva • Hannah K. • Tuba Khan • Khadija Khurshed • Adam Kice • David Kiddell • Nancy Kidder • Josh Kilen • Kim • Oliver Kim • Russell Kinch • Amanda K. King & Michael R. Swanson • Ben King • G. King • MaryEllen King • The Next J. King • Ryan King • Shawn T. King • Lori Kingston • Vaughan King • Brad Kirk • Doug Kirkland & Stacey Drohan • Steven Kirk • Alen Kiseljak • Bodhi Kish • Marina Kisley • Amie Kissel • Justin Kita • David Kitching • Jordie Polly K. • Daniel Klaassen • Matt Klassen • Matt Klawiter • Joyce Klein • Mats Kleivane • Arienne Klijn • Krzysztof

Klimonda • Jordan J. Klovstad • Matthew Klure • Matt Kluting • Jess KluznCannon • Melanie K. • Danielle Knight • M. A. Knight • Tami Knudson • Michael W. Kobb • Kobus, Matthew, Brittany & Baby • Matthew & Angella Kocian • John Koehler • David "Zankabo" Kohler • Michael S. Kokowicz • Andrew Konicki • Jing Koo • Zachary Kosarik • Konstantin Koslowski • Morgan & Rob Kostelnik • Michelle Kotary • Koteric • Joseph Kotzker • Aljaž Koželj • Kevin Kramer • Steve Krepelka • Mira Michelle & Jeevan Morgan Kreß-Jones • Bruce Kretschmer • Taylor Krieg • Kristina & Markus • Kari Kron • Kally Kruchten • Wulf C. Krueger • Caroline Kruger • Erik Krumholz • Shaz K. • Tiffany K. • Nick Kuhn • Aaron Kung • Kimberly Kunker • Larry Kuperman • Lynda Kupson • Christopher L. Kurth • Kevin Kurth • Eyal Kurz • Kurt Kuzek

— L —

Mat L. • Nikolai T. L. • Samantha L. • Kyle "Spacecat" Laauser • Melanie Labarre • Joshua Labonte • Llorente Lacap • Tracey Lachaine • Laurie Lachapelle • Steffen Lahr • Mary Lai • Sophie Lai • Jake Lake • Tom Lake • Peter Lakshmanan • Calen Lambert • Greg Lambert • Bradley Landress • Gary J. Landry Jr. • Florian Landsteiner • Adam Lane • Phoenix G. Lane • Jeremy Lange • Janice Langhorne • Eric Konrad Langley • Brad Lankford • Dorothy Lannert • Eldrin Lannister • Laura LaPenes • Damien Larcombe • Dora Larrabee • Ann-Karin T. Larsen • Bjarte Larsen • Mark Larsen • Shawn Larsen • Alex Larson • Rebecca Larson • Bryan J. Lash • Chris Last • Scott Latter • André Laude • Laura & John • Lauren • Joel Lavoie • Greg Lawlor • Laura Lawrence (Australia) • Paul Lawson • Shirley Lawson • Joey Lazz • Justin S. Leach • Darrell Leadbetter • Michael Leaich • Heather "elvenmageus" Leasor • Andreas Leathley • Babette LeBlanc • Jordyn LeClair • Ben Lederman • Joseph Ledford • Darren Lee • Jack Leek • Sandra K. Lee • Brian Lefebvre • Scherolyn A. Leggett • Ty Legge • Rainer Lehr • Erynn Lehtonen • Megan Leifker • Holger Leimeier • Michael Leinen • Carly R. Leis • Mark T. Lemke • Jerry & Zachary

Lencoski • Christiaan Lennaerts • John Lenz • Michael Lenzo • Jenna Leonardo • Paul Leonard • Hailey J. Leone • Kevin O. Lepard • Le Pop • Tarin Leslie • Jared Lessor • Nathen Leung • Aaron Levi • Sean Michael Levi • Blaine Lewis • Clint Lewis • Deighton M. Lewis • Olivia Lewis • S. Lewis • Joshua Lew • Lian • Eric Lienhard • Lillian • Jeffrey P. Limmer • Linas • Chad Lindaman • Adrienne Haataja Lindgren • Leila Lineberger • Roxanne Lingenfelter • Brooke R. Lingle • Lisa Link • Ken Lipinski • Chris Lira • Todd M. C. Li • Patricia Liu • Rainy Liu • Tellina Liu • Danny Live • Liz • Whit Lloyd • Dylan Lockwood • Jonas Lodewyckx • Brittni Loehr • C. R. Lofters • Philadelphia Logan • Jack Loh • The Lokos Family • Bill Lombardi • Sarah Longlands • Brent Longstaff • Barbara Lookerse • Arya Loomba • Georgia Loomes • Julia Looney • Kevin Looney • Tony Lopresti • Frank N. Loreti • Joe Lott • Nathan Loutrel • Stewart Love • Louise Lowenspets • Nate Lowery • Eun Ken Low • Casey Lozier • Boris Lubarsky • Mark Lubischer • Jon Lucina • Samuel Ludford • Andrea Luhman • Lynda J. Lum • Garry Lundberg • Suzanne Lundeen • John Lupo • Luthie & Eggie • Des Lynch • Duncan Lynch • Jae Lynch • Michael B. Lynch • Paul Lynch • D. Lynette • Mike Lynk • DeeDee Lynn • Bob Lyon • Andrew Lyons • Justin Lyons • Kristy Kimberly Lyons • Steve Lyon

— M —

A. J. M. • Anne M. • Brittney & Ashley M. • Camille M. • Connor M. • J. N. M. • Karen M. • Kaushik M. • M&M & Kitkat • Bradley MacDonald • Deb MacDonald • Dimitrios, Petra, Erika Angelika & Nikolaos Machikas • Brigette MacKenzie • Ken MacLean • Romney, Spencer & Tanner Madsen • Scott Madsen • Haley Mae • Richard Magaldi • Thomas Magers • Allie & Ben Mages • Jason Magnan • Jacob Magnusson • Steve Maguire • Gavin & Sarah Mahaley • Emmanuel MAHE • Mahiya & Ben • Todd Maines • MajikJack • Vincent Mak • Audrey Mal-Dulin • Eric Malchodi • Tyler & Tom Maley • Brendan Mallon • The

Malones • Lucy Ma • Steven Joseph Malzone • Amy Manahan • Naveen Mandadhi • Ra'eesah Mangera • Shana Mannes • Matthew Son-of-Gimli Manni • James Manning • Ken Mann • Adam Mansell • N. Manzanares • Marc • Lahman Marcel • Ruth Marcus • Danielle Mar • Nick Marinos • Marise • Mariya • Mark185 • Michael Markins • Tobias D. Markowitz • Michael Marks • Allison Marlo & Sean Mince • Andrew Marmor • Pedro Marroquin • Dexter Finnius "Ham Pants" Marshall • Gerry Marshall • James M. Marshall • Jonathan Marshall • Steven Marshall • Sue Marshal • Gene W. Marsh • Jordan Marsh • Marco Martagon-Villamil • Craig Martens • Ivan Martens • Ava Lee Martin • Brandon Martin • Brett Martin • Douglas Martin • Jenny J. Martinez • Laken Martinez • Richard Martinez • Kai Martin • Lucas Martin • Pam Martin & Greg Johnson • Richard Martin • Shannon & Lori Martin • Beth Martinson • Shaylla Mason-Wright • David K. Mason • Kristopher Horatio Mason • Rebecca Mate • Clarece Mather • Amy Mathew • Tim Mathis • Tiffany Ma • Michael Matlock • Chris Matosky • James Matson • Rebecca Matte • Matthew • Garypam Matthews • Jacob Matthews • Jason Matthews • Matt & Rebecca • Kálnoky Mátyás-Zsigmond • Zachary Matzo • Layla Maurer • Charlene Maxwell • Guy Mayer • Elizabeth Mayers • Yair Mayer • Scott Maynard • Josh Mayoral • Lindsey Mayoras • Beth Mayson • Stephen G. May • Omar Mazin • Steve Mazurek • Lily McAlister • Michael McAulay • Steven McAuliffe • David Robson McBride • Nate, Sarah, Owen & Kate McBride • My loving wife Christine McCall • Kat McCall & John Beutter • Chad L. McCance • Andy McCarl • Ryan McClelland • Stewart McClelland • Kelly McClenahan • David F. McCloskey • Jean McClure • Shane McCollum • John McCormick • Travis McCormick • Debbie McCoy • Mark McCoy • Kyle McCray • Ryan McCredie • Andrew Lee McCullough • Ed McCutchan • Bobby McDaniel • Gerald P. McDaniel • Greginald McDicken • Hunter McDole • J. P. McDonagh • Allison McDonald • Michael McDonald • Bryan McEntire • Chris McGann • Adam Mcgee • Mack McGehee • Sean

David McGrath • The McGraw Family • Troy McGuerra • Ryan S. McGuire • John R. McGuirt III • Michael McHugh • Phillip McIntyre-Dominica • Andy McKay • Rob McKenzie • Patrick McKernan • Aaron McKinley • Jack, Kayleigh & Henry McKinley • Bobby McKnight • Kieva McLaughlin • Christopher McLeod • Lee McLeod • Beth McMahon • William McMahon • Ian McNatt • Laura McNaughton • Dinah McNutt • Glenn McPhee • Denise McWilliams • Chris Meadows • Nate Mealy • Jed Mecham • Monica Medeiros • Edgar I. Medina • Morena Medina • Abbie Meeks • Hylda Renee Meeks • Meggs • Aaron Meier • Stephanie Meier • Tanya Meikle • Angela-Francesca Mejia • Brian & Amber Melican • Ashley & Megan Mellenthien • Alex Mellnik & Caitlin Cox • Mark & Stephani Melton • Piper & Kai Menda • Dominic & Sarah Meo • Deanna Mercer • M. Mercer • Nicole Merkulovich • Christine & Parker Merriman • David & Caitlin Messina • Jessi Lenore Metzger • Deborah Meyer • Sylke Meyerhuber • Ken Meyri • Michael • Neighborly Michaela • Miriam Michalak • Steve Michel • S. Michener • Mia & Thomas Mikloucich • Monica Mileti • Neil Millar • Galen W. Miller • Grant Fitz Miller • J. Lance Miller • Joe & Debbie Miller • Nathan Miller • Peter C. Miller • Sean Miller • Shira Miller • Daniel J. Milligan • Erin Millner • Dillon Mills • Kendall Mills • Nathan Mills • Elizabeth Milne • Mirkwrath • Michelle Mishmash • William Miskovetz • Shruti Misra • Annarose Mitchell • Bradford Mitchell • Addeson Moh • Kumail Hussain Mohammed • David Moldawer • Jakob Moll • Joe Molnar • Nabeel Moloo • Lieze Mondelaers • James Monsebroten • Kyndra Monterastelli & Anthony Tran • Scott Mooney • Andrea, Joshua & Henry Moore • Carl Moore • Colleen Moore • Dustin Moore • Mike Moore • Paul Raithe Moore • Robert Moore • Robin Moore • Sabre Addington Moore • Charles & Anna Moorhead • Jason Moos • Aaron & Corrie Moran • Serge Mora • Daniel Moretti • Jasmine Morgado • Clifford J. Morgan • Marleigh Morgan • Marvin D. Morgan Jr. • Victor Morgan • Floriana Morina • Lisa Morris • Patrick Morrison • Wayne Morris • Stuart Morse • Luka Mosashvili • Jason Moseley • Mo Moser • Katie Mosharo • Konner

& True Moshier • Celeste Moss • A. Motola • Chad Moulder • Elias Moya • Calvin Moy • Jeff & Kelly Moyer • Mrbill2705 • Steve Muchow • Nathan Muilenburg • Brenna, Keira & Arya Murphy • John Murphy • Paul Murphy • Sig Murphy • Julie Murray • Scott Murray, OCT • Sabrina Musson • Tony Muzi • Sean Myer • Perrin Myerson • Anna Mykkeltvedt • Eric Mylius

— N —

W. R. N. • Axel Nackaerts • Stephan Nagel • Michael Nagy • Thushrika Naidoo • Brett Nance • Sid Nanda • Jimmy Napier • Kristina Napier • Joe Narcisi • Narrew • Stephen Nash • Michael Natale • Natalie • Richard Neal • Denise & Dwayne Need • Kelvin Neely • Patrick Neff • Valerie Neff • Charlie Negyesi • Bev Nelson • Kate Nelson • Robert Nelson • Jeffrey Neuschatz • Paul E. Neveux, Jr. Ph.D. • Tracy Newman • Samantha Nguyen • Gordon Niamatali • Lucas Nicholes • Sandy Nickell • The Nickels • Erik Nickerson • Theo Nicolaides • Sasha Nicoletti • Joshua Niday • Anita Nielsen • Peter Nierenberger • Rajat Nigam • Chrissy Nilsen • Nimesa • Juliana Nine • Bob Nixon • Tyler Nixon • Genie Nizigiyimana • J. P. Noble • Tiago Nodari • Patrick Noffke • Noj • Mark Nolan • William Norbut • Øyvind Nordli • Norman • Cole Norman • Dan Norton • The Norton Family • Anthony, Devyn & Royce Noto • Benjamin Novo • Dino Nowak • Craig Nuckels • Francisco A. Nunez Sr. • Marcos Nuñez • Carrie Nusz • Steffen Nyeland • Matthew Nykamp

— O —

D. L. O. • Kerry O'Connor • Pablo Ortiz Monasterio O'Dogherty • Jonathan O'Donnell • Neil O'Dwyer • Sean O'Mahoney • Kyle O'Mara • Emmett P. O'Neal • Joanne O'Reilly • Elaine O'Sullivan • Janet L. Oblinger • Sean & Melissa Obrock • Oliver Ockenden • Elizabeth Ocskay • Calley Odum • Michael Offutt • Ol Deezer • Mosby Oliphant • Phillip

Olive • Linda Ollila-Scherbring • Lasse Olsen • Isai Olvera & Amy Hunter • Laurence Olver • Curtis & Tina Olyslager • Þórhanna Inga Ómarsdóttir • Michaelangelo & Mona Lisa Ondevilla • Michael Oney • Mariëlle Ooms-Voges • Andrea Orjuela • Tim Ormsby • Jennifer Orton • Troy Osgood • Joshua D. Ostrander • Kirsten Otting • Conny Otto • Lucia Otto • Otus • Ron Owens • Katie & Kyle Oxford

— P —

Brad P. • Dawson P. • Jackye P. • Pavel P. • pa4m3 • Daniel J. Pack • Lea W. Padgett • Johannes Paetsch • Richard L. Page • Ruth Anne Pajcic • Dan Palade • Christine Ann Palmer • Matthew Paluch • Licia L. Pannucci • Tony Pantev • Sotiris Papaefthymiou • Alexandra Papas • Romy Papas • Daryl Parat • Scott Pare • Emmanouil Paris • David Parish • Calvin Park • Jeremy Parker • K. P. Parker • Lynn & Jason Parker • Michael S. Parker • Dale Parrott • James F. Parsons • Alexander Pasik • Elke Passarge • Chirag A. Patel • Jay Patel • Stuart Paterson • M. Patino • Bill Patterson • Chana Patterson • Michelle Patterson • Nathaniel Patton • Allison Pauli • Phillip Paul • Robert Pavel • Dom Pavlek • Katie Pawlik • Jacob Pawson • Deric Paxson • Micah Payson-Lewis • James Payton • Sarah Peachey-Green • Joel Pearson • Kari Pearson • N. Scott Pearson • Stephanie Peck • Jakob Pedersen • Josh Peel • Cassandra Pehrson • Steven Peiper • Autumn PeLata • Joseph R. Pellagatti • The Pendleton Family • Lisa Pennie • Jed M. Perlowin • Scott Perry • Pet Connection • Mark Peters • Dale W. Peterson • Jay Peterson • Timothy Peters • Paul Petrie Jr. • John Petrila • Bjørn Tore Pettersen • Jesper Pettersen • Smokey & Oreo Pettigrew • Jackson Sawyer Pfau • Justine Phelps • Skylar Phelps • Robert Philbrick • Philina • Joyce & Gary Phillips • Katie Phillips • Nicole & Steven Phillips • Taylor A. Phillips • Michael E. Philpott • Bonnie J. Phlieger • Genevere Pierce-Butler • Darlene Pierce • Jennifer L. Pierce • Matt Pierce • Michael Pierce • Travis "Xuul" Pierce • Jim Pier • Jordan Pier • Mackenzie D. Pierson • Leslie Pietila • John

Pietrzyk • Liam Pietrzyk • The Pike Family • William C. Pike • Patrick Pilgrim • Katy Pilkington • Chanthu Pillai • Jett Pinckard • Goncalo Pinheiro & Sofia Sousa • Joseph C. Pisano • Sharon Su Plasser • Jake Platfoot • David Plaut • Rick Plevak • Brett Plouffe • Michele Plum • Carl Plunkett • Mario Poier • Anthony Polcino • Shawn F. Polka • Sarah Clardy Polk • Jordan Pollard • Jack Pond • Brett Ponds • Thomas & Amber Poon • T. J. Poon • Laura Pope • Jen Porn • Beverly J. Porter (Pollack) • J. Ryan Porter • Mike Porter • Zach Porter • Aliechia Post • Calvin Post • Suzi Po • Cody Poteet • Shana Potter-Monroe • Matt Potts • Max Potts • Terri Rizzo Potts • Brianna L.C. Poulos • Kevin Powell • Ryan Powell • Franklin E. Powers, Jr. • Elisa Prada • Craig Prather • Gianna Pratten • Andrew Preece • Daphne Press • Serina & Tim Pressey • Edmund Pribitkin • Dan Price • Joseph P. Price • Will Prier & Melissa Fuller • David Prince • Probably not a bear • Chris Prohaska • pTeranodon • Fiama Puccini • Cameron Pugh • Mike Pugliese • Emilia Marjaana Pulliainen • Chris Pullman • Gregory A. Purdom • Elaine Puri • Matthew Purse • Kimberly Purser • Hugh Pyle

— Q, R —

Lord Jason Query • Heather Quigg • Jay Quigley • Andrew Quimby • Ben Quinn • Andrea & Brian Quinney • Luis Quiñones • David Quist • Joel R. • Juuso R. • Pedro R. • Christomir Rackov • Steven J. Radu • Joe & Cindy Radvany • Hali Rae • Terri Ann Rae • Christine Ragan • Tristan Ragan • Becky Raine • Akilan Rajendran • Nanni Raj • Slobodan Rakovic • David Ramirez • Marcos Ramirez • David K. Ramm • Michael D. Ramm • Amanda Ramsey • The Randall Family • Ranger the Labrador Retriever • Katie Rapp • Ashyanna Keli Rodriguez • Jason Rathburn • Daniel Ratica • Laura Ratti • Kate Rausch • Johnny Ray • Ryan Ray • Chad Ream • Big Jon Reaper • Steve Reaume • Norman Rechlin • Chris Rees • Jen Regan • Kyle, Carissa & Melody Reger • Charlie Regnier • Cody Reichenau • Bob Reichert II • Jacob Reich • Maggie Reid • Brian

Reilly • Jim & Lórien Reilly • Bradley Reis • Teri J. Reiten • Renée Relin • Isadora & Silas Remillard • Amber Rendmeister • Paul Alexander Rennick • Lisa Whiting Renshaw • Jules Reston • Sarah Retza • Henrik Reuther • Frank Reynolds • Crystal Rhinehart • Joel Ribert • Mike & Tammie Rice • Patricia C. Richardson • Sonja Richardson • Christophor Rick • John Riddell • The Riders • George Ricky Rieckenberg • Cris Mendoza & Will Rielly • Ernst Riemer • Grant "WereTiger" Rietze • Dana Riggle • Audrey Riggs • Riley & Alexa • Keri L. Riley • Seamus Riley • Kendra Rindler • Mark Ringer • Keegan Rinker • Jett Rink • Jason Rippentrop • Lincoln Rivadeneira • Charles & Sonia Rivas • Smooth Rivera • Billy Rixham • Blandor Roach I • Joel Roath • William J. Robbins • Edwin T. Roberson • C. Roberts • Clifton Roberts • Derek J. Roberts • Elise Roberts • Gary M. Robertson • Rachel Robertson • Adele Robinson • Daniel A. Robinson • D. Keith Robinson • Michael Robinson • Matt Roccuzzo • Rochester87 • Paul Rockhold • Berit Röder & Andreas Hoth • John Rodgers • Steven R. Rodgers • Monica Rodrigues • Miguel Rodriguez • Thomas R. Roedel • Robert Rohe • Yuri M. Roh • Eduardo Rojas • Jose Rojas • Christopher Roland • Autumn Rolon • Stacey Romeo • Robert Romore • Matthew Roos • Evan Rose • Jon Rose • Jia-Min Rosendale • Kristen Roskob • Thomas Ross • Todd L. Ross • Pål Asmund Røste • Cathy May Row • David Rowe • Chris Roy • Jamin Ruark • Cheryl Ruckel • Adrian Rudloff • K Rudolph, Scout & Baloo too! • John & Glenda Ruggles • Jay Rumple • Hemal Ruparelia • Dale A. Russell • J. P. Russell • Monica Russell • Rae J. Russell • Jen Ruth • Jon Rutten • Charles L. Ryan Jr. • Marc Ryan • Nicholas Ryan • Mladen Ryhard • Rylan • Ryan Rymer

— S —

Audrey S. • Denise S. • Garren S. • M. F. S. • Mahima M. S. • Michelle S. • Patricia S. • Matthew, Breanna & McKinnon Saagman • Arthur Ariel Sabintsev • Dillon Sabo • Sabrina • Gabor Sacharovsky • Daniel V.

Sadler • Ian Sadler • Sam & Tiffany Sadler • Eric Sands • Megan Sager • Nejc Saje • Greg Sakowski • Mark Sakulich • Erik Salamanca • Daniel Sal • Tony Salva • Kushil Samarasekera • Samius • Robert Sample • Catherine Sampson • Matthew B. Sampson • Samuel & Connie • Monika "Mon" Samul • Jason Sandau • Catherine J. Sanders • Alex Sandilands • Sandy • Sarah • Michael Sargent • Abhilash Sarhadi • Anthony Sasinowski • The Saumur Family • Ames D. & Linda L. Saunders • Marc Saunders • Mike Saurers • Glen Sawa • Sax is my Axe • scarlettpdx • J. Schachtschneider • Logan Schack • Robert Schaefer • Jacob Schafer • Christy M. Schakel • William Scheer • R. H. Schellhaas • David L. Schenberg • Anna Scherer • Marc Schifer • Whitney Schiffler • Florian Schild • Michael Schipper • Dee & Jim Schlatter • Ethan J. Schlemer • Ben Schmidt • Catherine Schmidt • Dave Schmidt • Bryn Mae Schmiege • Doug Schneider • Paul Schneider • Thibaut Schneider • Dave Schoenberger • E. Schramm • Christopher Schroeder • René Schultze • Roy Schultz • Ryan Schultz • Angela Schwartz • Eric Schwartz • Mark, Sloan & Sydney Schwindt • Jeremy Scofield • Calvin Scott • Codi Scott • Ellen Scott • Pam & Bill Scott • Daniel Scrutchfield • Sam Seah • Ryan Seaman • Marianne Searle • Sebastiaan Henau • SebastianZeh • Rhea Secor • Nancy Sedwick • Austin Segrave • Brant Seibert • David R. Seid • Erinn & Ari Seifter • Suzan Sempels • Jose Javier Soriano Sempere • Matt Sencenbaugh • Seth • Gopakumar Sethuraman • A. Severin • Rick Severson • Michael Sewell • Chris Seymour • William J. Seymour • Daniel Sgranfetto • David Shaffer • Brett Shand • Shane • The Shaner • Anil Shanker • David Shapiro • Scott Shaputis • Brandon Sharp • Corey Shaw • David Shaw • Laura Shea • Indiana Shedden • Kendra Shedenhelm • Rob Sheffield • Jenny Sheldon • Jeremy Shelton • Anthony William Shenberger • Catherine Shenoy • Paul Sheppard • SHERIC • John W. Shioli • Shiro • Keisha, Kyle, Adele & Herbie of House Shivorderpstrassepy • Shannon & Brandi Shockley • Charles Shopsin • Maria Shugars • The Shumates • Patrick Shurr • Heath Shurtleff • Stephen & Bryn Shutt • Laura & Matthew Siadak • Sibi &

Amanda • Toine Siebelink • Matt Siedman • Brian Sieglaff • Teddy Sigman • Sigrun • Barbara Silcox • The Silsby Family • Pedro Silva • SilverMt • Gregory Silvius • James Simmons • Simoneta • Harper, Karen & Travis Simpson • Lainie Simpson • Susan Lee Simpson • Andy Sims • Carlee Brooke Sims • David Simser • Kainoe Sinclair • Anthony Sinnott • Mary Sisock • From Adel-Rehman Dedicated To Nanni Sitar • The Siu Family • The Six Crows • Sarah Sjöberg • Mike Skaggs • James S. Skala Jr. • Birgit Skerjanc • Daniel R. Skidmore • Sonia Skik • Christian Skjødt • Niklas Sköld • Tracy S. Skrabut • Eric Slaney • Ella & Dorian Sloat • Kristine Slot • Lyndon Smiling • B. Smith • Brad J. Smith • Calvin Smith • Carly Smith • Christine Smith • Cierra Smith • Elizabeth Smith • Jeff Smith • Joe "Call Me Doc" Smith • Katie Smith • Levi Smith • Paul & Scott Smith • Randy Smith • Ryan Smith • S. Brian Smith • Sharon R. Smith • Shawn Robert Smith • Spenser Smith • Dr. Zachary Smith • Kim Smits • Smokey "the Cat" Swadron • Nadia Smoliakova • Craig Snead • The Snelgrove Family • Maria Snelgrove • Bruce Snell • Davis Snider • Jennifer Grouling Snider • Vincent Snider • Jesse & Brittany Snyder • Kayla Snyder • Robin Snyder • Tommy L. Snyder • Danny Soares • Jarosław Sobieraj • Mattias Söderholm • Soesja • Stan Sokorac • David J. Soloski • Steve Soltz • R. Sommerfeld • Miroslav Sommer • Robin Sones • Jörg Sonnenberger • Matthew Sorenson • Saverio Sotola • Kara Southwick • Francisco Spaghi • Jen Spangrud • Jeff Sparks • Christina Speir • Jennifer Spencer • Michael Spencer • Sarah Sperry & Quinn McSperryn • Silke Spiel • Mike Spitzer • Matt Spooner • Brian Spradlin • Ian & Mia Spredemann Plasencia • Kyle Springs • Andrew Sprow • Eric Spurgeon • John Squire • Sarita M. Sridharan • Dr. Michael Stafford • Philippa Stahl • Leah Stain • Roel Stalman • Stefan Stammler • Mike Stamp • Jackie Standaert • Deanna Stanley • Devlon Stapleton • Andrew Starnes • Jeff Stathopulos • Andrew J. Statler • Aaron Statner • Leon Stauffer • Brent Steele • Stephanie Steenstrup • Gareth "G-Man" Stefanc • Larson Steffek • Jim, Calvin & Sylvia Steger • Erik Stegman • Chaim Steinberg • Maria Steingoltz • Jeremy Stein • Doug

Steinker • Steven Stelma • Matthew A. Stenning • The Stephan Family • Rick Stephens • Tim Stephens • Mike Stern • Andrii Stetskyi • Steven • Ryan Stevenson • Sarah Stevenson • Lark Steward • Dan "Mandalohr" Stewart • Debra Stewart • Erek Stewart • Joshua Stewart • Kevin Stewart • Matthew Stewart • Michelle Stewart • Stiliyana • Joshua Stingl • Ken Stith • Michael S. Stocks • Sean Stockton • Kim Stoker • The Stokes Family • Stokie • Elisabeth Hollingsworth Stone • John Stork • Jessica Stormrager • Melicent Stossel • Tim Stotter • Alexander Strandberg • Daniel W. Stratton • Thom Stratton • Strella • Matthew Strickland • Carole & Bill Strohm • Jenn Strohschein • Marcello Strologo • Stuart & Judith • S. Stuart • Corinna Stübing • Geri Studer • Kevin D. Stumpf • James Sturtevant • Sreevidya Subramanian • Jeff Suess • Matthew Sugarman • Craig Charles Suiter • Ben Suitt • Darren Sullivan • Elliot Sullivan • Joe Sullivan • Kevin Sullivan • Shawn Sullivan • Shawn & Lorrie Sullivan • Stephen Sullivan • Benjamin Summers • Susan & Eric • Ian Sutherland • Thanuja Suwarnan • Sven • Nate Swalve • Patrick Swanson • Jesica Swanstrom • Dustan Swartzentruber • Larry Swasey • Amanda Sweeney • Laurie Swensen • John Henry Swenson • The Swerbensky Family • Jason Swiger • Sam Swihart • Keith Swyers • Jeff Symes • Kathy Szabo • Johnathon Szaefer • Sarah Szardien • Carol Szpara

— T —

Alex T. • Ashli T. • Brandon T. • C. M. T. • D. T. • K. T. • Adam Taber • James Tabor • Kristin Lyn Taggart • Katarina Takahashi • C. Corbin Talley • Nicholas Talty • Laurence G. Tamaccio, Jr. • Margaret Tam • Gowtham Kumar Tangirala • Jade Tang • Hannah Tangney • Leslie Tanner • Péter Tarján • Tash • Andrea J. Tassinari • Lee Tatum • Jeff Taylor-Kantz • Taube • Andromeda Taylor-Wallace • Alex & Thurston Taylor • Brennan Taylor • Jim Taylor • Michael D. Taylor • Zenobia Taylor • Ayman Teaman • Myles Templin • Daniela Teofilova • Richard TerKeurst & Stephanie Maxwell • Hope Terrell • Jonathan

Terrington • Tess • Stephanie Tettamanti • Neen Tettenborn • Sherry Tew • The Thacker Family • Quinn Thacker • Hanson Thao • David Theis • Glenn Thomas • Greg Thomas • Justin Thomas • Terence S. Thomas • Bridget M. Thompson • Cheryl Thompson • L. R. Thompson • VIcky A. Thompson • Darrel Thormer • Jing H. Thorne • Marcus Thornson • Kaitlin Thorsen • Britta Threshie • Sandra Thwaites • Dion Tieman • Tim! • Reyn Time • Mat Timmerman • Scott Timpe • Tina & Marco • Karen Tinnesand • Geoffrey Titus • Tobi • Kelton Tobler • Ian K. Todd • Will Todd • togepreee • Vicky Tolonen • Tom • Robert F. Towell • Chase Townsend • M. J. Tracy • Austin Trainer • James Traino • Andriana Tran • J. K. L. Tran • Shawna J. Traver • M. & J. Treeson • Ben Trehet • Jamal Tresize • Michael Trick • Travis Triggs • Jedidiah Tritle • Triviadave • Chassity Tsaprailis • Evan Charles Tucker • John Tucker • Othniel Tucker • Elliot B. Tullis • Teresa Tung • Tupitza • Karen Turner • Nathan Turner • Niki & Toby Turner • Stanford Turner • Tasha Turner • Birgitte Turøy • Joonas Turtiainen • Shannon Tusler • Paul Tuson • Tycen • Mitchell Tyler • Tyson • Aris Tzikas

— U, V —

Gabriel Ubieta & Lysell Robles • Kollin Upton • Daniela Uslan • Marcus Utley • Kathryn Utroska • Pete Vagiakos • Teresa & Elizabeth Valcourt • Richard B. Valdez • Bridgette Valente • Stan Valnicek • Lynley Jane Van Allen & Christopher Fleegal • Gijs van Bilsen • Elise & Elena van Clief • Harro van der Klauw • Paulien van der Meer • Ron van der Stelt • Calvin van Dorn • Martijn van Hagen • Wendy van Ipkens • Patricia van Onckelen • Jan van Ryswyk • Robbie van Steenburg • Cory & Kaylea van Vliet • Kristy van Wyhe • Maelle Vance • Youri Vandevelde • Joseph Vanucchi • Harsh Varia • Veselka Vasileva • Michael F. Vassar • Alexey Vasyukov • Gabby Velasquez • Russell Ventimeglia • Teresa Verhoeven • Gunnar Ingi Vestmann • T. Veto • Noah Vick • Kari Victoria • Matthew Vidalis • Balaji Vijayan • Vikyle • C. A. Villagomez • Isidro

"Sid" Villarreal • Bruce Villas, MD • Rosie Vincent • Chris Vinson • Sarah Vissaux • Liana Roza Vitale • Vitaly • Layton Vitanza • Vlar • Cheryl L. Vo • Greg Vochis • David Vo • B. Vojslavek • Bryce Vollmer • Miranda Vollmer • Bastian von der Bantorfer Heide • Elizabeth Vorpahl • Ron Vutpakdi

— W —

Brian W. • John W. • K. H. W. • Nick W. • Pamela Wadhwa • Joshua Wagner-Smith • Wagner/Slavich • Lauren Wagner • Randal & Lucy Wagner • Nathan Wahlgren • Gordon Walker • Jonny Walker • Kathryn Walker • Walter J. Wallace III • William Wallace • Allen Wall • Anders Walløe • Jennifer L. Walsh • Inge B. Wang • John Wang • Carole-Ann Warburton • James Albert Ward • Susanne Ward • Alan Warenski • Greg Wargo • John Warren • Mack Wartella • Kenta Washington • Ryan Wasserman • Craig Watkins • Tyler Watkins • Nickolai Watson • Charles Watt • Emmett Wawrzynek • Jeffrey L. Wayman • wburningham • Matthäus Wdowiak • Malachi Weaver • Ryan Weaver • Sara Webb • Stephanie Webb • Cyrus Weber • Eric Wegner • Madison Wehrer • Erika Weilage • Eric J. Weis • Jonathan Weiss • Seth Weissman • David Welch • Carson Welker • Charles G. Weller III • Wendy Wells • Doug & Jeanne West • Robert Westgate • Keith West, Future Potentate of the Solar System • Sonora A. Weston • Kristina Wetterman • Doug Weyek • Weylin • Thomas J. Wheatley • Dan Wheeler • Joseph Wheeler • Whit Wheeler • Andrew M. White • Brian White • Clay Whitehead • Lara Whitehead • Holly White • Jonas White • Sam White • Stephen Robert White • William H. White • Jeff & Laurie Whiting • Philip J. Whyte • Pamela Wickert • Danielle Wiegert • Alex Wieker • Christopher "Baer" Wigelbeyer • Wicket M. Wigglestein • Kesed Wilbur • Rex Wilburn • Lindsay Wilcox • Ron Wilcox • Brad & Becky Wild • K. Wildeman • Anissa Wiley • Zebulon Wilkin • Pieter Willems • Stephen Willems • Tim Willemstein • Brandon Willey • Brittany Williams • Bryan M. Williams • Jim Williams • Joel

Williams Jr. • Kambrie Williams • Matt & Becca Williams • Rachel Kaleonani Williamson • Scott M. Williams • Jeanne Marie Willis • Scott Willis • James "Gregory" Willmann • L. Wills • Barbara L. Wilson • Damon Isaac Wilson • Durand Wilson • Mark Wilson • Marshan Wilson • Michael "V. B." Wilson • B. Win • Michael J. Wine • David Winter • Eric & Lauren Winter • Ian Winter • Nicholle Winters • Matt Winton • Clarissa Witherly • James Witt • Holly Wittsack • Ben, Zach & Steve Witzel • Scott Witzeling • Sissel Wiull • Megan Mear, wizard • Jeff Wolfe • Joshua Wolf • Jessica Wolfram • Mirjam Wolfsbergen • Jean Wong • Jason C. Wood • R. Scott Wood • Woody • John Woosley • Coriel Wormdahl • Colin Worth • Rebekah Wortman • Nicole Wright-Gilbo • Charles & Christine Wright • Jake Wright • Kyle Wright • Caleb & Anna Wunderlich • Wxaith • Cory & Rachel Wyborney • Rikkert Wyckmans • Stacey Wyman

— X, Y, Z —

Katherine Xu • Valerie Y. • Yogesh Yagnik • Yale & Jasmine • Susan Yamamoto • Lemuel Yap • Keith Yarborough • Brian A. Yates • Gail Yates • Kyle A. Yawn • Chista Yazdani • Alec Yeung • Ray & Zeke Yolo • Benjamin York • Lawrence B. York • Valerie R. York • Caitlin J. Young • Daniel Young • Deanna Young • Ryan Young • Anders M. Ytterdahl • Federico Z. • Allie Zaenger • Robert Zangari • Brandon Zarzyczny • Zan Zastrow • Ludwig Zemrau • Sean Zephyr • Jehnytssa Zetino • Jing Zhu • Lisa Zidar • Perrin Zideos • Sandra Zielinger • Anthony Zielinski • Liron Zilber • Chad Zilla • Mike Ziska • Andrew R. Zodda • Peter Zola • Zwieciu

About the Author

Michael J. Sullivan is a *New York Times, USA Today,* and *Washington Post* bestselling author who has been nominated for eight Goodreads Choice Awards. His first novel, *The Crown Conspiracy*, was released by Aspirations Media Inc. in October 2008. From 2009 through 2010, he self-published the next five of the six books of the Riyria Revelations, which were later sold and re-released by Hachette Book Group's Orbit imprint as three, two-book omnibus editions (*Theft of Swords, Rise of Empire, Heir of Novron*).

Michael's Riyria Chronicles series (a prequel to Riyria Revelations) has been both traditionally and self-published. The first two books were released by Orbit, and the next two by his own imprint, Riyria Enterprises, LLC. A fifth Riyria Chronicle, titled *Drumindor*, will be self-published in the near future.

For Penguin Random House's Del Rey imprint, Michael has published the first three books of The Legends of the First Empire: *Age of Myth, Age of Swords,* and *Age of War.* The last three books of the series will be distributed by Grim Oak Press and are titled *Age of Legend, Age of Death,* and *Age of Empyre.*

Michael is now writing The Rise and the Fall Trilogy. These three books are set in his fictional world of Elan several hundred years after the events of The Legends of the First Empire and one thousand years before the Riyria novels.

You can email Michael at michael@michaelsullivan-author.com.

About the Type

This book was set in Fournier, a typeface named for Pierre Simon Fournier (1712–1768), the youngest son of a French printing family. He started out engraving woodblocks and large capitals, then moved on to fonts of type. In 1736, he began his own foundry and made several important contributions in the field of type design; he is said to have cut 147 alphabets of his own creation. Fournier is probably best remembered as the designer of St. Augustine Ordinaire, a face that served as the model for the Monotype Corporation's Fournier, which was released in 1925.

WORKS BY MICHAEL J. SULLIVAN

THE LEGENDS OF THE FIRST EMPIRE
Age of Myth • *Age of Swords* • *Age of War*
Age of Legend • *Age of Death*
Forthcoming: *Age of Empyre* (May 2020)

THE RISE AND THE FALL
Nolyn (Summer 2020) • *Farilane* (Summer 2021)
Esrahaddon (Summer 2022)

THE RIYRIA REVELATIONS
Theft of Swords (contains *The Crown Conspiracy* & *Avempartha*)
Rise of Empire (contains *Nyphron Rising* & *The Emerald Storm*)
Heir of Novron (contains *Wintertide* & *Percepliquis*)

THE RIYRIA CHRONICLES
The Crown Tower • *The Rose and the Thorn*
The Death of Dulgath • *The Disappearance of Winter's Daughter*
Forthcoming: *Drumindor*

STANDALONE NOVELS
Hollow World (Sci-fi Thriller)

SHORT STORY ANTHOLOGIES
Heroes Wanted: "The Ashmoore Affair" (Fantasy: Riyria Chronicles)
Unfettered: "The Jester" (Fantasy: Riyria Chronicles)
Unbound: "The Game" (Fantasy: Contemporary)
Unfettered II: "Little Wren and the Big Forest" (Fantasy: Legends)
Blackguards: "Professional Integrity" (Fantasy: Riyria Chronicles)
The End: Visions of the Apocalypse: "Burning Alexandria" (Dystopian Sci-fi)
Triumph Over Tragedy: "Traditions" (Fantasy: Tales from Elan)
The Fantasy Faction Anthology: "Autumn Mist" (Fantasy: Contemporary)